P9-DDL-399

CONTENTS

To Michael and Darlene,
good friends.

RISKY BUSINESS

Chapter 1

"Watch your step, please. Please, watch your step. Thank you." Liz took a ticket from a sunburned man with palm trees on his shirt, then waited patiently for a woman with two bulging straw baskets to dig out another one.

"I hope you haven't lost it, Mabel. I told you to let me hold it."

"I haven't lost it," the woman said testily before she pulled out the little piece of blue cardboard.

"Thank you. Please take your seats." It was several more minutes before everyone was settled and she could take her own. "Welcome aboard the *Fantasy,* ladies and gentlemen."

With her mind on a half dozen other things, Liz began her opening monologue. She gave an absentminded nod to the man on the dock who cast off the ropes before she started the engine. Her voice was pleasant and easy as she took another look at her watch. They were already fifteen minutes behind schedule. She gave one last scan of the beach, skimming by lounge chairs, over bodies already stretched and oiled slick, like offerings to the sun. She couldn't hold the tour any longer.

The boat swayed a bit as she backed it from the dock and took an eastern course. Though her thoughts were scattered, she made the turn from the coast expertly. She could have navigated the boat with her eyes closed. The air that ruffled around her face was soft and already warming, though the hour was early. Harmless and powder-puff white, clouds dotted the horizon. The water, churned by the engine, was as blue as the guidebooks promised. Even after ten years, Liz took none of it for granted—especially her livelihood. Part of that depended on an atmosphere that made muscles relax and problems disappear.

Behind her in the long, bullet-shaped craft were eighteen people seated on padded benches. They were already murmuring about the fish and formations they saw through the glass bottom. She doubted if any of them thought of the worries they'd left behind at home.

"We'll be passing Paraiso Reef North," Liz began in a low, flowing voice. "Diving depths range from thirty to fifty feet. Visibility is excellent, so you'll be able to see star and brain corals, sea fans and sponges, as well as schools of sergeant majors, groupers and parrot fish. The grouper isn't one of your prettier fish, but it's versatile. They're all born female and produce eggs before they change sex and become functioning males."

Liz set her course and kept the speed steady. She went on to describe the elegantly colored angelfish, the shy, silvery smallmouth grunts, and the intriguing and dangerous sea urchin. Her clients would find the information useful when she stopped for two hours of snorkeling at Palancar Reef.

She'd made the run before, too many times to count. It might have become routine, but it was never monotonous. She felt now, as she always did, the freedom of open water, blue sky and the hum of engine with her at the controls. The boat was hers, as were three others, and the little concrete block dive shop close to shore. She'd worked for all of it, sweating through months when the bills were steep and the cash flow slight. She'd made it. Ten years of struggle had been a small price to pay for having something of her own. Turning her back on her country, leaving behind the familiar, had been a small price to pay for peace of mind.

The tiny, rustic island of Cozumel in the Mexican Caribbean promoted peace of mind. It was her home now, the only one that mattered. She was accepted there, respected. No one on the island knew of the humiliation and pain she'd gone through before she'd fled to Mexico. Liz rarely thought of it, though she had a vivid reminder.

Faith. Just the thought of her daughter made her smile. Faith was small and bright and precious, and so far away. Just six weeks, Liz thought, and she'd be home from school for the summer.

Sending her to Houston to her grandparents had been for the best, Liz reminded herself whenever the ache of loneliness became acute. Faith's education was more important than a mother's needs. Liz had worked, gambled, struggled so that Faith could have everything she was entitled to, everything she would have had if her father...

Determined, Liz set her mind on other things. She'd promised herself a decade before that she would cut Faith's father from her mind, just as he had cut her from his life. It had been a mistake, one made in naïveté and passion, one that had changed the course of her life forever. But she'd won something precious from it: Faith.

"Below, you see the wreck of a forty-passenger Convair airliner lying upside down." She slowed the boat so that her passengers could examine the wreck and the divers out for early explorations. Bubbles rose from air tanks like small silver disks. "The wreck's no tragedy," she continued. "It was sunk for a scene in a movie and provides divers with easy entertainment."

Her job was to do the same for her passengers, she reminded herself. It was simple enough when she had a mate on board. Alone, she had to captain the boat, keep up the light, informative banter, deal with snorkel equipment, serve lunch and count heads. It just hadn't been possible to wait any longer for Jerry.

She muttered to herself a bit as she increased speed. It wasn't so much that she minded the extra work, but she felt her paying customers were entitled to the best she could offer. She should have known better than to depend on him. She could have easily arranged for someone else to come along. As it was, she had two men on the dive boat and two more in the shop. Because her second dive boat was due to launch at noon, no one could be spared to mate the glass bottom on a day trip. And Jerry had come through before, she reminded herself. With him on board, the women passengers were so charmed that Liz didn't think they even noticed the watery world the boat passed over.

Who could blame them? she thought with a half smile. If she hadn't been immune to men in general, Jerry might have had her falling over her own feet. Most women had a difficult time resisting dark, cocky looks, a cleft chin and smoky gray eyes. Add to that a lean, muscular build and a glib tongue, and no female was safe.

But that hadn't been why Liz had agreed to rent him a room, or give him a part-time job. She'd needed the extra income, as well as the extra help, and she was shrewd enough to recognize an operator when she saw one. Previous experience had taught her that it made good business sense to have an operator on your side. She told herself he'd better have a good excuse for leaving her without a crew, then forgot him.

The ride, the sun, the breeze relaxed her. Liz continued to speak of the sea life below, twining facts she'd learned while studying marine biology in college with facts she'd learned firsthand in the waters of the Mexican Caribbean. Occasionally one of her passengers would ask a question or call out in excitement over something that skimmed beneath them. She answered, commented and instructed while keeping the flow light. Because three of her passengers were Mexican, she repeated all her information in Spanish. Because there were several children on board, she made certain the facts were fun.

If things had been different, she would have been a teacher. Liz had long since pushed that early dream from her mind, telling herself she was more suited to the business world. Her business world. She glanced over where the clouds floated lazily over the horizon. The sun danced white and sharp on the surface of blue water. Below, coral rose like castles or waved like fans. Yes, she'd chosen her world and had no regrets.

When a woman screamed behind her, Liz let off the throttle. Before she could turn, the scream was joined by another. Her first thought was that perhaps they'd seen one of the sharks that occasionally visited the reefs. Set to calm and soothe, Liz let the boat drift in the current. A woman was weeping in her husband's arms, another held her child's face protectively against her shoulder. The rest were staring down through the clear glass. Liz took off her sunglasses as she walked down the two steps into the cabin.

"Please try to stay calm. I promise you, there's nothing down there that can hurt you in here."

A man with a Nikon around his neck and an orange sun visor over a balding dome gave her a steady look.

"Miss, you'd better radio the police."

Liz looked down through the clear glass, through the crystal blue water. Her heart rose to her throat. She saw now why Jerry had stood her up. He was lying on the white sandy bottom with an anchor chain wrapped around his chest.

The moment the plane finished its taxi, Jonas gathered his garment bag and waited impatiently for the door to be opened. When it did, there was a whoosh of hot air and the drone of engines. With a quick nod to the flight attendant he strode down the steep metal stairs. He didn't have the time or the inclination to appreciate the palm trees, the bursts of flowers or the dreamy blue sky. He walked purposefully, eyes straight ahead and narrowed against the sun. In his dark suit and trim tie he could have been a businessman, one who'd come to Cozumel to work, not to play. Whatever grief, whatever anger he felt were carefully masked by a calm, unapproachable expression.

The terminal was small and noisy. Americans on vacation stood in groups laughing or wandered in confusion. Though he knew no Spanish, Jonas passed quickly through customs then into a small, hot alcove where men waited at podiums to rent cars and Jeeps. Fifteen minutes after landing, Jonas was backing a compact out of a parking space and heading toward town with a map stuck in the sun visor. The heat baked right through the windshield.

Twenty-four hours before, Jonas had been sitting in his large, elegantly furnished, air-conditioned office. He'd just won a long, tough case that had taken all his skill and mountains of research. His client was a free man, acquitted of a felony charge that carried a minimum sentence of ten years. He'd accepted his fee, accepted the gratitude and avoided as much publicity as possible.

Jonas had been preparing to take his first vacation in eighteen months. He'd felt satisfied, vaguely tired and optimistic. Two weeks in Paris seemed like the perfect reward for so many months of ten-hour days. Paris, with its ageless sophistication and cool parks, its stunning museums and incomparable food was precisely what suited Jonas Sharpe.

When the call had come through from Mexico, it had taken him several moments to understand. When he'd answered that he did indeed have a brother Jeremiah, Jonas's predominant thought had been that Jerry had gotten himself into trouble again, and he was going to have to bail him out.

By the time he'd hung up the phone, Jonas couldn't think at all. Numb, he'd given his secretary instructions to cancel his Paris arrangements and to make new ones for a flight to Cozumel the next day. Then Jonas had picked up the phone to call his parents and tell them their son was dead.

He'd come to Mexico to identify the body and take his brother home to bury. With a fresh wave of grief, Jonas experienced a sense of inevitability. Jerry had always lived on the edge of disaster. This time he'd stepped over. Since childhood Jerry had courted trouble—charmingly. He'd once joked that Jonas had taken to law so he could find the most efficient way to get his brother out of jams. Perhaps in a sense it had been true.

Jerry had been a dreamer. Jonas was a realist. Jerry had been unapologetically lazy, Jonas a workaholic. They were—had been—two sides of a coin. As Jonas drew up to the police station in San Miguel it was with the knowledge that part of himself had been erased.

The scene at port should have been painted. There were small fishing boats pulled up on the grass. Huge gray ships sat complacently at dock while tourists in flowered shirts or skimpy shorts strolled along the sea wall. Water lapped and scented the air.

Jonas got out of the car and walked to the police station to begin to wade through the morass of paperwork that accompanied a violent death.

Captain Moralas was a brisk, no-nonsense man who had been born on the island and was passionately dedicated to protecting it. He was approaching forty and awaiting the birth of his fifth child. He was proud of his position, his education and his family, though the order often varied. Basically, he was a quiet man who enjoyed classical music and a movie on Saturday nights.

Because San Miguel was a port, and ships brought sailors on leave, tourists on holiday, Moralas was no stranger to trouble or the darker side of human nature. He did, however, pride himself on the low percentage of violent crime on his island. The murder of the American bothered him in the way a pesky fly bothered a man sitting contentedly on his porch swing. A cop didn't have to work in a big city to recognize a professional hit. There was no room for organized crime on Cozumel.

But he was also a family man. He understood love, and he understood grief, just as he understood certain men were compelled to conceal both. In the cool, flat air of the morgue, he waited beside Jonas. The American stood a head taller, rigid and pale.

"This is your brother, Mr. Sharpe?" Though he didn't have to ask.

Jonas looked down at the other side of the coin. "Yes."

In silence, he backed away to give Jonas the time he needed.

It didn't seem possible. Jonas knew he could have stood for hours staring down at his brother's face and it would never seem possible. Jerry had always looked for the easy way, the biggest deal, and he hadn't always been an admirable man. But he'd always been so full of life. Slowly, Jonas laid his hand on his brother's. There was no life there now, and nothing he could do; no amount of maneuvering or pulling of strings would bring it back. Just as slowly he removed his hand. It didn't seem possible, but it was.

Moralas nodded to the attendant. "I'm sorry."

Jonas shook his head. Pain was like a dull-edged knife through the base of his skull. He coated it with ice. "Who killed my brother, Captain?"

"I don't know. We're investigating."

"You have leads?"

Moralas gestured and started down the corridor. "Your brother had been in Cozumel only three weeks, Mr. Sharpe. At the moment, we are interviewing everyone who had contact with him during that time." He opened a door and stepped out into the air, breathing deeply of the fresh air and the flowers. The man beside him didn't seem to notice the change. "I promise you, we will do everything possible to find your brother's killer."

The rage Jonas had controlled for so many hours bubbled toward the surface. "I don't know you." With a steady hand he drew out a cigarette, watching the captain with narrowed eyes as he lit it. "You didn't know Jerry."

"This is my island." Moralas's gaze remained locked with Jonas's. "If there's a murderer on it, I'll find him."

"A professional." Jonas blew out smoke that hung in the air with no breeze to brush it away. "We both know that, don't we?"

Moralas said nothing for a moment. He was still waiting to receive information on Jeremiah Sharpe. "Your brother was shot, Mr. Sharpe, so we're investigating to find out why, how and who. You could help me by giving me some information."

Jonas stared at the door a moment—the door that led down the stairs, down the corridor and to his brother's body. "I've got to walk," he murmured.

Moralas waited until they'd crossed the grass, then the road. For a moment, they walked near the sea wall in silence. "Why did your brother come to Cozumel?"

"I don't know." Jonas drew deeply on the cigarette until it burned into the filter. "Jerry liked palm trees."

"His business? His work?"

With a half laugh Jonas ground the smoldering filter underfoot. Sunlight danced in diamonds on the water. "Jerry liked to call himself a free-lancer. He was a drifter." And he'd brought complications to Jonas's life as often as he'd brought pleasure. Jonas stared hard at the water, remembering shared lives, diverse opinions. "For Jerry, it was always the next town and the next deal. The last I heard—two weeks ago—he was giving diving lessons to tourists."

"The Black Coral Dive Shop," Moralas confirmed. "Elizabeth Palmer hired him on a part-time basis."

"Palmer." Jonas's attention shifted away from the water. "That's the woman he was living with."

"Miss Palmer rented your brother a room," Moralas corrected, abruptly proper. "She was also among the group to discover your brother's body. She's given my department her complete cooperation."

Jonas's mouth thinned. How had Jerry described this Liz Palmer in their brief phone conversation weeks before? A sexy little number who made great tortillas. She sounded like another one of Jerry's tough ladies on the lookout for a good time and the main chance. "I'll need her address." At the captain's quiet look he only raised a brow. "I assume my brother's things are still there."

"They are. I have some of your brother's personal effects, those that he had on him, in my office. You're welcome to collect them and what remains at Miss Palmer's. We've already been through them."

Jonas felt the rage build again and smothered it. "When can I take my brother home?"

"I'll do my best to complete the paperwork today. I'll need you to make a statement. Of course, there are forms." He looked at Jonas's set profile and felt a new tug of pity. "Again, I'm sorry."

He only nodded. "Let's get it done."

Liz let herself into the house. While the door slammed behind her, she flicked switches, sending two ceiling fans whirling. The sound, for the moment, was company enough. The headache she'd lived with for over twenty-four hours was a dull, nagging thud just under her right temple. Going into the bathroom, she washed down two aspirin before turning on the shower.

She'd taken the glass bottom out again. Though it was off season, she'd had to turn a dozen people away. It wasn't every day a body was found off the coast, and the curious had come in force. Morbid, she thought, then stripped and stepped under the cold spray of the shower. How long would it take, she wondered, before she stopped seeing Jerry on the sand beneath the water?

True, she'd barely known him, but he'd been fun and interesting and good company. He'd slept in her daughter's bed and eaten in her kitchen. Closing her eyes, she let the water sluice over her, willing the headache away. She'd be better, she thought, when the police finished the investigation. It had been hard, very hard, when they'd come to her house and searched through Jerry's things. And the questions.

How much had she known about Jerry Sharpe? He'd been American, an operator, a womanizer. She'd been able to use all three to her benefit when he'd given diving lessons or acted as mate on one of her boats. She'd thought him harmless—sexy, attractive and basically lazy. He'd boasted of making it big, of wheeling a deal that would set him up in style. Liz had considered it so much hot air. As far as she was concerned, nothing set you up in style but years of hard work—or inherited wealth.

But Jerry's eyes had lit up when he'd talked of it, and his grin had been appealing. If she'd been a woman who allowed herself dreams, she would have believed him. But dreams were for the young and foolish. With a little tug of regret, she realized Jerry Sharpe had been both.

Now he was gone, and what he had left was still scattered in her daughter's room. She'd have to box it up, Liz decided as she turned off the taps. It was something, at least. She'd box up Jerry's things and ask that Captain Moralas what to do about them. Certainly his family would want whatever he'd left behind. Jerry had spoken of a brother, whom he'd affectionately referred to as "the stuffed shirt." Jerry Sharpe had been anything but stuffy.

As she walked to the bedroom, Liz wrapped her hair in the towel. She remembered the way Jerry had tried to talk his way between her sheets a few days after he'd moved in. Smooth talk, smooth hands. Though he'd had her backed into the doorway, kissing her before she'd evaded it, Liz had easily brushed him off. He'd taken her refusal good-naturedly, she recalled, and they'd remained on comfortable terms. Liz pulled on an oversized shirt that skimmed her thighs.

The truth was, Jerry Sharpe had been a good-natured, comfortable man with big dreams. She wondered, not for the first time, if his dreams had had something to do with his death.

She couldn't go on thinking about it. The best thing to do was to pack what had belonged to Jerry back into his suitcase and take it to the police.

It made her feel gruesome. She discovered that after only five minutes. Privacy, for a time, had been all but her only possession. To invade someone else's made her uneasy. Liz folded a faded brown T-shirt that boasted the wearer had hiked the Grand Canyon and tried not to think at all. But she kept seeing him there, joking about sleeping with one of Faith's collection of dolls. He'd fixed the window that had stuck and had cooked paella to celebrate his first paycheck.

Without warning, Liz felt the first tears flow. He'd been so alive, so young, so full of that cocky sense of confidence. She'd hardly had time to consider him a friend, but he'd slept in her daughter's bed and left clothes in her closet.

She wished now she'd listened to him more, been friendlier, more approachable. He'd asked her to have drinks with him and she'd brushed him off because she'd had paperwork to do. It seemed petty now, cold. If she'd given him an hour of her life, she might have learned who he was, where he'd come from, why he'd died.

When the knock at the door sounded, she pressed her hands against her cheeks. Silly to cry, she told herself, when tears never solved anything. Jerry Sharpe was gone, and it had nothing to do with her.

She brushed away the tears as she walked to the door. The headache was easing. Liz decided it would be best if she called Moralas right away and arranged to have the clothes picked up. She was telling herself she really wasn't involved at all when she opened the door.

For a moment she could only stare. The T-shirt she hadn't been aware of still holding slipped from her fingers. She took one stumbling step back as she felt a rushing sound fill her head. Because her vision dimmed, she blinked to clear it. The man in the doorway stared back at her accusingly.

"Jer-Jerry," she managed and nearly screamed when he took a step forward.

"Elizabeth Palmer?"

She shook her head, numb and terrified. She had no superstitions. She believed in action and reaction on a purely practical level. When someone died, they couldn't come back. And yet she stood in her living room with the fans whirling and watched Jerry Sharpe step over her threshold. She heard him speak to her again.

"Are you Liz Palmer?"

"I saw you." She heard her own voice rise with nerves but couldn't take her eyes from his face. The cocky good looks, the cleft chin, the smoky eyes under thick dark brows. It was a face that appealed to a woman's need to risk, or to her dreams of risking. "Who are you?"

"Jonas Sharpe. Jerry was my brother. My twin brother."

When she discovered her knees were shaking, she sat down quickly. No, not Jerry, she told herself as her heartbeat leveled. The hair was just as dark, just as full, but it lacked Jerry's unkempt shagginess. The face was just as attractive, just as ruggedly hewn, but she'd never seen Jerry's eyes so hard, so cold. And this man wore a suit as though he'd been born in one. His stance was one of restrained passion and impatience. It took her a moment, only a moment, before anger struck.

"You did that on purpose." Because her palms were damp she rubbed them against her knees. "It was a hideous thing to do. You knew what I'd think when I opened the door."

"I needed a reaction."

She sat back and took a deep, steadying breath. "You're a bastard, Mr. Sharpe."

For the first time in hours, his mouth curved…only slightly. "May I sit down?"

She gestured to a chair. "What do you want?"

"I came to get Jerry's things. And to talk to you."

As he sat, Jonas took a long look around. His was not the polite, casual glance a stranger indulges himself in when he walks into someone else's home, but a sharp-eyed, intense study of what belonged to Liz Palmer. It was a small living area, hardly bigger than his office. While he preferred muted colors and clean lines, Liz chose bright, contrasting shades and odd knickknacks. Several Mayan masks hung on the walls, and rugs of different sizes and hues were scattered over the floor. The sunlight, fading now, came in slats through red window blinds. There was a big blue pottery vase on a woven mat on the table, but the butter-yellow flowers in it were losing their petals. The table itself didn't gleam with polish, but was covered with a thin layer of dust.

The shock that had had her stomach muscles jumping had eased. She said nothing as he looked around the room because she was looking at him. A mirror image of Jerry, she thought. And weren't mirror images something like negatives? She didn't think he'd be fun to have around. She had a frantic need to order him out, to pitch him out quickly and finally. Ridiculous, she told herself. He was just a man, and nothing to her. And he had lost his brother.

"I'm sorry, Mr. Sharpe. This is a very difficult time for you."

His gaze locked on hers so quickly that she tensed again. She'd barely been aware of his inch-by-inch study of her room, but she couldn't remain unmoved by his study of her.

She wasn't what he'd expected. Her face was all angles—wide cheekbones, a long narrow nose and a chin that came to a suggestion of a point. She wasn't beautiful, but stunning in an almost uncomfortable way. It might have been the eyes, a deep haunted brown, that rose a bit exotically at the outer edge. It might have been the mouth, full and vulnerable. The shirt overwhelmed her body with its yards of material, leaving only long, tanned legs bare. Her hands, resting on the arms of her chair, were small, narrow and ringless. Jonas had thought he knew his brother's taste as well as his own. Liz Palmer didn't suit Jerry's penchant for the loud and flamboyant, or his own for the discreet sophisticate.

Still, Jerry had lived with her. Jonas thought grimly that she was taking the murder of her lover very well. "And a difficult time for you."

His long study had left her shaken. It had gone beyond natural curiosity and made her feel like a specimen, filed and labeled for further research. She tried to remember that grief took different forms in different people. "Jerry was a nice man. It isn't easy to—"

"How did you meet him?"

Words of sympathy cut off, Liz straightened in her chair. She never extended friendliness where it wasn't likely to be accepted. If he wanted facts only, she'd give him facts. "He came by my shop a few weeks ago. He was interested in diving."

Jonas's brow lifted as in polite interest but his eyes remained cold. "In diving."

"I own a dive shop on the beach—rent equipment, boat rides, lessons, day trips. Jerry was looking for work. Since he knew what he was doing, I gave it to him. He crewed on the dive boat, gave some of the tourists lessons, that sort of thing."

Showing tourists how to use a regulator didn't fit with Jonas's last conversation with his brother. Jerry had talked about cooking up a big deal. Big money, big time. "He didn't buy in as your partner?"

Something came into her face—pride, disdain, amusement. Jonas couldn't be sure. "I don't take partners, Mr. Sharpe. Jerry worked for me, that's all."

"All?" The brow came up again. "He was living here."

She caught the meaning, had dealt with it from the police. Liz decided she'd answered all the questions she cared to and that she'd given Jonas Sharpe more than enough of her time. "Jerry's things are in here." Rising, she walked out of the room. Liz waited at the doorway to her daughter's room until Jonas joined her. "I was just beginning to pack his clothes. You'd probably prefer to do that yourself. Take as much time as you need."

When she started to turn away, Jonas took her arm. He wasn't looking at her, but into the room with the shelves of dolls, the pink walls and lacy curtains. And at his brother's clothes tossed negligently over the back of a painted white chair and onto a flowered spread. It hurt, Jonas discovered, all over again.

"Is this all?" It seemed so little.

"I haven't been through the drawers or the closet yet. The police have." Suddenly weary, she pulled the towel from her head. Dark blond hair, still damp, tumbled around her face and shoulders. Somehow her face seemed even more vulnerable. "I don't know anything about Jerry's personal life, his personal belongings. This is my daughter's room." She turned her head until their eyes met. "She's away at school. This is where Jerry slept." She left him alone.

Twenty minutes was all he needed. His brother had traveled light. Leaving the suitcase in the living room, Jonas walked through the house. It wasn't large. The next bedroom was dim in the early evening light, but he could see a splash of orange over a rattan bed and a desk cluttered with files and papers. It smelled lightly of spice and talcum powder. Turning away, he walked toward the back and found the kitchen. And Liz.

It was when he smelled the coffee that Jonas remembered he hadn't eaten since morning. Without turning around, Liz poured a second cup. She didn't need him to speak to know he was there. She doubted he was a man who ever had to announce his presence. "Cream?"

Jonas ran a hand through his hair. He felt as though he were walking through someone else's dream. "No, black."

When Liz turned to offer the cup, he saw the quick jolt. "I'm sorry," she murmured, taking up her own cup. "You look so much like him."

"Does that bother you?"

"It unnerves me."

He sipped the coffee, finding it cleared some of the mists of unreality. "You weren't in love with Jerry."

Liz sent him a look of mild surprise. She realized he'd thought she'd been his brother's lover, but she hadn't thought he'd have taken the next step. "I only knew him a few weeks." Then she laughed, remembering another time, another life. "No, I wasn't in love with him. We had a business relationship, but I liked him. He was cocky and well aware of his own charms. I had a lot of repeat female customers over the past couple of weeks. Jerry was quite an operator," she murmured, then looked up, horrified. "I'm sorry."

"No." Interested, Jonas stepped closer. She was a tall woman, so their eyes stayed level easily. She smelled of the talcum powder and wore no cosmetics. Not Jerry's type, he thought again. But there was something about the eyes. "That's what he was, only most people never caught on."

"I've known others." And her voice was flat. "Not so harmless, not so kind. Your brother was a nice man, Mr. Sharpe. And I hope whoever... I hope they're found."

She watched the gray eyes ice over. The little tremor in her stomach reminded her that cold was often more dangerous than heat. "They will be. I may need to talk with you again."

It seemed a simple enough request, but she backed away from it. She didn't want to talk to him again, she didn't want to be involved in any way. "There's nothing else I can tell you."

"Jerry was living in your house, working for you."

"I don't know anything." Her voice rose as she spun away

to stare out the window. She was tired of the questions, tired of people pointing her out on the beach as the woman who'd found the body. She was tired of having her life turned upside down by the death of a man she had hardly known. And she was nervous, she admitted, because Jonas Sharpe struck her as a man who could keep her life turned upside down as long as it suited him. "I've talked to the police again and again. He worked for me. I saw him a few hours out of the day. I don't know where he went at night, who he saw, what he did. It wasn't my business as long as he paid for the room and showed up to work." When she looked back, her face was set. "I'm sorry for your brother, I'm sorry for you. But it's not my business."

He saw the nerves as her hands unclenched but interpreted them in his own way. "We disagree, Mrs. Palmer."

"Miss Palmer," she said deliberately, and watched his slow, acknowledging nod. "I can't help you."

"You don't know that until we talk."

"All right. I won't help you."

He inclined his head and reached for his wallet. "Did Jerry owe you anything on the room?"

She felt the insult like a slap. Her eyes, usually soft, usually sad, blazed. "He owed me nothing, and neither do you. If you've finished your coffee..."

Jonas set the cup on the table. "I've finished. For now." He gave her a final study. Not Jerry's type, he thought again, or his. But she had to know something. If he had to use her to find out, he would. "Good night."

Liz stayed where she was until the sound of the front door closing echoed back at her. Then she shut her eyes. None of her business, she reminded herself. But she could still see Jerry under her boat. And now, she could see Jonas Sharpe with grief hard in his eyes.

Chapter 2

Liz considered working in the dive shop the next thing to taking a day off. Taking a day off, actually staying away from the shop and the boats, was a luxury she allowed herself rarely, and only when Faith was home on holiday. Today, she'd indulged herself by sending the boats out without her so that she could manage the shop alone. Be alone. By noon, all the serious divers had already rented their tanks so that business at the shop would be sporadic. It gave Liz a chance to spend a few hours checking equipment and listing inventory.

The shop was a basic cinder-block unit. Now and again, she toyed with the idea of having the outside painted, but could never justify the extra expense. There was a cubbyhole she wryly referred to as an office where she'd crammed an old gray steel desk and one swivel chair. The rest of the room was crowded with equipment that lined the floor, was stacked on shelves or hung from hooks. Her desk had a dent in it the size of a man's foot, but her equipment was top grade and flawless.

Masks, flippers, tanks, snorkels could be rented individually or in any number of combinations. Liz had learned that the wider the choice, the easier it was to move items out and draw the customer back. The equipment was the backbone of her business. Prominent next to the wide square opening that was only closed at night with a heavy wooden shutter was a list, in English and Spanish, of her equipment, her services and the price.

When she'd started eight years before, Liz had stocked enough tanks and gear to outfit twelve divers. It had taken every penny she'd saved—every penny Marcus had given a young, dewy-eyed girl pregnant with his child. The girl had become a woman quickly, and that woman now had a business that could accommodate fifty divers from the skin out, dozens of snorkelers, underwater photographers, tourists who wanted an easy day on the water or gung-ho deep-sea fishermen.

The first boat she'd gambled on, a dive boat, had been christened *Faith,* for her daughter. She'd made a vow when she'd been eighteen, alone and frightened, that the child she carried would have the best. Ten years later, Liz could look around her shop and know she'd kept her promise.

More, the island she'd fled to for escape had become home. She was settled there, respected, depended on. She no longer looked over the expanses of white sand, blue water, longing for Houston or a pretty house with a flowing green lawn. She no longer looked back at the education she'd barely begun, or what she might have been. She'd stopped pining for a man who didn't want her or the child they'd made. She'd never go back. But Faith could. Faith could learn how to speak French, wear silk dresses and discuss wine and music. One day Faith would go back and mingle unknowingly with her cousins on their own level.

That was her dream, Liz thought as she carefully filled tanks. To see her daughter accepted as easily as she herself had been rejected. Not for revenge, Liz mused, but for justice.

"Howdy there, missy."

Crouched near the back wall, Liz turned and squinted against the sun. She saw a portly figure stuffed into a black-and-red wet suit, topped by a chubby face with a fat cigar stuck in the mouth.

"Mr. Ambuckle. I didn't know you were still on the island."

"Scooted over to Cancun for a few days. Diving's better here."

With a smile, she rose to go to her side of the opening. Ambuckle was a steady client who came to Cozumel two or three times a year and always rented plenty of tanks. "I could've told you that. See any of the ruins?"

"Wife dragged me to Tulum." He shrugged and grinned at her with popping blue eyes. "Rather be thirty feet down than climbing over rocks all day. Did get some snorkeling in. But a man doesn't fly all the way from Dallas just to paddle around. Thought I'd do some night diving."

Her smile came easily, adding something soft and approachable to eyes that were usually wary. "Fix you right up. How much longer are you staying?" she asked as she checked an underwater flash.

"Two more weeks. Man's got to get away from his desk."

"Absolutely." Liz had often been grateful so many people from Texas, Louisiana and Florida felt the need to get away.

"Heard you had some excitement while we were on the other side."

Liz supposed she should be used to the comment by now, but a shiver ran up her spine. The smile faded, leaving her face remote. "You mean the American who was murdered?"

"Put the wife in a spin. Almost couldn't talk her into coming back over. Did you know him?"

No, she thought, not as well as she should have. To keep her hands busy, she reached for a rental form and began to fill it out. "As a matter of fact, he worked here a little while."

"You don't say?" Ambuckle's small blue eyes sparkled a bit. But Liz supposed she should be used to that, as well.

"You might remember him. He crewed the dive boat the last time you and your wife went out."

"No kidding?" Ambuckle's brow creased as he chewed on the cigar. "Not that good-looking young man—Johnny, Jerry," he remembered. "Had the wife in stitches."

"Yes, that was him."

"Shame," Ambuckle murmured, but looked rather pleased to have known the victim. "Had a lot of zip."

"Yes, I thought so, too." Liz lugged the tanks through the door and set them on the stoop. "That should take care of it, Mr. Ambuckle."

"Add a camera on, missy. Want to get me a picture of one of those squids. Ugly things."

Amazed, Liz plucked one from the shelf and added it to the list on a printed form. She checked her watch, noted down the time and turned the form for Ambuckle's signature. After signing, he handed her bills for the deposit. She appreciated the fact that Ambuckle always paid in cash, American. "Thanks. Glad to see you back, Mr. Ambuckle."

"Can't keep me away, missy." With a whoosh and a grunt, he hefted the tanks on his shoulders. Liz watched him cross to the walkway before she filed the receipt. Unlocking her cash box, she stored the money.

"Business is good."

She jolted at the voice and looking up again stared at Jonas Sharpe.

She'd never again mistake him for Jerry, though his eyes were almost hidden this time with tinted glasses, and he wore shorts and an open shirt in lieu of a suit. There was a long gold chain around his neck with a small coin dangling. She recalled Jerry had worn one. But something in the way Jonas stood, something in the set of his mouth made him look taller and tougher than the man she'd known.

Because she didn't believe in polite fencing, Liz finished relocking the cash box and began to check the straps and fasteners on a shelf of masks. No faulty equipment went out of her shop. "I didn't expect to see you again."

"You should have." Jonas watched her move down the shelf. She seemed stronger, less vulnerable than she had when he'd seen her a week ago. Her eyes were cool, her voice remote. It made it easier to do what he'd come for. "You have quite a reputation on the island."

She paused long enough to look over her shoulder. "Really?"

"I checked," he said easily. "You've lived here for ten years. Built this place from the first brick and have one of the most successful businesses on the island."

She examined the mask in her hand meticulously. "Are you interested in renting some equipment, Mr. Sharpe? I can recommend the snorkeling right off this reef."

"Maybe. But I think I'd prefer to scuba."

"Fine. I can give you whatever you need." She set the mask down and chose another. "It isn't necessary to be certified to dive in Mexico; however, I'd recommend a few basic lessons before you go down. We offer two different courses—individual or group."

He smiled at her for the first time, a slow, appealing curving of lips that softened the toughness around his mouth. "I might take you up on that. Meantime, when do you close?"

"When I'm ready to." The smile made a difference, she realized, and she couldn't let it. In defense, she shifted her weight on one hip and sent him a look of mild insolence. "This is Cozumel, Mr. Sharpe. We don't run nine to five here. Unless you want to rent some equipment or sign up for a tour, you'll have to excuse me."

He reached in to close his hand over hers. "I didn't come back to tour. Have dinner with me tonight. We can talk."

She didn't attempt to free her hand but stared at him. Running a business had taught her to be scrupulously polite in any circumstances. "No, thank you."

"Drinks, then."

"No."

"Miss Palmer..." Normally, Jonas was known for his deadly, interminable patience. It was a weapon, he'd learned, in the courtroom and out of it. With Liz, he found it difficult to wield it. "I don't have a great deal to go on at this point, and the police haven't made any progress at all. I need your help."

This time Liz did pull away. She wouldn't be sucked in, that she promised herself, not by quiet words or intense eyes. She had her life to lead, a business to run, and most important, a daughter coming home in a matter of weeks. "I won't get involved. I'm sorry, even if I wanted to, there'd be nothing I could do to help.''

''Then it won't hurt to talk to me.''

''Mr. Sharpe.'' Liz wasn't known for her patience. ''I have very little free time. Running this business isn't a whim or a lark, but a great deal of work. If I have a couple of hours to myself in the evening, I'm not going to spend them being grilled by you. Now—''

She started to brush him off again when a young boy came running up to the window. He was dressed in a bathing suit and slick with suntan lotion. With a twenty-dollar bill crumpled in his hand, he babbled a request for snorkeling equipment for himself and his brother. He spoke in quick, excited Spanish as Liz checked out the equipment, asking if she thought they'd see a shark.

She answered him in all seriousness as she exchanged money for equipment. ''Sharks don't live in the reef, but they do visit now and again.'' She saw the light of adventure in his eyes. ''You'll see parrot fish.'' She held her hands apart to show him how big. ''And if you take some bread crumbs or crackers, the sergeant majors will follow you, lots of them, close enough to touch.''

''Will they bite?''

She grinned. ''Only the bread crumbs. Adios.''

He dashed away, kicking up sand.

''You speak Spanish like a native,'' Jonas observed, and thought it might come in handy. He'd also noticed the pleasure that had come into her eyes when she'd talked with the boy. There'd been nothing remote then, nothing sad or haunted. Strange, he mused, he'd never noticed just how much a barometer of feeling the eyes could be.

''I live here,'' she said simply. ''Now, Mr. Sharpe—''

''How many boats?''

''What?''

''How many do you have?''

She sucked in a deep breath and decided she could humor him for another five minutes. ''I have four. The glass bottom, two dive boats and one for deep-sea fishing.''

"Deep-sea fishing." That was the one, Jonas decided. A fishing boat would be private and isolated. "I haven't done any in five or six years. Tomorrow." He reached in his wallet. "How much?"

"It's fifty dollars a person a day, but I don't take the boat out for one man, Mr. Sharpe." She gave him an easy smile. "It doesn't make good business sense."

"What's your minimum?"

"Three. And I'm afraid I don't have anyone else lined up. So—"

He set four fifty-dollar bills on the counter. "The extra fifty's to make sure you're driving the boat." Liz looked down at the money. An extra two hundred would help buy the aqua bikes she'd been thinking about. Several of the other dive shops already had them and she kept a constant eye on competition. Aqua biking and wind surfing were becoming increasingly popular, and if she wanted to keep up... She looked back at Jonas Sharpe's dark, determined eyes and decided it wasn't worth it.

"My schedule for tomorrow's already set. I'm afraid I—"

"It doesn't make good business sense to turn down a profit, Miss Palmer." When she only moved her shoulders, he smiled again, but this time it wasn't so pleasant. "I'd hate to mention at the hotel that I couldn't get satisfaction at The Black Coral. It's funny how word of mouth can help or damage a small business."

Liz picked up the money, one bill at a time. "What business are you in, Mr. Sharpe?"

"Law."

She made a sound that might have been a laugh as she pulled out a form. "I should've guessed. I knew someone studying law once." She thought of Marcus with his glib, calculating tongue. "He always got what he wanted, too. Sign here. We leave at eight," she said briskly. "The price includes a lunch on board. If you want beer or liquor, you bring your own. The sun's pretty intense on the water, so you'd better buy some sunscreen." She glanced beyond him. "One of my dive boats is coming back. You'll have to excuse me."

"Miss Palmer..." He wasn't sure what he wanted to say to her, or why he was uncomfortable having completed a successful maneuver. In the end, he pocketed his receipt. "If you change your mind about dinner—"

"I won't."

"I'm at the El Presidente."

"An excellent choice." She walked through the doorway and onto the dock to wait for her crew and clients.

By seven-fifteen, the sun was up and already burning off a low ground mist. What clouds there were, were thin and shaggy and good-natured.

"Damn!" Liz kicked the starter on her motorbike and turned in a little U toward the street. She'd been hoping for rain.

He was going to try to get her involved. Even now, Liz could imagine those dark, patient gray eyes staring into hers, hear the quietly insistent voice. Jonas Sharpe was the kind of man who took no for an answer but was dogged enough to wait however long it took for the yes. Under other circumstances, she'd have admired that. Being stubborn had helped her start and succeed in a business when so many people had shaken their heads and warned her against it. But she couldn't afford to admire Jonas Sharpe. Budgeting her feelings was every bit as important as budgeting her accounts.

She couldn't help him, Liz thought again, as the soft air began to play around her face. Everything she'd known about Jerry had been said at least twice. Of course she was sorry, and had grieved a bit herself for a man she'd hardly known, but murder was a police matter. Jonas Sharpe was out of his element.

She was in hers, Liz thought as her muscles began to relax with the ride. The street was bumpy, patched in a good many places. She knew when to weave and sway. There were houses along the street with deep green grass and trailing vines. Already clothes were waving out on lines. She could hear an early newscast buzzing through someone's open win-

dow and the sound of children finishing chores or breakfast
before school. She turned a corner and kept her speed steady.

There were a few shops here, closed up tight. At the door
of a market, Señor Pessado fumbled with his keys. Liz tooted
her horn and exchanged waves. A cab passed her, speeding
down the road to the airport to wait for the early arrivals. In
a matter of moments, Liz caught the first scent of the sea. It
was always fresh. As she took the last turn, she glanced idly
in her rearview mirror. Odd, she thought—hadn't she seen
that little blue car yesterday? But when she swung into the
hotel's parking lot, it chugged past.

Liz's arrangement with the hotel had been of mutual benefit. Her shop bordered the hotel's beach and encouraged business on both sides. Still, whenever she went inside, as she did
today to collect the lunch for the fishing trip, she always remembered the two years she'd spent scrubbing floors and
making beds.

"*Buenos días,* Margarita."

The young woman with a bucket and mop started to smile.
"*Buenos días,* Liz. *¿Cómo està?*"

"*Bien.* How's Ricardo?"

"Growing out of his pants." Margarita pushed the button
of the service elevator as they spoke of her son. "Faith comes
home soon. He'll be glad."

"So will I." They parted, but Liz remembered the months
they'd worked together, changing linen, hauling towels, wash-
ing floors. Margarita had been a friend, like so many others
she'd met on the island who'd shown kindness to a young
woman who'd carried a child but had no wedding ring.

She could have lied. Even at eighteen Liz had been aware
she could have bought a ten-dollar gold band and had an easy
story of divorce or widowhood. She'd been too stubborn. The
baby that had been growing inside her belonged to her. Only
to her. She'd feel no shame and tell no lies.

By seven forty-five, she was crossing the beach to her shop,
lugging a large cooler packed with two lunches and a smaller
one filled with bait. She could already see a few tubes bobbing
on the water's surface. The water would be warm and clear

and uncrowded. She'd like to have had an hour for snorkeling herself.

"Liz!" The trim, small-statured man who walked toward her was shaking his head. There was a faint, pencil-thin mustache above his lip and a smile in his dark eyes. "You're too skinny to carry that thing."

She caught her breath and studied him up and down. He wore nothing but a skimpy pair of snug trunks. She knew he enjoyed the frank or surreptitious stares of women on the beach. "So're you, Luis. But don't let me stop you."

"So you take the fishing boat today?" He hefted the larger cooler and walked with her toward the shop. "I changed the schedule for you. Thirteen signed up for the glass bottom for the morning. We got both dive boats going out, so I told my cousin Miguel to help fill in today. Okay?"

"Terrific." Luis was young, fickle with women and fond of his tequila, but he could be counted on in a pinch. "I guess I'm going to have to hire someone on, at least part-time."

Luis looked at her, then at the ground. He'd worked closest with Jerry. "Miguel, he's not dependable. Here one day, gone the next. I got a nephew, a good boy. But he can't work until he's out of school."

"I'll keep that in mind," Liz said absently. "Let's just put this right on the boat. I want to check the gear."

On board, Liz went through a routine check on the tackle and line. As she looked over the big reels and massive rods, she wondered, with a little smirk, if the lawyer had ever done any big-game fishing. Probably wouldn't know a tuna if it jumped up and bit his toe, she decided.

The decks were clean, the equipment organized, as she insisted. Luis had been with her the longest, but anyone who worked for Liz understood the hard and fast rule about giving the clients the efficiency they paid for.

The boat was small by serious sport fishing standards, but her clients rarely went away dissatisfied. She knew the waters all along the Yucatan Peninsula and the habits of the game that teemed below the surface. Her boat might not have sonar and fish finders and complicated equipment, but she deter-

mined to give Jonas Sharpe the ride of his life. She'd keep
him so busy, strapped in a fighting chair, that he wouldn't
have time to bother her. By the time they docked again, his
arms would ache, his back would hurt and the only thing he'd
be interested in would be a hot bath and bed. And if he wasn't
a complete fool, she'd see to it that he had a trophy to take
back to wherever he'd come from.

Just where was that? she wondered as she checked the
gauges on the bridge. She'd never thought to ask Jerry. It
hadn't seemed important. Yet now she found herself wondering where Jonas came from, what kind of life he led there.
Was he the type who frequented elegant restaurants with an
equally elegant woman on his arm? Did he watch foreign
films and play bridge? Or did he prefer noisy clubs and hot
jazz? She hadn't been able to find his slot as easily as she did
with most people she met, so she wondered, perhaps too
much. Not my business, she reminded herself and turned to
call to Luis.

"I'll take care of everything here. Go ahead and open the
shop. The glass bottom should be ready to leave in half an
hour."

But he wasn't listening. Standing on the deck, he stared
back at the narrow dock. She saw him raise a shaky hand to
cross himself. *"Madre de Dios."*

"Luis?" She came down the short flight of stairs to join
him. "What—"

Then she saw Jonas, a straw hat covering his head, sunglasses shading his eyes. He hadn't bothered to shave, so that
the light growth of beard gave him a lazy, vagrant look accented by a faded T-shirt and brief black trunks. He didn't,
she realized, look like a man who'd play bridge. Knowing
what was going through Luis's mind, Liz shook his arm and
spoke quickly.

"It's his brother, Luis. I told you they were twins."

"Back from the dead," Luis whispered.

"Don't be ridiculous." She shook off the shudder his
words brought her. "His name is Jonas and he's nothing like
Jerry at all, really. You'll see when you talk to him. You're

prompt, Mr. Sharpe,'' she called out, hoping to jolt Luis out of his shock. "Need help coming aboard?''

"I can manage.'' Hefting a small cooler, Jonas stepped lightly on deck. "The *Expatriate*.'' He referred to the careful lettering on the side of the boat. "Is that what you are?''

"Apparently.'' It was something she was neither proud nor ashamed of. "This is Luis—he works for me. You gave him a jolt just now.''

"Sorry.'' Jonas glanced at the slim man hovering by Liz's side. There was sweat beading on his lip. "You knew my brother?''

"We worked together,'' Luis answered in his slow, precise English. "With the divers. Jerry, he liked best to take out the dive boat. I'll cast off.'' Giving Jonas a wide berth, Luis jumped onto the dock.

"I seem to affect everyone the same way,'' Jonas observed. "How about you?'' He turned dark, direct eyes to her. Though he no longer made her think of Jerry, he unnerved her just the same. "Still want to keep me at arm's length?''

"We pride ourselves in being friendly to all our clients. You've hired the *Expatriate* for the day, Mr. Sharpe. Make yourself comfortable.'' She gestured toward a deck chair before climbing the steps to the bridge and calling out to Luis. "Tell Miguel he gets paid only if he finishes out the day.'' With a final wave to Luis, she started the engine, then cruised sedately toward the open sea.

The wind was calm, barely stirring the water. Liz could see the dark patches that meant reefs and kept the speed easy. Once they were in deeper water, she'd open it up a bit. By midday the sun would be stunningly hot. She wanted Jonas strapped in his chair and fighting two hundred pounds of fish by then.

"You handle a wheel as smoothly as you do a customer.''

A shadow of annoyance moved in her eyes, but she kept them straight ahead. "It's my business. You'd be more comfortable on the deck in a chair, Mr. Sharpe.''

"Jonas. And I'm perfectly comfortable here.'' He gave her a casual study as he stood beside her. She wore a fielder's cap over her hair with white lettering promoting her shop. On her T-shirt, the same lettering was faded from the sun and frequent washings. He wondered, idly, what she wore under it. "How long have you had this boat?"

"Almost eight years. She's sound." Liz pushed the throttle forward. "The waters are warm, so you'll find tuna, marlin, swordfish. Once we're out you can start chumming."

"Chumming?"

She sent him a quick look. So she'd been right—he didn't know a line from a pole. "Bait the water," she began. "I'll keep the speed slow and you bait the water, attract the fish."

"Seems like taking unfair advantage. Isn't fishing supposed to be luck and skill?"

"For some people it's a matter of whether they'll eat or not." She turned the wheel a fraction, scanning the water for unwary snorkelers. "For others, it's a matter of another trophy for the wall."

"I'm not interested in trophies."

She shifted to face him. No, he wouldn't be, she decided, not in trophies or in anything else without a purpose. "What are you interested in?"

"At the moment, you." He put his hand over hers and let off the throttle. "I'm in no hurry."

"You paid to fish." She flexed her hand under his.

"I paid for your time," he corrected.

He was close enough that she could see his eyes beyond the tinted lenses. They were steady, always steady, as if he knew he could afford to wait. The hand still over hers wasn't smooth as she'd expected, but hard and worked. No, he wouldn't play bridge, she thought again. Tennis, perhaps, or hand ball, or something else that took sweat and effort. For the first time in years she felt a quick thrill race through her— a thrill she'd been certain she was immune to. The wind tossed the hair back from her face as she studied him.

"Then you wasted your money."

Her hand moved under his again. Strong, he thought, though her looks were fragile. Stubborn. He could judge that by the way the slightly pointed chin stayed up. But there was a look in her eyes that said I've been hurt, I won't be hurt again. That alone was intriguing, but added to it was a quietly simmering sexuality that left him wondering how it was his brother hadn't been her lover. Not, Jonas was sure, for lack of trying.

"If I've wasted my money, it won't be the first time. But somehow I don't think I have."

"There's nothing I can tell you." Her hand jerked and pushed the throttle up again.

"Maybe not. Or maybe there's something you know without realizing it. I've dealt in criminal law for over ten years. You'd be surprised how important small bits of information can be. Talk to me." His hand tightened briefly on hers. "Please."

She thought she'd hardened her heart, but she could feel herself weakening. Why was it she could haggle for hours over the price of scuba gear and could never refuse a softly spoken request? He was going to cause her nothing but trouble. Because she already knew it, she sighed.

"We'll talk." She cut the throttle so the boat would drift. "While you fish." She managed to smile a bit as she stepped away. "No chum."

With easy efficiency, Liz secured the butt of a rod into the socket attached to a chair. "For now, you sit and relax," she told him. "Sometimes a fish is hot enough to take the hook without bait. If you get one, you strap yourself in and work."

Jonas settled himself in the chair and tipped back his hat. "And you?"

"I go back to the wheel and keep the speed steady so we tire him out without losing him." She gathered her hair in one hand and tossed it back. "There're better spots than this, but I'm not wasting my gas when you don't care whether you catch a fish or not."

His lips twitched as he leaned back in the chair. "Sensible. I thought you would be."

"Have to be."

"Why did you come to Cozumel?" Jonas ignored the rod in front of him and took out a cigarette.

"You've been here for a few days," she countered. "You shouldn't have to ask."

"Parts of your own country are beautiful. If you've been here ten years, you'd have been a child when you left the States."

"No, I wasn't a child." Something in the way she said it had him watching her again, looking for the secret she held just beyond her eyes. "I came because it seemed like the right thing to do. It was the right thing. When I was a girl, my parents would come here almost every year. They love to dive."

"You moved here with your parents?"

"No, I came alone." This time her voice was flat. "You didn't pay two hundred dollars to talk about me, Mr. Sharpe."

"It helps to have some background. You said you had a daughter. Where is she?"

"She goes to school in Houston—that's where my parents live."

Toss a child, and the responsibility, onto grandparents and live on a tropical island. It might leave a bad taste in his mouth, but it wasn't something that would surprise him. Jonas took a deep drag as he studied Liz's profile. It just didn't fit. "You miss her."

"Horribly," Liz murmured. "She'll be home in a few weeks, and we'll spend the summer together. September always comes too soon." Her gaze drifted off as she spoke, almost to herself. "It's for the best. My parents take wonderful care of her and she's getting an excellent education—taking piano lessons and ballet. They sent me pictures from a recital, and…" Her eyes filled with tears so quickly that she hadn't any warning. She shifted into the wind and fought them back, but he'd seen them. He sat smoking silently to give her time to recover.

"Ever get back to the States?"

"No." Liz swallowed and called herself a fool. It had been the pictures, she told herself, the pictures that had come in yesterday's mail of her little girl wearing a pink dress.

"Hiding from something?"

She whirled back, tears replaced with fury. Her body was arched like a bow ready to launch. Jonas held up a hand.

"Sorry. I have a habit of poking into secrets."

She forced herself to relax, to strap back passion as she'd taught herself so long ago. "It's a good way to lose your fingers, Mr. Sharpe."

He chuckled. "That's a possibility. I've always considered it worth the risk. They call you Liz, don't they?"

Her brow lifted under the fringe that blew around her brow. "My friends do."

"It suits you, except when you try to be aloof. Then it should be Elizabeth."

She sent him a smoldering look, certain he was trying to annoy her. "No one calls me Elizabeth."

He merely grinned at her. "Why weren't you sleeping with Jerry?"

"I beg your pardon?"

"Yes, definitely Elizabeth. You're a beautiful woman in an odd sort of way." He tossed out the compliment as casually as he tossed the cigarette into the water. "Jerry had a...fondness for beautiful women. I can't figure out why you weren't lovers."

For a moment, only a moment, it occurred to her that no one had called her beautiful in a very long time. She'd needed words like that once. Then she leaned back on the rail, planted her hands and aimed a killing look. She didn't need them now.

"I didn't choose to sleep with him. It might be difficult for you to accept, as you share the same face, but I didn't find Jerry irresistible."

"No?" As relaxed as she was tensed, Jonas reached into the cooler, offering her a beer. When she shook her head, he popped the top on one for himself. "What did you find him?"

"He was a drifter, and he happened to drift into my life. I gave him a job because he had a quick mind and a strong back. The truth was, I never expected him to last over a month. Men like him don't."

Though he hadn't moved a muscle, Jonas had come to attention. "Men like him?"

"Men who look for the quickest way to easy street. He worked because he liked to eat, but he was always looking for the big strike—one he wouldn't have to sweat for."

"So you did know him," Jonas murmured. "What was he looking for here?"

"I tell you I don't know! For all I know he was looking for a good time and a little sun." Frustration poured out of her as she tossed a hand in the air. "I let him have a room because he seemed harmless and I could use the money. I wasn't intimate with him on any level. The closest he came to talking about what he was up to was bragging about diving for big bucks."

"Diving? Where?"

Fighting for control, she dragged a hand through her hair. "I wish you'd leave me alone."

"You're a realistic woman, aren't you, Elizabeth?"

Her chin was set when she looked back at him. "Yes."

"Then you know I won't. Where was he going to dive?"

"I don't know. I barely listened to him when he got started on how rich he was going to be."

"What did he say?" This time Jonas's voice was quiet, persuading. "Just try to think back and remember what he told you."

"He said something about making a fortune diving, and I joked about sunken treasure. And he said…" She strained to remember the conversation. It had been late in the evening, and she'd been busy, preoccupied. "I was working at home," Liz remembered. "I always seem to handle the books better at night. He'd been out, partying I thought, because he was a little unsteady when he came in. He pulled me out of the chair. I remember I started to swear at him but he looked so damn happy, I let it go. Really, I hardly listened because I was picking up all the papers he'd scattered, but he was saying something about the big time and buying champagne to celebrate. I told him he'd better stick to beer on his salary. That's when he talked about deals coming through and diving for big bucks. Then I made some comment about sunken treasure.…"

"And what did he say?"

"Sometimes you make more putting stuff in than taking it out." With a line between her brows, she remembered how he'd laughed when she'd told him to go sleep it off. "He made a pass neither one of us took seriously, and then...I think he made a phone call. I went back to work."

"When was this?"

"A week, maybe one week after I took him on."

"That must have been when he called me." Jonas looked out to sea. And he hadn't paid much attention, either, he reminded himself. Jerry had talked about coming home in style. But then he had always been talking about coming home in style. And the call, as usual, had been collect.

"Did you ever see him with anyone? Talking, arguing?"

"I never saw him argue with anyone. He flirted with the women on the beach, made small talk with the clients and got along just fine with everyone he worked with. I assumed he spent most of his free time in San Miguel. I think he cruised a few bars with Luis and some of the others."

"What bars?"

"You'll have to ask them, though I'm sure the police already have." She took a deep breath. It was bringing it all back again, too close. "Mr. Sharpe, why don't you let the police handle this? You're running after shadows."

"He was my brother." And more, what he couldn't explain, his twin. Part of himself had been murdered. If he were ever to feel whole again, he had to know why. "Haven't you wondered why Jerry was murdered?"

"Of course." She looked down at her hands. They were empty and she felt helpless. "I thought he must've gotten into a fight, or maybe he bragged to the wrong person. He had a bad habit of tossing what money he had around."

"It wasn't robbery or a mugging, Elizabeth. It was professional. It was business."

Her heart began a slow, painful thud. "I don't understand."

"Jerry was murdered by a pro, and I'm going to find out why."

Because her throat was suddenly dry, she swallowed. "If

you're right, then that's all the more reason to leave it to the police.''

He drew out his cigarettes again, but stared ahead to where the sky met the water. ''Police don't want revenge. I do.'' In his voice, she heard the calm patience and felt a shiver.

Staring, she shook her head. ''Even if you found the person who did it, what could you do?''

He took a long pull from his beer. ''As a lawyer, I suppose I'd be obliged to see they had their day in court. As a brother...'' He trailed off and drank again. ''We'll have to see.''

''I don't think you're a very nice man, Mr. Sharpe.''

''I'm not.'' He turned his head until his eyes locked on hers. ''And I'm not harmless. Remember, if I make a pass, we'll both take it seriously.''

She started to speak, then saw his line go taut. ''You've got a fish, Mr. Sharpe,'' she said dryly. ''You'd better strap in or he'll pull you overboard.''

Turning on her heel, she went back to the bridge, leaving Jonas to fend for himself.

Chapter 3

It was sundown when Liz parked her bike under the lean-to beside her house. She was still laughing. However much trouble Jonas had caused her, however much he had annoyed her in three brief meetings, she had his two hundred dollars. And he had a thirty-pound marlin—whether he wanted it or not. We deliver, she thought as she jingled her keys.

Oh, it had been worth it, just to see his face when he'd found himself on the other end of the wire from a big, bad-tempered fish. Liz believed he'd have let it go if she hadn't taken the time for one last smirk. Stubborn, she thought again. Yes, any other time she'd have admired it, and him.

Though she'd been wrong about his not being able to handle a rod, he'd looked so utterly perplexed with the fish lying at his feet on the deck that she'd nearly felt sorry for him. But his luck, or the lack of it, had helped her make an easy exit once they'd docked. With all the people crowding around to get a look at his catch and congratulate him, Jonas hadn't been able to detain her.

Now she was ready for an early evening, she thought. And a rainy one if the clouds moving in from the east delivered. Liz let herself into the house, propping the door open to bring in the breeze that already tasted of rain. After the fans were whirling, she turned on the radio automatically. Hurricane season might be a few months off, but the quick tropical storms were unpredictable. She'd been through enough of them not to take them lightly.

In the bedroom she prepared to strip for the shower that would wash the day's sweat and salt from her skin. Because it was twilight, she was already reaching for the light switch when a stray thought stopped her. Hadn't she left the blinds up that morning? Liz stared at them, tugged snugly over the windowsill. Odd, she was sure she'd left them up, and why wasn't the cord wrapped around its little hook? She was fanatical about that kind of detail, she supposed because ropes on a boat were always secured.

She hesitated, even after light spilled into the room. Then she shrugged. She must have been more distracted that morning than she'd realized. Jonas Sharpe, she decided, was taking up too much of her time, and too many of her thoughts. A man like him was bound to do so, even under different circumstances. But she'd long since passed the point in her life where a man could dominate it. He only worried her because he was interfering in her time, and her time was a precious commodity. Now that he'd had his way, and his talk, there should be no more visits. She remembered, uncomfortably, the way he'd smiled at her. It would be best, she decided, if he went back to where he'd come from and she got on with her own routine.

To satisfy herself, Liz walked over to the first shade and secured the cord. From the other room, the radio announced an evening shower before music kicked in. Humming along with it, she decided to toss together a chicken salad before she logged the day's accounts.

As she straightened, the breath was knocked out of her by an arm closing tightly around her neck. The dying sun caught a flash of silver. Before she could react, she felt the quick prick of a knife blade at her throat.

"Where is it?"

The voice that hissed in her ear was Spanish. In reflex, she brought her hands to the arm around her neck. As her nails dug in, she felt hard flesh and a thin metal band. She gasped for air, but stopped struggling when the knife poked threateningly at her throat.

"What do you want?" In terror her mind skimmed forward. She had less than fifty dollars cash and no jewelry of value except a single strand of pearls left by her grandmother. "My purse is in on the table. You can take it."

The vicious yank on her hair had her gasping in pain. "Where did he put it?"

"Who? I don't know what you want."

"Sharpe. Deal's off, lady. If you want to live, you tell me where he put the money."

"I don't know." The knife point pricked the vulnerable skin at her throat. She felt something warm trickle down her skin. Hysteria bubbled up behind it. "I never saw any money. You can look—there's nothing here."

"I've already looked." He tightened his hold until her vision grayed from lack of air. "Sharpe died fast. You won't be so lucky. Tell me where it is and nothing happens."

He was going to kill her. The thought ran in her head. She was going to die for something she knew nothing about. Money...he wanted money and she only had fifty dollars. Faith. As she felt herself on the verge of unconsciousness, she thought of her daughter. Who would take care of her? Liz bit down on her lip until the pain cleared her mind. She couldn't die.

"Please..." She let herself go limp in his arms. "I can't tell you anything. I can't breathe."

His hold loosened just slightly. Liz slumped against him and when he shifted, she brought her elbow back with all her strength. She didn't bother to turn around but ran blindly. A rug slid under her feet, but she stumbled ahead, too terrified to look back. She was already calling for help when she hit the front door.

Her closest neighbor was a hundred yards away. She vaulted the little fence that separated the yards and sprinted toward the house. She stumbled up the steps, sobbing. Even as the door opened, she heard the sound of a car squealing tires on the rough gravel road behind her.

"He tried to kill me," she managed, then fainted.

*   *   *

"There is no further information I can give you, Mr. Sharpe." Moralas sat in his neat office facing the waterfront. The file on his desk wasn't as thick as he would have liked. Nothing in his investigation had turned up a reason for Jerry Sharpe's murder. The man who sat across from him stared straight ahead. Moralas had a photo of the victim in the file, and a mirror image a few feet away. "I wonder, Mr. Sharpe, if your brother's death was a result of something that happened before his coming to Cozumel."

"Jerry wasn't running when he came here."

Moralas tidied his papers. "Still, we have asked for the cooperation of the New Orleans authorities. That was your brother's last known address."

"He never had an address," Jonas murmured. Or a conventional job, a steady woman. Jerry had been a comet, always refusing to burn itself out. "I've told you what Miss Palmer said. Jerry was cooking up a deal, and he was cooking it up in Cozumel."

"Yes, having to do with diving." Always patient, Moralas drew out a thin cigar. "Though we've already spoken with Miss Palmer, I appreciate your bringing me the information."

"But you don't know what the hell to do with it."

Moralas flicked on his lighter, smiling at Jonas over the flame. "You're blunt. I'll be blunt as well. If there was a trail to follow to your brother's murder, it's cold. Every day it grows colder. There were no fingerprints, no murder weapon, no witnesses." He picked up the file, gesturing with it. "That doesn't mean I intend to toss this in a drawer and forget about it. If there is a murderer on my island, I intend to find him. At the moment, I believe the murderer is miles away, perhaps in your own country. Procedure now is to backtrack on your brother's activities until we find something. To be frank, Mr. Sharpe, you're not doing yourself or me any good by being here."

"I'm not leaving."

"That is, of course, your privilege—unless you interfere

with police procedure.'' At the sound of the buzzer on his desk, Moralas tipped his ash and picked up the phone.

''Moralas.'' There was a pause. Jonas saw the captain's thick, dark brows draw together. ''Yes, put her on. Miss Palmer, this is Captain Moralas.''

Jonas stopped in the act of lighting a cigarette and waited. Liz Palmer was the key, he thought again. He had only to find what lock she fit.

''When? Are you injured? No, please stay where you are, I'll come to you.'' Moralas was rising as he hung up the phone. ''Miss Palmer has been attacked.''

Jonas was at the door first. ''I'm coming with you.''

His muscles ached with tension as the police car raced out of town toward the shore. He asked no questions. In his mind, Jonas could see Liz as she'd been on the bridge hours before—tanned, slim, a bit defiant. He remembered the self-satisfied smirk she'd given him when he'd found himself in a tug-of-war with a thirty-pound fish. And how neatly she'd skipped out on him the moment they'd docked.

She'd been attacked. Why? Was it because she knew more than she'd been willing to tell him? He wondered if she were a liar, an opportunist or a coward. Then he wondered how badly she'd been hurt.

As they pulled down the narrow drive, Jonas glanced toward Liz's house. The door was open, the shades drawn. She lived there alone, he thought, vulnerable and unprotected. Then he turned his attention to the little stucco building next door. A woman in a cotton dress and apron came onto the porch. She carried a baseball bat.

''You are the police.'' She nodded, satisfied, when Moralas showed his identification. ''I am Señora Alderez. She's inside. I thank the Virgin we were home when she came to us.''

''Thank you.''

Jonas stepped inside with Moralas and saw her. She was sitting on a patched sofa, huddled forward with a glass of wine in both hands. Jonas saw the liquid shiver back and forth as her hands trembled. She looked up slowly when they came in, her gaze passing over Moralas to lock on Jonas. She stared, with no expression in those deep, dark eyes. Just as slowly, she looked back at her glass.

"Miss Palmer." With his voice very gentle, Moralas sat down beside her. "Can you tell me what happened?"

She took the smallest of drinks, pressed her lips together briefly, then began as though she were reciting. "I came home at sunset. I didn't close the front door or lock it. I went straight into the bedroom. The shades were down, and I thought I'd left them up that morning. The cord wasn't secured, so I went over and fixed it. That's when he grabbed me—from behind. He had his arm around my neck and a knife. He cut me a little." In reflex, she reached up to touch the inch-long scratch her neighbor had already cleaned and fussed over. "I didn't fight because he had the knife at my throat and I thought he would kill me. He was going to kill me." She brought her head up to look directly into Moralas's eyes. "I could hear it in his voice."

"What did he say to you, Miss Palmer?"

"He said, 'Where is it?' I didn't know what he wanted. I told him he could take my purse. He was choking me and he said, 'Where did he put it?' He said Sharpe." This time she looked at Jonas. When she lifted her head, he saw that bruises were already forming on her throat. "He said the deal was off and he wanted the money. If I didn't tell him where it was he'd kill me, and I wouldn't die quickly, the way Jerry had. He didn't believe me when I said I didn't know anything." She spoke directly to Jonas. As she stared at him he felt the guilt rise.

Patient, Moralas touched her arm to bring her attention back to him. "He let you go?"

"No, he was going to kill me." She said it dully, without fear, without passion. "I knew he would whether I told him anything or not, and my daughter—she needs me. I slumped as if I'd fainted, then I hit him. I think I hit him in the throat with my elbow. And I ran."

"Can you identify the man?"

"I never saw him. I never looked."

"His voice."

"He spoke Spanish. I think he was short because his voice was right in my ear. I don't know anything else. I don't know anything about money or Jerry or anything else." She looked back into her glass, abruptly terrified she would cry. "I want to go home."

"As soon as my men make certain it's safe. You'll have police protection, Miss Palmer. Rest here. I'll come back for you and take you home."

She didn't know if it had been minutes or hours since she'd fled through the front door. When Moralas took her back, it was dark with the moon just rising. An officer would remain outside in her driveway and all her doors and windows had been checked. Without a word, she went through the house into the kitchen.

"She was lucky." Moralas gave the living room another quick check. "Whoever attacked her was careless enough to be caught off guard."

"Did the neighbors see anything?" Jonas righted a table that had been overturned in flight. There was a conch shell on the floor that had cracked.

"A few people noticed a blue compact outside the house late this afternoon. Senora Alderez saw it drive off when she opened the door to Miss Palmer, but she couldn't identify the make or the plates. We will, of course, keep Miss Palmer under surveillance while we try to track it down."

"It doesn't appear my brother's killer's left the island."

Moralas met Jonas's gaze blandly. "Apparently whatever deal your brother was working on cost him his life. I don't intend for it to cost Miss Palmer hers. I'll drive you back to town."

"No. I'm staying." Jonas examined the pale pink shell with the crack spreading down its length. He thought of the mark on Liz's throat. "My brother involved her." Carefully, he set the damaged shell down. "I can't leave her alone."

"As you wish." Moralas turned to go when Jonas stopped him.

"Captain, you don't still think the murderer's hundreds of miles away."

Moralas touched the gun that hung at his side. "No, Mr. Sharpe, I don't. *Buenas noches.*"

Jonas locked her door himself, then rechecked the windows before he went back to the kitchen. Liz was pouring her second cup of coffee. "That'll keep you up."

Liz drank half a cup, staring at him. She felt nothing at the moment, no anger, no fear. "I thought you'd gone."

"No." Without invitation, he found a mug and poured coffee for himself.

"Why are you here?"

He took a step closer, to run a fingertip gently down the mark on her throat. "Stupid question," he murmured.

She backed up, fighting to maintain the calm she'd clung to. If she lost control, it wouldn't be in front of him, in front of anyone. "I want to be alone."

He saw her hands tremble before she locked them tighter on the cup. "You can't always have what you want. I'll bunk in your daughter's room."

"No!" After slamming the cup down, she folded her arms across her chest. "I don't want you here."

With studied calm, he set his mug next to hers. When he took her shoulders, his hands were firm, not gentle. When he spoke, his voice was brisk, not soothing. "I'm not leaving you alone. Not now, not until they find Jerry's killer. You're involved whether you like it or not. And so, damn it, am I."

Her breath came quickly, too quickly, though she fought to steady it. "I wasn't involved until you came back and started hounding me."

He'd already wrestled with his conscience over that. Neither one of them could know if it were true. At the moment, he told himself it didn't matter. "However you're involved, you are. Whoever killed Jerry thinks you know something. You'll have an easier time convincing me you don't than you will them. It's time you started thinking about cooperating with me."

"How do I know you didn't send him here to frighten me?"

His eyes stayed on hers, cool and unwavering. "You don't.

I could tell you that I don't hire men to kill women, but you wouldn't have to believe it. I could tell you I'm sorry.'' For the first time, his tone gentled. He lifted a hand to brush the hair back from her face and his thumb slid lightly over her cheekbone. Like the conch shell, she seemed delicate, lovely and damaged. ''And that I wish I could walk away, leave you alone, let both of us go back to the way things were a few weeks ago. But I can't. We can't. So we might as well help each other.''

''I don't want your help.''

''I know. Sit down. I'll fix you something to eat.''

She tried to back away. ''You can't stay here.''

''I am staying here. Tomorrow, I'm moving my things from the hotel.''

''I said—''

''I'll rent the room,'' he interrupted, turning away to rummage through the cupboards. ''Your throat's probably raw. This chicken soup should be the best thing.''

She snatched the can from his hand. ''I can fix my own dinner, and you're not renting a room.''

''I appreciate your generosity.'' He took the can back from her. ''But I'd rather keep it on a business level. Twenty dollars a week seems fair. You'd better take it, Liz,'' he added before she could speak. ''Because I'm staying, one way or the other. Sit down,'' he said again and looked for a pot.

She wanted to be angry. It would help keep everything else bottled up. She wanted to shout at him, to throw him bodily out of her house. Instead she sat because her knees were too weak to hold her any longer.

What had happened to her control? For ten years she'd been running her own life, making every decision by herself, for herself. For ten years, she hadn't asked advice, she hadn't asked for help. Now something had taken control and decisions out of her hands, something she knew nothing about. Her life was part of a game, and she didn't know any of the rules.

She looked down and saw the tear drop on the back of her hand. Quickly, she reached up and brushed others from her cheeks. But she couldn't stop them. One more decision had been taken from her.

"Can you eat some toast?" Jonas asked her as he dumped the contents of the soup in a pan. When she didn't answer, he turned to see her sitting stiff and pale at the table, tears running unheeded down her face. He swore and turned away again. There was nothing he could do for her, he told himself. Nothing he could offer. Then, saying nothing, he came to the table, pulled a chair up beside her and waited.

"I thought he'd kill me." Her voice broke as she pressed a hand to her face. "I felt the knife against my throat and thought I was going to die. I'm so scared. Oh God, I'm so scared."

He drew her against him and let her sob out the fear. He wasn't used to comforting women. Those he knew well were too chic to shed more than a delicate drop or two. But he held her close during a storm of weeping that shook her body and left her gasping.

Her skin was icy, as if to prove the fact that fear made the blood run cold. She couldn't summon the pride to draw herself away, to seek a private spot as she'd always done in a crisis. He didn't speak to tell her everything would be fine; he didn't murmur quiet words of comfort. He was simply there. When she was drained, he still held her. The rain began slowly, patting the glass of the windows and pinging on the roof. He still held her.

When she shifted away, he rose and went back to the stove. Without a word, he turned on the burner. Minutes later he set a bowl in front of her then went back to ladle some for himself. Too tired to be ashamed, Liz began to eat. There was no sound in the kitchen but the slow monotonous plop of rain on wood, tin and glass.

She hadn't realized she could be hungry, but the bowl was empty almost before she realized it. With a little sigh, she pushed it away. He was tipped back in his chair, smoking in silence.

"Thank you."

"Okay." Her eyes were swollen, accentuating the vulnerability that always haunted them. It tugged at him, making him uneasy. Her skin, with its ripe, warm honey glow was pale, making her seem delicate and defenseless. She was a woman, he realized, that a man had to keep an emotional distance from. Get too close and you'd be sucked right in. It wouldn't do to care about her too much when he needed to use her to help both of them. From this point on, he'd have to hold the controls.

"I suppose I was more upset than I realized."

"You're entitled."

She nodded, grateful he was making it easy for her to skim over what she considered an embarrassing display of weakness. "There's no reason for you to stay here."

"I'll stay anyway."

She curled her hand into a fist, then uncurled it slowly. It wasn't possible for her to admit she wanted him to, or that for the first time in years she was frightened of being alone. Since she had to cave in, it was better to think of the arrangement on a practical level.

"All right, the room's twenty a week, first week in advance."

He grinned as he reached for his wallet. "All business?"

"I can't afford anything else." After putting the twenty on the counter, she stacked the bowls. "You'll have to see to your own food. The twenty doesn't include meals."

He watched her take the bowls to the sink and wash them. "I'll manage."

"I'll give you a key in the morning." She took a towel and meticulously dried the bowls. "Do you think he'll be back?" She tried to make her voice casual, and failed.

"I don't know." He crossed to her to lay a hand on her shoulder. "You won't be alone if he does."

When she looked at him, her eyes were steady again. Something inside him unknotted. "Are you protecting me, Jonas, or just looking for your revenge?"

"I do one, maybe I'll get the other." He twined the ends of her hair around his finger, watching the dark gold spread over his skin. "You said yourself I'm not a nice man."

''What are you?'' she whispered.

''Just a man.'' When his gaze lifted to hers, she didn't believe him. He wasn't just a man, but a man with patience, with power and with violence. ''I've wondered the same about you. You've got secrets, Elizabeth.''

She was breathless. In defense, she lifted her hand to his. ''They've got nothing to do with you.''

''Maybe they don't. Maybe you do.''

It happened very slowly, so slowly she could have stopped it. Yet she seemed unable to move. His arms slipped around her, drawing her close with an arrogant sort of laziness that should have been his undoing. Instead, Liz watched, fascinated, as his mouth lowered to hers.

She'd just thought of him as a violent man, but his lips were soft, easy, persuading. It had been so long since she'd allowed herself to be persuaded. With barely any pressure, with only the slightest hint of power, he sapped the will she'd always relied on. Her mind raced with questions, then clouded over to a fine, smoky mist. She wasn't aware of how sweetly, how hesitantly her mouth answered his.

Whatever impulse had driven him to kiss her was lost in the reality of mouth against mouth. He'd expected her to resist, or to answer with fire and passion. To find her so soft, yielding, unsteady, had his own desire building in a way he'd never experienced. It was as though she'd never been kissed before, never been held close to explore what man and woman have for each other. Yet she had a daughter, he reminded himself. She'd had a child, she was young, beautiful. Other men had held her like this. Yet he felt like the first and had no choice but to treat her with care.

The more she gave, the more he wanted. He'd known needs before. The longer he held her, the longer he wanted to. He understood passions. But a part of himself he couldn't understand held back, demanded restraint. She wanted him—he could feel it. But even as his blood began to swim, his hands, as if under their own power, eased her away.

Needs, so long unstirred, churned in her. As she stared back at him, Liz felt them spring to life, with all their demands and risks. It wouldn't happen to her again. But even as she renewed the vow she felt the soft, fluttering longings waltz through her. It couldn't happen again. But the eyes that were wide and on his reflected confusion and hurt and hope. It was a combination that left Jonas shaken.

"You should get some sleep," he told her, and took care not to touch her again.

So that was all, Liz thought as the flicker of hope died. It was foolish to believe, even for a moment, anything could change. She brought her chin up and straightened her shoulders. Perhaps she'd lost control of many things, but she could still control her heart. "I'll give you a receipt for the rent and the key in the morning. I get up at six." She took the twenty-dollar bill she'd left on the counter and walked out.

Chapter 4

The jury was staring at him. Twelve still faces with blank eyes were lined behind the rail. Jonas stood before them in a small, harshly lit courtroom that echoed with his own voice. He carried stacks of law books, thick, dusty and heavy enough to make his arms ache. But he knew he couldn't put them down. Sweat rolled down his temples, down his back as he gave an impassioned closing plea for his client's acquittal. It was life and death, and his voice vibrated with both. The jury remained unmoved, disinterested. Though he struggled to hold them, the books began to slip from his grasp. He heard the verdict rebound, bouncing off the courtroom walls.

Guilty. Guilty. Guilty.

Defeated, empty-handed, he turned to the defendant. The man stood, lifting his head so that they stared, eye to eye, twin images. Himself? Jerry. Desperate, Jonas walked to the bench. In black robes, Liz sat above him, aloof with distance. But her eyes were sad as she slowly shook her head. "I can't help you."

Slowly, she began to fade. He reached up to grab her hand, but his fingers passed through hers. All he could see were her dark, sad eyes. Then she was gone, his brother was gone, and he was left facing a jury—twelve cold faces who smiled smugly back at him.

Jonas lay still, breathing quickly. He found himself staring back at the cluster of gaily dressed dolls on the shelf beside the bed. A flamenco dancer raised her castanets. A princess held a glass slipper. A spiffily dressed Barbie relaxed in a pink convertible, one hand raised in a wave.

Letting out a long breath, Jonas ran a hand over his face and sat up. It was like trying to sleep in the middle of a party, he decided. No wonder he'd had odd dreams. On the opposing wall was a collection of stuffed animals ranging from the dependable bear to something that looked like a blue dust rag with eyes.

Coffee, Jonas thought, closing his own. He needed coffee. Trying to ignore the dozens of smiling faces surrounding him, he dressed. He wasn't sure how or where to begin. The coin on his chain dangled before he pulled a shirt over his chest. Outside, birds were sending up a clatter. At home there would have been the sound of traffic as Philadelphia awoke for the day. He could see a bush close to the window where purple flowers seemed to crowd each other for room. There were no sturdy elms, no tidy evergreen hedges or chain-link fences. No law books would help him with what he had to do. There was nothing familiar, no precedents to follow. Each step he took would be taken blindly, but he had to take them. He smelled the coffee the moment he left the room.

Liz was in the kitchen dressed in a T-shirt and what appeared to be the bottoms of a skimpy bikini. Jonas wasn't a man who normally awoke with all batteries charged, but he didn't miss a pair of long, honey-toned legs. Liz finished buttering a piece of toast.

"Coffee's on the stove," she said without turning around. "There're some eggs in the refrigerator. I don't stock cereal when Faith's away."

"Eggs are fine," he mumbled, but headed for the coffee.

"Use what you want, as long as you replace it." She turned up the radio to listen to the weather forecast. "I leave in a half hour, so if you want a ride to your hotel, you'll have to be ready."

Jonas let the first hot taste of coffee seep into his system. "My car's in San Miguel."

Liz sat down at the table to go over that day's schedule. "I can drop you by the El Presidente or one of the other hotels on the beach. You'll have to take a cab from there."

Jonas took another sip of coffee and focused on her fully. She was still pale, he realized, so that the marks on her neck stood out in dark relief. The smudges under her eyes made him decide she'd slept no better than he had. He tossed off his first cup of coffee and poured another.

"Ever consider taking a day off?"

She looked at him for the first time. "No," she said simply and lowered her gaze to her list again.

So they were back to business, all business, and don't cross the line. "Don't you believe in giving yourself a break, Liz?"

"I've got work to do. You'd better fix those eggs if you want to have time to eat them. The frying pan's in the cupboard next to the stove."

He studied her for another minute, then with a restless movement of his shoulders prepared to cook his breakfast. Liz waited until she was sure his back was to her before she looked up again.

She'd made a fool of herself the night before. She could almost accept the fact that she'd broken down in front of him because he'd taken it so matter-of-factly. But when she added the moments she'd stood in his arms, submissive, willing, hoping, she couldn't forgive herself. Or him.

He'd made her feel something she hadn't felt in a decade. Arousal. He'd made her want what she'd been convinced she didn't want from a man. Affection. She hadn't backed away or brushed him aside as she'd done with any other man who'd approached her. She hadn't even tried. He'd made her feel soft again, then he'd shrugged her away.

So it would be business, she told herself. Straight, impersonal business as long as he determined to stay. She'd put the rent money aside until she could manage the down payment on the aqua bikes. Jonas sat at the table with a plate of eggs that sent steam rising toward the ceiling.

"Your key." Liz slid it over to him. "And your receipt for the first week's rent."

Without looking at it, Jonas tucked the paper in his pocket. "Do you usually take in boarders?"

"No, but I need some new equipment." She rose to pour another cup of coffee and wash her plate. The radio announced the time before she switched it off. She was ten minutes ahead of schedule, but as long as she continued to get up early enough, they wouldn't have to eat together. "Do you usually rent a room in a stranger's house rather than a hotel suite?"

He tasted the eggs and found himself vaguely dissatisfied with his own cooking. "No, but we're not strangers anymore."

Liz watched him over the rim of her cup. He looked a little rough around the edges this morning, she decided. It added a bit too much sexuality to smooth good looks. She debated offering him a razor, then rejected the notion. Too personal. "Yes, we are."

He continued to eat his eggs so that she thought he'd taken her at her word. "I studied law at Notre Dame, apprenticed with Neiram and Barker in Boston, then opened my own practice five years ago in Philadelphia." He added some salt, hoping it would jazz up his cooking. "I specialize in criminal law. I'm not married, and live alone. In an apartment," he added. "On weekends I'm remodeling an old Victorian house I bought in Chadd's Ford."

She wanted to ask him about the house—was it big, did it have those wonderful high ceilings and rich wooden floors? Were the windows tall and mullioned? Was there a garden where roses climbed on trellises? Instead she turned to rinse out her cup. "That doesn't change the fact that we're strangers."

"Whether we know each other or not, we have the same problem."

The cup rattled in the sink as it slipped from her hand. Silently, Liz picked it up again, rinsed it off and set it in the drainer. She'd chipped it, but that was a small matter at the moment. "You've got ten minutes," she said, but he took her arm before she could skirt around him.

"We do have the same problem, Elizabeth." His voice was quiet, steady. She could have hated him for that alone.

"No, we don't. You're trying to avenge your brother's death. I'm just trying to make a living."

"Do you think everything would settle down quietly if I were back in Philadelphia?"

She tugged her arm uselessly. "Yes!" Because she knew she lied, her eyes heated.

"One of the first impressions I had of you was your intelligence. I don't know why you're hiding on your pretty little island, Liz, but you've got a brain, a good one. We both know that what happened to you last night would have happened with or without me."

"All right." She relaxed her arm. "What happened wasn't because of you, but because of Jerry. That hardly makes any difference to my position, does it?"

He stood up slowly, but didn't release her arm. "As long as someone thinks you knew what Jerry was into, you're the focus. As long as you're the focus, I'm standing right beside you, because directly or indirectly, you're going to lead me to Jerry's killer."

Liz waited a moment until she was sure she could speak calmly. "Is that all people are to you, Jonas? Tools? Means to an end?" She searched his face and found it set and remote. "Men like you never look beyond their own interests."

Angry without knowing why, he cupped her face in his hand. "You've never known a man like me."

"I think I have," she said softly. "You're not unique, Jonas. You were raised with money and expectations, you went to the best schools and associated with the best people. You had your goal set and if you had to step on or over a few people on the way to it, it wasn't personal. That's the worst of it," she said on a long breath. "It's never personal." Lifting her chin, she pushed his hand from her face. "What do you want me to do?"

Never in his life had anyone made him feel so vile. With

a few words she'd tried and condemned him. He remembered the dream, and the blank, staring eyes of the jury. He swore at her and turned to pace to the window. He couldn't back away now, no matter how she made him feel because he was right—whether he was here or in Philadelphia, she was still the key.

There was a hammock outside, bright blue and yellow strings stretched between two palms. He wondered if she ever gave herself enough time to use it. He found himself wishing he could take her hand, walk across the yard and lie with her on the hammock with nothing more important to worry about than swatting at flies.

"I need to talk to Luis," he began. "I want to know the places he went with Jerry, the people he may have seen Jerry talk to."

"I'll talk to Luis." When Jonas started to object, Liz shook her head. "You saw his reaction yesterday. He wouldn't be able to talk to you because you make him too nervous. I'll get you a list."

"All right." Jonas fished for his cigarettes and found with some annoyance that he'd left them in the bedroom. "I'll need you to go with me, starting tonight, to the places Luis gives you."

A feeling of stepping into quicksand came strongly. "Why?"

He wasn't sure of the answer. "Because I have to start somewhere."

"Why do you need me?"

And even less sure of this one. "I don't know how long it'll take, and I'm not leaving you alone."

She lifted a brow. "I have police protection."

"Not good enough. In any case, you know the language, the customs. I don't. I need you." He tucked his thumbs in his pockets. "It's as simple as that."

Liz walked over to turn off the coffee and move the pot to a back burner. "Nothing's simple," she corrected. "But I'll get your list, and I'll go along with you under one condition."

"Which is?"

She folded her hands. Jonas was already certain by her stance alone that she wasn't set to bargain but to lay down the rules. "That no matter what happens, what you find out or don't find out, you're out of this house and out of my life when my daughter comes home. I'll give you four weeks, Jonas—that's all."

"It'll have to be enough."

She nodded and started out of the room. "Wash your dishes. I'll meet you out front."

The police car still sat in the driveway when Jonas walked out the front door. A group of children stood on the verge of the road and discussed it in undertones. He heard Liz call one of them by name before she took out a handful of coins. Jonas didn't have to speak Spanish to recognize a business transaction. Moments later, coins in hand, the boy raced back to his friends.

"What was that about?"

Liz smiled after them. Faith would play with those same children throughout the summer. "I told them they were detectives. If they see anyone but you or the police around the house, they're to run right home and call Captain Moralas. It's the best way to keep them out of trouble."

Jonas watched the boy in charge pass out the coins. "How much did you give them?"

"Twenty pesos apiece."

He thought of the current rate of exchange and shook his head. "No kid in Philadelphia would give you the time of day for that."

"This is Cozumel," she said simply and wheeled out her bike.

Jonas looked at it, then at her. The bike would have sent a young teenager into ecstasies. "You drive this thing?"

Something in his tone made her want to smile. Instead, she kept her voice cool. "This thing is an excellent mode of transportation."

"A BMW's an excellent mode of transportation."

She laughed. He hadn't heard her laugh so easily since he'd met her. When she looked back at him, her eyes were warm and friendly. Jonas felt the ground shift dangerously under his feet. "Try to take your BMW on some of the back roads to the coast or into the interior." She swung a leg over the seat. "Hop on, Jonas, unless you want to hike back to the hotel."

Though he had his doubts, Jonas sat behind her. "Where do I put my feet?"

She glanced down and didn't bother to hide the grin. "Well, if I were you, I'd keep them off the ground." With this she started the engine then swung the bike around in the driveway. After adjusting for the added weight, Liz kept the speed steady. Jonas kept his hands lightly at her hips as the bike swayed around ruts and potholes.

"Are there roads worse than this?"

Liz sped over a bump. "What's wrong with this?"

"Just asking."

"If you want sophistication, try Cancun. It's only a few minutes by air."

"Ever get there?"

"Now and again. Last year Faith and I took the *Expatriate* over and spent a couple of days seeing the ruins. We have some shrines here. They're not well restored, but you shouldn't miss them. Still, I wanted her to see the pyramids and walled cities around Cancun."

"I don't know much about archaeology."

"You don't have to. All you need's an imagination."

She tooted the horn. Jonas saw an old, bent man straighten from the door of a shop and wave. "Señor Pessado," she said. "He gives Faith candy they both think I don't know about."

Jonas started to ask her about her daughter, then decided to wait for a better time. As long as she was being expansive, it was best to keep things less personal. "Do you know a lot of people on the island?"

"It's like a small town, I suppose. You don't necessarily have to know someone to recognize their face. I don't know a lot of people in San Miguel or on the east coast. I know a few people from the interior because we worked at the hotel."

"I didn't realize your shop was affiliated with the hotel."

"It's not." She paused at a stop sign. "I used to work in the hotel. As a maid." Liz gunned the engine and zipped across the intersection.

He looked at her hands, lean and delicate on the handlebars. He studied her slender shoulders, thought of the slight hips he was even now holding. It was difficult to imagine her lugging buckets and pails. "I'd have thought you more suited to the front desk or the concierge."

"I was lucky to find work at all, especially during the off season." She slowed the bike a bit as she started down the long drive to El Presidente. She'd indulge herself for a moment by enjoying the tall elegant palms that lined the road and the smell of blooming flowers. She was taking one of the dive boats out today, with five beginners who'd need instruction and constant supervision, but she wondered about the people inside the hotel who came to such a place to relax and to play.

"Is it still gorgeous inside?" she asked before she could stop herself.

Jonas glanced ahead to the large stately building. "Lots of glass," he told her. "Marble. The balcony of my room looks out over the water." She steered the bike to the curb. "Why don't you come in? See for yourself."

She was tempted. Liz had an affection for pretty things, elegant things. It was a weakness she couldn't allow herself. "I have to get to work."

Jonas stepped onto the curb, but put his hand over hers before she could drive away. "I'll meet you at the house. We'll go into town together."

She only nodded before turning the bike back toward the road. Jonas watched her until the sound of the motor died away. Just who was Elizabeth Palmer? he wondered. And why was it becoming more and more important that he find out?

By evening she was tired. Liz was used to working long hours, lugging equipment, diving, surfacing. But after a fairly easy day, she was tired. It should have made her feel secure to have had the young policeman identify himself to her and join her customers on the dive boat. It should have eased her mind that Captain Moralas was keeping his word about protection. It made her feel caged.

All during the drive home, she'd been aware of the police cruiser keeping a discreet distance. She'd wanted to run into her house, lock the door and fall into a dreamless, private sleep. But Jonas was waiting. She found him on the phone in her living room, a legal pad on his lap and a scowl on his face. Obviously a complication at his office had put him in a nasty mood. Ignoring him, Liz went to shower and change.

Because her wardrobe ran for the most part to beachwear, she didn't waste time studying her closet. Without enthusiasm, she pulled out a full cotton skirt in peacock blue and matched it with an oversized red shirt. More to prolong her time alone than for any other reason, she fiddled with her little cache of makeup. She was stalling, brushing out her braided hair, when Jonas knocked on her door. He didn't give her time to answer before he pushed it open.

"Did you get the list?"

Liz picked up a piece of notepaper. She could, of course, snap at him for coming in, but the end result wouldn't change. "I told you I would."

He took the paper from her to study it. He'd shaved, she noticed, and wore a casually chic jacket over bone-colored slacks. But the smoothness and gloss didn't mesh with the toughness around his mouth and in his eyes. "Do you know these places?"

"I've been to a couple of them. I don't really have a lot of time for bar- or club-hopping."

He glanced up and his curt answer slipped away. The shades behind her were up as she preferred them, but the light coming through the windows was pink with early evening. Though she'd buttoned the shirt high over her throat, her hair was brushed back, away from her face. She'd dawdled over the makeup, but her hand was always conservative. Her lashes were darkened, the lids lightly touched with shadow. She'd brushed some color over her cheeks but not her lips.

"You should be careful what you do to your eyes," Jonas

murmured, absently running his thumb along the top curve of her cheek. "They're a problem."

She felt the quick, involuntary tug but stood still. "A problem?"

"My problem." Uneasy, he tucked the paper in his pocket and glanced around the room. "Are you ready?"

"I need my shoes."

He didn't leave her as she'd expected, instead wandering around her room. It was, as was the rest of the house, furnished simply but with jarring color. The spicy scent he'd noticed before came from a wide green bowl filled with potpourri. On the wall were two colored sketches, one of a sunset very much like the quietly brilliant one outside the window, and another of a storm-tossed beach. One was all serenity, the other all violence. He wondered how much of each were inside Elizabeth Palmer. Prominent next to the bed was a framed photograph of a young girl.

She was all smiles in a flowered blouse tucked at the shoulders. Her hair came to a curve at her jawline, black and shiny. A tooth was missing, adding charm to an oval, tanned face. If it hadn't been for the eyes, Jonas would never have connected the child with Liz. They were richly, deeply brown, slightly tilted. Still, they laughed out of the photo, open and trusting, holding none of the secrets of her mother's.

"This is your daughter."

"Yes." Liz slipped on the second shoe before taking the photo out of Jonas's hand and setting it down again.

"How old is she?"

"Ten. Can we get started? I don't want to be out late."

"Ten?" A bit stunned, Jonas stopped her with a look. He'd assumed Faith was half that age, a product of a relationship Liz had fallen into while on the island. "You can't have a ten-year-old child."

Liz glanced down at the picture of her daughter. "I do have a ten-year-old child."

"You'd have been a child yourself."

"No. No, I wasn't." She started to leave again, and again he stopped her.

"Was she born before you came here?"

Liz gave him a long, neutral look. "She was born six months after I moved to Cozumel. If you want my help, Jonas, we go now. Answering questions about Faith isn't part of our arrangement."

But he didn't let go of her hand. As it could become so unexpectedly, his voice was gentle. "He was a bastard, wasn't he?"

She met his eyes without wavering. Her lips curved, but not with humor. "Yes. Oh yes, he was."

Without knowing why he was compelled to, Jonas bent and just brushed her lips with his. "Your daughter's lovely, Elizabeth. She has your eyes."

She felt herself softening again, too much, too quickly. There was understanding in his voice without pity. Nothing could weaken her more. In defense she took a step back. "Thank you. Now we have to go. I have to be up early tomorrow."

The first club they hit was noisy and crowded with a high percentage of American clientele. In a corner booth, a man in a tight white T-shirt spun records on a turntable and announced each selection with a display of colored lights. They ordered a quick meal in addition to drinks while Jonas hoped someone would have a reaction to his face.

"Luis said they came in here a lot because Jerry liked hearing American music." Liz nibbled on hot nachos as she looked around. It wasn't the sort of place she normally chose to spend an evening. Tables were elbow to elbow, and the music was pitched to a scream. Still, the crowd seemed good-natured enough, shouting along with the music or just shouting to each other. At the table beside them a group of people experimented with a bottle of tequila and a bowl of lemon wedges. Since they were a group of young gringos, she assumed they'd be very sick in the morning.

It was definitely Jerry's milieu, Jonas decided. Loud, just this side of wild and crammed to the breaking point. "Did Luis say if he spoke with anyone in particular?"

"Women." Liz smiled a bit as she sampled a tortilla. "Luis was very impressed with Jerry's ability to...interest the ladies."

"Any particular lady?"

"Luis said there was one, but Jerry just called her baby."

"An old trick," Jonas said absently.

"Trick?"

"If you call them all baby, you don't mix up names and complicate the situation."

"I see." She sipped her wine and found it had a delicate taste.

"Could Luis describe her?"

"Only that she was a knockout—a Mexican knockout, if that helps. She had lots of hair and lots of hip. Luis's words," Liz added when Jonas gave her a mild look. "He also said there were a couple of men Jerry talked to a few times, but he always went over to them, so Luis didn't know what they spoke about. One was American, one was Mexican. Since Luis was more interested in the ladies, he didn't pay any attention. But he did say Jerry would cruise the bars until he met up with them, then he'd usually call it a night."

"Did he meet them here?"

"Luis said it never seemed to be in the same place twice."

"Okay, finish up. We'll cruise around ourselves."

By the fourth stop, Liz was fed up. She noticed that Jonas no more than toyed with a drink at each bar, but she was tired of the smell of liquor. Some places were quiet, and on the edge of seamy. Others were raucous and lit with flashing lights. Faces began to blur together. There were young people, not so young people. There were Americans out for exotic nightlife, natives celebrating a night on the town. Some courted on dance floors or over tabletops. She saw those who seemed to have nothing but time and money, and others who sat alone nursing a bottle and a black mood.

"This is the last one," Liz told him as Jonas found a table at a club with a crowded dance floor and recorded music.

Jonas glanced at his watch. It was barely eleven. Action

rarely heated up before midnight. "All right," he said easily, and decided to distract her. "Let's dance."

Before she could refuse, he was pulling her into the crowd. "There's no room," she began, but his arms came around her.

"We'll make some." He had her close, his hand trailing up her back. "See?"

"I haven't danced in years," she muttered, and he laughed.

"There's no room anyway." Locked together, jostled by the crowd, they did no more than sway.

"What's the purpose in all this?" she demanded.

"I don't know until I find it. Meantime, don't you ever relax?" He rubbed his palm up her back again, finding the muscles taut.

"No."

"Let's try it this way." His gaze skimmed the crowd as he spoke. "What do you do when you're not working?"

"I think about working."

"Liz."

"All right, I read—books on marine life mostly."

"Busman's holiday?"

"It's what interests me."

Her body shifted intimately against his. Jonas forgot to keep his attention on the crowd and looked down at her. "*All* that interests you?"

He was too close. Liz tried to ease away and found his arms very solid. In spite of her determination to remain unmoved, her heart began to thud lightly in her head. "I don't have time for anything else."

She wore no perfume, he noted, but carried the scent of powder and spice. He wondered if her body would look as delicate as it felt against his. "It sounds as though you limit yourself."

"I have a business to run," she murmured. Would it be the same if he kissed her again? Sweet, overpowering. His lips were so close to hers, closer still when he ran his hand through her hair and drew her head back. She could almost taste him.

"Is making money so important?"

"It has to be," she managed, but could barely remember why. "I need to buy some aqua bikes."

Her eyes were soft, drowsy. They made him feel invulnerable. "Aqua bikes?"

"If I don't keep up with the competition..." He pressed a kiss to the corner of her mouth.

"The competition?" he prompted.

"I...the customers will go someplace else. So I..." The kiss teased the other corner.

"So?"

"I have to buy the bikes before the summer season."

"Of course. But that's weeks away. I could make love with you dozens of times before then. Dozens," he repeated as she stared at him. Then he closed his mouth over hers.

He felt her jolt—surprise, resistance, passion—he couldn't be sure. He only knew that holding her had led to wanting her and wanting to needing. By nature, he was a man who preferred his passion in private, quiet spots of his own choosing. Now he forgot the crowded club, loud music and flashing lights. They no longer swayed, but were hemmed into a corner of the dance floor, surrounded, pressed close. Oblivious.

She felt her head go light, heard the music fade. The heat from his body seeped into hers and flavored the kiss. Hot, molten, searing. Though they stood perfectly still, Liz had visions of racing. The breath backed up in her lungs until she released it with a shuddering sigh. Her body, coiled like a spring, went lax on a wave of confused pleasure. She strained closer, reaching up to touch his face. Abruptly the music changed from moody to rowdy. Jonas shifted her away from flailing arms.

"Poor timing," he murmured.

She needed a minute. "Yes." But she meant it in a more general way. It wasn't a matter of time and place, but a matter of impossibility. She started to move away when Jonas's grip tightened on her. "What is it?" she began, but only had to look at his face.

Cautiously, she turned to see what he stared at. A woman in a skimpy red dress stared back at him. Liz recognized the shock in her eyes before the woman turned and fled, leaving her dance partner gaping.

"Come on." Without waiting for her, Jonas sprinted through the crowd. Dodging, weaving and shoving when she had to, Liz dashed after him.

The woman had barely gotten out to the street when Jonas caught up to her. "What are you running away from?" he demanded. His fingers dug into her arms as he held her back against a wall.

"Por favor, no comprendo," she murmured and shook like a leaf.

"Oh yes, I think you do." With his fingers bruising her arms, Jonas towered over her until she nearly squeaked in fear. "What do you know about my brother?"

"Jonas." Appalled, Liz stepped between them. "If this is the way you intend to behave, you'll do without my help." She turned away from him and touched the woman's shoulder. *"Lo siento mucho,"* she began, apologizing for Jonas. "He's lost his brother. His brother, Jerry Sharpe. Did you know him?"

She looked at Liz and whispered. "He has Jerry's face. But he's dead—I saw in the papers."

"This is Jerry's brother, Jonas. We'd like to talk to you."

As Liz had, the woman had already sensed the difference between Jonas and the man she'd known. She'd never have cowered away from Jerry for the simple reason that she'd known herself to be stronger and more clever. The man looming over her now was a different matter.

"I don't know anything."

"Por favor. Just a few minutes."

"Tell her I'll make it worth her while," Jonas added before she could refuse again. Without waiting for Liz to translate, he reached for his wallet and took out a bill. He saw fear change to speculation.

"A few minutes," she agreed, but pointed to an outdoor café. "There."

Jonas ordered two coffees and a glass of wine. "Ask her her name," he told Liz.

"I speak English." The woman took out a long, slim cigarette and tapped it on the tabletop. "I'm Erika. Jerry and I were friends." More relaxed, she smiled at Jonas. "You know, good friends."

"Yes, I know."

"He was very good-looking," she added, then caught her bottom lip between her teeth. "Lots of fun."

"How long did you know him?"

"A couple of weeks. I was sorry when I heard he was dead."

"Murdered," Jonas stated.

Erika took a deep drink of wine. "Do you think it was because of the money?"

Every muscle in his body tensed. Quickly, he shot Liz a warning look before she could speak. "I don't know—it looks that way. How much did he tell you about it?"

"Oh, just enough to intrigue me. You know." She smiled again and held out her cigarette for a light. "Jerry was very charming. And generous." She remembered the little gold bracelet he'd bought for her and the earrings with the pretty blue stones. "I thought he was very rich, but he said he would soon be much richer. I like charming men, but I especially like rich men. Jerry said when he had the money, we could take a trip." She blew out smoke again before giving a philosophical little shrug. "Then he was dead."

Jonas studied her as he drank coffee. She was, as Luis had said, a knockout. And she wasn't stupid. He was also certain her mind was focusing on one point, and one point alone. "Do you know when he was supposed to have the money?"

"Sure, I had to take off work if we were going away. He called me—it was Sunday. He was so excited. 'Erika,' he said, 'I hit the jackpot.' I was a little mad because he hadn't shown up Saturday night. He told me he'd done some quick business in Acapulco and how would I like to spend a few weeks in Monte Carlo?" She gave Jonas a lash-fluttering smile. "I decided to forgive him. I was packed," she added, blowing smoke past Jonas's shoulder. "We were supposed to leave

Tuesday afternoon. I saw in the papers Monday night that he was dead. The papers said nothing about the money.''

"Do you know who he had business with?''

"No. Sometimes he would talk to another American, a skinny man with pale hair. Other times he would see a Mexican. I didn't like him—he had *mal ojo*.''

"Evil eye,'' Liz interpreted. "Can you describe him?''

"Not pretty,'' she said offhandedly. "His face was pitted. His hair was long in the back, over his collar and he was very thin and short.'' She glanced at Jonas again with a sultry smile that heated the air. "I like tall men.''

"Do you know his name?''

"No. But he dressed very nicely. Nice suits, good shoes. And he wore a silver band on his wrist, a thin one that crossed at the ends. It was very pretty. Do you think he knows about the money? Jerry said it was lots of money.''

Jonas merely reached for his wallet. "I'd like to find out his name,'' he told her and set a fifty on the table. His hand closed over hers as she reached for it. "His name, and the name of the American. Don't hold out on me, Erika.''

With a toss of her head, she palmed the fifty. "I'll find out the names. When I tell you, it's another fifty.''

"When you tell me.'' He scrawled Liz's number on the back of a business card. "Call this number when you have something.''

"Okay.'' She slipped the fifty into her purse as she stood up. "You know, you don't look as much like Jerry as I thought.'' With the click of high heels, she crossed the pavement and went back into the club.

"It's a beginning,'' Jonas murmured as he pushed his coffee aside. When he looked over, he saw Liz studying him. "Problem?''

"I don't like the way you work.''

He dropped another bill on the table before he rose. "I don't have time to waste on amenities.''

"What would you have done if I hadn't calmed her down? Dragged her off to the nearest alley and beaten it out of her?''

He drew out a cigarette, struggling with temper. "Let's go home, Liz."

"I wonder if you're any different from the men you're looking for." She pushed back from the table. "Just as a matter of interest, the man who broke into my house and attacked me wore a thin band at his wrist. I felt it when he held the knife to my throat."

She watched as his gaze lifted from the flame at the end of the cigarette and came to hers. "I think you two might recognize each other when the time comes."

Chapter 5

"Always check your gauges," Liz instructed, carefully indicating each one on her own equipment as she spoke. "Each one of these gauges is vital to your safety when you dive. That's true if it's your first dive or your fiftieth. It's very easy to become so fascinated not only by the fish and coral, but the sensation of diving itself, that you can forget you're dependent on your air tank. Always be certain you start your ascent while you have five or ten minutes of air left."

She'd covered everything, she decided, in the hour lesson. If she lectured any more, her students would be too impatient to listen. It was time to give them a taste of what they were paying for.

"We'll dive as a group. Some of you may want to explore on your own, but remember, always swim in pairs. As a final precaution, check the gear of the diver next to you."

Liz strapped on her own weight belt as her group of novices followed instructions. So many of them, she knew, looked on scuba diving as an adventure. That was fine, as long as they remembered safety. Whenever she instructed, she stressed the what ifs just as thoroughly as the how tos. Anyone who went down under her supervision would know what steps to take under any circumstances. Diving accidents were most often the result of carelessness. Liz was never careless with herself or with her students. Most of them were talking excitedly as they strapped on tanks.

"This group." Luis hefted his tank. "Very green."

"Yeah." Liz helped him with the straps. As she did with all her employees, Liz supplied Luis's gear. It was checked just as thoroughly as any paying customer's. "Keep an eye on the honeymoon couple, Luis. They're more interested in each other than their regulators."

"No problem." He assisted Liz with her tank, then stepped back while she cinched the straps. "You look tired, kid."

"No, I'm fine."

When she turned, he glanced at the marks on her neck. The story had already made the rounds. "You sure? You don't look so fine."

She lifted a brow as she hooked on her diving knife. "Sweet of you."

"Well, I mean it. You got me worried about you."

"No need to worry." As Liz pulled on her mask, she glanced over at the roly-poly fatherly type who was struggling with his flippers. He was her bodyguard for the day. "The police have everything under control," she said, and hoped it was true. She wasn't nearly as sure about Jonas.

He hadn't shocked her the night before. She'd sensed that dangerously waiting violence in him from the first. But seeing his face as he'd grabbed Erika, hearing his voice, had left her with a cold, flat feeling in her stomach. She didn't know him well enough to be certain if he would choose to control the violence or let it free. More, how could she know he was capable of leashing it? Revenge, she thought, was never pretty. And that's what he wanted. Remembering the look in his eyes, Liz was very much afraid he'd get it.

The boat listed, bringing her back to the moment. She couldn't think about Jonas now, she told herself. She had a business to run and customers to satisfy.

"Miss Palmer." A young American with a thin chest and a winning smile maneuvered over to her. "Would you mind giving me a check?"

"Sure." In her brisk, efficient way, Liz began to check gauges and hoses.

"I'm a little nervous," he confessed. "I've never done this sort of thing before."

"It doesn't hurt to be a little nervous. You'll be more careful. Here, pull your mask down. Make sure it's comfortable but snug."

He obeyed, and his eyes looked wide and pale through the glass. "If you don't mind, I think I'll stick close to you down there."

She smiled at him. "That's what I'm here for. The depth here is thirty feet," she told the group in general. "Remember to make your adjustments for pressure and gravity as you descend. Please keep the group in sight at all times." With innate fluidity, she sat on the deck and rolled into the water. With Luis on deck, and Liz treading a few feet away, they waited until each student made his dive. With a final adjustment to her mask, Liz went under.

She'd always loved it. The sensation of weightlessness, the fantasy of being unimpeded, invulnerable. From near the surface, the sea floor was a spread of white. She loitered there a moment, enjoying the cathedral like view. Then, with an easy kick, she moved down with her students.

The newlyweds were holding hands and having the time of their lives. Liz reminded herself to keep them in sight. The policeman assigned to her was plodding along like a sleepy sea turtle. He'd keep her in sight. Most of the others remained in a tight group, fascinated but cautious. The thin American gave her a wide-eyed look that was a combination of pleasure and nerves and stuck close by her side. To help him relax, Liz touched his shoulder and pointed up. In an easy motion, she turned on her back so that she faced the surface. Sunlight streaked thinly through the water. The hull of the dive boat was plainly visible. He nodded and followed her down.

Fish streamed by, some in waves, some on their own. Though the sand was white, the water clear, there was a montage of color. Brain coral rose up in sturdy mounds, the color of saffron. Sea fans, as delicate as lace, waved pink and purple in the current. She signaled to her companion and watched a school of coral sweepers, shivering with metallic tints, turn as a unit and skim through staghorn coral.

It was a world she understood as well, perhaps better, than the one on the surface. Here, in the silence, Liz often found the peace of mind that eluded her from day to day. The scientific names of the fish and formations they passed were no strangers to her. Once she'd studied them diligently, with dreams of solving mysteries and bringing the beauty of the world of the sea to others. That had been another life. Now she coached tourists and gave them, for hourly rates, something memorable to take home after a vacation. It was enough.

Amused, she watched an angelfish busy itself by swallowing the bubbles rising toward the surface. To entertain her students, she poked at a small damselfish. The pugnacious male clung to his territory and nipped at her. To the right, she saw sand kick up and cloud the water. Signaling for caution, Liz pointed out the platelike ray that skimmed away, annoyed by the intrusion.

The new husband showed off a bit, turning slow somersaults for his wife. As divers gained confidence, they spread out a little farther. Only her bodyguard and the nervous American stayed within an arm span at all times. Throughout the thirty-minute dive, Liz circled the group, watching individual divers. By the time the lesson was over, she was satisfied that her customers had gotten their money's worth. This was verified when they surfaced.

"Great!" A British businessman on his first trip to Mexico clambered back onto the deck. His face was reddened by the sun but he didn't seem to mind. "When can we go down again?"

With a laugh, Liz helped other passengers on board. "You have to balance your down time with your surface time. But we'll go down again."

"What was that feathery-looking stuff?" someone else asked. "It grows like a bush."

"It's a gorgonian, from the Gorgons of mythology." She slipped off her tanks and flexed her muscles. "If you remember, the Gorgons had snakes for hair. The whip gorgonian has a resilient skeletal structure and undulates like a snake with the current.''

More questions were tossed out, more answers supplied. Liz noticed the American who'd stayed with her, sitting by himself, smiling a little. Liz moved around gear then dropped down beside him.

''You did very well.''

''Yeah?'' He looked a little dazed as he shrugged his shoulders. ''I liked it, but I gotta admit, I felt better knowing you were right there. You sure know what you're doing.''

''I've been at it a long time.''

He sat back, unzipping his wet suit to his waist. ''I don't mean to be nosy, but I wondered about you. You're American, aren't you?''

It had been asked before. Liz combed her fingers through her wet hair. ''That's right.''

''From?''

''Houston.''

''No kidding.'' His eyes lit up. ''Hell, I went to school in Texas. Texas A and M.''

''Really?'' The little tug she felt rarely came and went. ''So did I, briefly.''

''Small world,'' he said, pleased with himself. ''I like Texas. Got a few friends in Houston. I don't suppose you know the Dresscots?''

''No.''

''Well, Houston isn't exactly small-town U.S.A.'' He stretched out long, skinny legs that were shades paler than his arms but starting to tan. ''So you went to Texas A and M.''

''That's right.''

''What'd you study?''

She smiled and looked out to sea. ''Marine biology.''

''Guess that fits.''

''And you?''

''Accounting.'' He flashed his grin again. ''Pretty dry stuff. That's why I always take a long breather after tax time.''

"Well, you chose a great place to take it. Ready to go down again?"

He took a long breath as if to steady himself. "Yeah. Hey, listen, how about a drink after we get back in?"

He was attractive in a mild sort of way, pleasant enough. She gave him an apologetic smile as she rose. "It sounds nice, but I'm tied up."

"I'll be around for a couple of weeks. Some other time?"

"Maybe. Let's check your gear."

By the time the dive boat chugged into shore, the afternoon was waning. Her customers, most of them pleased with themselves, wandered off to change for dinner or spread out on the beach. Only a few loitered near the boat, including her bodyguard and the accountant from America. It occurred to Liz that she might have been a bit brisk with him.

"I hope you enjoyed yourself, Mr...."

"Trydent. But it's Scott, and I did. I might just try it again."

Liz smiled at him as she helped Luis and another of her employees unload the boat. "That's what we're here for."

"You, ah, ever give private lessons?"

Liz caught the look. Perhaps she hadn't been brisk enough. "On occasion."

"Then maybe we could—"

"Hey, there, missy."

Liz shaded her eyes. "Mr. Ambuckle."

He stood on the little walkway, his legs bulging out of the short wet suit. What hair he had was sleeked wetly back. Beside him, his wife stood wearily in a bathing suit designed to slim down wide hips. "Just got back in!" he shouted. "Had a full day of it."

He seemed enormously pleased with himself. His wife looked at Liz and rolled her eyes. "Maybe I should take you out as crew, Mr. Ambuckle."

He laughed, slapping his side. "Guess I'd rather dive than anything." He glanced at his wife and patted her shoulder. "Almost anything. Gotta trade in these tanks, honey, and get me some fresh ones."

"Going out again?"

"Tonight. Can't talk the missus into it."

"I'm crawling into bed with a good book," she told Liz. "The only water I want to see is in the tub."

With a laugh, Liz jumped down to the walkway. "At the moment, I feel the same way. Oh, Mr. and Mrs. Ambuckle, this is Scott Trydent. He just took his first dive."

"Well now." Expansive, Ambuckle slapped him on the back. "How'd you like it?"

"Well, I—"

"Nothing like it, is there? You want try it at night, boy. Whole different ball game at night."

"I'm sure, but—"

"Gotta trade in these tanks." After slapping Scott's back again, Ambuckle hefted his tanks and waddled off toward the shop.

"Obsessed," Mrs. Ambuckle said, casting her eyes to the sky. "Don't let him get started on you, Mr. Trydent. You'll never get any peace."

"No, I won't. Nice meeting you, Mrs. Ambuckle." Obviously bemused, Scott watched her wander back toward the hotel. "Quite a pair."

"That they are." Liz lifted her own tanks. She stored them separately from her rental equipment. "Goodbye, Mr. Trydent."

"Scott," he said again. "About that drink—"

"Thanks anyway," Liz said pleasantly and left him standing on the walkway. "Everything in?" she asked Luis as she stepped into the shop.

"Checking it off now. One of the regulators is acting up."

"Set it aside for Jose to look at." As a matter of habit, she moved into the back to fill her tanks before storage. "All the boats are in, Luis. We shouldn't have too much more business now. You and the rest can go on as soon as everything's checked in. I'll close up."

"I don't mind staying."

"You closed up last night," she reminded him. "What do

you want?'' She tossed a grin over her shoulder. ''Overtime?
Go on home, Luis. You can't tell me you don't have a date.''

He ran a fingertip over his mustache. ''As a matter of
fact...''

''A hot date?'' Liz lifted a brow as air hissed into her tank.

''Is there any other kind?''

Chuckling, Liz straightened. She noticed Ambuckle trudg-
ing across the sand with his fresh tanks. Her other employees
talked among themselves as the last of the gear was stored.
''Well, go make yourself beautiful then. The only thing I have
a date with is the account books.''

''You work too much,'' Luis mumbled.

Surprised, Liz turned back to him. ''Since when?''

''Since always. It gets worse every time you send Faith
back to school. Better off if she was here.''

That her voice cooled only slightly was a mark of her affection for Luis. ''No, she's happy in Houston with my parents. If I thought she wasn't, she wouldn't be there.''

''She's happy, sure. What about you?''

Her brows drew together as she picked her keys from a
drawer. ''Do I look unhappy?''

''No.'' Tentatively, he touched her shoulder. He'd known
Liz for years, and understood there were boundaries she
wouldn't let anyone cross. ''But you don't look happy either.
How come you don't give one of these rich American tourists
a spin? That one on the boat—his eyes popped out every time
he looked at you.''

The exaggeration made her laugh, so she patted his cheek.
''So you think a rich American tourist is the road to happiness?''

''Maybe a handsome Mexican.''

''I'll think about it—after the summer season. Go home,''
she ordered.

''I'm going.'' Luis pulled a T-shirt over his chest. ''You
look out for that Jonas Sharpe,'' he added. ''He's got a different kind of look in his eyes.''

Liz waved him off. *''Hasta luego.''*

When the shop was empty, Liz stood, jingling her keys and

looking out onto the beach. People traveled in couples, she noted, from the comfortably married duo stretched out on lounge chairs, to the young man and woman curled together on a beach towel. Was it an easy feeling, she wondered, to be half of a set? Or did you automatically lose part of yourself when you joined with another?

She'd always thought of her parents as separate people, yet when she thought of one, the other came quickly to mind. Would it be a comfort to know you could reach out your hand and someone else's would curl around it?

She held out her own and remembered how hard, how strong, Jonas's had been. No, he wouldn't make a relationship a comfortable affair. Being joined with him would be demanding, even frightening. A woman would have to be strong enough to keep herself intact, and soft enough to allow herself to merge. A relationship with a man like Jonas would be a risk that would never ease.

For a moment, she found herself dreaming of it, dreaming of what it had been like to be held close and kissed as though nothing and no one else existed. To be kissed like that always, to be held like that whenever the need moved you—it might be worth taking chances for.

Stupid, she thought quickly, shaking herself out of it. Jonas wasn't looking for a partner, and she wasn't looking for a dream. Circumstances had tossed them together temporarily. Both of them had to deal with their own realities. But she felt a sense of regret and a stirring of wishes.

Because the feeling remained, just beyond her grasp, Liz concentrated hard on the little details that needed attending to before she could close up. The paperwork and the contents of the cash box were transferred to a canvas portfolio. She'd have to swing out of her way to make a night deposit, but she no longer felt safe taking the cash or the checks home. She spent an extra few minutes meticulously filling out a deposit slip.

It wasn't until she'd picked up her keys again that she remembered her tanks. Tucking the portfolio under the counter, she turned to deal with her own gear.

It was perhaps her only luxury. She'd spent more on her personal equipment than she had on all the contents of her closet and dresser. To Liz, the wet suit was more exciting than any French silks. All her gear was kept separate from the shop's inventory. Unlocking the door to the closet, Liz hung up her wet suit, stored her mask, weight belt, regulator. Her knife was sheathed and set on a shelf. After setting her tanks side by side, she shut the door and prepared to lock it again. After she'd taken two steps away she looked down at the keys again. Without knowing precisely why, she moved each one over the ring and identified it.

The shop door, the shop window, her bike, the lock for the chain, the cash box, the front and back doors of her house, her storage room. Eight keys for eight locks. But there was one more on her ring, a small silver key that meant nothing to her at all.

Puzzled, she counted off the keys again, and again found one extra. Why should there be a key on her ring that didn't belong to her? Closing her fingers over it, she tried to think if anyone had given her the key to hold. No, it didn't make sense. Brows drawn together, she studied the key again. Too small for a car or door key, she decided. It looked like the key to a locker, or a box or... Ridiculous, she decided on a long breath. It wasn't her key but it was on her ring. Why?

Because someone put it there, she realized, and opened her hand again. Her keys were often tossed in the drawer at the shop for easy access for Luis or one of the other men. They needed to open the cash box. And Jerry had often worked in the shop alone.

With a feeling of dread, Liz slipped the keys into her pocket. Jonas's words echoed in her head. *"You're involved, whether you want to be or not."*

Liz closed the shop early.

Jonas stepped into the dim bar to the scent of garlic and the wail of a squeaky jukebox. In Spanish, someone sang of endless love. He stood for a moment, letting his eyes adjust, then skimmed his gaze over the narrow booths. As agreed, Erika sat all the way in the back, in the corner.

"You're late." She waved an unlit cigarette idly as he joined her.

"I passed it the first time. This place isn't exactly on the tourist route."

She closed her lips over the filter as Jonas lit her cigarette. "I wanted privacy."

Jonas glanced around. There were two men at the bar, each deep in separate bottles. Another couple squeezed themselves together on one side of a booth. The rest of the bar was deserted. "You've got it."

"But I don't have a drink."

Jonas slid out from the booth and bought two drinks at the bar. He set tequila and lime in front of Erika and settled for club soda. "You said you had something for me."

Erica twined a string of colored beads around her finger. "You said you would pay fifty for a name."

In silence, Jonas took out his wallet. He set fifty on the table, but laid his hand over it. "You have the name."

Erika smiled and sipped at her drink. "Maybe. Maybe you want it bad enough to pay another fifty."

Jonas studied her coolly. This was the type his brother had always been attracted to. The kind of woman whose hard edge was just a bit obvious. He could give her another fifty, Jonas mused, but he didn't care to be taken for a sucker. Without a word, he picked up the bill and tucked it into his pocket. He was halfway out of the booth when Erika grabbed his arm.

"Okay, don't get mad. Fifty." She sent him an easy smile as he settled back again. Erika had been around too long to let an opportunity slip away. "A girl has to make a living, *sí?* The name is Pablo Manchez—he's the one with the face."

"Where can I find him?"

"I don't know. You got the name."

With a nod, Jonas took the bill out and passed it to her. Erika folded it neatly into her purse. "I'll tell you something else, because Jerry was a sweet guy." Her gaze skimmed the bar again as she leaned closer to Jonas. "This Manchez, he's bad. People got nervous when I asked about him. I heard he was mixed up in a couple of murders in Acapulco last year. He's paid, you know, to..." She made a gun out of her hand and pushed down her thumb. "When I hear that, I stop asking questions."

"What about the other one, the American?"

"Nothing. Nobody knows him. But if he hangs out with Manchez, he's not a Boy Scout." Erika tipped back her drink. "Jerry got himself in some bad business."

"Yeah."

"I'm sorry." She touched the bracelet on her wrist. "He gave me this. We had some good times."

The air in the bar was stifling him. Jonas rose and hesitated only a moment before he took out another bill and set it next to her drink. "Thanks."

Erika folded the bill as carefully as the first. *"De nada."*

She'd wanted him to be home. When Liz found the house empty, she made a fist over the keys in her hand and swore in frustration. She couldn't sit still; her nerves had been building all during the drive home. Outside, Moralas's evening shift was taking over.

For how long? she wondered. How long would the police sit patiently outside her house and follow her through her daily routine? In her bedroom, Liz closed the canvas bag of papers and cash in her desk. She regretted not having a lock for it, as well. Sooner or later, she thought, Moralas would back off on the protection. Then where would she be? Liz looked down at the key again. She'd be alone, she told herself bluntly. She had to do something.

On impulse, she started into her daughter's room. Perhaps Jerry had left a case, a box of some kind that the police had overlooked. Systematically she searched Faith's closet. When she found the little teddy bear with the worn ear, she brought it down from the shelf. She'd bought it for Faith before she'd been born. It was a vivid shade of purple, or had been so many years before. Now it was faded a bit, a little loose at the seams. The ear had been worn down to a nub because

Faith had always carried him by it. They'd never named it, Liz recalled. Faith had merely called it *mine* and been satisfied.

On a wave of loneliness that rocked her, Liz buried her face against the faded purple pile. "Oh, I miss you, baby," she murmured. "I don't know if I can stand it."

"Liz?"

On a gasp of surprise, Liz stumbled back against the closet door. When she saw Jonas, she put the bear behind her back. "I didn't hear you come in," she said, feeling foolish.

"You were busy." He came toward her to gently pry the bear from her fingers. "He looks well loved."

"He's old." She cleared her throat and took the toy back again. But she found it impossible to stick it back on the top shelf. "I keep meaning to sew up the seams before the stuffing falls out." She set the bear down on Faith's dresser. "You've been out."

"Yes." He'd debated telling her of his meeting with Erika, and had decided to keep what he'd learned to himself, at least for now. "You're home early."

"I found something." Liz reached in her pocket and drew out her keys. "This isn't mine."

Jonas frowned at the key she indicated. "I don't know what you mean."

"I mean this isn't my key, and I don't know how it got on my ring."

"You just found it today?"

"I found it today, but it could have been put on anytime. I don't think I would've noticed." With the vain hope of distancing herself, Liz unhooked it from the others and handed it to Jonas. "I keep these in a drawer at the shop when I'm there. At home, I usually toss them on the kitchen counter. I can't think of any reason for someone to put it with mine unless they wanted to hide it."

Jonas examined the key. "'The Purloined Letter,'" he murmured.

"What?"

"It was one of Jerry's favorite stories when we were kids.

I remember when he tested out the theory by putting a book he'd bought for my father for Christmas on the shelf in the library.''

''So do you think it was his?''

''I think it would be just his style.''

Liz picked up the bear again, finding it comforted her. ''It doesn't do much good to have a key when you don't have the lock.''

''It shouldn't be hard to find it.'' He held the key up by the stem. ''Do you know what it is?''

''A key.'' Liz sat on Faith's bed. No, she hadn't distanced herself. The quicksand was bubbling again.

''To a safe-deposit box.'' Jonas turned it over to read the numbers etched into the metal.

''Do you think Captain Moralas can trace it?''

''Eventually,'' Jonas murmured. The key was warm in his hand. It was the next step, he thought. It had to be. ''But I'm not telling him about it.''

''Why?''

''Because he'd want it, and I don't intend to give it to him until I open the lock myself.''

She recognized the look easily enough now. It was still revenge. Leaving the bear on her daughter's bed, Liz rose. ''What are you going to do, go from bank to bank and ask if you can try the key out? You won't have to call the police, they will.''

''I've got some connections—and I've got the serial number.'' Jonas pocketed the key. ''With luck, I'll have the name of the bank by tomorrow afternoon. You may have to take a couple of days off.''

''I can't take a couple of days off, and if I could, why should I need to?''

''We're going to Acapulco.''

She started to make some caustic comment, then stopped. ''Because Jerry told Erika he'd had business there?''

''If Jerry was mixed up in something, and he had something important or valuable, he'd tuck it away. A safe-deposit box in Acapulco makes sense.''

"Fine. If that's what you believe, have a nice trip." She started to brush past him. Jonas only had to shift his body to bar the door.

"We go together."

The word "together" brought back her thoughts on couples and comfort. And it made her remember her conclusion about Jonas. "Look, Jonas, I can't drop everything and follow you on some wild-goose chase. Acapulco is very cosmopolitan. You won't need an interpreter."

"The key was on your ring. The knife was at your throat. I want you where I can see you."

"Concerned?" Her face hardened, muscle by muscle. "You're not concerned with me, Jonas. And you're certainly not concerned *about* me. The only thing you care about is your revenge. I don't want any part of it, or you."

He took her by the shoulders until she was backed against the door. "We both know that's not true. We've started something." His gaze skimmed down, lingered on her lips. "And it's not going to stop until we're both finished with it."

"I don't know what you're talking about."

"Yes, you do." He pressed closer so that their bodies met and strained, one against the other. He pressed closer to prove something, perhaps only to himself. "Yes, you do," he repeated. "I came here to do something, and I intend to do it. I don't give a damn if you call it revenge."

Her heart was beating lightly at her throat. She wouldn't call it fear. But his eyes were cold and close. "What else?"

"Justice."

She felt an uncomfortable twinge, remembering her own feelings on justice. "You're not using your law books, Jonas."

"Law doesn't always equal justice. I'm going to find out what happened to my brother and why." He skimmed his hand over her face and tangled his fingers in her hair. He didn't find silk and satin, but a woman of strength. "But there's more now. I look at you and I want you." He reached out, taking her face in his hand so that she had no choice but to look directly at him. "I hold you and I forget what I have to do. Damn it, you're in my way."

At the end of the words, his mouth was crushed hard on hers. He hadn't meant to. He hadn't had a choice. Before he'd been gentle with her because the look in her eyes requested it. Now he was rough, desperate, because the power of his own needs demanded it.

He frightened her. She'd never known fear could be a source of exhilaration. As her heart pounded in her throat, she let him pull her closer, still closer to the edge. He dared her to jump off, to let herself tumble down into the unknown. To risk.

His mouth drew desperately from hers, seeking passion, seeking submission, seeking strength. He wanted it all. He wanted it mindlessly from her. His hands were reaching for her as if they'd always done so. When he found her, she stiffened, resisted, then melted so quickly that it was nearly impossible to tell one mood from the next. She smelled of the sea and tasted of innocence, a combination of mystery and sweetness that drove him mad.

Forgetting everything but her, he drew her toward the bed and fulfillment.

"No." Liz pushed against him, fighting to bring herself back. They were in her daughter's room. "Jonas, this is wrong."

He took her by the shoulders. "Damn it, it may be the only thing that's right."

She shook her head, and though unsteady, backed away. His eyes weren't cold now. A woman might dream of having a man look at her with such fire and need. A woman might toss all caution aside if only to have a man want her with such turbulent desire. She couldn't.

"Not for me. I don't want this, Jonas." She reached up to push back her hair. "I don't want to feel like this."

He took her hand before she could back away. His head was swimming. There had been no other time, no other place, no other woman that had come together to make him ache. "Why?"

"I don't make the same mistake twice."

"This is now, Liz."

"And it's my life." She took a long, cleansing breath and found she could face him squarely. "I'll go with you to Acapulco because the sooner you have what you want, the sooner you'll go." She gripped her hands together tightly, the only outward sign that she was fighting herself. "You know Moralas will have us followed."

He had his own battles to fight. "I'll deal with that."

Liz nodded because she was sure he would. "Do what you have to do. I'll make arrangements for Luis to take over the shop for a day or two."

When she left him alone, Jonas closed his hands over the key again. It would open a lock, he thought. But there was another lock that mystified and frustrated him. Idly, he picked up the bear Liz had left on the bed. He looked from it to the key in his hand. Somehow he'd have to find a way to bring them together.

Chapter 6

Acapulco wasn't the Mexico Liz understood and loved. It wasn't the Mexico she'd fled to a decade before, nor where she'd made her home. It was sophisticated and ultra modern with spiraling high-rise hotels crowded together and gleaming in tropical sunlight. It was swimming pools and trendy shops. Perhaps it was the oldest resort in Mexico, and boasted countless restaurants and nightclubs, but Liz preferred the quietly rural atmosphere of her own island.

Still she had to admit there was something awesome about the city, cupped in the mountains and kissed by a magnificent bay. She'd lived all her life in flat land, from Houston to Cozumel. The mountains made everything else seem smaller, and somehow protected. Over the water, colorful parachutes floated, allowing the adventurous a bird's-eye view and a stunning ride. She wondered fleetingly if skimming through the sky would be as liberating as skimming through the water.

The streets were crowded and noisy, exciting in their own way. It occurred to her that she'd seen more people in the hour since they'd landed at the airport than she might in a week on Cozumel. Liz stepped out of the cab and wondered if she'd have time to check out any of the dive shops.

Jonas had chosen the hotel methodically. It was luxuriously expensive—just Jerry's style. The villas overlooked the Pacific and were built directly into the mountainside. Jonas took a suite, pocketed the key and left the luggage to the bellman.

"We'll go to the bank now." It had taken him two days to match the key with a name. He wasn't going to waste any more time.

Liz followed him out onto the street. True, she hadn't come to enjoy herself, but a look at their rooms and a bite of lunch didn't seem so much to ask. Jonas was already climbing into a cab. "I don't suppose you'd considered making that a request."

He gave her a brief look as she slammed the cab door. "No." After giving the driver their direction, Jonas settled back. He could understand Jerry drifting to Acapulco, with its jet-set flavor, frantic nightlife and touches of luxury. When Jerry landed in a place for more than a day, it was a city that had the atmosphere of New York, London, Chicago. Jerry had never been interested in the rustic, serene atmosphere of a spot like Cozumel. So since he'd gone there, stayed there, he'd had a purpose. In Acapulco, Jonas would find out what it was.

As to the woman beside him, he didn't have a clue. Was she caught up in the circumstances formed before they'd ever met, or was he dragging her in deeper than he had a right to? She sat beside him, silent and a little sulky. Probably thinking about her shop, Jonas decided, and wished he could send her safely back to it. He wished he could turn around, go back to the villa and make love with her until they were both sated.

She shouldn't have appealed to him at all. She wasn't witty, flawlessly polished or classically beautiful. But she did appeal to him, so much so that he was spending his nights awake and restless, and his days on the edge of frustration. He wanted her, wanted to fully explore the tastes of passion she'd given him. He wanted to arouse her until she couldn't think of accounts or customers or schedules. Perhaps it was a matter of wielding power—he could no longer be sure. But mostly, inexplicably, he wanted to erase the memory of how she'd looked when he'd walked into her daughter's room and found her clutching a stuffed bear.

When the cab rolled up in front of the bank, Liz stepped
out on the curb without a word. There were shops across the
streets, boutiques where she could see bright, wonderful
dresses on cleverly posed mannequins. Even with the distance,
she caught the gleam and glimmer of jewelry. A limousine
rolled by, with smoked glass windows and quiet engine. Liz
looked beyond the tall, glossy buildings to the mountains, and
space.

"I suppose this is the sort of place that appeals to you."

He'd watched her survey. She didn't have to speak for him
to understand that she'd compared Acapulco with her corner
of Mexico and found Acapulco lacking. "Under certain circumstances." Taking her arm, Jonas led her inside.

The bank was, as banks should be, quiet and sedate. Clerks
wore neat suits and polite smiles. What conversation there
was, was carried on in murmurs. Jerry, he thought, had always
preferred the ultraconservative in storing his money, just as
he'd preferred the wild in spending it. Without hesitation,
Jonas strolled over to the most attractive teller. "Good afternoon."

She glanced up. It only took a second for her polite smile
to brighten. "Mr. Sharpe, *Buenos días.* It's nice to see you
again."

Beside him, Liz stiffened. He's been here before, she
thought. Why hadn't he told her? She sent a long, probing
look his way. Just what game was he playing?

"It's nice to see you." He leaned against the counter, urbane and, she noted, flirtatious. The little tug of jealousy was
as unexpected as it was unwanted. "I wondered if you'd remember me."

The teller blushed before she glanced cautiously toward her
supervisor. "Of course. How can I help you today?"

Jonas took the key out of his pocket. "I'd like to get into
my box." He simply turned and stopped Liz with a look when
she started to speak.

"I'll arrange that for you right away." The teller took a
form, dated it and passed it to Jonas. "If you'll just sign
here."

Jonas took her pen and casually dashed off a signature. Liz read: *Jeremiah C. Sharpe.* Though she looked up quickly, Jonas was smiling at the teller. Because her supervisor was hovering nearby, the teller stuck to procedure and checked the signature against the card in the files. They matched perfectly.

"This way, Mr. Sharpe."

"Isn't that illegal?" Liz murmured as the teller led them from the main lobby.

"Yes." Jonas gestured for her to proceed him through the doorway.

"And does it make me an accessory?"

He smiled at her, waiting while the teller drew the long metal box from its slot. "Yes. If there's any trouble, I'll recommend a good lawyer."

"Great. All I need's another lawyer."

"You can use this booth, Mr. Sharpe. Just ring when you're finished."

"Thanks." Jonas nudged Liz inside, shut, then locked, the door.

"How did you know?"

"Know what?" Jonas set the box on a table.

"To go to that clerk? When she first spoke to you, I thought you'd been here before."

"There were three men and two women. The other woman was into her fifties. As far as Jerry would've been concerned, there would have been only one clerk there."

That line of thinking was clear enough, but his actions weren't. "You signed his name perfectly."

Key in hand, Jonas looked at her. "He was part of me. If we were in the same room, I could have told you what he was thinking. Writing his name is as easy as writing my own."

"And was it the same for him?"

It could still hurt, quickly and unexpectedly. "Yes, it was the same for him."

But Liz remembered Jerry's good-natured description of his brother as a stuffed shirt. The man Liz was beginning to know didn't fit. "I wonder if you understood each other as well as both of you thought.'' She looked down at the box again. None of her business, she thought, and wished it were as true as she'd once believed. ''I guess you'd better open it.''

He slipped the key into the lock, then turned it soundlessly. When he drew back the lid, Liz could only stare. She'd never seen so much money in her life. It sat in neat stacks, tidily banded, crisply American. Unable to resist, Liz reached out to touch.

''God, it looks like thousands.'' She swallowed. ''Hundreds of thousands.''

His face expressionless, Jonas flipped through the stacks. The booth became as quiet as a tomb. ''Roughly three hundred thousand, in twenties and fifties.''

''Do you think he stole it?'' she murmured, too overwhelmed to notice Jonas's hands tighten on the money. ''This must be the money the man who broke into my house wanted.''

''I'm sure it is.'' Jonas set down a stack of bills and picked up a small bag. ''But he didn't steal it.'' He forced his emotions to freeze. ''I'm afraid he earned it.''

''How?'' she demanded. ''No one earns this kind of money in a matter of days, and I'd swear Jerry was nearly broke when I hired him. I know Luis lent him ten thousand pesos before his first paycheck.''

''I'm sure he was.'' He didn't bother to add that he'd wired his brother two hundred before Jerry had left New Orleans. Carefully, Jonas reached under the stack of money and pulled out a small plastic bag, dipped in a finger and tasted. But he'd already known.

''What is that?''

His face expressionless, Jonas sealed the bag. He couldn't allow himself any more grief. ''Cocaine.''

Horrified, Liz stared at the bag. ''I don't understand. He lived in my house. I'd have known if he were using drugs.''

Jonas wondered if she realized just how innocent she was of the darker side of humanity. Until that moment, he hadn't fully realized just how intimate he was with it. ''Maybe,

maybe not. In any case, Jerry wasn't into this sort of thing. At least not for himself.''

Liz sat down slowly. ''You mean he sold it?''

''Dealt drugs?'' Jonas nearly smiled. ''No, that wouldn't have been exciting enough.'' In the corner of the box was a small black address book. Jonas took it out to leaf through it. ''But smuggling,'' he murmured. ''Jerry could have justified smuggling. Action, intrigue and fast money.''

Her mind was whirling as she tried to focus back on the man she'd known so briefly. Liz had thought she'd understood him, categorized him, but he was more of a stranger now than when he'd been alive. It didn't seem to matter anymore who or what Jerry Sharpe had been. But the man in front of her mattered. ''And you?'' she asked. ''Can you justify it?''

He glanced down at her, over the book in his hands. His eyes were cold, so cold that she could read nothing in them at all. Without answering, Jonas went back to the book.

''He'd listed initials, dates, times and some numbers. It looks as though he made five thousand a drop. Ten drops.''

Liz glanced over at the money again. It no longer seemed crisp and neat but ugly and ill used. ''That only makes fifty thousand. You said there was three hundred.''

''That's right.'' Plus a bag of uncut cocaine with a hefty street value. Jonas took out his own book and copied down the pages from his brother's.

''What are we going to do with this?''

''Nothing.''

''Nothing?'' Liz rose again, certain she'd stepped into a dream. ''Do you mean just leave it here? Just leave it here in this box and walk away?''

With the last of the numbers copied, Jonas replaced his brother's book. ''Exactly.''

''Why did we come if we're not going to do anything with it?''

He slipped his own book into his jacket. ''To find it.''

''Jonas.'' Before he could close the lid she had her hand on his wrist. ''You have to take it to the police. To Captain Moralas.''

In a deliberate gesture, he removed her hand, then picked up the bag of coke. She understood rejection and braced herself against it. But it wasn't rejection she saw in his face; it was fury. "You want to take this on the plane, Liz? Any idea on what the penalty is in Mexico for carrying controlled substances?"

"No."

"And you don't want to." He closed the lid, locked it. "For now, just forget you saw anything. I'll handle this in my own way."

"No."

His emotions were raw and tangled, his patience thin. "Don't push me, Liz."

"Push you?" Infuriated, she grabbed his shirtfront and planted her feet. "You've pushed me for days. Pushed me right into the middle of something that's so opposed to the way I've lived I can't even take it all in. Now that I'm over my head in drug smuggling and something like a quarter of a million dollars, you tell me to forget it. What do you expect me to do, go quietly back and rent tanks? Maybe you've finished using me now, Jonas, but I'm not ready to be brushed aside. There's a murderer out there who thinks I know where the money is." She stopped as her skin iced over. "And now I do."

"That's just it," Jonas said quietly. For the second time, he removed her hands, but this time he held on to her wrists. Frightened, he thought. He was sure her pulse beat with fear as well as anger. "Now you do. The best thing for you to do now is stay out of it, let them focus on me."

"Just how am I supposed to do that?"

The anger was bubbling closer, the anger he'd wanted to lock in the box with what had caused it. "Go to Houston, visit your daughter."

"How can I?" she demanded in a whisper that vibrated in the little room. "They might follow me." She looked down at the long, shiny box. "They would follow me. I won't risk my daughter's safety."

She was right, and because he knew it, Jonas wanted to

rage. He was boxed in, trapped between love and loyalty and right and wrong. Justice and the law. "We'll talk to Moralas when we get back." He picked up the box again, hating it.

"Where are we going now?"

Jonas unlocked the door. "To get a drink."

Rather than going with Jonas to the lounge, Liz took some time for herself. Because she felt he owed her, she went into the hotel's boutique, found a simple one-piece bathing suit and charged it to the room. She hadn't packed anything but a change of clothes and toiletries. If she was stuck in Acapulco for the rest of the evening, she was going to enjoy the private pool each villa boasted.

The first time she walked into the suite, she was dumbfounded. Her parents had been reasonably successful, and she'd been raised in a quietly middle-class atmosphere. Nothing had prepared her for the sumptuousness of the two-bedroom suite overlooking the Pacific. Her feet sank cozily into the carpet. Softly colored paintings were spaced along ivory-papered walls. The sofa, done in grays and greens and blues, was big enough for two to sprawl on for a lazy afternoon nap.

She found a phone in the bathroom next to a tub so wide and deep that she was almost tempted to take her dip there. The sink was a seashell done in the palest of pinks.

So this is how the rich play, she mused as she wandered to the bedroom where her overnight bag was set at the end of a bed big enough for three. The drapes of her balcony were open so that she could see the tempestuous surf of the Pacific hurl up and spray. She pulled the glass doors open, wanting the noise.

This was the sort of world Marcus had told her of so many years before. He'd made it seem like a fairy tale with gossamer edges. Liz had never seen his home, had never been permitted to, but he'd described it to her. The white pillars, the white balconies, the staircase that curved up and up. There were servants to bring you tea in the afternoons, a stable where grooms waited to saddle glossy horses. Champagne was drunk from French crystal. It had been a fairy tale, and she hadn't wanted it for herself. She had only wanted him.

A young girl's foolishness, Liz thought now. In her naive way, she'd made a prince out of a man who was weak and selfish and spoiled. But over the years she had thought of the house he'd talked of and pictured her daughter on those wide, curving stairs. That had been her sense of justice.

The image wasn't as clear now, not now that she'd seen wealth in a long metal box and understood where it had come from. Not when she'd seen Jonas's eyes when he'd spoken of his kind of justice. That hadn't been a fairy tale with gossamer edges, but grimly real. She had some thinking to do. But before she could plan for the rest of her life, and for her daughter's, she had to get through the moment.

Jonas. She was bound to him through no choice of her own. And perhaps he was bound to her in the same way. Was that the reason she was drawn to him? Because they were trapped in the same puzzle? If she could only explain it away, maybe she could stop the needs that kept swimming through her. If she could only explain it away, maybe she would be in control again.

But how could she explain the feelings she'd experienced on the silent cab ride back to the hotel? She had had to fight the desire to put her arms around him, to offer comfort when nothing in his manner had indicated he needed or wanted it. There were no easy answers—no answers at all to the fact that she was slowly, inevitably falling in love with him.

It was time to admit that, she decided, because you could never face anything until it was admitted. You could never solve anything until it was faced. She'd lived by that rule years before during the biggest crisis of her life. It still held true.

So she loved him, or very nearly loved him. She was no longer naive enough to believe that love was the beginning of any answer. He would hurt her. There were no ifs about that. He'd steal from her the one thing she'd managed to hold fast to for ten years. And once he'd taken her heart, what would it mean to him? She shook her head. No more than such things ever mean to those who take them.

Jonas Sharpe was a man on a mission, and she was no more to him than a map. He was ruthless in his own patient way. When he had finished what he'd come to do, he would turn away from her, go back to his life in Philadelphia and never think of her again.

Some women, Liz thought, were doomed to pick the men who could hurt them the most. Making her mind a blank, Liz stripped and changed to her bathing suit. But Jonas, thoughts of Jonas, kept slipping through the barriers.

Maybe if she talked to Faith—if she could touch her greatest link with normality, things would snap back into focus. On impulse, Liz picked up the phone beside her bed and began the process of placing the call. Faith would just be home from school, Liz calculated, growing more excited as she heard the clinks and buzzes on the receiver. When the phone began to ring, she sat on the bed. She was already smiling.

"Hello?"

"Mom?" Liz felt the twin surges of pleasure and guilt as she heard her mother's voice. "It's Liz."

"Liz!" Rose Palmer felt identical surges. "We didn't expect to hear from you. Your last letter just came this morning. Nothing's wrong, is it?"

"No, no, nothing's wrong." Everything's wrong. "I just wanted to talk to Faith."

"Oh, Liz, I'm so sorry. Faith's not here. She has her piano lesson today."

The letdown came, but she braced herself against it. "I forgot." Tears threatened, but she forced them back. "She likes the lessons, doesn't she?"

"She loves them. You should hear her play. Remember when you were taking them?"

"I had ten thumbs." She managed to smile. "I wanted to thank you for sending the pictures. She looks so grown up. Momma, is she...looking forward to coming back?"

Rose heard the need, felt the ache. She wished, not for the

first time, that her daughter was close enough to hold. "She's marking off the days on her calendar. She bought you a present."

Liz had to swallow. "She did?"

"It's supposed to be a surprise, so don't tell her I told you."

"I won't." She dashed tears away, grateful she could keep her voice even. It hurt, but was also a comfort to be able to speak to someone who knew and understood Faith as she did. "I miss her. The last few weeks always seem the hardest."

Her voice wasn't as steady as she thought—and a mother hears what others don't. "Liz, why don't you come home? Spend the rest of the month here while she's in school?"

"No, I can't. How's Dad?"

Rose fretted impatiently at the change of subject, then subsided. She'd never known anyone as thoroughly stubborn as her daughter. Unless it was her granddaughter. "He's fine. Looking forward to coming down and doing some diving."

"We'll take one of the boats out—just the four of us. Tell Faith I…tell her I called," she finished lamely.

"Of course I will. Why don't I have her call you back when she gets home? The car pool drops her off at five."

"No. No, I'm not home. I'm in Acapulco—on business." Liz let out a long breath to steady herself. "Just tell her I miss her and I'll be waiting at the airport. You know I appreciate everything you're doing. I just—"

"Liz." Rose interrupted gently. "We love Faith. And we love you."

"I know." Liz pressed her fingers to her eyes. She did know, but was never quite sure what to do about it. "I love you, too. It's just that sometimes things get so mixed up."

"Are you all right?"

She dropped her hand again, and her eyes were dry. "I will be when you get there. Tell Faith I'm marking off the days too."

"I will."

"Bye, Momma."

She hung up and sat until the churning emptiness had run

its course. If she'd had more confidence in her parents' support, more trust in their love, would she have fled the States and started a new life on her own? Liz dragged a hand through her hair. She'd never be sure of that, nor could she dwell on it. She'd burned her own bridges. The only thing that was important was Faith, and her happiness.

An hour later, Jonas found her at the pool. She swam laps in long, smooth strokes, her body limber. She seemed tireless, and oddly suited to the private luxury. Her suit was a flashy red, but the cut so simple that it relied strictly on the form it covered for style.

He counted twenty laps before she stopped, and wondered how many she'd completed before he'd come down. It seemed to him as if she swam to drain herself of some tension or sorrow, and that with each lap she'd come closer to succeeding. Waiting, he watched her tip her head back in the water so that her hair slicked back. The marks on her neck had faded. As she stood, water skimmed her thigh.

"I've never seen you relaxed," Jonas commented. But even as he said the words, he could see her muscles tense again. She turned away from her contemplation of the mountains and looked at him.

He was tired, she realized, and wondered if she should have seen it before. There was a weariness around his eyes that hadn't been there that morning. He hadn't changed his clothes, and had his hands tucked into the pockets of bone-colored slacks. She wondered if he'd been up to the suite at all.

"I didn't bring a suit with me." Liz pushed against the side of the pool and hitched herself out. Water rained from her. "I charged this one to the room."

The thighs were cut nearly to the waist. Jonas caught himself wondering just how the skin would feel there. "It's nice."

Liz picked up her towel. "It was expensive."

He only lifted a brow. "I could deduct it from the rent."

Her lips curved a little as she rubbed her hair dry. "No,

you can't. But since you're a lawyer, I imagine you can find a way to deduct it from something else. I saved the receipt.''

He hadn't thought he could laugh. ''I appreciate it. You know, I get the impression you don't think much of lawyers.''

Something came and went in her eyes. ''I try not to think of them at all.''

Taking the towel from her, he gently dried her face. ''Faith's father's a lawyer?''

Without moving, she seemed to shift away from him. ''Leave it alone, Jonas.''

''You don't.''

''Actually I do, most of the time. Maybe it's been on my mind the past few weeks, but that's my concern.''

He draped the towel around her shoulders and, holding the ends, drew her closer. ''I'd like you to tell me about it.''

It was his voice, she thought, so calm, so persuasive, that nearly had her opening both mind and heart. She could almost believe as she looked at him that he really wanted to know, to understand. The part of her that was already in love with him needed to believe he might care. ''Why?''

''I don't know. Maybe it's that look that comes into your eyes. It makes a man want to stroke it away.''

Her chin came up a fraction. ''There's no need to feel sorry for me.''

''I don't think sympathy's the right word.'' Abruptly weary, he dropped his forehead to hers. He was tired of fighting demons, of trying to find answers. ''Damn.''

Uncertain, she stood very still. ''Are you all right?''

''No. No, I'm not.'' He moved away from her to walk to the end of the path where a plot of tiny orange flowers poked up through white gravel. ''A lot of things you said today were true. A lot of things you've said all along are true. I can't do anything about them.''

''I don't know what you want me to say now.''

''Nothing.'' Hideously tired, he ran both hands over his face. ''I'm trying to live with the fact that my brother's dead, and that he was murdered because he decided to make some easy money drug-trafficking. He had a good brain, but he always chose to use it in the wrong way. Every time I look in the mirror, I wonder why.''

Liz was beside him before she could cut off her feelings. He hurt. It was the first time she'd seen below the surface to the pain. She knew what it was like to live with pain. "He was different, Jonas. I don't think he was bad, just weak. Mourning him is one thing—blaming yourself for what he did, or for what happened to him, is another.''

He hadn't known he needed comfort, but her hand resting on him had something inside him slowly uncurling. "I was the only one who could reach him, keep him on some kind of level. There came a point where I just got tired of running both our lives.''

"Do you really believe you could have prevented him from doing what he did?''

"Maybe. That's something else I have to live with.''

"Just a minute.'' She took his shirtfront in much the same way she had that afternoon. There was no sympathy now, but annoyance on her face. He hadn't known he needed that, as well. "You were brothers, twins, but you were separate people. Jerry wasn't a child to be guided and supervised. He was a grown man who made his decisions.''

"That's the trouble. Jerry never grew up.''

"And you did,'' she tossed back. "Are you going to punish yourself for it?''

He'd been doing just that, Jonas realized. He'd gone home, buried his brother, comforted his parents and blamed himself for not preventing something he knew in his heart had been inevitable. "I have to find out who killed him, Liz. I can't set the rest aside until I do.''

"We'll find them.'' On impulse, she pressed her cheek to his. Sometimes the slightest human contact could wash away acres of pain. "Then it'll be over.''

He wasn't sure he wanted it to be, not all of it. He ran a hand down her arm, needing the touch of her skin. He found it chilled. "The sun's gone down.'' He wrapped the towel around her in a gesture that would have been mere politeness with another woman. With Liz, it was for protection. "You'd better get out of that wet suit. We'll have dinner."

"Here?"

"Sure. The restaurant's supposed to be one of the best."

Liz thought of the elegance of their suite and the contents of her overnight bag. "I didn't bring anything to wear."

He laughed and swung an arm around her. It was the first purely frivolous thing he'd heard her say. "Charge something else."

"But—"

"Don't worry, I've got the best crooked accountant in Philadelphia."

Chapter 7

Because she'd been certain she would never sleep away from home, in a hotel bed, Liz was surprised to wake to full sunlight. Not only had she slept, she realized, she'd slept like a rock for eight hours and was rested and ready to go. True, it was just a little past six, and she had no business to run, but her body was tuned to wake at that hour. A trip to Acapulco didn't change that.

It had changed other things, she reminded herself as she stretched out in the too-big bed. Because of it, she'd become inescapably tangled in murder and smuggling. Putting the words together made her shake her head. In a movie, she might have enjoyed watching the melodrama. In a book, she'd have turned the page to read more. But in her own life, she preferred the more mundane. Liz was too practical to delude herself into believing she could distance herself from any part of the puzzle any longer. For better or worse, she was personally involved in this melodrama. That included Jonas Sharpe. The only question now was which course of action to take.

She couldn't run. That had never been a choice. Liz had already concluded she couldn't hide behind Moralas and his men forever. Sooner or later the man with the knife would come back, or another man more determined or more desperate. She wouldn't escape a second time. The moment she'd looked into the safe-deposit box, she'd become a full-fledged player in the game. Which brought her back full circle to Jonas. She had no choice but to put her trust in him now. If he were to give up on his brother's murder and return to Philadelphia she would be that much more alone. However much she might wish it otherwise, Liz needed him just as much as he needed her.

Other things had changed, she thought. Her feelings for him were even more undefined and confusing than they had started out to be. Seeing him as she had the evening before, hurt and vulnerable, had touched off more than impersonal sympathy or physical attraction. It had made her feel a kinship, and the kinship urged her to help him, not only for her own welfare, but for his. He suffered, for his brother's loss, but also for what his brother had done. She'd loved once, and had suffered, not only because of loss but because of disillusionment.

A lifetime ago? Liz wondered. Did we ever really escape from one lifetime to another? It seemed years could pass, circumstances could change, but we carried our baggage with us through each phase. If anything, with each phase we had to carry a bit more. There was little use in thinking, she told herself as she climbed from the bed. From this point on, she had little choice but to act.

Jonas heard her the moment she got up. He'd been awake since five, restless and prowling. For over an hour he'd been racking his brain and searching his conscience for a way to ease Liz out of a situation his brother, and he himself had locked her into. He'd already thought of several ways to draw attention away from her to himself, but that wouldn't guarantee Liz's safety. She wouldn't go to Houston, and he understood her feelings about endangering her daughter in any way.

As the days passed, he felt he was coming to understand her better and better. She was a loner, but only because she saw it as the safest route. She was a businesswoman, but only because she looked to her daughter's welfare first. Inside, he thought, she was a woman with dreams on hold and love held in bondage. She had steered both toward her child and denied herself. And, Jonas added, she'd convinced herself she was content.

That was something else he understood, because until a few weeks before he had also convinced himself he was content. It was only now, after he'd had the opportunity to look at his life from a distance that he realized he had merely been drifting. Perhaps, when the outward trimmings were stripped away, he hadn't been so different from his brother. For both of them, success had been the main target, they had simply aimed for it differently. Though Jonas had a steady job, a home of his own, there had never been an important woman. He'd put his career first. Jonas wasn't certain he'd be able to do so again. It had taken the loss of his brother to make him realize he needed something more, something solid. Exploring the law was only a job. Winning cases was only a transitory satisfaction. Perhaps he'd known it for some time. After all, he'd bought the old house in Chadd's Ford to give himself something permanent. When had he started thinking about sharing it?

Still, thinking about his own life didn't solve the problem of Liz Palmer and what he was going to do with her. She couldn't go to Houston, he thought again, but there were other places she could go until he could assure her that her life could settle back the way she wanted it. His parents were his first thought, and the quiet country home they'd retired to in Lancaster. If he could find a way to slip her out of Mexico, she would be safe there. It would even be possible to have her daughter join her. Then his conscience would ease. Jonas had no doubt that his parents would accept them both, then dote on them.

Once he'd done what he'd come to do, he could go to Lancaster himself. He'd like to see Liz there, in surroundings he was used to. He wanted time to talk with her about simple things. He wanted to hear her laugh again, as she had only once in all the days he'd known her. Once they were there, away from the ugliness, he might understand his feelings better. Perhaps by then he'd be able to analyze what had happened inside him when she'd pressed her cheek against his and had offered unconditional support.

He'd wanted to hold on to her, to just hold on and the hell with the world. There was something about her that made him think of lazy evenings on cool porches and long Sunday afternoon walks. He couldn't say why. In Philadelphia he rarely took time for such things. Even socializing had become business. And he'd seen for himself that she never gave herself an idle hour. Why should he, a man dedicated to his work, think of lazing days away with a woman obsessed by hers?

She remained a mystery to him, and perhaps that was an answer in itself. If he thought of her too often, too deeply, it was only because while his understanding was growing, he still knew so little. If it sometimes seemed that discovering Liz Palmer was just as important as discovering his brother's killer, it was only because they were tied together. How could he take his mind off one without taking his mind off the other? Yet when he thought of her now, he thought of her stretched out on his mother's porch swing, safe, content and waiting for him.

Annoyed with himself, Jonas checked his watch. It was after nine on the East Coast. He'd call his office, he thought. A few legal problems might clear his mind. He'd no more than picked up the receiver when Liz came out from her bedroom.

"I didn't know you were up," she said, and fiddled nervously with her belt. Odd, she felt entirely different about sharing the plush little villa with him than she did her home. After all, she reasoned, at home he was paying rent.

"I thought you'd sleep longer." He replaced the receiver again. The office could wait.

"I never sleep much past six." Feeling awkward, she wandered to the wide picture window. "Terrific view."

"Yes, it is."

"I haven't stayed in a hotel in…in years," she finished. "When I came to Cozumel, I worked in the same hotel where I'd stayed with my parents. It was an odd feeling. So's this."

"No urge to change the linen or stack the towels?"

When she chuckled, some of the awkwardness slipped away. "No, not even a twinge."

"Liz, when we're finished with all this, when it's behind us, will you talk to me about that part of your life?"

She turned to him, away from the window, but they both felt the distance. "When we're finished with this, there won't be any reason to."

He rose and came to her. In a gesture that took her completely by surprise, he took both of her hands. He lifted one, then the other, to his lips and watched her eyes cloud. "I can't be sure of that," he murmured. "Can you?"

She couldn't be sure of anything when his voice was quiet, his hands gentle. For a moment, she simply absorbed the feeling of being a woman cared for by a man. Then she stepped back, as she knew she had to. "Jonas, you told me once we had the same problem. I didn't want to believe it then, but it was true. It is true. Once that problem is solved, there really isn't anything else between us. Your life and mine are separated by a lot more than miles."

He thought of his house and his sudden need to share it. "They don't have to be."

"There was a time I might have believed that."

"You're living in the past." He took her shoulders, but this time his hands weren't as gentle. "You're fighting ghosts."

"I may have my ghosts, but I don't live in the past. I can't afford to." She put her hands to his wrists, but let them lie there only a moment before she let go. "I can't afford to pretend to myself about you."

He wanted to demand, he wanted to pull her with him to the sofa and prove to her that she was wrong. He resisted. It wasn't the first time he'd used courtroom skill, courtroom tactics, to win on a personal level. "We'll leave it your way for now," he said easily. "But the case isn't closed. Are you hungry?"

Unsure whether she should be uneasy or relieved, Liz nodded. "A little."

"Let's have breakfast. We've got plenty of time before the plane leaves."

*   *   *

She didn't trust him. Though Jonas kept the conversation light and passionless throughout breakfast, Liz kept herself braced for a countermove. He was a clever man, she knew. He was a man, she was certain, who made sure he got his own way no matter how long it took. Liz considered herself a woman strong enough to keep promises made, even when they were to herself. No man, not even Jonas, was going to make her change the course she'd set ten years before. There was only room enough for two loves in her life. Faith and her work.

"I can't get used to eating something at this hour of the morning that's going to singe my stomach lining."

Liz swallowed the mixture of peppers, onions and eggs. "Mine's flame resistant. You should try my chili."

"Does that mean you're offering to cook for me?"

When Liz glanced up she wished he hadn't been smiling at her in just that way. "I suppose I could make enough for two as easily as enough for one. But you don't seem to have any trouble in the kitchen."

"Oh, I can cook. It's just that once I've finished, it never seems worth the bother." He leaned forward to run a finger down her hand from wrist to knuckle. "Tell you what—I'll buy the supplies and even clean up the mess if you handle the chili."

Though she smiled, Liz drew her hand away. "The question is, can you handle the chili? It might burn right through a soft lawyer's stomach."

Appreciating the challenge, he took her hand again. "Why don't we find out? Tonight."

"All right." She flexed her fingers, but he merely linked his with them. "I can't eat if you have my hand."

He glanced down. "You have another one."

He made her laugh when she'd been set to insist. "I'm entitled to two."

"I'll give it back. Later."

"Hey, Jerry!"

The easy smile on Jonas's face froze. Only his eyes changed, locking on to Liz's, warning and demanding. His hand remained on hers, but the grip tightened. The message was very clear—she was to do nothing, say nothing until he'd tallied the odds. He turned, flashing a new smile. Liz's stomach trembled. It was Jerry's smile, she realized. Not Jonas's.

"Why didn't you tell me you were back in town?" A tall, tanned man with sandy blond hair and a trim beard dropped a hand on Jonas's shoulder. Liz caught the glint of a diamond on his finger. He was young, she thought, determined to store everything she could, barely into his thirties, and dressed with slick, trendy casualness.

"Quick trip," Jonas said as, like Liz, he took in every detail. "Little business..." He cast a meaningful glance toward Liz. "Little pleasure."

The man turned and stared appreciatively at Liz. "Is there any other way?"

Thinking fast, Liz offered her hand. "Hello. Since Jerry's too rude to introduce us, we'll have to do it ourselves. I'm Liz Palmer."

"David Merriworth." He took her hand between both of his. They were smooth and uncalloused. "Jerry might have trouble with manners, but he's got great taste."

She smiled, hoping she did it properly. "Thank you."

"Pull up a chair, Merriworth." Jonas took out a cigarette. "As long as you keep your hands off my lady." He said it in the good-natured, only-kidding tone Jerry had inevitably used, but his eyes were Jonas's, warning her to tread carefully.

"Wouldn't mind a quick cup of coffee." David pulled over a chair after he checked his watch. "Got a breakfast meeting in a few minutes. So how are things on Cozumel?" He inclined his head ever so slightly. "Getting in plenty of diving?"

Jonas allowed his lips to curve and kept his eyes steady. "Enough."

"Glad to hear it. I was going to check in with you myself, but I've been in the States for a couple weeks. Just got back in last night." He used two sugars after the waiter set a fresh cup of coffee beside him. "Business is good, buddy. Real good."

"What business are you in, Mr. Merriworth?"

He gave Liz a big grin before he winked at Jonas. "Sales, sweetheart. Imports, you might say."

"Really." Because her throat was dry she drank more coffee. "It must be fascinating."

"It has its moments." He turned in his chair so that he could study her face. "So where did Jerry find you?"

"On Cozumel." She sent Jonas a steady look. "We're partners."

David lowered his cup. "That so?"

They were in too deep, Jonas thought, for him to contradict her. "That's so," he agreed.

David picked up his cup again with a shrug. "If it's okay with the boss, it doesn't bother me."

"I do things my way," Jonas drawled. "Or I don't do them."

Amused, and perhaps admiring, David broke into a smile. "That never changes. Look, I've been out of touch for a few weeks. The drops still going smooth?"

With those words, Jonas's last hopes died. What he'd found in the safe-deposit box had been real, and it had been Jerry's. He buttered a roll as though he had all the time in the world. Beneath the table, Liz touched his leg once, hoping he'd take it as comfort. He never looked at her. "Why shouldn't they?"

"It's the classiest operation I've ever come across," David commented, taking a cautious glance around to other tables. "Wouldn't like to see anything screw it up."

"You worry too much."

"You're the one who should worry," David pointed out. "I don't have to deal with Manchez. You weren't around last year when he took care of those two Colombians. I was. You deal with supplies, I stick with sales. I sleep better."

"I just dive," Jonas said, and tapped out his cigarette. "And I sleep fine."

"He's something, isn't he?" David sent Liz another grin. "I knew Jerry here was just the man the boss was looking for. You keep diving, kid." He tipped his cup at Jonas. "It makes me look good."

"Sounds like you two have known each other for a while," Liz said with a smile. Under the table, she twisted the napkin in her lap.

"Go way back, don't we, Jer?"

"Yeah. We go back."

"First time we hooked up was six, no, seven years ago. We were working a pigeon drop in L.A. We'd have had that twenty thousand out of that old lady if her daughter hadn't caught on." He took out a slim cigarette case. "Your brother got you out of that one, didn't he? The East Coast lawyer."

"Yeah." Jonas remembered posting the bond and pulling the strings.

"Now I've been working out of here for almost five. A real businessman." He slapped Jonas's arm. "Hell of a lot better than the pigeon drop, huh, Jerry?"

"Pays better."

David let out a roar of laughter. "Why don't I show you two around Acapulco tonight?"

"Gotta get back." Jonas signaled for the check. "Business."

"Yeah, I know what you mean." He nodded toward the restaurant's entrance. "Here's my customer now. Next time you drop down, give a call."

"Sure."

"And give my best to old Clancy." With another laugh, David gave them each a quick salute. They watched him stride across the room and shake hands with a dark-suited man.

"Don't say anything here," Jonas murmured as he signed the breakfast check. "Let's go."

Liz's crumpled napkin slid to the floor as she rose to walk out with him. He didn't speak again until they had the door of the villa closed behind them.

"You had no business telling him we were partners."

Because she'd been ready for the attack, she shrugged it off. "He said more once I did."

"He'd have said just as much if you'd made an excuse and left the table."

She folded her arms. "We have the same problem, remember?"

He didn't care to have his own words tossed back at him. "The least you could have done was to give him another name."

"Why? They know who I am. Sooner or later he's going to talk to whoever's in charge and get the whole story."

She was right. He didn't care for that either. "Are you packed?"

"Yes."

"Then let's check out. We'll go to the airport."

"And then?"

"And then we go straight to Moralas."

"You've been very busy." Moralas held on to his temper as he rocked back in his chair. "Two of my men wasted their valuable time looking for you in Acapulco. You might have told me, Mr. Sharpe, that you planned to take Miss Palmer on a trip."

"I thought a police tail in Acapulco might be inconvenient."

"And now that you have finished your own investigation, you bring me this." He held up the key and examined it. "This which Miss Palmer discovered several days ago. As a lawyer, you must understand the phrase 'withholding evidence.'"

"Of course." Jonas nodded coolly. "But neither Miss Palmer nor myself could know the key was evidence. We speculated, naturally, that it might have belonged to my brother. Withholding a speculation is hardly a crime."

"Perhaps not, but it is poor judgment. Poor judgment often translates into an offense."

Jonas leaned back in his chair. If Moralas wanted to argue law, they'd argue law. "If the key belonged to my brother, as executor of his estate, it became mine. In any case, once it was proved to me that the key did indeed belong to Jerry, and that the contents of the safe-deposit box were evidence,

I brought both the key and a description of the contents to you.''

"Indeed. And do you also speculate as to how your brother came to possess those particular items?''

"Yes.''

Moralas waited a beat, then turned to Liz. "And you, Miss Palmer—you also have your speculations?''

She had her hands gripped tightly in her lap, but her voice was matter-of-fact and reasonable. "I know that whoever attacked me wanted money, obviously a great deal of money. We found a great deal.''

"And a bag of what Mr. Sharpe...speculates is cocaine.'' Moralas folded his hands on the desk with the key under them. "Miss Palmer, did you at any time see Mr. Jeremiah Sharpe in possession of cocaine?''

"No.''

"Did he at any time speak to you of cocaine or drug-trafficking?''

"No, of course not. I would have told you.''

"As you told me about the key?'' When Jonas started to protest, Moralas waved him off. "I will need a list of your customers for the past six weeks, Miss Palmer. Names and, wherever possible, addresses.''

"My customers? Why?''

"It's more than possible that Mr. Sharpe used your shop for his contacts.''

"My shop.'' Outraged, she stood up. "My boats? Do you think he could have passed drugs under my nose without me being aware?''

Moralas took out a cigar and studied it. "I very much hope you were unaware, Miss Palmer. You will bring me the list of clients by the end of the week.'' He glanced at Jonas. "Of course, you are within your rights to demand a warrant. It will simply slow down the process. And I, of course, am within my rights to hold Miss Palmer as a material witness.''

Jonas watched the pale blue smoke circle toward the ceiling. It was tempting to call Moralas's bluff simply as an exercise in testing two ends of the law. And in doing so, he and the captain could play tug-of-war with Liz for hours. "There are times, Captain, when it's wiser not to employ certain rights. I think I'm safe in saying that the three of us in this room want basically the same thing." He rose and flicked his lighter at the end of Moralas's cigar. "You'll have your list, Captain. And more."

Moralas lifted his gaze and waited.

"Pablo Manchez," Jonas said, and was gratified to see Moralas's eyes narrow.

"What of Manchez?"

"He's on Cozumel. Or was," Jonas stated. "My brother met with him several times in local bars and clubs. You may also be interested in David Merriworth, an American working out of Acapulco. Apparently he's the one who put my brother onto his contacts in Cozumel. If you contact the authorities in the States, you'll find that Merriworth has an impressive rap sheet."

In his precise handwriting, Moralas noted down the names, though he wasn't likely to forget them. "I appreciate the information. However, in the future, Mr. Sharpe, I would appreciate it more if you stayed out of my way. *Buenas tardes,* Miss Palmer."

Moments later, Liz strode out to the street. "I don't like being threatened. That's what he was doing, wasn't it?" she demanded. "He was threatening to put me in jail."

Very calm, even a bit amused, Jonas lit a cigarette. "He was pointing out his options, and ours."

"He didn't threaten to put you in jail," Liz muttered.

"He doesn't worry as much about me as he does about you."

"Worry?" She stopped with her hand gripping the handle of Jonas's rented car.

"He's a good cop. You're one of his people."

She looked back toward the police station with a scowl. "He has a funny way of showing it." A scruffy little boy scooted up to the car and gallantly opened the door for her. Even as he prepared to hold out a hand, Liz was digging for a coin.

"Gracias."

He checked the coin, grinned at the amount and nodded approval. *"Buenas tardes, señorita."* Just as gallantly he closed the door for her while the coin disappeared into a pocket.

"It's a good thing you don't come into town often," Jonas commented.

"Why?"

"You'd be broke in a week."

Liz found a clip in her purse and pulled back her hair. "Because I gave a little boy twenty-five pesos?"

"How much did you give the other kid before we went in to Moralas?"

"I bought something from him."

"Yeah." Jonas swung away from the curb. "You look like a woman who can't go a day without a box of Chiclets."

"You're changing the subject."

"That's right. Now tell me where I can find the best place for buying ingredients for chili."

"You want me to cook for you tonight?"

"It'll keep your mind off the rest. We've done everything we can do for the moment," he added. "Tonight we're going to relax."

She would have liked to believe he was right. Between nerves and anger, she was wound tight. "Cooking's supposed to relax me?"

"Eating is going to relax you. It's just an unavoidable circumstance that you have to cook it first."

It sounded so absurd that she subsided. "Turn left at the next corner. I tell you what to buy, you buy it, then you stay out of my way."

"Agreed."

"And you clean up."

"Absolutely."

"Pull over here," she directed. "And remember, you asked for it."

Liz never skimped when she cooked, even taking into account that authentic Mexican spices had more zing than the sort sold in the average American supermarket. She'd developed a taste for Mexican food and Yucatan specialties when she'd been a child, exploring the peninsula with her parents. She wasn't an elaborate cook, and when alone would often make do with a sandwich, but when her heart was in it, she could make a meal that would more than satisfy.

Perhaps, in a way, she wanted to impress him. Liz found she was able to admit it while she prepared a Mayan salad for chilling. It was probably very natural and harmless to want to impress someone with your cooking. After peeling and slicing an avocado, she found, oddly enough, she was relaxing.

So much of what she'd done in the past few days had been difficult or strange. It was a relief to make a decision no more vital than the proper way to slice her fruits and vegetables. In the end, she fussed with the arrangement a bit more, pleased with the contrasting colors of greens and oranges and cherry tomatoes. It was, she recalled, the only salad she could get Faith to eat because it was the only one Faith considered pretty enough. Liz didn't realize she was smiling as she began to sauté onions and peppers. She added a healthy dose of garlic and let it all simmer.

"It already smells good," Jonas commented as he strode through the doorway.

She only glanced over her shoulder. "You're supposed to stay out of my way."

"You cook, I take care of the table."

Liz only shrugged and turned back to the stove. She measured, stirred and spiced until the kitchen was filled with a riot of scent. The sauce, chunky with meat and vegetables, simmered and thickened on low heat. Pleased with herself, she wiped her hands on a cloth and turned around. Jonas was sitting comfortably at the table watching her.

"You look good," he told her. "Very good."

It seemed so natural, their being together in the kitchen with a pot simmering and a breeze easing its way through the screen. It made her remember how hard it was not to want such simple things in your life. Liz set the cloth down and found she didn't know what to do with her hands. "Some men think a woman looks best in front of a stove."

"I don't know. It's a toss-up with the way you looked at the wheel of a boat. How long does that have to cook?"

"About a half hour."

"Good." He rose and went to the counter where he'd left two bottles. "We have time for some wine."

A little warning signal jangled in her brain. Liz decided she needed a lid for the chili. "I don't have the right glasses."

"I already thought of that." From a bag beside the bottle, he pulled out two thin-stemmed wineglasses.

"You've been busy," she murmured.

"You didn't like me hovering over you in the market. I had to do something." He drew out the cork, then let the wine breathe.

"These candles aren't mine."

He turned to see Liz fiddling with the fringe of one of the woven mats he'd set on the table. In the center were two deep blue tapers that picked up the color in the border of her dishes.

"They're ours," Jonas told her.

She twisted the fringe around one finger, let it go, then twisted it again. The last time she'd burned candles had been during a power failure. These didn't look sturdy, but slender and frivolous. "There wasn't any need to go to all this trouble. I don't—"

"Do candles and wine make you uneasy?"

Dropping the fringe, she let her hands fall to her sides. "No, of course not."

"Good." He poured rich red wine into both glasses. Walking to her, he offered one. "Because I find them relaxing. We did agree to relax."

She sipped, and though she wanted to back away, held her ground. "I'm afraid you may be looking for more than I can give."

"No." He touched his glass to hers. "I'm looking for exactly what you can give."

Recognizing when she was out of her depth, Liz turned toward the refrigerator. "We can start on the salad."

He lit the candles and dimmed the lights. She told herself it didn't matter. Atmosphere was nothing more than a pleasant addition to a meal.

"Very pretty," Jonas told her when she'd mixed the dressing and arranged avocado slices. "What's it called?"

"It's a Mayan salad." Liz took the first nibble and was satisfied. "I learned the recipe when I worked at the hotel. Actually, that's where most of my cooking comes from."

"Wonderful," Jonas decided after the first bite. "It makes me wish I'd talked you into cooking before."

"A one time only." She relaxed enough to smile. "Meals aren't—"

"Included in the rent," Jonas finished. "We might negotiate."

This time she laughed at him and chose a section of grapefruit. "I don't think so. How do you manage in Philadelphia?"

"I have a housekeeper who'll toss together a casserole on Wednesdays." He took another bite, enjoying the contrast of crisp greens and spicy dressing. "And I eat out a lot."

"And parties? I suppose you go to a lot of parties."

"Some business, some pleasure." He'd almost forgotten what it was like to sit in a kitchen and enjoy a simple meal. "To be honest, it wears a bit. The cruising."

"Cruising?"

"When Jerry and I were teenagers, we might hop in the car on a Friday night and cruise. The idea was to see what teenage girls had hopped in their cars to cruise. The party circuit's just adult cruising."

She frowned a bit because it didn't seem as glamorous as she'd imagined. "It seems rather aimless."

"Doesn't seem. Is."

"You don't appear to be a man who does anything without a purpose."

"I've had my share of aimless nights," he murmured. "You come to a point where you realize you don't want too many more." That was just it, he realized. It wasn't the work, the hours spent closeted with law books or in a courtroom. It was the nights without meaning that left him wanting more. He lifted the wine to top off her glass, but his eyes stayed on hers. "I came to that realization very recently."

Her blood began to stir. Deliberately, Liz pushed her wine aside and rose to go to the stove. "We all make decisions at certain points in our lives, realign our priorities."

"I have the feeling you did that a long time ago."

"I did. I've never regretted it."

That much was true, he thought. She wasn't a woman for regrets. "You wouldn't change it, would you?"

Liz continued to spoon chili into bowls. "Change what?"

"If you could go back eleven years and take a different path, you wouldn't do it."

She stopped. From across the room he could see the flicker of candlelight in her eyes as she turned to him. More, he could see the strength that softness and shadows couldn't disguise. "That would mean I'd have to give up Faith. No, I wouldn't do it."

When she set the bowls on the table, Jonas took her hand. "I admire you."

Flustered, she stared down at him. "What for?"

"For being exactly what you are."

Chapter 8

No smooth phrases, no romantic words could have affected her more deeply. She wasn't used to flattery, but flattery, Liz was sure, could be brushed easily aside by a woman who understood herself. Sincere and simple approval was a different matter. Perhaps it was the candlelight, the wine, the intimacy of the small kitchen in the empty house, but she felt close to him, comfortable with him. Without being aware of it happening, Liz dropped her guard.

"I couldn't be anything else."

"Yes, you could. I'm glad you're not."

"What are you?" she wondered as she sat beside him.

"A thirty-five-year-old lawyer who's just realizing he's wasted some time." He lifted his glass and touched it to hers. "To making the best of whatever there is."

Though she wasn't certain she understood him, Liz drank, then waited for him to eat.

"You could fuel an engine with this stuff." Jonas dipped his spoon into the chili again and tasted. Hot spice danced on his tongue. "It's great."

"Not too hot for your Yankee stomach?"

"My Yankee stomach can handle it. You know, I'm surprised you haven't opened a restaurant, since you can cook like this."

She wouldn't have been human if the compliment hadn't pleased her. "I like the water more than I like the kitchen."

"I can't argue with that. So you picked this up in the kitchen when you worked at the hotel?"

"That's right. We'd take a meal there. The cook would show me how much of this and how much of that. He was very kind," Liz remembered. "A lot of people were kind."

He wanted to know everything—the small details, the feelings, the memories. Because he did, he knew he had to probe with care. "How long did you work there?"

"Two years. I lost count of how many beds I made."

"Then you started your own business?"

"Then I started the dive shop." She took a thin cracker and broke it in two. "It was a gamble, but it was the right one."

"How did you handle it?" He waited until she looked over at him. "With your daughter?"

She withdrew. He could hear it in her voice. "I don't know what you mean."

"I wonder about you." He kept the tone light, knowing she'd never respond to pressure. "Not many women could have managed all you've managed. You were alone, pregnant, making a living."

"Does that seem so unusual?" It made her smile to think of it. "There are only so many choices, aren't there?"

"A great many people would have made a different one."

With a nod, she accepted. "A different one wouldn't have been right for me." She sipped her wine as she let her mind drift back. "I was frightened. Quite a bit at first, but less and less as time when on. People were very good to me. It might have been different if I hadn't been lucky. I went into labor when I was cleaning room 328." Her eyes warmed as if she'd just seen something lovely. "I remember holding this stack of towels in my hand and thinking, 'Oh God, this is it, and I've only done half my rooms.'" She laughed and went back to her meal. Jonas's bowl sat cooling.

"You worked the day your baby was born?"

"Of course. I was healthy."

"I know men who take the day off if they need a tooth filled."

She laughed again and passed him the crackers. "Maybe women take things more in stride."

Only some women, he thought. Only a few exceptional women. "And afterward?"

"Afterward I was lucky again. A woman I worked with knew Señora Alderez. When Faith was born, her youngest had just turned five. She took care of Faith during the day, so I was able to go right back to work."

The cracker crumbled in his hand. "It must have been difficult for you."

"The only hard part was leaving my baby every morning, but the señora was wonderful to Faith and to me. That's how I found this house. Anyway, one thing led to another. I started the dive shop."

He wondered if she realized that the more simply she described it, the more poignant it sounded. "You said the dive shop was a gamble."

"Everything's a gamble. If I'd stayed at the hotel, I never would have been able to give Faith what I wanted to give her. And I suppose I'd have felt cheated myself. Would you like some more?"

"No." He rose to take the bowls himself while he thought out how to approach her. If he said the wrong thing, she'd pull away again. The more she told him, the more he found he needed to know. "Where did you learn to dive?"

"Right here in Cozumel, when I was just a little older than Faith." As a matter of habit she began to store the leftovers while Jonas ran water in the sink. "My parents brought me. I took to it right away. It was like, I don't know, learning to fly I suppose."

"Is that why you came back?"

"I came back because I'd always felt peaceful here. I needed to feel peaceful."

"But you must have still been in school in the States."

"I was in college." Crouching, Liz shifted things in the refrigerator to make room. "My first year. I was going to be a marine biologist, a teacher who'd enlighten class after class on the mysteries of the sea. A scientist who'd find all the answers. It was such a big dream. It overwhelmed everything else to the point where I studied constantly and rarely went out. Then I—'' She caught herself. Straightening slowly, she closed the refrigerator. ''You'll want the lights on to do those dishes.''

''Then what?'' Jonas demanded, taking her shoulder as she hit the switch.

She stared at him. Light poured over them without the shifting shadows of candles. ''Then I met Faith's father, and that was the end of dreams.''

The need to know eclipsed judgment. He forgot to be careful. ''Did you love him?''

''Yes. If I hadn't, there'd have been no Faith.''

It wasn't the answer he'd wanted. ''Then why are you raising her alone?''

''That's obvious, isn't it?'' Anger surged as she shoved his hand aside. ''He didn't want me.''

''Whether he did or didn't, he was responsible to you and the child.''

''Don't talk to me about responsibility. Faith's my responsibility.''

''The law sees things otherwise.''

''Keep your law,'' she snapped. ''He could quote it chapter and verse, and it didn't mean a thing. We weren't wanted.''

''So you let pride cut you off from your rights?'' Impatient with her, he stuck his hands in his pockets and strode back to the sink. ''Why didn't you fight for what you were entitled to?''

''You want the details, Jonas?'' Memory brought its own particular pain, its own particular shame. Liz concentrated on the anger. Going back to the table, she picked up her glass of wine and drank deeply.

''I wasn't quite eighteen. I was going to college to study exactly what I wanted to study so I could do exactly what I wanted to do. I considered myself a great deal more mature than some of my classmates who flitted around from class to class more concerned about where the action would be that night. I spent most of my evenings in the library. That's where I met him. He was in his last year and knew if he didn't pass the bar there'd be hell to pay at home. His family had been in law or politics since the Revolution. You'd understand about family honor, wouldn't you?''

The arrow hit the mark, but he only nodded.

''Then you should understand the rest. We saw each other every night in the library, so it was natural that we began to talk, then have a cup of coffee. He was smart, attractive, wonderfully mannered and funny.'' Almost violently, she blew out the candles. The scent carried over and hung in the room. ''I fell hard. He brought me flowers and took me for long quiet drives on Saturday nights. When he told me he loved me, I believed him. I thought I had the world in the palm of my hand.''

She set the wine down again, impatient to be finished. Jonas said nothing. ''He told me we'd be married as soon as he established himself. We'd sit in his car and look at the stars and he'd tell me about his home in Dallas and the wonderful rooms. The parties and the servants and the chandeliers. It was like a story, a lovely happily-ever-after story. Then one day his mother came.'' Liz laughed, but gripped the back of her chair until her knuckles were white. She could still feel the humiliation.

''Actually, she sent her driver up to the dorm to fetch me. Marcus hadn't said a thing about her visiting, but I was thrilled that I was going to meet her. At the curb was this fabulous white Rolls, the kind you only see in movies. When the driver opened the door for me, I was floating. Then I got in and she gave me the facts of life. Her son had a certain position to maintain, a certain image to project. She was sure I was a very nice girl, but hardly suitable for a Jensann of Dallas.''

Jonas's eyes narrowed at the name, but he said nothing. Restless, Liz went to the stove and began to scrub the surface. ''She told me she'd already spoken with her son and he understood the relationship had to end. Then she offered me a check as compensation. I was humiliated, and worse, I was pregnant. I hadn't told anyone yet, because I'd just found out that morning. I didn't take her money. I got out of the Rolls and went straight to Marcus. I was sure he loved me enough to toss it all aside for me, and for our baby. I was wrong.''

Her eyes were so dry that they hurt. Liz pressed her fingers to them a moment. ''When I went to see him, he was very logical. It had been nice; now it was over. His parents held the purse strings and it was important to keep them happy. But he wanted me to know we could still see each other now and again, as long as it was on the side. When I told him about the baby, he was furious. How could I have done such a thing? *I*.''

Liz tossed the dishrag into the sink so that hot, soapy water heaved up. ''It was as though I'd conceived the baby completely on my own. He wouldn't have it, he wouldn't have some silly girl who'd gotten herself pregnant messing up his life. He told me I had to get rid of it. It—as though Faith were a thing to be erased and forgotten. I was hysterical. He lost his temper. There were threats. He said he'd spread word that I was sleeping around and his friends would back him up. I'd never be able to prove the baby was his. He said my parents would be embarrassed, perhaps sued if I tried to press it. He tossed around a lot of legal phrases that I couldn't understand, but I understood he was finished with me. His family had a lot of pull at the college, and he said he'd see that I was dismissed. Because I was foolish enough to believe everything he said, I was terrified. He gave me a check and told me to go out of state—better, out of the country—to take care of things. That way no one would have to know.

''For a week I did nothing. I went through my classes in a daze, thinking I'd wake up and find out it had all been a bad dream. Then I faced it. I wrote my parents, telling them what I could. I sold the car they'd given me when I graduated from high school, took the check from Marcus and came to Cozumel to have my baby.''

He'd wanted to know, even demanded, but now his insides were raw. ''You could have gone to your parents.''

"Yes, but at the time Marcus had convinced me they'd be ashamed. He told me they'd hate me and consider the baby a burden."

"Why didn't you go to his family? You were entitled to be taken care of."

"Go to them?" He'd never heard venom in her voice before. "Be taken care of by them? I'd have gone to hell first."

He waited a moment, until he was sure he could speak calmly. "They don't even know, do they?"

"No. And they never will. Faith is mine."

"And what does Faith know?"

"Only what she has to know. I'd never lie to her."

"And do you know that Marcus Jensann has his sights set on the senate, and maybe higher?"

Her color drained quickly and completely. "You know him?"

"By reputation."

Panic came and went, then returned in double force. "He doesn't know Faith exists. None of them do. They can't."

Watching her steadily, he took a step closer. "What are you afraid of?"

"Power. Faith is mine, she's going to stay mine. None of them will ever touch her."

"Is that why you stay here? Are you hiding from them?"

"I'll do whatever's necessary to protect my child."

"He's still got you running scared." Furious for her, Jonas took her arms. "He's got a frightened teenager strapped inside of you who's never had the chance to stretch and feel alive. Don't you know a man like that wouldn't even remember who you are? You're still running away from a man who wouldn't recognize you on the street."

She slapped him hard enough to make his head snap back. Breathing fast, she backed away from him, appalled by a show of violence she hadn't been aware of possessing. "Don't tell me what I'm running from," she whispered. "Don't tell me what I feel." She turned and fled. Before she'd reached the front door he had her again, whirling her around, gripping her hard. He no longer knew why his anger was so fierce, only that he was past the point of controlling it.

"How much have you given up because of him?" Jonas demanded. "How much have you cut out of your life?"

"It's my life!" she shouted at him.

"And you won't share it with anyone but your daughter. What the hell are you going to do when she's grown? What the hell are you going to do in twenty years when you have nothing but your memories?"

"Don't." Tears filled her eyes too quickly to be blinked away.

He grabbed her close again, twisting until she had to look at him. "We all need someone. Even you. It's about time someone proved it to you."

"No."

She tried to turn her head but he was quick. With his mouth crushed on hers she struggled, but her arms were trapped between their bodies and his were ironlike around her. Emotions already mixed with fear and anger became more confused with passion. Liz fought not to give in to any of them as his mouth demanded both submission and response.

"You're not fighting me," he told her. His eyes were close, searing into hers. "You're fighting yourself. You've been fighting yourself since the first time we met."

"I want you to let me go." She wanted her voice to be strong, but it trembled.

"Yes. You want me to let you go just as much as you want me not to. You've been making your own decisions for a long time, Liz. This time I'm making one for you."

Her furious protest was lost against his mouth as he pressed her down to the sofa. Trapped under him, her body began to heat, her blood began to stir. Yes, she was fighting herself. She had to fight herself before she could fight him. But she was losing.

She heard her own moan as his lips trailed down her throat, and it was a moan of pleasure. She felt the hard line of his body against hers as she arched under him, but it wasn't a movement of protest. Want me, she seemed to say. Want me for what I am.

Her pulse began to thud in parts of her body that had been quiet for so many years. Life burst through her like a torrid wind through thin glass until every line of defense was shattered. With a desperate groan, she took his face in her hands and dragged his mouth back to hers.

She could taste the passion, the life, the promises. She wanted them all. Recklessness, so long chained within, tore free and ruled. A sound bubbled in her throat she wasn't even aware was a laugh as she wrapped herself around him. She wanted. He wanted. The hell with the rest.

He wasn't sure what had driven him—anger, need, pain. All he knew now was that he had to have her, body, soul and mind. She was wild beneath him, but no longer in resistance. Every movement was a demand that he take more, give more, and nothing seemed fast enough. She was a storm set to rage, a fire desperate to consume. Whatever he'd released inside of her had whipped out and taken him prisoner.

He pulled the shirt over her head and tossed it aside. His heartbeat thundered. She was so small, so delicate. But he had a beast inside him that had been caged too long. He took her breast in his mouth and sent them both spinning. She tasted so fresh: a cool, clear glass of water. She smelled of woman at her most unpampered and most seductive. He felt her body arch against his, taut as a bowstring, hot as a comet. The innocence that remained so integral a part of her trembled just beneath wanton passion. No man alive could have resisted it; any man alive might have wished for it. His mouth was buried at her throat when he felt the shirt rip away from his back.

She hardly knew what she was doing. Touching him sent demands to her brain that she couldn't deny. She wanted to feel him against her, flesh to flesh, to experience an intimacy she'd so long refused to allow herself. There'd been no one else. As Liz felt her skin fused to his she understood why. There was only one Jonas. She pulled his mouth back to hers to taste him again.

He drew off her slacks so that she was naked, but she didn't feel vulnerable. She felt invulnerable. Hardly able to breathe, she struggled with his. Then she gave him no choice. Desperate for that final release, she wrapped her legs around him and drew him into her until she was filled. At the shock of that first ragged peak, her eyes flew open. Inches away, he watched her face. Her mouth trembled open, but before she could catch her breath, he was driving her higher, faster. She couldn't tell how long they balanced on the edge, trapped between pleasure and fulfillment. Then his arms came around her, hers around his. Together, they broke free.

She didn't speak. Her system leveled slowly, and she was helpless to hurry it. He didn't move. He'd shifted his weight, but his arms had come around her and stayed there. She needed him to speak, to say something that would put what had happened in perspective. She'd only had one other lover and had learned not to expect.

Jonas rested his forehead against her shoulder a moment. He was wrestling with his own demons. ''I'm sorry, Liz.''

He could have said nothing worse. She closed her eyes and forced her emotions to drain. She nearly succeeded. Steadier, she reached for the tangle of clothes on the floor. ''I don't need an apology.'' With her clothes in a ball in her arm, she walked quickly to the bedroom.

On a long breath, Jonas sat up. He couldn't seem to find the right buttons on Liz Palmer. Every move he made seemed to be a move in reverse. It still stunned him that he'd been so rough with her, left her so little choice in the final outcome. He'd be better off hiring her a private bodyguard and moving himself back to the hotel. It was true he didn't want to see her hurt and felt a certain responsibility for her welfare, but he didn't seem to be able to act on it properly. When she'd stood in the kitchen telling him what she'd been through, something had begun to boil in him. That it had taken the form of passion in the end wasn't something easily explained or justified. His apology had been inadequate, but he had little else.

Drawing on his pants, Jonas started for his room. It

shouldn't have surprised him to find himself veering toward Liz's. She was just pulling on a robe. "It's late, Jonas."

"Did I hurt you?"

She sent him a look that made guilt turn over in his stomach. "Yes. Now I want to take a shower before I go to bed."

"Liz, there's no excuse for being so rough, and there's no making it up to you, but—"

"Your apology hurt me," she interrupted. "Now if you've said all you have to say, I'd like to be alone."

He stared at her a moment, then dragged a hand through his hair. How could he have convinced himself he understood her when she was now and always had been an enigma? "Damn it, Liz, I wasn't apologizing for making love to you, but for the lack of finesse. I practically tossed you on the ground and ripped your clothes off."

She folded her hands and tried to keep calm. "I ripped yours."

His lips twitched, then curved. "Yeah, you did."

Humor didn't come into her eyes. "And do you want an apology?"

He came to her then and rested his hands on her shoulders. Her robe was cotton and thin and whirling with bright color. "No. I guess what I'd like is for you to say you wanted me as much as I wanted you."

Her courage weakened, so she looked beyond him. "I'd have thought that was obvious."

"Liz." His hand was gentle as he turned her face back to his.

"All right. I wanted you. Now—"

"Now," he interrupted. "Will you listen?"

"There's no need to say anything."

"Yes, there is." He walked with her to the bed and drew her down to sit. Moonlight played over their hands as he took hers. "I came to Cozumel for one reason. My feelings on that haven't changed but other things have. When I first met you I thought you knew something, were hiding something. I linked everything about you to Jerry. It didn't take long for me to see there was something else. I wanted to know about you, for myself.''

"Why?''

"I don't know. It's impossible not to care about you." At her look of surprise, he smiled. "You project this image of pure self-sufficiency and still manage to look like a waif. Tonight, I purposely maneuvered you into talking about Faith and what had brought you here. When you told me I couldn't handle it.''

She drew her hand from his. "That's understandable. Most people have trouble handling unwed mothers.''

Anger bubbled as he grabbed her hand again. "Stop putting words in my mouth. You stood in the kitchen talking and I could see you, young, eager and trusting, being betrayed and hurt. I could see what it had done to you, how it had closed you off from things you wanted to do.''

"I told you I don't have any regrets.''

"I know." He lifted her hand and kissed it. "I guess for a moment I needed to have them for you.''

"Jonas, do you think anyone's life turns out the way they plan it as children?''

He laughed a little as he slipped an arm around her and drew her against him. Liz sat still a moment, unsure how to react to the casual show of affection. Then she leaned her head against his shoulder and closed her eyes. "Jerry and I were going to be partners.''

"In what?''

"In anything.''

She touched the coin on the end of his chain. "He had one of these.''

"Our grandparents gave them to us when we were kids. They're identical five-dollar gold pieces. Funny, I always wore mine heads up. Jerry wore his heads down." He closed his fingers over the coin. "He stole his first car when we were sixteen.''

Her fingers crept up to his. "I'm sorry.''

"The thing was he didn't need to—we had access to any

car in the garage. He told me he just wanted to see if he could get away with it.''

''He didn't make life easy for you.''

''No, he didn't make life easy. Especially for himself. But he never did anything out of meanness. There were times I hated him, but I never stopped loving him.''

Liz drew closer. ''Love hurts more than hate.''

He kissed the top of her head. ''Liz, I don't suppose you've ever talked to a lawyer about Faith.''

''Why should I?''

''Marcus has a responsibility, a financial responsibility at the least, to you and Faith.''

''I took money from Marcus once. Not again.''

''Child support payments could be set up very quietly. You could stop working seven days a week.''

Liz took a deep breath and pulled away until she could see his face. ''Faith is my child, has been my child only since the moment Marcus handed me a check. I could have had the abortion and gone back to my life as I'd planned it. I chose not to. I chose to have the baby, to raise the baby, to support the baby. She's never given me anything but pleasure from the moment she was born, and I have no intention of sharing her.''

''One day she's going to ask you for his name.''

Liz moistened her lips, but nodded. ''Then one day I'll tell her. She'll have her own choice to make.''

He wouldn't press her now, but there was no reason he couldn't have his law clerk begin to investigate child support laws and paternity cases. ''Are you going to let me meet her? I know the deal is for me to be out of the house and out of your life when she gets back. I will, but I'd like the chance to meet her.''

''If you're still in Mexico.''

''One more question.''

The smile came more easily. ''One more.''

''There haven't been any other men, have there?''

The smile faded. ''No.''

He felt twin surges of gratitude and guilt. "Then let me show you how it should be."

"There's no need—"

Gently, he brushed the hair back from her face. "Yes, there is. For both of us." He kissed her eyes closed. "I've wanted you from the first." His mouth on hers was as sweet as spring rain and just as gentle. Slowly, he slipped the robe from her shoulders, following the trail with warm lips. "Your skin's like gold," he murmured, then traced a finger over her breasts where the tone changed. "And so pale. I want to see all of you."

"Jonas—"

"All of you," he repeated, looking into her eyes until the heat kindled again. "I want to make love with all of you."

She didn't resist. Never in her life had anyone ever touched her with such reverence, looked at her with such need. When he urged her back, Liz lay on the bed, naked and waiting.

"Lovely," Jonas murmured. Her body was milk and honey in the moonlight. And her eyes were dark—dark and open and uncertain. "I want you to trust me." He began a slow journey of exploration at her ankles. "I want to know when I look at you that you're not afraid of me."

"I'm not afraid of you."

"You have been. Maybe I've even wanted you to be. No more."

His tongue slid over her skin and teased the back of her knees. The jolt of power had her rising up and gasping. "Jonas."

"Relax." He ran a hand lightly up her hip. "I want to feel your bones melt. Lie back, Liz. Let me show you how much you can have."

She obeyed, only because she hadn't the strength to resist. He murmured to her, stroking, nibbling, until she was too steeped in what he gave to give in return. But he wanted her that way, wanted to take her as though she hadn't been touched before. Not by him, not by anyone. Slowly, thoroughly and with great, great patience he seduced and pleasured. He thought as his mouth skimmed up her thigh that he could hear her skin hum.

She'd never known anything could be like this—so deep, so dark. There was a freedom here, she discovered, that she'd once only associated with diving down through silent fathoms. Her body could float, her limbs could be weightless, but she could feel every touch, every movement. Dreamlike, sensations drifted over her, so soft, so misty, each blended into the next. How long could it go on? Perhaps, after all, there were forevers.

She was lean, with muscles firm in her legs. Like a dancer's he thought, disciplined and trained. The scent from the bowl on her dresser spiced the air, but it was her fragrance, cool as a waterfall, that swam in his head. His mind emptied of everything but the need to delight her. Love, when unselfish, has incredible power.

His tongue plunged into the heat and his hands gripped hers as she arched, stunned at being flung from a floating world to a churning one. He drew from her, both patient and relentless, until she shuddered to climax and over. When her hands went limp in his, he brought them back to his body and pleasured himself.

She hadn't known passion could stretch so far or a body endure such a barrage of sensations. His hands, rough at the palm, showed her secrets she'd never had the chance to imagine. His lips, warmed from her own skin, opened mysteries and whispered the answers. He gentled her, he enticed her, he stroked with tenderness and he devoured. Gasping for air, she had no choice but to allow him whatever he wanted, and to strain for him to show her more.

When he was inside of her she thought it was all, and more, than she could ever want. If this was love, she'd never tasted it. If this was passion, she'd only skimmed its surface. Now it was time to risk the depths. Willing, eager, she held on to him.

It was trust he felt from her, and trust that moved him unbearably. He thought he'd needed before, desired before, but never so completely. Though he knew what it was to be part of another person, he'd never expected to feel the merger again. Strong, complex, unavoidable, the emotion swamped him. He belonged to her as fully as he'd wanted her to belong to him.

He took her slowly, so that the thrill that coursed through her seemed endless. His skin was moist when she pressed her lips to his throat. The pulse there was as quick as her own. A giddy sense of triumph moved through her, only to be whipped away with passion before it could spread.

Then he drew her up to him, and her body, liquid and limber with emotion, rose like a wave to press against his. Wrapped close, mouths fused, they moved together. Her hair fell like rain down her back. She could feel his heartbeat fast against her breast.

Still joined, they lowered again. The rhythm quickened. Desperation rose. She heard him breathe her name before the gates burst open and she was lost in the flood.

Chapter 9

She woke slowly, with a long, lazy stretch. Keeping her eyes closed, Liz waited for the alarm to ring. It wasn't often she felt so relaxed, even when waking, so she pampered herself and absorbed the luxury of doing nothing. In an hour, she mused, she'd be at the dive shop shifting through the day's schedule. The glass bottom, she thought, frowning a little. Was she supposed to take it out? Odd that she couldn't remember. Then with a start, it occurred to her that she didn't remember because she didn't know. She hadn't handled the schedule in two days. And last night...

She opened her eyes and looked into Jonas's.

"I could watch your mind wake up." He bent over and kissed her. "Fascinating."

Liz closed her fingers over the sheet and tugged it a little higher. What was she supposed to say? She'd never spent the night with a man, never awoken with one. She cleared her throat and wondered if every man awoke as sexily disheveled as Jonas Sharpe. "How did you sleep?" she managed, and felt ridiculous.

"Fine." He smiled as he brushed her hair from her cheek with a fingertip. "And you?"

"Fine." Her fingers moved restlessly on the sheet until he

closed his hands over them. His eyes were warm and heavy and made her heart pound.

"It's a little late to be nervous around me, Elizabeth."

"I'm not nervous." But color rose to her cheeks when he pressed his lips to her naked shoulder.

"Still, it's rather flattering. If you're nervous…" He turned his head so the tip of his tongue could toy with her ear. "Then you're not unmoved. I wouldn't like to think you felt casually about being with me—yet."

Was it possible to want so much this morning what she'd sated herself with the night before? She didn't think it should be, and yet her body told her differently. She would, as she always did, listen to her intellect first. "It must be almost time to get up." One hand firmly on the sheets, she rose on her elbows to look at the clock. "That's not right." She blinked and focused again. "It can't be eight-fifteen."

"Why not?" He slipped a hand beneath the sheet and stroked her thigh.

"Because." His touch had her pulses speeding. "I always set it for six-fifteen."

Finding her a challenge, Jonas brushed light kisses over her shoulder, down her arm. "You didn't set it last night."

"I always—" She cut herself off. It was hard enough to try to think when he was touching her, but when she remembered the night before, it was nearly impossible to understand why she had to think. Her mind hadn't been on alarms and schedules and customers when her body had curled into Jonas's to sleep. Her mind, as it was now, had been filled with him.

"Always what?"

She wished he wouldn't distract her with fingertips sliding gently over her skin. She wished he could touch her everywhere at once. "I always wake up at six, whether I set it or not."

"You didn't this time." He laughed as he eased her back down. "I suppose I should be flattered again."

"Maybe I flatter you too much," she murmured and started

to shift away. He simply rolled her back to him. "I have to get up."

"No, you don't."

"Jonas, I'm already late. I have to get to work."

Sunlight dappled over her face. He wanted to see it over the rest of her. "The only thing you have to do is make love with me." He kissed her fingers, then slowly drew them from the sheet. "I'll never get through the day without you."

"The boats—"

"Are already out, I'm sure." He cupped her breast, rubbing his thumb back and forth over the nipple. "Luis seems competent."

"He is. I haven't been in for two days."

"One more won't hurt."

Her body vibrated with need that slowly wound itself into her mind. Her arms came up to him, around him. "No, I guess it won't."

She hadn't stayed in bed until ten o'clock since she'd been a child. Liz felt as irresponsible as one as she started the coffee. True, Luis could handle the shop and the boats as well as she, but it wasn't his job. It was hers. Here she was, brewing coffee at ten o'clock, with her body still warm from loving. Nothing had been the same since Jonas Sharpe had arrived on her doorstep.

"It's useless to give yourself a hard time for taking a morning off," Jonas said from behind her.

Liz popped bread into the toaster. "I suppose not, since I don't even know today's schedule."

"Liz." Jonas took her by the arms and firmly turned her around. He studied her, gauging her mood before he spoke. "You know, back in Philadelphia I'm considered a workaholic. I've had friends express concern over the workload I take on and the hours I put in. Compared to you, I'm retired."

Her brows drew together as they did when she was concentrating. Or annoyed. "We each do what we have to do."

"True enough. It appears what I have to do is harass you until you relax."

She had to smile. He said it so reasonably and his eyes were laughing. "I'm sure you have a reputation for being an expert on harassment."

"I majored in it at college."

"Good for you. But I'm an expert at budgeting my own time. And there's my toast." He let her pluck it out, waited until she'd buttered it, then took a piece for himself.

"You mentioned diving lessons."

She was still frowning at him when she heard the coffee begin to simmer. She reached for one cup, then relented and took two. "What about them?"

"I'll take one. Today."

"Today?" She handed him his coffee, drinking her own standing by the stove. "I'll have to see what's scheduled. The way things have been going, both dive boats should already be out."

"Not a group lesson, a private one. You can take me out on the *Expatriate*."

"Luis usually takes care of the private lessons."

He smiled at her. "I prefer dealing with the management."

Liz dusted crumbs from her fingers. "All right then. It'll cost you."

He lifted his cup in salute. "I never doubted it."

Liz was laughing when Jonas pulled into a narrow parking space at the hotel. "If he'd picked your pocket, why did you defend him?"

"Everyone's entitled to representation," Jonas reminded her. "Besides, I figured if I took him on as a client, he'd leave my wallet alone."

"And did he?"

"Yeah." Jonas took her hand as they crossed the sidewalk to the sand. "He stole my watch instead."

She giggled, a foolish, girlish sound he'd never heard from her. "And did you get him off?"

"Two years probation. There, it looks like business is good."

Liz shielded her eyes from the sun and looked toward the

shop. Luis was busily fitting two couples with snorkel gear. A glance to the left showed her only the *Expatriate* remained in dock. "Cozumel's becoming very popular," she murmured.

"Isn't that the idea?"

"For business?" She moved her shoulders. "I'd be a fool to complain."

"But?"

"But sometimes I think it would be nice if it could block out the changes. I don't want to see the water choked with suntan oil. *Hola,* Luis."

"Liz!" His gaze passed over Jonas briefly before he grinned at her. "We thought maybe you deserted us. How did you like Acapulco?"

"It was…different," she decided, and was already scooting behind the counter to find the daily schedule. "Any problems?"

"Jose took care of a couple repairs. I brought Miguel back to fill in, but I keep an eye on him. Got this—what do you call it—brochure on the aqua bikes." He pulled out a colorful pamphlet, but Liz only nodded.

"The Brinkman party's out diving. Did we take them to Palancar?"

"Two days in a row. Miguel likes them. They tip good."

"Hmm. You're handling the shop alone."

"No problem. Hey, there was a guy." He screwed up his face as he tried to remember the name. "Skinny guy, American. You know the one you took out on the beginners' trip?"

She flipped through the receipts and was satisfied. "Trydent?"

"*Sí,* that was it. He came by a coupla times."

"Rent anything?"

"No." Luis wiggled his eyebrows at her. "He was looking for you."

Liz shrugged it off. If he hadn't rented anything, he didn't interest her. "If everything's under control here, I'm going to take Mr. Sharpe out for a diving lesson."

Luis looked quickly at Jonas, then away. The man made

him uneasy, but Liz looked happier than she had in weeks. "Want me to get the gear?"

"No, I'll take care of it." She looked up and smiled at Jonas. "Write Mr. Sharpe up a rental form and give him a receipt for the gear, the lesson and the boat trip. Since it's..." She trailed off as she checked her watch. "Nearly eleven, give him the half-day rate."

"You're all heart," Jonas murmured as she went to the shelves to choose his equipment.

"You got the best teacher," Luis told him, but couldn't manage more than another quick look at Jonas.

"I'm sure you're right." Idly, Jonas swiveled the newspaper Luis had tossed on the counter around to face him. He missed being able to sit down with the morning paper over coffee. The Spanish headlines told him nothing. "Anything going on I should know about?" Jonas asked, indicating the paper.

Luis relaxed a bit as he wrote. Jonas's voice wasn't so much like Jerry's when you weren't looking at him. "Haven't had a chance to look at it yet. Busy morning."

Going with habit, Jonas turned the paper over. There, in a faded black-and-white picture, was Erika. Jonas's fingers tightened. He glanced back and saw that Liz was busy, her back to him. Without a word, he slid the paper over the receipt Luis was writing.

"Hey, that's the—"

"I know," Jonas said in an undertone. "What does it say?"

Luis bent over the paper to read. He straightened again very slowly, and his face was ashen. "Dead," he whispered. "She's dead."

"How?"

Luis's fingers opened and closed on the pen he held. "Stabbed."

Jonas thought of the knife held at Liz's throat. "When?"

"Last night." Luis had to swallow twice. "They found her last night."

"Jonas," Liz called from the back, "how much do you weigh?"

Keeping his eyes on Luis, Jonas turned the paper over again. "One seventy. She doesn't need to hear this now," he added under his breath. He pulled bills from his wallet and laid them on the counter. "Finish writing the receipt."

After a struggle, Luis mastered his own fear and straightened. "I don't want anything to happen to Liz."

Jonas met the look with a challenge that held for several humming seconds before he relaxed. The smaller man was terrified, but he was thinking of Liz. "Neither do I. I'm going to see nothing does."

"You brought trouble."

"I know." His gaze shifted beyond Luis to Liz. "But if I leave, the trouble doesn't."

For the first time, Luis forced himself to study Jonas's face. After a moment, he blew out a long breath. "I liked your brother, but I think it was him who brought trouble."

"It doesn't matter anymore who brought it. I'm going to look out for her."

"Then you look good," Luis warned softly. "You look real good."

"First lesson," Liz said as she unlocked her storage closet. "Each diver carries and is responsible for his own gear." She jerked her head back to where Jonas's was stacked. With a last look at Luis, he walked through the doorway to gather it up.

"Preparing for a dive is twice as much work as diving itself," she began as she hefted her tanks. "It's a good thing it's worth it. We'll be back before sundown, Luis. *Hasta luego.*"

"Liz." She stopped, turning back to where Luis hovered in the doorway. His gaze passed over Jonas, then returned to her. *"Hasta luego,"* he managed, and closed his fingers over the medal he wore around his neck.

The moment she was on board, Liz restacked her gear. As a matter of routine, she checked all the *Expatriate*'s gauges. "Can you cast off?" she asked Jonas.

He ran a hand down her hair, surprising her. She looked so competent, so in charge. He wondered if by staying close he was protecting or endangering. It was becoming vital to believe the first. "I can handle it."

She felt her stomach flutter as he continued to stare at her. "Then you'd better stop looking at me and do it."

"I like looking at you." He drew her close, just to hold her. "I could spend years looking at you."

Her arms came up, hesitated, then dropped back to her sides. It would be so easy to believe. To trust again, give again, be hurt again. She wanted to tell him of the love growing inside her, spreading and strengthening with each moment. But if she told him she'd no longer have even the illusion of control. Without control, she was defenseless.

"I clocked you on at eleven," she said, but couldn't resist breathing deeply of his scent and committing it to memory.

Because she made him smile again, he drew her back. "I'm paying the bill, I'll worry about the time."

"Diving lesson," she reminded him. "And you can't dive until you cast off."

"Aye, aye, sir." But he gave her a hard, breath-stealing kiss before he jumped back on the dock.

Liz drew air into her lungs and let it out slowly before she turned on the engines. All she could hope was that she looked more in control than she felt. He was winning a battle, she mused, that he didn't even know he was fighting. She waited for Jonas to join her again before she eased the throttle forward.

"There are plenty of places to dive where we don't need the boat, but I thought you'd enjoy something away from the beaches. Palancar is one of the most stunning reefs in the Caribbean. It's probably the best place to start because the north end is shallow and the wall slopes rather than having a sheer vertical drop-off. There are a lot of caves and passageways, so it makes for an interesting dive."

"I'm sure, but I had something else in mind."

"Something else?"

Jonas took a small book out of his pocket and flipped through it. "What do these numbers look like to you?"

Liz recognized the book. It was the same one he'd used in

Acapulco to copy down the numbers from his brother's book in the safe-deposit box. He still had his priorities, she reminded herself, then drew back on the throttle to let the boat idle.

The numbers were in precise, neat lines. Any child who'd paid attention in geography class would recognize them. "Longitude and latitude."

He nodded. "Do you have a chart?"

He'd planned this since he'd first seen the numbers, she realized. Their being lovers changed nothing else. "Of course, but I don't need it for this. I know these waters. That's just off the coast of Isla Mujeres." Liz adjusted her course and picked up speed. Perhaps, she thought, the course had already been set for both of them long before this. They had no choice but to see it through. "It's a long trip. You might as well relax."

He put his hands on her shoulders to knead. "We won't find anything, but I have to go."

"I understand."

"Would you rather I go alone?"

She shook her head violently, but said nothing.

"Liz, this had to be his drop point. By tomorrow, Moralas will have the numbers and send his own divers down. I have to see for myself."

"You're chasing shadows, Jonas. Jerry's gone. Nothing you can do is going to change that."

"I'll find out why. I'll find out who. That'll be enough."

"Will it?" With her hand gripping the wheel hard, she looked over her shoulder. His eyes were close, but they held that cool, set look again. "I don't think so—not for you." Liz turned her face back to the sea. She would take him where he wanted to go.

Isla Mujeres, Island of Women, was a small gem in the water. Surrounded by reefs and studded with untouched lagoons, it was one of the perfect retreats of the Caribbean. Party boats from the continental coast or one of the other islands cruised there daily to offer their customers snorkeling or diving at its best. It had once been known by pirates and blessed by a goddess. Liz anchored the boat off the southwest coast. Once again, she became the teacher.

"It's important to know and understand both the name and the use of every piece of equipment. It's not just a matter of stuffing in a mouthpiece and strapping on a tank. No smoking," she added as Jonas took out a cigarette. "It's ridiculous to clog up your lungs in the first place, and absurd to do it before a dive."

Jonas set the pack on the bench beside him. "How long are we going down?"

"We'll keep it under an hour. The depth here ranges to eighty feet. That means the nitrogen in your air supply will be over three times denser than what your system's accustomed to. In some people at some depths, this can cause temporary imbalances. If you begin to feel light-headed, signal to me right away. We'll descend in stages to give your body time to get used to the changes in pressure. We ascend the same way in order to give the nitrogen time to expel. If you come up too quickly, you risk decompression sickness. It can be fatal." As she spoke, she spread out the gear with the intention of explaining each piece. "Nothing is to be taken for granted in the water. It is not your milieu. You're dependent on your equipment and your own good sense. It's beautiful and it's exciting, but it's not an amusement park."

"Is this the same lecture you give on the dive boat?"

"Basically."

"You're very good."

"Thank you." She picked up a gauge. "Now—"

"Can we get started?" he asked and reached for his wet suit.

"We are getting started. You can't dive without a working knowledge of your equipment."

"That's a depth gauge." He nodded toward her hand as he stripped down to black briefs. "A very sophisticated one. I wouldn't think most dive shops would find it necessary to stock that quality."

"This is mine," she murmured. "But I keep a handful for rentals."

"I don't think I mentioned that you have the best-tended equipment I've ever seen. It isn't in the same league with your personal gear, but it's quality. Give me a hand, will you?"

Liz rose to help him into the tough, stretchy suit. "You've gone down before."

"I've been diving since I was fifteen." Jonas pulled up the zipper before bending over to check the tanks himself.

"Since you were fifteen." Liz yanked off her shirt and tossed it aside. Fuming, she pulled off her shorts until she wore nothing but a string bikini and a scowl. "Then why did you let me go on that way?"

"I liked hearing you." Jonas glanced up and felt his blood surge. "Almost as much as I like looking at you."

She wasn't in the mood to be flattered, less in the mood to be charmed. Without asking for assistance, she tugged herself into her wet suit. "You're still paying for the lesson."

Jonas grinned as he examined his flippers. "I never doubted it."

She strapped on the rest of her gear in silence. It was difficult even for her to say if she were really angry. All she knew was the day, and dive, weren't as simple as they had started out to be. Lifting the top of a bench, she reached into a compartment and took out two short metal sticks shaped like bats.

"What's this for?" Jonas asked as she handed him one.

"Insurance." She adjusted her mask. "We're going down to the caves where the sharks sleep."

"Sharks don't sleep."

"The oxygen content in the water in the cave keeps them quiescent. But don't think you can trust them."

Without another word, she swung over the side and down the ladder.

The water was as clear as glass, so she could see for more than a hundred feet. As she heard Jonas plunge in beside her, Liz turned to assure herself he did indeed know what he was doing. Catching her skeptical look, Jonas merely circled his thumb and forefinger, then pointed down.

He was tense. Liz could feel it from him, though she understood it had nothing to do with his skill underwater. His brother had dived here once—she was as certain of it as Jonas. And the reason for his dives had been the reason for his death. She no longer had to think whether she was angry. In a gesture as personal as a kiss, she reached out a hand and took his.

Grateful, Jonas curled his fingers around hers. He didn't know what he was looking for, or even why he continued to look when already he'd found more than he'd wanted to. His brother had played games with the rules and had lost. Some would say there was justice in that. But they'd shared birth. He had to go on looking, and go on hoping.

Liz saw the first of the devilfish and tugged on Jonas's hands. Such things never failed to touch her spirit. The giant manta rays cruised together, feeding on plankton and unconcerned with the human intruders. Liz kicked forward, delighted to swim among them. Their huge mouths could crush and devour crustaceans. Their wingspan of twenty feet and more was awesome. Without fear, Liz reached out to touch. Pleasure came easily, as it always did to her in the sea. Her eyes were laughing as she reached out again for Jonas.

They descended farther, and some of his tension began to dissolve. There was something different about her here, a lightness, an ease that dissolved the sadness that always seemed to linger in her eyes. She looked free, and more, as happy as he'd ever seen her. If it were possible to fall in love in a matter of moments, Jonas fell in love in those, forty feet below the surface with a mermaid who'd forgotten how to dream.

Everything she saw, everything she could touch fascinated her. He could see it in the way she moved, the way she looked at everything as though it were her first dive. If he could have found a way, he would have stayed with her there, surrounded by love and protected by fathoms.

They swam deeper, but leisurely. If something evil had been begun, or been ended there, it had left no trace. The sea was calm and silent and full of life too lovely to exist in the air.

When the shadow passed over, Liz looked up. In all her dives, she'd never seen anything so spectacular. Thousands upon thousands of silvery grunts moved together in a wave so dense that they might have been one creature. Eyes wide with the wonder of it, Liz lifted her arms and took her body up. The wave swayed as a unit, avoiding intrusion. Delighted, she signaled for Jonas to join her. The need to share the magic was natural. This was the pull of the sea that had driven her to study, urged to explore and invited her once to dream. With her fingers linked with Jonas's, she propelled them closer. The school of fish split in half so that it became two unified forms swirling on either side of them. The sea teemed with them, thick clouds of silver so tightly grouped that they seemed fused together.

For a moment she was as close to her own fantasies as she had ever been, floating free, surrounded by magic, with her lover's hand in hers. Impulsively, she wrapped her arms around Jonas and held on. The clouds of fish swarmed around them, linked into one, then swirled away.

He could feel her pulse thud when he reached for her wrist. He could see the fascinated delight in her eyes. Hampered by his human frailty in the water, he could only touch his hand to her cheek. When she lifted her own to press it closer, it was enough. Side by side they swam toward the seafloor.

The limestone caves were eerie and compelling. Once Jonas saw the head of a moray eel slide out and curve, either in curiosity or warning. An old turtle with barnacles crusting his back rose from his resting place beneath a rock and swam between them. Then at the entrance to a cave, Liz pointed and shared another mystery.

The shark moved across the sand, as a dog might on a hearth rug. His small, black eyes stared back at them as his gills slowly drew in water. While they huddled just inside the entrance, their bubbles rising up through the porous limestone and toward the surface, the shark shifted restlessly. Jonas reached for Liz's hand to draw her back, but she moved a bit closer, anxious to see.

In a quick move, the shark shot toward the entrance. Jonas

was grabbing for Liz and his knife, when she merely poked at the head with her wooden bat. Without pausing, the shark swam toward the open sea and vanished.

He wanted to strangle her. He wanted to tell her how fascinating she was to watch. Since he could do neither, Jonas merely closed a hand over her throat and gave her a mock shake. Her laughter had bubbles dancing.

They swam on together, parting from time to time to explore separate interests. He decided she'd forgotten his purpose in coming, but thought it was just as well. If she could take this hour for personal freedom, he was glad of it. For him, there were demands.

The water and the life in it were undeniably beautiful, but Jonas noticed other things. They hadn't seen another diver and their down time was nearly up. The caves where the sharks slept were also a perfect place to conceal a cache of drugs. Only the very brave or the very foolish would swim in their territory at night. He thought of his brother and knew Jerry would have considered it the best kind of adventure. A man with a reason could swim into one of the caves while the sharks were out feeding, and leave or take whatever he liked.

Liz hadn't forgotten why Jonas had come. Because she thought she could understand a part of what he was feeling, she gave him room. Here, eighty feet below the surface, he was searching for something, anything, to help him accept his brother's death. And his brother's life.

It would come to an end soon, Liz reflected. The police had the name of the go-between in Acapulco. And the other name that Jonas had given them, she remembered suddenly. Where had he gotten that one? She looked toward him and realized there were things he wasn't telling her. That, too, would end soon, she promised herself. Then she found herself abruptly out of air.

She didn't panic. Liz was too well trained to panic. Immediately, she checked her gauge and saw that she had ten full minutes left. Reaching back, she ran a hand down her hose and found it unencumbered. But she couldn't draw air.

Whatever the gauge said, her life was on the line. If she swam toward the surface, her lungs would be crushed by the pressure. Forcing herself to stay calm, she swam in a diagonal toward Jonas. When she caught his ankle, she tugged sharply. The smile he turned with faded the moment he saw her eyes. Recognizing her signal, he immediately removed his regulator and passed it to her. Liz drew in air. Nodding, she handed it back to him. Their bodies brushing, her hand firm on his shoulder, they began their slow ascent.

Buddy-breathing, they rose closer to the surface, restraining themselves from rushing. What took only a matter of minutes seemed to drag on endlessly. The moment Liz's head broke water, she pushed back her mask and gulped in fresh air.

"What happened?" Jonas demanded, but when he felt her begin to shake, he only swore and pulled her with him to the ladder. "Take it easy." His hand was firm at her back as she climbed up.

"I'm all right." But she collapsed on a bench, without the energy to draw off her tanks. Her body shuddered once with relief as Jonas took the weight from her. With her head between her knees, she waited for the mists to clear. "I've never had anything like that happen," she managed. "Not at eighty feet."

He was rubbing her hands to warm them. "What did happen?"

"I ran out of air."

Enraged, he took her by the shoulders and dragged her back to a sitting position. "Ran out of air? That's unforgivably careless. How can you give lessons when you haven't the sense to watch your own gauges?"

"I watched my gauge." She drew air in and let it out slowly. "I should have had another ten minutes."

"You rent diving equipment, for God's sake! How can you be negligent with your own? You might've died."

The insult to her competence went a long way toward smothering the fear. "I'm never careless," she snapped at him. "Not with rental equipment or my own." She dragged the mask from her head and tossed it on the bench. "Look at my gauge. I should have had ten minutes left."

He looked, but it didn't relieve his anger. "Your equipment should be checked. If you go down with a faulty gauge you're inviting an accident."

"My equipment has been checked. I check it myself after every dive, and it was fine before I stored it. I filled those tanks myself." The alternative came to her even as she finished speaking. Her face, already pale, went white. "God, Jonas, I filled them myself. I checked every piece of equipment the last time I went down."

He closed a hand over hers hard enough to make her wince. "You keep it in the shop, in that closet."

"I lock it up."

"How many keys?"

"Mine—and an extra set in the drawer. They're rarely used because I always leave mine there when I go out on the boats."

"But the extra set would have been used when we were away?"

The shaking was starting again. This time it wasn't as simple to control it. "Yes."

"And someone used the key to the closet to get in and tamper with your equipment."

She moistened her lips. "Yes."

The rage ripped inside him until he was nearly blind with it. Hadn't he just promised to watch out for her, to keep her safe? With intensely controlled movements, he pulled off his flippers and discarded his mask. "You're going back. You're going to pack, then I'm putting you on a plane. You can stay with my family until this is over."

"No."

"You're going to do exactly what I say."

"No," she said again and managed to draw the strength to stand. "I'm not going anywhere. This is the second time someone's threatened my life."

"And they're not going to have a chance to do it again."

"I'm not leaving my home."

"Don't be a fool." He rose. Knowing he couldn't touch her, he unzipped his wet suit and began to strip it off. "Your business isn't going to fall apart. You can come back when it's safe."

"I'm not leaving." She took a step toward him. "You came here looking for revenge. When you have it, you can leave and be satisfied. Now I'm looking for answers. I can't leave because they're here."

Struggling to keep his hands gentle, he took her face between them. "I'll find them for you."

"You know better than that, don't you, Jonas? Answers don't mean anything unless you find them yourself. I want my daughter to be able to come home. Until I find those answers, until it's safe, she can't." She lifted her hands to his face so that they stood as a unit. "We both have reasons to look now."

He sat, took his pack of cigarettes and spoke flatly. "Erika's dead."

The anger that had given her the strength to stand wavered. "What?"

"Murdered." His voice was cold again, hard again. "A few days ago I met her, paid her for a name."

Liz braced herself against the rail. "The name you gave to the captain."

Jonas lit his cigarette, telling himself he was justified to put fear back into her eyes. "That's right. She asked some questions, got some answers. She told me this Pablo Manchez was bad, a professional killer. Jerry was killed by a pro. So, it appears, was Erika."

"She was shot?"

"Stabbed," Jonas corrected and watched Liz's hand reach involuntarily for her own neck. "That's right." He drew violently on the cigarette then hurled it overboard before he rose. "You're going back to the States until this is all over."

She turned her back on him a moment, needing to be certain she could be strong. "I'm not leaving, Jonas. We have the same problem."

"Liz—"

"No." When she turned back her chin was up and her eyes were clear. "You see, I've run from problems before, and it doesn't work."

"This isn't a matter of running, it's a matter of being sensible."

"You're staying."

"I don't have a choice."

"Then neither do I."

"Liz, I don't want you hurt."

She tilted her head as she studied him. She could believe that, she realized, and take comfort in it. "Will you go?"

"I can't. You know I can't."

"Neither can I." She wrapped her arms around him, pressed her cheek to his shoulder in a first spontaneous show of need or affection. "Let's go home," she murmured. "Let's just go home."

Chapter 10

Every morning when Liz awoke she was certain Captain Moralas would call to tell her it was all over. Every night when she closed her eyes, she was certain it was only a matter of one more day. Time went on.

Every morning when Liz awoke she was certain Jonas would tell her he had to leave. Every night when she slept in his arms, she was certain it was the last time. He stayed.

For over ten years her life had had a certain purpose. Success. She'd started the struggle toward it in order to survive and to provide for her child. Somewhere along the way she'd learned the satisfaction of being on her own and making it work. In over ten years, Liz had gone steadily forward without detours. A detour could mean failure and the loss of independence. It had been barely a month since Jonas had walked into her house and her life. Since that time the straight road she had followed had forked. Ignoring the changes hadn't helped, fighting them hadn't worked. Now it no longer seemed she had the choice of which path to follow.

Because she had to hold on to something, she worked every day, keeping stubbornly to her old routine. It was the only aspect of her life that she could be certain she could control. Though it brought some semblance of order to her life, it didn't keep Liz's mind at rest. She found herself studying her customers with suspicion. Business thrived as the summer season drew closer. It didn't seem as important as it had even weeks before, but she kept the shop open seven days a week.

Jonas had taken the fabric of her life, plucked at a few threads and changed everything. Liz had come to the point that she could admit nothing would ever be quite the same again, but she had yet to come to the point that she knew what to do about it. When he left, as she knew he would, she would have to learn all over again how to suppress longings and black out dreams.

They would find Jerry Sharpe's killer. They would find the man with the knife. If she hadn't believed that, Liz would never have gone on day after day. But after the danger was over, after all questions were answered, her life would never be as it had been. Jonas had woven himself into it. When he went away, he'd leave a hole behind that would take all her will to mend.

Her life had been torn before. Liz could comfort herself that she had put it together again. The shape had been different, the texture had changed, but she had put it together. She could do so again. She would have to.

There were times when she lay in bed in the dark, in the early hours of the morning, restless, afraid she would have to begin those repairs before she was strong enough.

Jonas could feel her shift beside him. He'd come to understand she rarely slept peacefully. Or she no longer slept peacefully. He wished she would lean on him, but knew she never would. Her independence was too vital, and opposingly, her insecurity was too deep to allow her to admit a need for another. Even the sharing of a burden was difficult for her. He wanted to soothe. Through his adult life, Jonas had carefully chosen companions who had no problems, required no advice, no comfort, no support. A woman who required such things required an emotional attachment he had never been willing to make. He wasn't a selfish man, simply a cautious one. Throughout his youth, and through most of his adult life, he'd picked up the pieces his brother had scattered. Consciously or unconsciously, Jonas had promised himself he'd never be put in the position of having to do so for anyone else.

Now he was drawing closer and closer to a woman who elicited pure emotion, then tried to deflect it. He was falling in love with a woman who needed him but refused to admit it. She was strong and had both the intelligence and the will to take care of herself. And she had eyes so soft, so haunted, that a man would risk anything to protect her from any more pain.

She had completely changed his life. She had altered the simple, tidy pattern he'd been weaving for himself. He *needed* to soothe, to protect, to share. There was nothing he could do to change that. Whenever he touched her, he came closer to admitting there was nothing he would do.

The bed was warm and the room smelled of the flowers that grew wild outside the open window. Their scent mixed with the bowl of potpourri on Liz's dresser. Now and then the breeze ruffled through palm fronds so that the sound whispered but didn't disturb. Beside him was a woman whose body was slim and restless. Her hair spread over her pillow and onto his, carrying no more fragrance than wind over water. The moonlight trickled in, dipping into corners, filtering over the bed so he could trace her silhouette. As she tossed in sleep, he drew her closer. Her muscles were tense, as though she were prepared to reject the gift of comfort even before it was offered. Slowly, as her breath whispered at his throat, he began to massage her shoulders. Strong shoulders, soft skin. He found the combination irresistible. She murmured, shifting toward him, but he didn't know if it was acceptance or request. It didn't matter.

She felt so good there; she felt right there. All questions, all doubts could wait for the sunrise. Before dawn they would share the need that was in both of them. In the moonlight, in the quiet hours, each would have what the other could offer. He touched his mouth lightly, ever so lightly, to hers.

She sighed, but it was only a whisper of a sound—a sigh in sleep as her body relaxed against his. If she dreamed now, she dreamed of easy things, calm water, soft grass. He trailed a hand down her back, exploring the shape of her. Long, lean, slender and strong. He felt his own body warm and pulse. Passion, still sleepy, began to stir.

She seemed to wake in stages. First her skin, then her blood, then muscle by muscle. Her body was alert and throbbing before her mind raced to join it. She found herself wrapped around Jonas, already aroused, already hungry. When his mouth came to hers again, she answered him.

There was no hesitation in her this time, no moment of doubt before desire overwhelmed reason. She wanted to give herself to him as fully as it was possible to give. It wouldn't be wise to speak her feelings out loud. It couldn't be safe to tell him with words that her heart was stripped of defenses and open for him. But she could show him, and by doing so give them both the pleasure of love without restrictions.

Her arms tightened around him as her mouth roamed madly over his. She drew his bottom lip inside the heat, inside the moistness of her mouth and nibbled, sucked until his breath came fast and erratic. She felt the abrupt tension as his body pressed against hers and realized he, too, could be seduced. He, too, could be aroused beyond reason. And she realized with a heady sort of wonder that she could be the seducer, she could arouse.

She shifted her body under his, tentatively, but with a slow rhythm that had him murmuring her name and grasping for control. Instinctively she sought out vulnerabilities, finding them one by one, learning from them, taking from them. Her tongue flicked over his throat, seeking then enjoying the subtle, distinct taste of man. His pulse was wild there, as wild as hers. She shifted again until she lay across him and his body was hers for the taking.

Her hands were inexperienced so that her stroking was soft and hesitant. It drove him mad. No one had ever been so sweetly determined to bring him pleasure. She pressed kisses over his chest, slowly, experimentally, then rubbed her cheek over his skin so that the touch both soothed and excited.

His body was on fire, yet it seemed to float free so that he could feel the passage of air breathe cool over his flesh. She touched, and the heat spread like brushfire. She tasted and the moistness from her lips was like the whisper of a night breeze, cooling, calming.

"Tell me what you want." She looked up and her eyes were luminous in the moonlight, dark and beautiful. "Tell me what to do."

It was almost more than he could bear, the purity of the request, the willingness to give. He reached up so that his hands were lost in her hair. He could have kept her there forever, arched above him with her skin glowing gold in the thin light, her hair falling pale over her shoulders, her eyes shimmering with need. He drew her down until their lips met again. Hunger exploded between them. She didn't need to be told, she didn't need to be taught. Her body took over so that her own desire drove them both.

Jonas let reason go, let control be damned. Gripping her hips, he drew her up, then brought her to him, brought himself into her with a force that had her gasping in astonished pleasure. As she shuddered again, then again, he reached for her hands. Their fingers linked as she arched back and let her need set the pace. Frantic. Desperate. Uncontrollable. Pleasure, pain, delight, terror all whipped through her, driving her on, thrusting her higher.

He couldn't think, but he could feel. Until that moment, he wouldn't have believed it possible to feel so much so intensely. Sensations racked him, building and building and threatening to explode until the only sound he could hear was the roar of his own heart inside his head. With his eyes half open he could see her above him, naked and glorious in the moonlight. And when she plunged him beyond sensation, beyond sight and reason, he could still see her. He always would.

It didn't seem possible. It didn't, Liz thought, seem reasonable that she could be managing the shop, dealing with customers, stacking equipment when her system was still soaking up every delicious sensation she'd experienced just before dawn. Yet she was there, filling out forms, giving advice, quoting prices and making change. Still it was all mechanical. She'd been wise to delegate the diving tours and remain on shore.

She greeted her customers, some old and some new, and tried not to think too deeply about the list she'd been forced to give Moralas. How many of them would come to the Black Coral for equipment or lessons if they knew that by doing only that they were under police investigation? Jerry Sharpe's murder, and her involvement in it, could endanger her business far more than a slow season or a rogue hurricane.

Over and above her compassion, her sympathy and her hopes that Jonas could put his mind and heart at rest was a desperate need to protect her own, to guard what she'd built from nothing for her daughter. No matter how she tried to bury it, she couldn't completely block out the resentment she felt for being pulled into a situation that had been none of her making.

Yet there was a tug-of-war waging inside of her. Resentment for the disruption of her life battled against the longing to have Jonas remain in it. Without the disruption, he never would have come to her. No matter how much she tried, she could never regret the weeks they'd had together. She promised herself that she never would. It was time to admit that she had a great scope of love that had been trapped inside her. Rejected once, it had refused to risk again. But Jonas had released it, or perhaps she'd released it herself. Whatever happened, however it ended, she'd been able to love again.

"You're a hard lady to pin down."

Startled out of her own thoughts, Liz looked up. It took her a moment to remember the face, and a moment still to link a name with it. "Mr. Trydent." She rose from her desk to go to the counter. "I didn't realize you were still on the island."

"I only take one vacation a year, so I like to make the most of it." He set a tall paper cup that bounced with ice on the counter. "I figured this was the only way to get you to have a drink with me."

Liz glanced at the cup and wondered if she'd been businesslike or rude. At the moment she would have liked nothing better than to be alone with her own thoughts, but a customer was a customer. "That's nice of you. I've been pretty tied up."

"No kidding." He gave her a quick smile that showed straight teeth and easy charm. "You're either out of town or out on a boat. So I thought about the mountain and Mohammed." He glanced around. "Things are pretty quiet now."

"Lunchtime," Liz told him. "Everyone who's going out is already out. Everyone else is grabbing some food or a siesta before they decide how to spend the afternoon."

"Island living."

She smiled back. "Exactly. Tried any more diving?"

He made a face. "I let myself get talked into a night dive with Mr. Ambuckle before he headed back to Texas. I'm planning on sticking to the pool for the rest of my vacation."

"Diving's not for everyone."

"You can say that again." He drank from the second cup he'd brought, then leaned on the counter. "How about dinner? Dinner's for everyone."

She lifted a brow, a little surprised, a little flattered that he seemed bent on a pursuit. "I rarely eat out."

"I like home cooking."

"Mr. Trydent—"

"Scott," he corrected.

"Scott, I appreciate the offer, but I'm…" How did she put it? Liz wondered. "I'm seeing someone."

He laid a hand on hers. "Serious?"

Not sure whether she was embarrassed or amused, Liz drew her hand away. "I'm a serious sort of person."

"Well." Scott lifted his cup, watching her over the rim as he drank. "I guess we'd better stick to business then. How about explaining the snorkeling equipment to me?"

With a shrug, Liz glanced over her shoulder. "If you can swim, you can snorkel."

"Let's just say I'm cautious. Mind if I come in and take a look?"

She'd been ungracious enough for one day, Liz decided. She sent him a smile. "Sure, look all you want." When he'd skirted around the counter and through the door, she walked with him to the back shelves. "The snorkel's just a hollow tube with a mouthpiece," she began as she took one down to offer it. "You put this lip between your teeth and breathe normally through your mouth. With the tube attached to a face mask, you can paddle around on the surface indefinitely."

"Okay. How about all the times I see these little tubes disappear under the water?"

"When you want to go down, you hold your breath and let out a bit of air to help you descend. The trick is to blow out and clear the tube of water when you surface. Once you get the knack, you can go down and up dozens of times without ever taking your face out of the water."

Scott turned the snorkel over in his hand. "There's a lot to see down there."

"A whole world."

He was no longer looking at the snorkel, but at her. "I guess you know a lot about the water and the reefs in this area. Know much about Isla Mujeres?"

"Excellent snorkeling and diving." Absently, Liz took down a mask to show him how to attach the snorkel. "We offer full- and half-day trips. If you're adventurous enough, there are caves to explore."

"And some are fairly remote," he said idly.

"For snorkeling you'd want to stay closer to the reefs, but an experienced diver could spend days around the caves."

"And nights." Scott passed the snorkel through his fingers as he watched her. "I imagine a diver could go down there at night and be completely undisturbed."

She wasn't certain why she felt a trickle of alarm. Automatically, she glanced over his shoulder to where her police guard half dozed in the sun. Silly, she told herself with a little shrug. She'd never been one to jump at shadows. "It's a dangerous area for night diving."

"Some people prefer danger, especially when it's profitable."

Her mouth was dry, so she swallowed as she replaced the mask on the shelf. "Perhaps. I don't."

This time his smile wasn't so charming or his eyes so friendly. "Don't you?"

"I don't know what you mean."

"I think you do." His hand closed over her arm. "I think you know exactly what I mean. What Jerry Sharpe skimmed off the top and dumped in that safe-deposit box in Acapulco was petty cash, Liz." He leaned closer as his voice lowered. "There's a lot more to be made. Didn't he tell you?"

She had a sudden, fierce memory of a knife probing against her throat. "He didn't tell me anything. I don't know anything." Before she could evade, he had her backed into a corner. "If I scream," she managed in a steady voice, "there'll be a crowd of people here before you can take a breath."

"No need to scream." He held up both hands as if to show her he meant no harm. "This is a business discussion. All I want to know is how much Jerry told you before he made the mistake of offending the wrong people."

When she discovered she was trembling, Liz forced herself to stop. He wouldn't intimidate her. What weapon could he hide in a pair of bathing trunks and an open shirt? She straightened her shoulders and looked him directly in the eye. "Jerry didn't tell me anything. I said the same thing to your friend when he had the knife at my throat. It didn't satisfy him, so he put a damaged gauge on my tanks."

"My partner doesn't understand much about finesse," Scott said easily. "I don't carry knives, and I don't know enough about your diving equipment to mess with the gauges. What I know about is you, and I know plenty. You work too hard, Liz, getting up at dawn and hustling until sundown. I'm just trying to give you some options. Business, Liz. We're just going to talk business."

It was his calm, reasonable attitude that had her temper whipping out. He could be calm, he could be reasonable, and people were dead. "I'm not Jerry and I'm not Erika, so keep that in mind. I don't know anything about the filthy business you're into, but the police do, and they'll know more. If you think you can frighten me by threatening me with a knife or damaging my equipment, you're right. But that doesn't stop me from wishing every one of you to hell. Now get out of my shop and leave me alone.''

He studied her face for a long ten seconds, then backed an inch or two away. ''You've got me wrong, Liz. I said this was a business discussion. With Jerry gone, an experienced diver would come in handy, especially one who knows the waters around here. I'm authorized to offer you five thousand dollars. Five thousand American dollars for doing what you do best. Diving. You go down, drop off one package and pick up another. No names, no faces. Bring the package back to me unopened and I hand you five thousand in cash. Once or twice a week, and you can build up a nice little nest egg. I'd say a woman raising a kid alone could use some extra money.''

Fear had passed into fury; she clenched her hands together. ''I told you to get out,'' she repeated. ''I don't want your money.''

He smiled and touched a finger to her cheek. ''Give it some thought. I'll be around if you change your mind.''

Liz waited for her breathing to level as she watched him walk away. With deliberate movements, she locked the shop, then walked directly to her police guard. ''I'm going home,'' she told him as he sprang to attention. ''Tell Captain Moralas to meet me there in half an hour.'' Without waiting for a reply, she strode across the sand.

Fifteen minutes later, Liz slammed into her house. The ride home hadn't calmed her. At every turn she'd been violated. At every turn, her privacy and peace had been disrupted. This last incident was the last she'd accept. She might have been able to handle another threat, another demand. But he'd offered her a job. Offered to pay her to smuggle cocaine, to take over the position of a man who'd been murdered. Jonas's brother.

A nightmare, Liz thought as she paced from window to window. She wished she could believe it was a nightmare. The cycle was drawing to a close, and she felt herself being trapped in the center. What Jerry Sharpe had started, she and Jonas would be forced to finish, no matter how painful. No matter how deadly. Finish it she would, Liz promised herself. The cycle would be broken, no matter what she had to do. She would be finished with it so her daughter could come home safely. Whatever she had to do, she would see to that.

At the sound of a car approaching, Liz went to the front window. Jonas, she thought, and felt her heart sink. Did she tell him now that she'd met face-to-face with the man who might have killed his brother? If he had the name, if he knew the man, would he race off in a rage for the revenge he'd come so far to find? And if he found his revenge, could the cycle ever be broken? Instead, she was afraid it would revolve and revolve around them, smothering everything else. She saw Jonas, a man of the law, a man of patience and compassion, shackled forever within the results of his own violence. How could she save him from that and still save herself?

Her hand was cold as she reached for the door and opened it to meet him. He knew there was something wrong before he touched her. "What are you doing home? I went by the shop and it was closed."

"Jonas." She did the only thing she knew how. She drew him against her and held on. "Moralas is on his way here."

"What happened?" A little skip of panic ran through him before he could stop it. He held her away, searching her face. "Did something happen to you? Were you hurt?"

"No, I'm not hurt. Come in and sit down."

"Liz, I want to know what happened."

She heard the sound of a second engine and looked down the street to see the unmarked car. "Moralas is here," she murmured. "Come inside, Jonas. I'd rather go through this only once."

There was really no decision to be made, Liz told herself as she moved away from the door to wait. She would give Moralas and Jonas the name of the man who had approached her. She would tell them exactly what he'd said. By doing so she would take herself one step further away from the investigation. They would have a name, a face, a location. They would have motive. It was what the police wanted, it was what she wanted. She glanced at Jonas as Moralas came up the front walk. It was what Jonas wanted. What he needed. And by giving it to him, she would take herself one step further way from him.

"Miss Palmer." Moralas took off his hat as he entered, glanced briefly at Jonas and waited.

"Captain." She stood by a chair but didn't sit. "I have some information for you. There's an American, a man named Scott Trydent. Less than an hour ago he offered me five thousand dollars to smuggle cocaine off the reef of Isla Mujeres."

Moralas's expression remained impassive. He tucked his hat under his arm. "And have you had previous dealings with this man?"

"He joined one of my diving classes. He was friendly. Today he came by the shop to talk to me. Apparently he believed that I..." She trailed off to look at Jonas. He stood very still and very quiet just inside the door. "He thought that Jerry had told me about the operation. He'd found out about the safe-deposit box. I don't know how. It was as though he knew every move I've made for weeks." As her nerves began to fray, she dragged a hand through her hair. "He told me that I could take over Jerry's position, make the exchange in the caves near Isla Mujeres and be rich. He knows..." She had to swallow to keep her voice from trembling. "He knows about my daughter."

"You would identify him?"

"Yes. I don't know if he killed Jerry Sharpe." Her gaze shifted to Jonas again and pleaded. "I don't know, but I could identify him."

Moralas watched the exchange before crossing the room. "Please sit down, Miss Palmer."

"You'll arrest him?" She wanted Jonas to say something, anything, but he continued to stand in silence. "He's part of the cocaine ring. He knows about Jerry's Sharpe's murder. You have to arrest him."

"Miss Palmer." Moralas urged her down on the sofa, then sat beside her. "We have names. We have faces. The smug-

gling ring currently operating in the Yucatan Peninsula is under investigation by both the Mexican and the American gov-
ernments. The names you and Mr. Sharpe have given me are
not unfamiliar. But there is one we don't have. The person
who organizes, the person who undoubtedly ordered the murder of Jerry Sharpe. This is the name we need. Without it, the
arrest of couriers, of salesmen, is nothing. We need this name,
Miss Palmer. And we need proof.''

"I don't understand. You mean you're just going to let
Trydent go? He'll just find someone else to make the drops.''

"It won't be necessary for him to look elsewhere if you
agree.''

"No.'' Before Liz could take in Moralas's words, Jonas
was breaking in. He said it quietly, so quietly that chills began
to race up and down her spine. He took out a cigarette. His
hands were rock steady. Taking his time, he flicked his lighter
and drew until the tip glowed red. He blew out a stream of
smoke and locked his gaze on Moralas. "You can go to hell.''

"Miss Palmer has the privilege to tell me so herself.''

"You're not using her. If you want someone on the inside,
someone closer to the names and proof, I'll make the drop.''

Moralas studied him, saw the steady nerves and untiring
patience along with simmering temper. If he'd had a choice,
he'd have preferred it. "It isn't you who has been asked.''

"Liz isn't going down.''

"Just a minute.'' Liz pressed both hands to her temples.
"Are you saying you want me to see Trydent again, to tell
him I'll take the job? That's crazy. What purpose could there
be?''

"You would be a decoy.'' Moralas glanced down at her
hands. Delicate, yes, but strong. There was nothing about Elizabeth Palmer he didn't know. "The investigation is closing
in. We don't want the ring to change locations at this point.
If the operation appears to go smoothly, there should be no
move at this time. You've been the stumbling block, Miss
Palmer, for the ring, and the investigation.''

"How?'' Furious, she started to stand. Moralas merely put
a hand on her arm.

"Jerry Sharpe lived with you, worked for you. He had a weakness for women. Neither the police nor the smugglers have been sure exactly what part you played. Jerry Sharpe's brother is now living in your home. The key to the safe-deposit box was found by you."

"Guilty by association, Captain?" Her voice took on that ice-sharp edge Jonas had heard only once or twice before. "Have I had police protection, or have I been under surveillance?"

Moralas's tone never altered. "One serves the same purpose as the other."

"If I'm under suspicion, haven't you considered that I might simply take the money and run?"

"That's precisely what we want you to do."

"Very clever." Jonas wasn't certain how much longer he could hold on to his temper. It would have given him great satisfaction to have picked Moralas up bodily and thrown him out of the house. Out of Liz's life. "Liz double-crosses them, annoying the head of the operation. It's then necessary to eliminate her the way my brother was eliminated."

"Except that Miss Palmer will be under police protection at all times. If this one drop goes as we plan, the investigation will end, and the smugglers, along with your brother's killer, will be caught and punished. This is what you want?"

"Not if it means risking Liz. Plant your own pigeon, Moralas."

"There isn't time. With your cooperation, Miss Palmer, we can end this. Without it, it could take months."

Months? she thought. Another day would be a lifetime. "I'll do it."

Jonas was beside her in a heartbeat, pulling her off the couch. "Liz—"

"My daughter comes home in two weeks." She put her hands on his arms. "She won't come back to anything like this."

"Take her someplace else." Jonas gripped her shoulders until his fingers dug into flesh. "We'll go someplace else."

"Where?" she demanded. "Every day I tell myself I'm

pulling away from this thing and every day it's a lie. I've been in it since Jerry walked in the door. We can't change that. Until it's over, really over, nothing's going to be right.''

He knew she was right, had known it from the first moment. But too much had changed. There was a desperation in him now that he'd never expected to feel. It was all for her. ''Come back to the States with me. It will be over.''

''Will it? Will you forget your brother was murdered? Will you forget the man who killed him?'' His fingers tightened, his eyes darkened, but he said nothing. Her breath came out in a sigh of acceptance. ''No, it won't be over until we finish it. I've run before, Jonas. I promised myself I'd never run again.''

''You could be killed.''

''I've done nothing and they've nearly killed me twice.'' She dropped her head on his chest. ''Please help me.''

He couldn't force her to bend his way. Two of the things he most admired in her were her capacity to give and her will to stand firm. He could plead with her, he could argue, but he could never lie. If she ran, if they ran, they'd never be free of it. His arm came around her. Her hair smelled of summer and sea air. And before the summer ended, he promised himself, she'd be free. They'd both be free.

''I go with her.'' He met Moralas's eyes over her head.

''That may not be possible.''

''I'll make it possible.''

Chapter 11

She'd never been more frightened in her life. Every day she worked in the shop, waiting for Scott Trydent to approach. Every evening she locked up, went home and waited for the phone to ring. Jonas said little. She no longer knew what he did with the hours they were apart, but she was aware that he was planning his own move, in his own time. It only frightened her more.

Two days passed until her nerves were stretched thinner and tighter than she would have believed possible. On the beach, people slept or read novels, lovers walked by arm in arm. Children chattered and ran. Snorkelers splashed around the reef. She wondered why nothing seemed normal, or if it ever would again. At sundown she emptied her cash box, stacked gear and began to lock up.

"How about that drink?"

Though she'd thought she'd braced herself for the moment when it would begin, Liz jolted. Her head began to throb in a slow, steady rhythm she knew would last for hours. In the pit of her stomach she felt the twist come and go from panicked excitement. From this point on, she reminded herself, she had no room to panic. She turned and looked at Scott. "I was wondering if you'd come back."

"Told you I'd be around. I always figure people need a couple of days to mull things over."

She had a part to play, Liz reminded herself. She had to do it well. Carefully, she finished locking up, then turned back to him. She didn't smile. It was to be a business discussion, cut and dry. "We can get a drink over there." She pointed to the open-air thatched-roof restaurant overhanging the reef. "It's public."

"Suits me." Though he offered his hand, she ignored it and began to walk.

"You used to be friendlier."

"You used to be a customer." She sent him a sideways look. "Not a business partner."

"So..." She saw him glance right, then left. "You've mulled."

"You need a diver, I need money." Liz walked up the two wooden stairs and chose a chair that had her back to the water. Seconds after she sat, a man settled himself into a corner table. One of Moralas's, she thought, and ordered herself to be calm. She'd been briefed and rebriefed. She knew what to say, how to say it, and that the waiter who would serve them carried a badge and a gun. "Jerry didn't tell me a great deal," she began, and ordered an American soft drink. "Just that he made the drop and collected the money."

"He was a good diver."

Liz swallowed the little bubble of fear. "I'm better."

Scott grinned at her. "So I'm told."

A movement beside her had her glancing over, then freezing. A dark man with a pitted face took the chair beside her. Liz knew he wore a thin silver band on his wrist before she looked for it.

"Pablo Manchez, Liz Palmer. Though I think you two have met."

"*Señorita.*" Manchez's thin mouth curved as he took her hand.

"Tell your friend to keep his hands to himself." Calmly, Jonas pulled a chair up to the table. "Why don't you introduce me, Liz?" When she could do no more than stare at him, he settled back. "I'm Jonas Sharpe. Liz and I are partners." He leveled his gaze to Manchez. This was the man, he thought, whom he'd come thousands of miles to see. This was the man he'd kill. Jonas felt the hatred and the fury rise. But he knew how to strap the emotions and wait. "I believe you knew my brother."

Manchez's hand dropped from Liz's and went to his side. "Your brother was greedy and stupid."

Liz held her breath as Jonas reached in his pocket. Slowly, he pulled out his cigarettes. "I'm greedy," he said easily as he lit one. "But I'm not stupid. I've been looking for you." He leaned across the table. With a slow smile, he offered Manchez the cigarettes.

Manchez took one and broke off the filter. His hands were beautiful, with long spidery fingers and narrow palms. Liz fought back a shudder as she looked at them. "So you found me."

Jonas was still smiling as he ordered a beer. "You need a diver."

Scott sent Manchez a warning look. "We have a diver."

"What you have is a team. Liz and I work together." Jonas blew out a stream of smoke. "Isn't that right, Liz?"

He wanted them. He wasn't going to back off until he had them. And she had no choice. "That's right."

"We don't need no team." Manchez started to rise.

"You need us." Jonas took his beer as it was served. "We already know a good bit about your operation. Jerry wasn't good at keeping secrets." Jonas took a swig from the bottle. "Liz and I are more discreet. Five thousand a drop?"

Scott waited a beat, then held a hand up, signaling Manchez. "Five. If you want to work as a team, it's your business how you split it."

"Fifty-fifty." Liz spread her fingers around Jonas's beer. "One of us goes down, one stays in the dive boat."

"Tomorrow night. Eleven o'clock. You come to the shop. Go inside. You'll find a waterproof case. It'll be locked."

"So will the shop," Liz put in. "How does the case get inside?"

Manchez blew smoke between his teeth. "I got no problem getting in."

"Just take the case," Scott interrupted. "The coordinates will be attached to the handle. Take the boat out, take the case down, leave it. Then come back up and wait exactly an hour. That's when you dive again. All you have to do is take the case that's waiting for you back to the shop and leave it."

"Sounds smooth," Jonas decided. "When do we get paid?"

"After you do the job."

"Half up front." Liz took a long swallow of beer and hoped her heart would settle. "Leave twenty-five hundred with the case or I don't dive."

Scott smiled. "Not as trusting as Jerry."

She gave him a cold, bitter look. "And I intend to stay alive."

"Just follow the rules."

"Who makes them?" Jonas took the beer back from Liz. Her hand slipped down to his leg and stayed steady.

"You don't want to worry about that," Manchez advised. The cigarette was clamped between his teeth as he smiled. "He knows who you are."

"Just follow the coordinates and keep an eye on your watch." Scott dropped bills on the table as he rose. "The rest is gravy."

"Stay smart, Jerry's brother." Manchez gave them both a slow smile. *"Adios, señorita."*

Jonas calmly finished his beer as the two men walked away.

"You weren't supposed to interfere during the meeting," Liz began in a furious undertone. "Moralas said—"

"The hell with Moralas." He crushed out his cigarette, watching as the smoke plumed up. "Is that the man who put the bruises on your neck?"

Her hand moved up before she could stop it. Halfway to her throat, Liz curled her fingers into a ball and set her hand on the table. "I told you I didn't see him."

Jonas turned his head. His eyes, as they had before, reminded her of frozen smoke. "Was it the man?"

He didn't need to be told. Liz leaned closer and spoke softly. "I want it over, Jonas. And I don't need revenge. You were supposed to let me meet with Scott and set things up by myself."

In an idle move, he tilted the candle on the table toward him and lit it. "I changed my mind."

"Damn you, you could've messed everything up. I don't want to be involved but I am. The only way to get uninvolved is to finish it. How do we know they won't just back off now that you've come into it?"

"Because you're right in the middle, and you always have been." Before she could speak, he took her arm. His face was close, his voice cool and steady. "I was going to use you. From the minute I walked into your house, I was going to use you to get to Jerry's killer. If I had to walk all over you, if I had to knock you out of the way or drag you along with me, I was going to use you. Just the way Moralas is going to use you. Just the way the others are going to use you." The heat of the candle flickered between them as he drew her closer. "The way Jerry used you."

She swallowed the tremor and fought against the pain. "And now?"

He didn't speak. They were so close that he could see himself reflected in her eyes. In them, surrounding his own reflection, he saw the doubts and the defiance. His hand came to the back of her neck, held there until he could feel the rhythm of her pulse. With a simmering violence, he pulled her against him and covered her mouth with his. A flare that was passion, a glimmer that was hope—he didn't know which to reach for. So he let her go.

"No one's going to hurt you again," he murmured. "Especially not me."

It was the longest day of her life. Liz worked and waited as the hours crawled by. Moralas's men mixed with the vacationers on the beach. So obviously, it seemed to Liz, that she wondered everyone else didn't notice them as though they wore badges around their necks. Her boats went out, returned and went out again. Tanks and equipment were checked and rented. She filled out invoices and accepted credit cards as if there were some importance to daily routine. She wished for the day to end. She hoped the night would never come.

A thousand times she thought of telling Moralas she couldn't go through with it. A thousand times she called herself a coward. But as the sun went down and the beach began to clear, she realized courage wasn't something that could be willed into place. She would run, if she had the choice. But as long as she was in danger, Faith was in danger. When the sun went down, she locked the shop as if it were the end of any ordinary day. Before she'd pocketed her keys, Jonas was beside her.

"There's still time to change your mind."

"And do what? Hide?" She looked out at the beach, at the sea, at the island that was her home. And her prison. Why had she never seen it as a prison until Jonas had come to it? "You've already told me how good I am at hiding."

"Liz—"

She shook her head to stop him. "I can't talk about it. I just have to do it."

They drove home in silence. In her mind, Liz went over her instructions, every point, every word Moralas had pushed at her. She was to follow the routine, make the exchange, then turn the case with the money over to the police who'd be waiting near the dock. She'd wait for the next move. And while she waited, she'd never be more than ten feet away from a cop. It sounded foolproof. It made her stomach churn.

There was a man walking a dog along the street in front of her house. One of Moralas's men. The man whittling on her neighbor's porch had a gun under his denim vest. Liz tried to look at neither of them.

"You're going to have a drink, some food and a nap," Jonas ordered as he steered her inside.

"Just the nap."

"The nap first then." After securing the lock, Jonas followed her into the bedroom. He lowered the shades. "Do you want anything?"

It was still so hard to ask. "Would you lie down with me?"

He came to her. She was already curled on her side, so he drew her back against him and wrapped her close. "Will you sleep?"

"I think so." In sleep she could find escape, if only temporarily. But she didn't close her eyes. "Jonas?"

"Hmm?"

"After tonight—after we've finished, will you hold me like this again?"

He pressed his lips to her hair. He didn't think he could love her any more. He was nearly certain if he told her she'd pull away. "As long as you want. Just sleep."

Liz let her eyes close and her mind empty.

The case was small, the size of an executive briefcase. It seemed too inconspicuous to be the catalyst for so much danger. Beside it, on the counter of Liz's shop, was an envelope. Inside was a slip of paper with longitude and latitude printed. With the slip of paper were twenty-five one-hundred-dollar bills.

"They kept their part of the bargain," Jonas commented.

Liz merely shoved the envelope into a drawer. "I'll get my equipment."

Jonas watched her. She'd rather do this on her own, he reflected. She'd rather not think she had someone to lean on, to turn to. He took her tanks before she could heft them. She was going to learn, he reminded himself, that she had a great deal more than that. "The coordinates?"

"The same that were in Jerry's book." She found herself amazingly calm as she waited to lock the door behind him. They were being watched. She was aware that Moralas had staked men in the hotel. She was just as certain Manchez was somewhere close. She and Jonas didn't speak again until they were on the dive boat and had cast off. "This could end it." She glanced at him as she set her course.

"This could end it."

She was silent for a moment. All during the evening hours

she'd thought about what she would say to him, how she would say it. "Jonas, what will you do?"

The flame of his lighter hissed, flared, then was quiet. "What I have to do."

The fear tasted like copper in her mouth, but it had nothing to do with herself and everything to do with Jonas. "If we make the exchange tonight, turn the second case over to Moralas. They'll have to come out in the open. Manchez, and the man who gives the orders."

"What are you getting at, Liz?"

"Manchez killed your brother."

Jonas looked beyond her. The sea was black. The sky was black. Only the hum of the motor broke the silence. "He was the trigger."

"Are you going to kill him?"

Slowly, he turned back to her. The question had been quiet, but her eyes weren't. They sent messages, posed argument, issued pleas. "It doesn't involve you."

That hurt deeply, sharply. With a nod, she followed the shimmer of light on the water. "Maybe not. But if you let hate rule what you do, how you think, you'll never be free of it. Manchez will be dead, Jerry will still be dead and you..." She turned to look at him again. "You'll never really be alive again."

"I didn't come all this way, spend all this time, to let Manchez walk away. He kills for money and because he enjoys it. He enjoys it," Jonas repeated viciously. "You can see it in his eyes."

And she had. But she didn't give a damn about Manchez. "Do you remember telling me once that everyone was entitled to representation?"

He remembered. He remembered everything he'd once believed in. He remembered how Jerry had looked in the cold white light of the morgue. "It didn't have anything to do with this."

"I suppose you change the rules when it's personal."

"He was my brother."

"And he's dead." With a sigh she lifted her face so that

the wind could cool her skin. "I'm sorry, Jonas. Jerry's dead and if you go through with what you've planned, you're going to kill something in yourself." And, though she couldn't tell him, something in her. "Don't you trust the law?"

He tossed his cigarette into the water, then leaned on the rail. "I've been playing with it for years. It's the last thing I'd trust."

She wanted to go to him but didn't know how. Still, no matter what he did, she was beside him. "Then you'll have to trust yourself. And so will I."

Slowly, he crossed to her. Taking her face in his hands, he tried to understand what she was telling him, what she was still holding back. "Will you?"

"Yes."

He leaned to press a kiss to her forehead. Inside there was a need, a fierce desire to tell her to head the boat out to sea and keep going. But that would never work, not for either of them. They stood on the boat together, and stood at the crossroads. "Then start now." He kissed her again before he turned and lifted one of the compartment seats. Liz frowned as she saw the wet suit.

"What are you doing?"

"I arranged to have Luis leave this here for me."

"Why? We can't both go down."

Jonas stripped down to his trunks. "That's right. I'm diving, you're staying with the boat."

Liz stood very straight. It wouldn't do any good to lose her temper. "The arrangements were made on all sides, Jonas. I'm diving."

"I'm changing the arrangements." He tugged the wet suit up to his waist before he looked at her. "I'm not taking any more chances with you."

"You're not taking chances with me. I am. Jonas, you don't know these waters. I do. You've never gone down here at night. I have."

"I'm about to."

"The last thing we need right now is for you to start behaving like an overprotective man."

He nearly laughed as he snapped the suit over his shoulders. "That's too bad, then, because that's just what we've got."

"I told Manchez and Trydent I was going down."

"I guess your reputation's shot when you lie to murderers and drug smugglers."

"Jonas, I'm not in the mood for jokes."

He strapped on his diver's knife, adjusted his weight belt, then reached for his mask. "Maybe not. And maybe you're not in the mood to hear this. I care about you. Too damn much." He reached out, gripping her chin. "My brother dragged you into this because he never wasted two thoughts about anyone else in his life. I pulled you in deeper because all I was thinking about was payback. Now I'm thinking about you, about us. You're not going down. If I have to tie you to the wheel, you're not going down."

"I don't want you to go." She balled her fists against his chest. "If I was down, all I'd think about was what I was doing. If I stay up here, I won't be able to stop thinking about what could happen to you."

"Time me." He lifted the tanks and held them out to her. "Help me get them on."

Hadn't she told herself weeks before that he wasn't a man who'd lose an argument? Her hands trembled a bit as she slipped the straps over his shoulders. "I don't know how to handle being protected."

He hooked the tanks as he turned back to her. "Practice."

She closed her eyes. It was too late for talk, too late for arguments. "Bear northeast as you dive. The cave's at eighty feet." She hesitated only a moment, then picked up a spear gun. "Watch out for sharks."

When he was over the side, she lowered the case to him. In seconds, he was gone and the sea was black and still. In her mind, Liz followed him fathom by fathom. The water would be dark so that he would be dependent on his gauges and the thin beam of light. Night creatures would be feeding. Squid, the moray, barracuda. Sharks. Liz closed her mind to it.

She should have forced him to let her go. How? Pacing the

deck, she pushed the hair back from her face. He'd gone to protect her. He'd gone because he cared about her. Shivering, she sat down to rub her arms warm again. Was this what it was like to be cared for by a man? Did it mean you had to sit and wait? She was up again and pacing. She'd lived too much of her life doing to suddenly become passive. And yet... To hear him say he cared. Liz sat again and waited.

She'd checked her watch four times before she heard him at the ladder. On a shudder of relief, she dashed over to the side to help him. "I'm going down the next time," she began.

Jonas pulled off his light, then his tanks. "Forget it." Before she could protest, he dragged her against him. "We've got an hour," he murmured against her ear. "You want to spend it arguing?"

He was wet and cold. Liz wrapped herself around him. "I don't like being bossed around."

"Next time you can boss me around." He dropped onto a bench and pulled her with him. "I'd forgotten what it was like down there at night. Fabulous." And it was nearly over, he told himself. The first step had been taken, the second one had to follow. "I saw a giant squid. Scared the hell out of him with the light. I swear he was thirty feet long."

"They get bigger." She rested her head on his shoulder and tried to relax. They had an hour. "I was diving with my father once. We saw one that was nearly sixty."

"Made you nervous?"

"No. I was fascinated. I remember I swam close enough to touch the tentacles. My father gave me a twenty-minute lecture when we surfaced."

"I imagine you'd do the same thing with Faith."

"I'd be proud of her," Liz began, then laughed. "Then I'd give her a twenty-minute lecture."

For the first time that night he noticed the stars. The sky was alive with them. It made him think of his mother's porch swing and long summer nights. "Tell me about her."

"You don't want to get me started."

"Yes, I do." He slipped an arm around her shoulder. "Tell me about her."

With a half smile, Liz closed her eyes. It was good to think of Faith, to talk of Faith. A picture began to emerge for Jonas of a young girl who liked school because there was plenty to do and lots of people. He heard the love and the pride, and the wistfulness. He saw the dark, sunny-faced girl in the photo and learned she spoke two languages, liked basketball and hated vegetables.

"She's always been sweet," Liz reflected. "But she's no angel. She's very stubborn, and when she's crossed, her temper isn't pretty. Faith wants to do things herself. When she was two she'd get very annoyed if I wanted to help her down the stairs."

"Independence seems to run in the family."

Liz moved her shoulders. "We've needed it."

"Ever thought about sharing?"

Her nerves began to hum. Though she shifted only a bit, it was away from him. "When you share, you have to give something up. I've never been able to afford to give up anything."

It was an answer he'd expected. It was an answer he intended to change. "It's time to go back down."

Liz helped him back on with his tanks. "Take the spear gun. Jonas…" He was already at the rail before she ran to him. "Hurry back," she murmured. "I want to go home. I want to make love with you."

"Hell of a time to bring that up." He sent her a grin, curled and fell back into the water.

Within five minutes Liz was pacing again. Why hadn't she thought to bring any coffee? She'd concentrate on that. In little more than an hour they could be huddled in her kitchen with a pot brewing. It wouldn't matter that there would be police surrounding the house. She and Jonas would be inside. Together. Perhaps she was wrong about sharing. Perhaps… When she heard the splash at the side of the boat, she was at the rail like a shot.

"Jonas, did something happen? Why—" She found herself looking down the barrel of a .22.

"Señorita." Manchez tossed his mask and snorkel onto a bench as he climbed over the side. *"Buenas noches."*

"What are you doing here?" She struggled to sound indignant as the blood rushed from her face. No, she wasn't brave, she realized. She wasn't brave at all. "We had a deal."

"You're an amateur," he told her. "Like Sharpe was an amateur. You think we'd just forget about the money?"

"I don't know anything about the money Jerry took." She gripped the rail. "I've told you that all along."

"The boss decided you were a loose end, pretty lady. You do us a favor and make this delivery. We do you a favor. We kill you quickly."

She didn't look at the gun again. She didn't dare. "If you keep killing your divers, you're going to be out of business."

"We're finished in Cozumel. When your friend brings up the case, I take it and go to Merida. I live in style. You don't live at all."

She wanted to sit because her knees were shaking. She stood because she thought she might never be able to again. "If you're finished in Cozumel, why did you set up this drop?"

"Clancy likes things tidy."

"Clancy?" The name David Merriworth had mentioned, Liz remembered, and strained to hear any sound from the water.

"There's a few thousand in cocaine down there, that's all. A few thousand dollars in the case coming up. The boss figures it's worth the investment to make it look like you were doing the dealing with Sharpe. Then you two have an argument and shoot each other. Case closed."

"You killed Erika too, didn't you?"

"She asked too many questions." He lowered the gun. "You ask too many questions."

Light flooded the boat and the water so quickly that Liz's first instinct was to freeze. Before the next reaction had fully registered, she was tumbling into the water and diving blind.

How could she warn Jonas? Liz groped frantically in the water as lights played on the surface above her. She had no tanks, no mask, no protection. Any moment he'd be surfacing, unaware of any danger. He had no protection but her.

Without equipment, she'd be helpless in a matter of moments. She fought to stay down, keeping as close to the ladder as she dared. Her lungs were ready to burst when she felt the movement in the water. Liz turned toward the beam of light.

When he saw her, his heart nearly stopped. She looked like a ghost clinging to the hull of the boat. Her hair was pale and floating out in the current, her face was nearly as white as his light. Before his mind could begin to question, he was pushing his mouthpiece between her lips and giving her air. There could be no communication but emotion. He felt the fear. Jonas steadied the spear gun in his arm and surfaced.

"Mr. Sharpe." Moralas caught him in the beam of a spotlight. Liz rose up beside him. "We have everything under control." On the deck of her boat, Liz saw Manchez handcuffed and flanked by two divers. "Perhaps you will give my men and their prisoner a ride back to Cozumel."

She felt Jonas tense. The spear gun was set and aimed. Even through the mask, she could see his eyes burning, burning as only ice can. "Jonas, please." But he was already starting up the ladder. She hauled herself over the rail and tumbled onto the deck, cold and dripping. "Jonas, you can't. Jonas, it's over."

He barely heard her. All his emotion, all his concentration was on the man who stood only feet away. Their eyes were locked. It gave him no satisfaction to watch the blood drain from Manchez's face, or the knowledge leap frantically into his eyes. It was what he'd come for, what he'd promised himself. The medallion on the edge of his chain dangled and reminded him of his brother. His brother was dead. No satisfaction. Jonas lowered the gun.

Manchez tossed back his head. "I'll get out," he said quietly. The smile started to spread. "I'll get out."

The spear shot out and plowed into the deck between Manchez's feet. Liz saw the smile freeze on his face an instant before one formed on Jonas's. "I'll be waiting."

* * *

Could it really be over? It was all Liz could think when she awoke, warm and dry, in her own bed. She was safe, Jonas was safe, and the smuggling ring on Cozumel was broken. Of course, Jonas had been furious. Manchez had been watched, they had been watched, but the police had made their presence known only after Liz had been held at gunpoint.

But he'd gotten what he'd come for, she thought. His brother's killer was behind bars. He'd face a trial and justice. She hoped it was enough for Jonas.

The morning was enough for her. The normality of it. Happy, she rolled over and pressed her body against Jonas's. He only drew her closer.

"Let's stay right here until noon."

She laughed and nuzzled against his throat. "I have—"

"A business to run," he finished.

"Exactly. And for the first time in weeks I can run it without having this urge to look over my shoulder. I'm happy." She looked at him, then tossed her arms around his neck and squeezed. "I'm so happy."

"Happy enough to marry me?"

She went still as a stone, then slowly, very slowly drew away. "What?"

"Marry me. Come home with me. Start a life with me."

She wanted to say yes. It shocked her that her heart burned to say yes. Pulling away from him was the hardest thing she'd ever done. "I can't."

He stopped her before she could scramble out of bed. It hurt, he realized, more than he could possibly have anticipated. "Why?"

"Jonas, we're two different people with two totally separate lives."

"We stopped having separate lives weeks ago." He took her hands. "They're not ever going to be separate again."

"But they will." She drew her hands away. "After you're back in Philadelphia for a few weeks, you'll barely remember what I look like."

He had her wrists handcuffed in his hands. The fury that surfaced so seldom in him seemed always on simmer when

he was around her. "Why do you do that?" he demanded.
"Why can't you ever take what you're given?" He swung
her around until she was beneath him on the bed. "I love
you."

"Don't." She closed her eyes as the wish nearly eclipsed
the reason. "Don't say that to me."

Shut out. She was shutting him out. Jonas felt the panic
come first, then the anger. Then the determination. "I will say
it. If I say it enough, sooner or later you'll start to believe it.
Do you think all these nights have been a game? Haven't you
felt it? Don't you feel anything?"

"I thought I felt something once before."

"You were a child." When she started to shake her head,
he gripped her tighter. "Yes, you were. In some ways you
still are, but I know what goes through you when you're with
me. I know. I'm not a ghost, I'm not a memory. I'm real and
I want you."

"I'm afraid of you," she whispered. "I'm afraid because
you make me want what I can't have. I won't marry you,
Jonas, because I'm through taking chances with my life and
I won't take chances with my child's life. Please let me go."

He released her, but when she stood, his arms went around
her. "It isn't over for us."

She dropped her head against his chest, pressed her cheek
close. "Let me have the few days we have left. Please let me
have them."

He lifted her chin. Everything he needed to know was in
her eyes. A man who knew and who planned to win could
afford to wait. "You haven't dealt with anyone as stubborn
as you are before this. And you haven't nearly finished dealing with me." Then his hand gentled as he stroked her hair.
"Get dressed. I'll take you to work."

Because he acted as though nothing had been said, Liz relaxed. It was impossible, and she knew it. They'd known each
other only weeks, and under circumstances that were bound
to intensify any feelings. He cared. She believed that he cared,
but love—the kind of love needed to build a marriage—was
too much to risk.

She loved. She loved so much that she pushed him away when she wanted to pull him closer. He needed to go back to his life, back to his world. After time had passed, if he thought of her he'd think with gratitude that she had closed a door he'd opened on impulse. She would think of him. Always.

By the time Liz was walking toward the shop, she'd settled her mind. "What are you going to do today?"

"Me?" Jonas, too, had settled his mind. "I'm going to sit in the sun and do nothing."

"Nothing?" Incredulous, Liz stared at him. "All day?"

"It's known as relaxing, or taking a day off. If you do it several days running, it's called a vacation. I was supposed to have one in Paris."

Paris, she thought. It would suit him. She wondered briefly how the air smelled in Paris. "If you get bored, I'm sure one of the boats could use the extra crew."

"I've had enough diving for a few days, thanks." Jonas plopped down on a chaise in front of the shop. It was the best place to keep an eye on her.

"Miguel." Liz automatically looked around for Luis. "You're here early."

"I came with Luis. He's checking out the dive boat—got an early tour."

"Yes, I know." But she wouldn't trust Miguel to run the shop alone for long. "Why don't you help him? I'll take care of the counter."

"*Bueno.* Oh, there were a couple of guys looking at the fishing boat. Maybe they want to rent."

"I'll take a look. You go ahead." Walking back, she crouched beside Jonas. "Keep an eye on the shop for me, will you? I've got a couple of customers over by the *Expatriate.*"

Jonas adjusted his sunglasses. "What do you pay per hour?"

Liz narrowed her eyes. "I might cook dinner tonight."

With a smile, he got up to go behind the counter. "Take all the time you need."

He made her laugh. Liz strolled down the walkway and to the pier, drinking up the morning. She could use a good fishing cruise. The aqua bikes had been ordered, but they still had to be paid for. Besides, she'd like the ride herself. It made her think of Jonas and his unwanted catch a few weeks before. Liz laughed again as she approached the men beside her boat.

"Buenos días," she began. "Mr. Ambuckle." Beaming a smile, Liz held out a hand. "I didn't know you were back. Is this one of your quick weekend trips?"

"That's right." His almost bald head gleamed in the sun as he patted her hand. "When the mood strikes me I just gotta move."

"Thinking about some big-game fishing this time around?"

"Funny you should mention it. I was just saying to my associate here that I only go for the big game."

"Only the big game." Scott Trydent turned around and pushed back his straw hat. "That's right, Clancy."

"Now don't turn around, honey." Ambuckle's fingers clamped over hers before she could move. "You're going to get on the boat, nice and quiet. We have some talking to do, then we might just take a little ride."

"How long have you been using my dive shop to smuggle?" Liz saw the gun under Scott's jacket. She couldn't signal to Jonas, didn't dare.

"For the past couple of years I've found your shop's location unbeatable. You know, they ship that stuff up from Colombia and dump in Miami. The way the heat's been on the past few years, you take a big chance using the regular routes. It takes longer this way, but I lose less merchandise."

"And you're the organizer," she murmured. "You're the man the police want."

"I'm a businessman," he said with a smile. "Let's get on board, little lady."

"The police are watching," Liz told him as she climbed on deck.

"The police have Manchez. If he hadn't tried to pull a double cross, the last shipment would have gone down smooth."

"A double cross?"

"That's right," Scott put in as he flanked her. "Pablo decided he could make more free-lancing than by being a company man.''

''And by reporting on his fellow employee, Mr. Trydent moves up in rank. I work my organization on the incentive program.''

Scott grinned at Ambuckle. ''Can't beat the system.''

''You had Jerry Sharpe killed.'' Struggling to believe what was happening, Liz stared at the round little man who'd chatted with her and rented her tanks. ''You had him shot.''

''He stole a great deal of money from me.'' Ambuckle's face puckered as he thought of it. ''A great deal. I had Manchez dispose of him. The truth is, I'd considered you as a liaison for some time. It seemed simpler, however, just to use your shop. My wife's very fond of you.''

''Your wife.'' Liz thought of the neat, matronly woman in skirted bathing suits. ''She knows you smuggle drugs, and she knows you kill people?''

''She thinks we have a great stockbroker.'' Ambuckle grinned. ''I've been moving snow for ten years, and my wife wouldn't know coke from powdered sugar. I like to keep business and family separate. The little woman's going to be sick when she finds out you had an accident. Now we're going to take a little ride. And we're going to talk about the three hundred thousand our friend Jerry slipped out from under my nose. Cast off, Scott.''

''No!'' Thinking only of survival, Liz made a lunge toward the dock. Ambuckle had her on the deck with one shove. He shook his head, dusted his hands and turned to her. ''I'd wanted to keep this from getting messy. You know, I switched gauges on your tanks, figuring you'd back off. Always had a soft spot for you, little lady. But business is business.'' With a wheezy sigh, he turned to Scott. ''Since you've taken over Pablo's position, I assume you know how to deal with this.''

''I certainly do.'' He took out a revolver. His eyes locked on Liz's. When she caught her breath, he turned the barrel toward Ambuckle. ''You're under arrest.'' With his other hand, he pulled out a badge. ''You have the right to remain silent…'' It was the last thing Liz heard before she buried her face in her hands and wept.

Chapter 12

"I want to know what the hell's been going on." They were in Moralas's office, but Jonas wouldn't sit. He stood behind Liz's chair, his fingers curled tight over the back rung. If anyone had approached her, he would have struck first and asked questions later. He'd already flattened the unfortunate detective who'd tried to hold him back when he'd seen Liz on the deck of the *Expatriate* with Scott.

With his hands folded on his desk, Moralas gave Jonas a long, quiet look. "Perhaps the explanation should come from your countryman."

"Special Agent Donald Scott." The man Liz had known as Scott Trydent sat on the corner of Moralas's desk. "Sorry for the deception, Liz." Though his voice was calm and matter-of-fact, it couldn't mask the excitement that bubbled from him. As he sipped his coffee, he glanced up at Jonas. Explanations wouldn't go over easily with this one, he thought. But he'd always believed the ends justified the means. "I've been after that son of a bitch for three years." He drank again, savoring triumph. "It took us two before we could infiltrate the ring, and even then I couldn't make contact with the head man. To get to him I had to go through more channels than you do with the Company. He's been careful. For the past eight months I've been working with Manchez as Scott Trydent. He was the closest I could get to Ambuckle until two days ago.''

"You used her." Jonas's hand went to Liz's shoulder. "You put her right in the middle."

"Yeah. The problem was, for a long time we weren't sure just how involved she was. We knew about your shop, Liz. We knew you were an experienced diver. In fact, there isn't anything about you my organization didn't know. For some time, you were our number-one suspect.''

"Suspect?'' She had her hands folded neatly in her lap, but the anger was boiling. "You suspected me.''

"You left the U.S. over ten years ago. You've never been back. You have both the contacts and the means to have run the ring. You keep your daughter off the island for most of the year and in one of the best schools in Houston.''

"That's my business.''

"Details like that become our business. When you took Jerry Sharpe in and gave him a job, we leaned even further toward you. He thought differently, but then we weren't using him for his opinions.''

She felt Jonas's fingers tighten and reached up to them as she spoke. "Using him?''

"I contacted Jerry Sharpe in New Orleans. He was someone else we knew everything about. He was a con, an operator, but he had style.'' He took another swig of coffee as he studied Jonas. "We made him a deal. If he could get on the inside, feed us information, we'd forget about a few... indiscretions. I liked your brother,'' Scott said to Jonas. "Really liked him. If he'd been able to settle a bit, he'd have made a hell of a cop. 'Conning the bad guys,' he called it.''

"Are you saying Jerry was working for you?'' Jonas felt his emotions race toward the surface. The portrait he'd barely been able to force himself to accept was changing.

"That's right.'' Scott took out a cigarette and watched the match flare as he struck it. "I liked him—I mean that. He had a way of looking at things that made you forget they were so lousy.''

That was Jerry, Jonas thought. To give himself a moment,

he walked to the window. He could see the water lapping calmly against the hulls of boats. He could see the sun dancing down on it and children walking along the sea wall. The scene had been almost the same the day he'd arrived on Cozumel. Some things remained the same; others altered constantly. "What happened?"

"He had a hard time following orders. He wanted to push them too fast too far. He told me once he had something to prove, to himself and to the other part of him. The better part of him."

Jonas turned slowly. The pain came again, an ache. Liz saw it in his eyes and went to stand with him. "Go on."

"He got the idea into his head to rip off the money from a shipment. I didn't know about it until he called me from Acapulco. He figured he'd put the head man in a position where he'd have to deal personally. I told him to stay put, that we were scrubbing him. He'd have been taken back to the States and put somewhere safe until the job was over." He tossed the match he'd been holding into an ashtray on Moralas's desk. "He didn't listen. He came back to Cozumel and tried to deal with Manchez himself. It was over before I knew. Even if I'd have known, I can't be sure I could've stopped it. We don't like to lose civilians, Mr. Sharpe. I don't like to lose friends."

The anger drained from him degree by degree. It would have been so like Jerry, Jonas thought. An adventure, the excitement, the impulsiveness. "Go on."

"Orders came down to put the pressure on Liz." Scott gave a half laugh that had nothing to do with humor. "Orders from both sides. It wasn't until after your trip to Acapulco that we were sure you weren't involved in the smuggling. You stopped being a suspect and became the decoy."

"I came to the police." She looked at Moralas. "I came to you. You didn't tell me."

"I wasn't aware of Agent Scott's identity until yesterday. I knew only that we had a man on the inside and that it was necessary to use you."

"You were protected," Scott put in. "There wasn't a day

you weren't guarded by Moralas's men and by mine. Your being here complicated things," he said to Jonas. "You were pushing too close to the bone. I guess you and Jerry had more in common than looks."

Jonas felt the weight on the chain around his neck. "Maybe we did."

"Well, we'd come to the point where we had to settle for Manchez and a few others or go for broke. We went for broke."

"The drop we made. It was a setup."

"Manchez had orders to do whatever he had to to get back the money Jerry had taken. They didn't know about the safe-deposit box." He blew out a stream of smoke. "I had to play it pretty fast and loose to keep that under wraps. But then we didn't know about it either, until you led us to it. As far as Ambuckle was concerned, you had the money, and he was going to get it back. He wanted it to look as though you'd been running the smuggling operation together. When you were found dead, the heat would be off of him. He planned to lie low a while, then pick up business elsewhere. I had that from Manchez. You were set up," he agreed. "So was he. I got to Merriworth, made enough noise about how Manchez was about to double-cross to set him off. When Manchez was snorkeling to your boat, I was on the phone with the man I knew as Clancy. I got a promotion, and Clancy came back to deal with you himself."

Liz tried to see it as he did, as a chess game, as any game with pawns. She couldn't. "You knew who he was yesterday morning and you still had me get on that boat."

"There were a dozen sharpshooters in position. I had a gun, Ambuckle didn't. We wanted him to order Liz's murder, and we wanted him to tell her as much as possible. When this goes to court, we want it tidy. We want him put away for a long time. You're a lawyer, Sharpe. You know how these things can go. We can make a clean collar, have a stack of evidence and lose. I've watched too many of these bastards walk." He blew out smoke between set teeth. "This one's not walking anywhere but into federal prison."

"There is still the question of whether these men will be tried in your country or mine." Moralas spoke softly, and didn't move when Scott whirled on him.

"Look, Moralas—"

"This will be discussed later. You have my thanks and my apologies," he said to Jonas and Liz. "I regret we saw no other way."

"So do I," Liz murmured, then turned to Scott. "Was it worth it?"

"Ambuckle brought thousands of pounds of cocaine into the States. He's responsible for more than fifteen murders in the U.S. and Mexico. Yeah, it was worth it."

She nodded. "I hope you understand that I never want to see you again." After closing her hand around Jonas's she managed a smile. "You were a lousy student."

"Sorry we never had that drink." He looked back at Jonas. "Sorry about a lot of things."

"I appreciate what you told me about my brother. It makes a difference."

"I'm recommending him for a citation. They'll send it to your parents."

"It'll mean a great deal to them." He offered his hand and meant it. "You were doing your job—I understand that. We all do what we have to do."

"That doesn't mean I don't regret it."

Jonas nodded. Something inside him was free, completely free. "As to putting Liz through hell for the past few weeks…" Very calmly, Jonas curled his hand into a fist and planted it solidly on Scott's jaw. The thin man snapped a chair in half as he crashed into it on his way to the floor.

"Jonas!" Stunned, Liz could do no more than stare. Then, incredibly, she felt the urge to giggle. With one hand over her mouth, she leaned into Jonas and let the laughter come. Moralas remained contentedly at his desk, sipping coffee.

Scott rubbed his jaw gingerly. "We all do what we have to do," he murmured.

Jonas only turned his back. "Goodbye, Captain."

Moralas stayed where he was. "Goodbye, Mr. Sharpe." He

rose and, in a rare show of feeling, took Liz's hand and kissed it. *"Vaya con dios."*

He waited until the door had shut behind them before he looked down at Scott again. "Your government will, of course, pay for the chair."

He was gone. She'd sent him away. After nearly two weeks, Liz awoke every morning with the same thoughts. Jonas was gone. It was for the best. After nearly two weeks she awoke every morning struggling to convince herself. If she'd followed her heart, she would have said yes the moment he'd asked her to marry him. She would have left everything she'd built behind and gone with him. And ruined his life, perhaps her own.

He was already back in his own world, poring through law books, facing juries, going to elegant dinner parties. By now, she was sure his time in Cozumel was becoming vague. After all, he hadn't written. He hadn't called. He'd left the day after Ambuckle had been taken into custody without another word about love. He'd conquered his ghosts when he'd faced Manchez and had walked away whole.

He was gone, and she was once more standing on her own. As she was meant to, Liz thought. She'd have no regrets. That she'd promised herself. What she'd given to Jonas had been given without conditions or expectations. What he'd given to her she'd never lose.

The sun was high and bright, she thought. The air was as mellow as quiet music. Her lover was gone, but she, too, was whole. A month of memories could be stretched to last a lifetime. And Faith was coming home.

Liz pulled her bike into a parking space and listened to the thunder of a plane taking off. Even now Faith and her parents were crossing the Gulf. Liz left her bike and walked toward the terminal. It was ridiculous to feel nervous, she told herself, but she couldn't prevent it. It was ridiculous to arrive at the airport nearly an hour early, but she'd have gone mad at home. She skirted around a bed of marigolds and geraniums. She'd buy flowers, she decided. Her mother loved flowers.

Inside the terminal, the air was cool and full of noise. Tourists came and went but rarely passed the shops without a last-minute purchase. Liz started in the first store and worked her way down, buying consistently and strictly on impulse. By the time she arrived at the gate, she carried two shopping bags and an armful of dyed carnations.

Any minute, she thought. She'd be here any minute. Liz shifted both bags to one hand and nervously brushed at her hair. Passengers waited for their flights by napping in the black plastic chairs or reading guidebooks. She watched a woman check her lipstick in a compact mirror and wondered if she had time to run into the ladies room to examine her own face. Gnawing on her lip, she decided she couldn't leave, even for a moment. Neither could she sit, so she paced back and forth in front of the wide windows and watched the planes come and go. It was late. Planes were always late when you were waiting for them. The sky was clear and blue. She knew it was equally clear in Houston because she'd been checking the weather for days. But the plane was late. Impatient, she walked back to security to ask about the status. She should have known better.

Liz got a shrug and the Mexican equivalent of It'll be here when it comes. In another ten minutes, she was ready to scream. Then she saw it. She didn't have to hear the flight announcement to know. With her heart thudding dully, she waited by the door.

Faith wore blue striped pants and a white blouse. Her hair's grown, Liz thought as she watched her daughter come down the steps. She's grown—though she knew it would never do to tell Faith so. She'd just wrinkle her nose and roll her eyes. Her palms were wet. Don't cry, don't cry, Liz ordered herself. But the tears were already welling. Then Faith looked up and saw her. With a grin and a wave she was racing forward. Liz dropped her bags and reached out for her daughter.

"Mom, I got to sit by the window, but I couldn't see our house." As she babbled, Faith held her mother's neck in a stranglehold. "I brought you a present."

With her face buried against Faith's throat, Liz drew in the scents—powder, soap and chocolate from the streak on the front of the white blouse. "Let me look at you." Drawing her back, Liz soaked up the sight of her. She's beautiful, Liz realized with a jolt. Not just cute or sweet or pretty any longer. Her daughter was beautiful.

I can't let her go again. It hit her like a wall. I'll never be able to let her go again. "You've lost a tooth," Liz managed as she brushed back her daughter's hair.

"Two." Faith grinned to show the twin spaces. "Grandma said I could put them under my pillow, but I brought them with me so I can put them under my real pillow. Will I get pesos?"

"Yes." Liz kissed one cheek, then the other. "Welcome home."

With her hand firmly in Faith's, Liz rose to greet her parents. For a moment she just looked at them, trying to see them as a stranger would. Her father was tall and still slim, though his hairline was creeping back. He was grinning at her the way he had whenever she'd done something particularly pleasing to him. Her mother stood beside him, lovely in her tidy way. She looked now, as she'd always looked to Liz, like a woman who'd never had to handle a crisis more stressful than a burned roast. Yet she'd been as solid and as sturdy as a rock. There were tears in her eyes. Liz wondered abruptly if the beginning of the summer left her mother as empty as the end of the summer left her.

"Momma." Liz reached out and was surrounded. "Oh, I've missed you. I've missed you all so much." *I want to go home*. The thought surged up inside her and nearly poured out. She needed to go home.

"Mom." Faith tugged on the pocket of her jeans. "Mom."

Giddy, Liz turned and scooped her up. "Yes." She covered her face with kisses until Faith giggled. "Yes, yes, yes!"

Faith snuggled in. "You have to say hello to Jonas."

"What?"

"He came with us. You have to say hi."

"I don't—" Then she saw him, leaning against the window, watching—waiting patiently. The blood rushed out of her head to her heart until she was certain something would burst. Holding onto Faith, Liz stood where she was. Jonas walked to her, took her face in both hands and kissed her hard.

"Nice to see you," he murmured, then bent down to pick up the bags Liz had dropped. "I imagine these are for you," he said as he handed Liz's mother the flowers.

"Yes." Liz tried to gather the thoughts stumbling through her mind. "I forgot."

"They're lovely." She sent her daughter a smile. "Jonas is going to drive us to the hotel. I invited him to dinner tonight. I hope you don't mind. You always make enough."

"No, I... Of course."

"We'll see you then." She gave Liz another brief kiss. "I know you want to get Faith home and have some time together. We'll see you tonight."

"But I—"

"Our bags are here. We're going to deal with customs."

Before Liz could say another word, she was alone with her daughter.

"Can we stop by and see Señor Pessado?"

"Yes," Liz said absently.

"Can I have some candy?"

Liz glanced down to the chocolate stain on Faith's blouse. "You've already had some."

Faith just smiled. She knew she could depend on Señor Pessado. "Let's go home now."

Liz waited until Faith was unpacked, until the crystal bird Faith had bought her was hanging in the window and her daughter had consumed two tacos and a pint of milk.

"Faith..." She wanted her voice to be casual. "When did you meet Mr. Sharpe?"

"Jonas? He came to Grandma's house." Faith turned the doll Liz had brought her this way and that for inspection.

"To Grandma's? When?"

"I don't know." She decided to call the doll Cassandra

because it was pretty and had long hair. "Can I have my ice cream now?"

"Oh—yes." Liz walked over to get it out of the freezer. "Faith, do you know why he went to Grandma's?"

"He wanted to talk to her, I guess. To Grandpa, too. He stayed for dinner. I knew Grandma liked him because she made cherry pies. I liked him, too. He can play the piano really good." Faith eyed the ice cream and was satisfied when her mother added another scoop. "He took me to the zoo."

"What?" The bowl nearly slipped out of Liz's hand as she set it down. "Jonas took you to the zoo?"

"Last Saturday. We fed popcorn to the monkeys, but mostly we ate it." She giggled as she shoveled in ice cream. "He tells funny stories. I scraped my knee." Remembering suddenly, Faith pulled up her slacks to show off her wound.

"Oh, baby." It was small and already scabbed over, but Liz brushed a kiss over it anyway. "How'd you do this?"

"At the zoo. I was running. I can run really fast in my new sneakers, but I fell down. I didn't cry."

Liz rolled the slacks down. "I'm sure you didn't."

"Jonas didn't get mad or anything. He cleaned it all up with his handkerchief. It was pretty messy. I bled a lot." She smiled at that, pleased with herself. "He said I have pretty eyes just like you."

A little thrill of panic raced through her, but she couldn't stop herself. "Did he? What else did he say?"

"Oh, we talked about Mexico and about Houston. He wondered which I liked best."

Liz rested her hands on her daughter's knees. This is what matters, she realized. This was all that really mattered. "What did you tell him?"

"I like it best where you are." She scraped the bottom of the bowl. "He said he liked it best there, too. Is he going to be your boyfriend?"

"My—" Liz managed, just barely, to suppress the laugh. "No."

"Charlene's mother has a boyfriend, but he isn't as tall as Jonas and I don't think he ever took Charlene to the zoo.

Jonas said sometime maybe we could go see the Liberty Bell.
Do you think we can?''

Liz picked up the ice cream dish and began to wash it.
''We'll see,'' she muttered.

. ''Listen, someone's coming.'' Faith was up like a shot and
dashing for the front door. ''It's Jonas!'' With a whoop, she
was out of the door and running full steam.

''Faith!'' Liz hurried from the kitchen and reached the
porch in time to see Faith hurl herself at Jonas. With a laugh,
he caught her, tossed her in the air then set her down again
in a move so natural that it seemed he'd been doing so all his
life. Liz knotted the dishcloth in her hands.

''You came early.'' Pleased, Faith hung on to his hand.
''We were talking about you.''

''Were you?'' He tousled Faith's hair but looked up at Liz.
''That's funny, because I was thinking about you.''

''We're going to make paella because that's what Grandpa
likes best. You can help.''

''Faith—''

''Love to,'' Jonas interrupted. ''After I talk to your
mother.'' At the foot of the stairs he crouched down to Faith's
level. ''I'd really like to talk to your mom alone.''

Faith's mouth screwed up. ''Why?''

''I have to convince her to marry me.''

He ignored Liz's gasp and watched for Faith's reaction. Her
eyes narrowed and her mouth pursed. ''She said you weren't
her boyfriend. I asked.''

He grinned and leaned closer. ''I just have to talk her into
it.''

''Grandma says nobody can ever talk my mom into anything. She has a hard head.''

''So do I, and I make a living talking people into things.
But maybe you could put in a few good words for me later.''

As Faith considered, her eyes brightened. ''Okay. Mom,
can I see if Roberto's home? You said he had new puppies.''

Liz stretched out the cloth then balled it again. ''Go ahead,
but just for a little while.''

Jonas straightened as he watched Faith race toward the

house across the street. "You've done an excellent job with your daughter, Elizabeth."

"She's done a great deal of it herself."

He turned and saw the nerves on her face. It didn't displease him. But he remembered the way she'd looked when she had opened her arms to Faith at the airport. He wanted, he would, see her look that way again. "Do you want to talk inside?" he began as he walked up the steps. "Or right here?"

"Jonas, I don't know why you've come back, but—"

"Of course you know why I've come back. You're not stupid."

"We don't have anything to talk about."

"Fine." He closed the distance quickly. She didn't resist, though she told herself she would. When he dragged her against him, she went without hesitation. Her mouth locked hungrily to his, and for a moment, just for a moment, the world was right again. "If you don't want to talk, we'll go inside and make love until you see things a little more clearly."

"I see things clearly." Liz put her hands on his arms and started to draw away.

"I love you."

He felt the shudder, saw the flash of joy in her eyes before she looked away. "Jonas, this isn't possible."

"Wrong. It's entirely possible—in fact, it's already done. The point is, Liz, you need me."

Her eyes narrowed to slits. "What I need I take care of."

"That's why I love you," he said simply and took the wind out of her sails.

"Jonas—"

"Are you going to tell me you haven't missed me?" She opened her mouth, then shut it again. "Okay, so you take the Fifth on that one." He stepped back from her. "Are you going to deny that you've spent some sleepless nights in the past couple of weeks, that you've thought about what happened between us? Are you going to stand here and look at me now and tell me you're not in love with me?"

She'd never been able to lie well. Liz turned and meticulously spread the dishcloth over the porch rail. "Jonas, I can't run my life on my feelings."

"From now on you can. Did you like the present Faith brought you?"

"What?" Confused, she turned back. "Yes, of course I did."

"Good. I brought you one too." He took a box out of his pocket. Liz saw the flash of diamond and nearly had her hand behind her back before he caught it in his. Firmly, he slipped the ring on. "It's official."

She wouldn't even look at it. She couldn't stop herself. The diamond was shaped in a teardrop and as white and glossy as a wish. "You're being ridiculous," she told him, but couldn't make herself take it off.

"You're going to marry me." He took her shoulders and leaned her back against a post. "That's not negotiable. After that, we have several options. I can give up my practice and live in Cozumel. You can support me."

She let out a quick breath that might have been a laugh. "Now you're really being ridiculous."

"You don't like that one. Good, I didn't care for it either. You can come back to Philadelphia with me. I'll support you."

Her chin went up. "I don't need to be supported."

"Excellent. We agree on the first two options." He ran his hands through her hair and discovered he wasn't feeling as patient as he'd thought he would. "Now, you can come back to the States. We'll take a map and you can close your eyes and pick a spot. That's where we'll live."

"We can't run our lives this way." She pushed him aside to walk down the length of the porch and back. But part of her was beginning to believe they could. "Don't you see how impossible it is?" she demanded as much of herself as of him. "You have your career. I have my business. I'd never be a proper wife for someone like you."

"You're the only wife for someone like me." He grabbed her shoulders again. No, he wasn't feeling patient at all.

"Damn it, Liz, you're the only one. If the business is important to you, keep it. Have Luis run it. We can come back a half a dozen times a year if you want. Start another business. We'll go to Florida, to California, anywhere you want where they need a good dive shop. Or..." He waited until he was sure he had her full attention. "You could go back to school."

He saw it in her eyes—the surprise, the dream, then the denial. "That's over."

"The hell it is. Look at you—it's what you want. Keep the shop, build another, build ten others, but give yourself something for yourself."

"It's been more than ten years."

He lifted a brow. "You said once you wouldn't change anything."

"And I meant it, but to go back now, after all this time."

"Afraid?"

Her eyes narrowed; her spine stiffened. "Yes."

He laughed, delighted with her. "Woman, in the past few weeks, you've been through hell and out again. And you're afraid of a few college courses?"

With a sigh, she turned away. "I might not be able to make it."

"So what?" He whirled her back again. "So you fall flat on your face. I'll be right there falling down with you. It's time for risking, Liz. For both of us."

"Oh, I want to believe you." She lifted a hand to rest it on his face. "I want to. I do love you, Jonas. So much."

She was locked against him again, lost in him. "I need you, Liz. I'm not going back without you."

She clung to him a moment, almost ready to believe. "But it's not just me. You have to understand I can't do whatever I'd like."

"Faith?" He drew her back again. "I've spent the past weeks getting to know her. My main objective when I started was to ingratiate myself. I figured the only way to get to you was through her."

So she'd already surmised. "Afternoons at the zoo?"

"That's right. Thing was, I didn't know she was as easy to fall for her as her mother. I want her."

The hand Liz had lifted to her hair froze. "I don't understand."

"I want her to be mine—legally, emotionally. I want you to agree to let me adopt her."

"Adopt…" Whatever she might have expected from him, it hadn't been this. "But she's—"

"Yours?" he interrupted. "No, she's going to be ours. You're going to have to share her. And if you're set on her going to school in Houston, we'll live in Houston. Within the year I expect she should have a brother or sister because she needs family as much as we do."

He was offering her everything, everything she'd ever wanted and had refused to believe in. She had only to hold out her hand. The idea terrified her. "She's another man's child. How will you be able to forget that?"

"She's your child," he reminded her. "You told me yourself she was your child only. Now she's going to be mine." Taking her hands, he kissed them. "So are you."

"Jonas, do you know what you're doing? You're asking for a wife who'll have to start from scratch and a half-grown daughter. You're complicating your life."

"Yeah, and maybe I'm saving it."

And hers. Her blood was pumping again, her skin was tingling. For the first time in years she could look at her life and see no shadows. She closed her eyes and breathed deeply before she turned. "Be sure," she whispered. "Be absolutely sure. If I let myself go, if I say yes and you change your mind, I'll hate you for the rest of my life."

He took her by the shirtfront. "In one week, we're going to my parents' farm in Lancaster, calling the local minister, justice of the peace or witch doctor and we're getting married. Adoption papers are being drawn up. When we settle in as a family, we're all having the same name. You and Faith and I."

With a sigh, Liz leaned back again against the post and studied his face. It was beautiful, she decided. Strong, passionate, patient. Her life was going to be bound up with that face. It was as real as flesh and blood and as precious as dreams. Her lover was back, her child was with her and nothing was impossible.

"When I first met you, I thought you were the kind of man who always got what he wanted."

"And you were right." He took her hands again and held them. "Now what are we going to tell Faith?" he demanded.

Her lips curved slowly. "I guess we'd better tell her you talked me into it."

* * * * *

STORM WARNING

For Mom,
who wouldn't let my brothers clobber me—
even when I deserved it.

Chapter 1

The Pine View Inn was nestled comfortably in the Blue Ridge Mountains. After leaving the main road, the meandering driveway crossed a narrow ford just wide enough for one car. The inn was situated a short distance beyond the ford.

It was a lovely place, full of character, the lines so clean they disguised the building's rambling structure. It was three stories high, built of brick that had been weathered to a soft rose, the facade interspersed with narrow, white-shuttered windows. The hipped roof had faded long ago to a quiet green, and three straight chimneys rose from it. A wide wooden porch made a white skirt around the entire house and doors opened out to it from all four sides.

The surrounding lawn was smooth and well tended. There was less than an acre, house included, before the trees and outcroppings of rock staked their claim on the land. It was as if nature had decided that the house could have this much and no more. The effect was magnificent. The house and mountains stood in peaceful coexistence, neither detracting from the other's beauty.

As she pulled her car to the informal parking area at the side of the house, Autumn counted five cars, including her aunt's vintage Chevy. Though the season was still weeks off, it appeared that the inn already had several guests.

There was a light April chill in the air. The daffodils had yet to open, and the crocuses were just beginning to fade. A few azalea buds showed a trace of color. The day was poised and waiting for spring. The higher, surrounding mountains clung to their winter brown, but touches of green were creeping up them. It wouldn't be gloomy brown and gray for long.

Autumn swung her camera case over one shoulder and her purse over the other—the purse was of secondary importance. Two large suitcases also had to be dragged from the trunk. After a moment's struggle, she managed to arrange everything so that she could take it all in one load, then mounted the steps. The door, as always, was unlocked.

There was no one about. The sprawling living room which served as a lounge was empty, though a fire crackled in the grate. Setting down her cases, Autumn entered the room. Nothing had changed.

Rag rugs dotted the floor; hand-crocheted afghans were draped on the two patchworked sofas. At the windows were chintz priscillas and the Hummel collection was still on the mantel. Characteristically, the room was neat, but far from orderly. There were magazines here and there, an overflowing sewing basket, a group of pillows piled for comfort rather than style on the windowseat. The ambience was friendly with a faintly distracted charm. Autumn thought with a smile that the room suited her aunt perfectly.

She felt an odd pleasure. It was always reassuring to find that something loved hasn't changed. Taking a last quick glance around the room, she ran a hand through her hair. It hung past her waist and was tousled from the long drive with open windows. She gave idle consideration to digging out a brush, but promptly forgot when she heard footsteps down the hall.

"Oh, Autumn, there you are." Typically, her aunt greeted her as though Autumn had just spent an hour at the local supermarket rather than a year in New York. "I'm glad you got in before dinner. We're having pot roast, your favorite."

Not having the heart to remind her aunt that pot roast was her brother Paul's favorite, Autumn smiled. "Aunt Tabby, it's so good to see you!'' Quickly she walked over and kissed her aunt's cheek. The familiar scent of lavender surrounded her.

Aunt Tabby in no way resembled the cat her name brought to mind. Cats are prone to snobbishness, disdainfully tolerating the rest of the world. They are known for speed, agility and cunning. Aunt Tabby was known for her vague meanderings, disjointed conversations and confused thinking. She had no guile. Autumn adored her.

Drawing her aunt away, Autumn studied her closely. ''You look wonderful.'' It was invariably true. Aunt Tabby's hair was the same deep chestnut as her niece's, but it was liberally dashed with gray. It suited her. She wore it short, curling haphazardly around her small round face. Her features were all small-scaled—mouth, nose, ears, even her hands and feet. Her eyes were a mistily faded blue. Though she was halfway through her fifties, her skin refused to wrinkle; it was smooth as a girl's. She stood a half-foot shorter than Autumn and was pleasantly round and soft. Beside her, Autumn felt like a gangly toothpick. Autumn hugged her again, then kissed her other cheek. ''Absolutely wonderful.''

Aunt Tabby smiled up at her. ''What a pretty girl you are. I always knew you would be. But so awfully thin.'' She patted Autumn's cheek and wondered how many calories were in pot roast.

With a shrug, Autumn thought of the ten pounds she had gained when she'd stopped smoking. She had lost them again almost as quickly.

''Nelson always was thin,'' Aunt Tabby added, thinking of her brother, Autumn's father.

''Still is,'' Autumn told her. She set her camera case on a table and grinned at her aunt. ''Mom's always threatening to sue for divorce.''

''Oh well.'' Aunt Tabby clucked her tongue and looked thoughtful. ''I don't think that's wise after all the years they've been married.'' Knowing the jest had been lost, Autumn merely nodded in agreement. ''I gave you the room you always liked, dear. You can still see the lake from the window. The leaves will be full soon though, but... Remember when you fell in when you were a little girl? Nelson had to fish you out.''

''That was Will,'' Autumn reminded her, thinking back on the day her younger brother had toppled into the lake.

''Oh?'' Aunt Tabby looked faintly confused a moment, then smiled disarmingly. ''He learned to swim quite well, didn't he? Such an enormous young man now. It always surprised me. There aren't any children with us at the moment,'' she added, flowing from sentence to sentence with her own brand of logic.

''I saw several cars. Are there many people here?'' Autumn stretched her cramped muscles as she wandered the room. It smelled of sandalwood and lemon oil.

''One double and five singles,'' she told her. ''One of the singles is French and quite fond of my apple pie. I must go check on my blueberry cobbler,'' she announced suddenly. ''Nancy is a marvel with a pot roast, but helpless with baking. George is down with a virus.''

She was already making for the door as Autumn tried to puzzle out the last snatch of information.

''I'm sorry to hear that,'' she replied with what she hoped was appropriate sympathy.

''I'm a bit shorthanded at the moment, dear, so perhaps you can manage your suitcases yourself. Or you can wait for one of the gentlemen to come in.''

George, Autumn remembered. Gardener, bellboy and bartender.

''Don't worry, Aunt Tabby. I can manage.''

''Oh, by the way, Autumn.'' She turned back, but Autumn knew her aunt's thoughts were centered on the fate of her cobbler. ''I have a little surprise for you—oh, I see Miss Bond is coming in.'' Typically, she interrupted herself, then smiled. ''She'll keep you company. Dinner's at the usual time. Don't be late.''

Obviously relieved that both her cobbler and her niece were about to be taken care of, she bustled off, her heels tapping cheerfully on the hardwood floor.

Autumn turned to watch her designated companion enter through the side door. She found herself gaping.

Julia Bond. Of course, Autumn recognized her instantly. There could be no other woman who possessed such shimmering, golden beauty. How many times had she sat in a crowded theater and watched Julia's charm and talent transcend the movie screen? In person, in the flesh, her beauty didn't diminish. It sparkled, all the more alive in three dimensions.

Small, with exquisite curves just bordering on lush, Julia Bond was a magnificent example of womanhood at its best. Her cream-colored linen slacks and vivid blue cashmere sweater set off her coloring to perfection. Pale golden hair framed her face like sunlight. Her eyes were a deep summer blue. The full, shapely mouth lifted into a smile even as the famous brows arched. For a moment, Julia stood, fingering her silk scarf. Then she spoke, her voice smoky, exactly as Autumn had known it would be. "What fabulous hair."

It took Autumn a moment to register the comment. Her mind was blank at seeing Julia Bond step into her aunt's lounge as casually as she would have strolled into the New York Hilton. The smile, however, was full of charm and so completely unaffected that Autumn was able to form one in return.

"Thank you. I'm sure you're used to being stared at, Miss Bond, but I apologize anyway."

Julia sat, with a grace that was at once insolent and admirable, in a wingback chair. Drawing out a long, thin cigarette, she gave Autumn a full-power smile. "Actors adore being stared at. Sit down." She gestured. "I have a feeling I've at last found someone to talk to in this place."

Autumn's obedience was automatic, a tribute to the actress's charm.

"Of course," Julia continued, still studying Autumn's face, "you're entirely too young and too attractive." Settling back, she crossed her legs. Somehow, she managed to transform the wingback chair, with the small darning marks in the left arm, into a throne. "Then your coloring and mine offset each other nicely. How old are you, darling?"

"Twenty-five." Captivated, Autumn answered without thinking.

Julia laughed, a low bubbling sound that flowed and ebbed like a wave. "Oh, so am I. Perennially." She tossed her head in amusement, then left it cocked to the side. Autumn's fingers itched for her camera. "What's your name, darling, and what brings you to solitude and pine trees?"

"Autumn," she responded as she pushed her hair off her shoulders. "Autumn Gallegher. My aunt owns the inn."

"Your aunt?" Julia's face registered surprise and more amusement. "That dear fuzzy little lady is your aunt?"

"Yes." A grin escaped at the accuracy of the description. "My father's sister." Relaxed, Autumn leaned back. She was doing her own studying, thinking in angles and shadings.

"Incredible," Julia decided with a shake of her head. "You don't look like her. Oh, the hair," she corrected with an envious glance. "I imagine hers was once your color. Magnificent. I know women who would kill for that shade, and you seem to have about three feet of it." With a sigh, she drew delicately on her cigarette. "So, you've come to pay your aunt a visit."

There was nothing condescending in her attitude. Her eyes were interested and Autumn began to find her not only charming but likable. "For a few weeks. I haven't seen her in nearly a year. She wrote and asked me to come down, so I'm taking my vacation all at one time."

"What do you do?" Julia pursed her lips. "Model?"

"No." Autumn's laughter came quickly at the thought of it. "I'm a photographer."

"Photographer!" Julia exclaimed. She glowed with pleasure. "I'm very fond of photographers. Vanity, I suppose."

"I imagine photographers are fond of you for the same reason."

"Oh, my dear." When Julia smiled, Autumn recognized both pleasure and amusement. "How sweet."

"Are you alone, Miss Bond?" Her sense of curiosity was ingrained. Autumn had already forgotten to be overwhelmed.

"Julia, please, or you'll remind me of the half-decade that separates our ages. The color of that sweater suits you," she commented, eyeing Autumn's crewneck. "I never could wear gray. Sorry, darling," she apologized with a lightning-quick smile. "Clothes are a weakness of mine. Am I alone?" The smile deepened. "Actually, this little hiatus is a mixture of business and pleasure. I'm in between husbands at the moment—a glorious interlude." Julia tossed her head. "Men are delightful, but husbands can be dreadfully inhibiting. Have you ever had one?"

"No." The grin was irrepressible. From the tone, Julia might have asked if Autumn had ever owned a cocker spaniel.

"I've had three." Julia's eyes grew wicked and delighted. "In this case, the third was *not* the charm. Six months with an English baron was quite enough."

Autumn remembered the photos she had seen of Julia with a tall, aristocratic Englishman. She had worn tweed brilliantly.

"I've taken a vow of abstinence," Julia continued. "Not against men—against marriage."

"Until the next time?" Autumn ventured.

"Until the next time," Julia agreed with a laugh. "At the moment, I'm here for platonic purposes with Jacques Le-Farre."

"The producer?"

"Of course." Again, Autumn felt the close scrutiny. "He'll take one look at you and decide he has a new star on the horizon. Still, that might be an interesting diversion." She frowned a moment, then shrugged it away. "The other residents of your aunt's cozy inn have offered little in the way of diversions thus far."

"Oh?" Automatically, Autumn shook her head as Julia offered her a cigarette.

"We have Dr. and Mrs. Spicer," Julia began. One perfectly shaped nail tapped against the arm of her chair. There was something different in her attitude now. Autumn was sensitive to moods, but this was too subtle a change for her to identify.

"The doctor himself might be interesting," Julia continued. "He's very tall and nicely built, smoothly handsome with just the right amount of gray at the temples."

She smiled. Just then Autumn thought Julia resembled a very pretty, well-fed cat.

"The wife is short and unfortunately rather dumpy. She spoils whatever attractiveness she might have with a continually morose expression." Julia demonstrated it with terrifying skill. Autumn's laughter burst out before she could stop it.

"How unkind," Autumn chided, smiling still.

"Oh, I know." A graceful hand waved in dismissal. "I have no patience for women who let themselves go, then look daggers at those who don't. He's fond of fresh air and walking in the woods, and she grumbles and mopes along after him." Julia paused, giving Autumn a wary glance. "How do you feel about walking?"

"I like it." Hearing the apology in her voice, Autumn grinned.

"Oh well." Julia shrugged at eccentricities. "It takes all kinds. Next, we have Helen Easterman." The oval, tinted nails began to tap again. Her eyes drifted from Autumn's to the view out the window. Somehow, Autumn didn't think she was seeing mountains and pine trees. "She says she's an art teacher, taking time off to sketch nature. She's rather attractive, though a bit overripe, with sharp little eyes and an unpleasant smile. Then, there's Steve Anderson." Julia gave her slow, cat smile again. Describing men, Autumn mused, was more to her taste. "He's rather delicious. Wide shoulders, California blond hair. Nice blue eyes. And he's embarrassingly rich. His father owns, ah…"

"Anderson Manufacturing?" Autumn prompted and was rewarded with a beam of approval.

"How clever of you."

"I heard something about Steve Anderson aiming for a political career."

"Mmm, yes. It would suit him." Julia nodded. "He's very

well-mannered and has a disarmingly boyish smile—that's always a political asset.''

"It's a sobering thought that government officials are elected on their smiles.''

"Oh, politics.'' Julia wrinkled her nose and shrugged away the entire profession. "I had an affair with a senator once. Nasty business, politics.'' She laughed at some private joke.

Not certain whether her comment had been a romantic observation or a general one, Autumn didn't pursue it. "So far,'' Autumn said, "it seems an unlikely menagerie for Julia Bond and Jacques LeFarre to join.''

"Show business.'' With a smile, she lit another cigarette, then waved it at Autumn. "Stick with photography, Autumn, no matter what promises Jacques makes you. We're here due to a whim of the last and most interesting character in our little play. He's a genius of a writer. I did one of his screenplays a few years back. Jacques wants to produce another, and he wants me for the lead.'' She dragged deep on the cigarette. "I'm willing—really good scripts aren't that easy to come by—but our writer is in the middle of a novel. Jacques thinks the novel could be turned into a screenplay, but our genius resists. He told Jacques he was coming here to write in peace for a few weeks, and that he'd think it over. The charming LeFarre talked him into allowing us to join him for a few days.''

Autumn was both fascinated and confused. Her question was characteristically blunt. "Do you usually chase writers around this way? I'd think it would be more the other way around.''

"And you'd be right,'' Julia said flatly. With only the movement of her eyebrows, her expression turned haughty. "But Jacques is dead set on producing this man's work, and he caught me at a weak moment. I had just finished reading one of the most appalling scripts. Actually,'' she amended with a grimace, "three of the most appalling scripts. My work feeds me, but I won't do trash. So...'' Julia smiled and moved her hands. "Here I am.''

"Chasing a reluctant writer.''

"It has its compensations."

I'd like to shoot her with the sun at her back. Low sun, just going down. The contrasts would be perfect. Autumn pulled herself back from her thoughts and caught up with Julia's conversation. "Compensations?" she repeated.

"The writer happens to be incredibly attractive, in that carelessly rugged sort of way that no one can pull off unless he's born with it. A marvelous change of pace," she added with a wicked gleam, "from English barons. He's tall and bronzed with black hair that's just a bit too long and always disheveled. It makes a woman itch to get her fingers into it. Best, he has those dark eyes that say 'go to hell' so eloquently. He's an arrogant devil." Her sigh was pure feminine approval. "Arrogant men are irresistible, don't you think?"

Autumn murmured something while she tried to block out the suspicions Julia's words were forming. It had to be someone else, she thought frantically. Anyone else.

"And, of course, Lucas McLean's talent deserves a bit of arrogance."

The color drained from Autumn's face and left it stiff. Waves of almost forgotten pain washed over her. *How could it hurt so much after all this time?* She had built the wall so carefully, so laboriously—how could it crumble into dust at the sound of a name? She wondered, dully, what sadistic quirk of fate had brought Lucas McLean back to torment her.

"Why, darling, what's the matter?"

Julia's voice, mixed with concern and curiosity, penetrated. As if coming up for air, Autumn shook her head. "Nothing." She shook her head again and swallowed. "It was just a surprise to hear that Lucas McLean is here." Drawing a deep breath, she met Julia's eyes. "I knew him…a long time ago."

"Oh, I see."

And she did see, Autumn noted, very well. Sympathy warred with speculation in both her face and voice. Autumn shrugged, determined to treat it lightly.

"I doubt he remembers me." Part of her prayed with fervor it was true, while another prayed at cross-purposes. Would he forget? she wondered. Could he?

"Autumn, darling, yours is a face no man is likely to forget." Through a mist of smoke, Julia studied her. "You were very young when you fell in love with him?"

"Yes." Autumn was trying, painfully, to rebuild her protective wall and wasn't surprised by the question. "Too young, too naive." She managed a brittle smile and for the first time in six months accepted a cigarette. "But I learn quickly."

"It seems the next few days might prove interesting, after all."

"Yes." Autumn's agreement lacked enthusiasm. "So it does." She needed time to be alone, to steady herself. "I have to take my bags up," she said as she rose.

While Autumn stretched her slender arms toward the ceiling, Julia smiled. "I'll see you at dinner."

Nodding, Autumn gathered up her camera case and purse and left the room.

In the hall, she struggled with her suitcases, camera and purse before beginning the task of transporting them up the stairs. Throughout the slow trek up the stairs, Autumn relieved tension by muttering and swearing. *Lucas McLean,* she thought and banged a suitcase against her shin. She nearly convinced herself that her ill humor was a result of the bruise she'd just given herself. Out of breath and patience, she reached the hallway outside her room and dumped everything on the floor with an angry thud.

"Hello, Cat. No bellboy?"

The voice—and the ridiculous nickname—knocked a few of her freshly mortared bricks loose. After a brief hesitation, Autumn turned to him. The pain wouldn't show on her face. She'd learned that much. But the pain was there, surprisingly real and physical. It reminded her of the day her brother had swung a baseball bat into her stomach when she had been twelve. *I'm not twelve now,* she reminded herself. She met Lucas's arrogant smile with one of her own.

"Hello, Lucas. I heard you were here. The Pine View Inn is bursting with celebrities."

He was the same, she noted. Dark and lean and male. There

was a ruggedness about him, accented by rough black brows and craggy, demanding features that couldn't be called handsome. Oh, no, that was much too tame a word for Lucas McLean. Arousing, irresistible. Fatal. Those words suited him better.

His eyes were nearly as black as his hair. They kept secrets easily. He carried himself well, with a negligent grace that was natural rather than studied. His not-so-subtle masculine power drifted with him as he ambled closer and studied her.

It was then that Autumn noticed how hellishly tired he looked. There were shadows under his eyes. He needed a shave. The creases in his cheeks were deeper than she remembered—and she remembered very well.

"You look like yesterday." He grabbed a handful of her hair as he fastened his eyes on hers. She wondered how she could have ever thought herself over him. No woman ever got over Lucas. Sheer determination kept her eyes level.

"You," she countered as she opened her door, "look like hell. You need some sleep."

Lucas leaned on the doorjamb before she could drag her cases inside and slam the door. "Having trouble with one of my characters," he said smoothly. "She's a tall, willowy creature with chestnut hair that ripples down her back. Narrow hipped, with legs that go right up to her waist."

Bracing herself, Autumn turned back and stared at him. Carefully, she erased any expression from her face.

"She has a child's mouth," he continued, dropping his glance to hers a moment. "And a small nose, somewhat at odds with high, elegant cheekbones. Her skin is ivory with touches of warmth just under the surface. Her eyes are long lidded and ridiculously lashed—green that melts into amber, like a cat's."

Without comment, she listened to his description of herself. She gave him a bored, disinterested look he would never have seen on her face three years before. "Is she the murderer or the corpse?" It pleased Autumn to see his brows lift in surprise before they drew together in a frown.

"I'll send you a copy when it's done." He searched her

face, then a shutter came down, leaving his expression unreadable. That, too, she noted, hadn't changed.

"You do that." After giving her cases a superhuman tug,
jettisoning them into her room, Autumn rested against the
door. Her smile had no feeling. "You'll have to excuse me,
Lucas, I've had a long drive and want a bath."

She closed the door firmly and with finality, in his face.

Autumn's movements then became brisk. There was un-
packing to do and a bath to draw and a dress to choose for
dinner. Those things would give her time to recover before
she allowed herself to think, to feel. When she slipped into
lingerie and stockings, her nerves were steadier. The worst of
it had been weathered. Surely, she mused, the first meeting,
the first exchange of words were the most difficult. She had
seen him. She had spoken to him. She had survived. Success
made her bold. For the first time in nearly two years, Autumn
allowed herself to remember.

She had been so much in love. Her assignment had been
an ordinary one—a picture layout of mystery novelist Lucas
McLean. The result had been six months of incredible joy
followed by unspeakable hurt.

He had overwhelmed her. She'd never met anyone like him.
She knew now that there was no one else like him. He was
a law unto himself. He had been brilliant, compelling, selfish
and moody. After the first shock of learning he was interested
in her, Autumn had floated along on a cloud of wonder and
admiration. And love.

His arrogance, as Julia had said, was irresistible. His phone
calls at three in the morning had been treasured. The last time
she had been held in his arms, experiencing the wild demands
of his mouth, had been as exciting as the first. She had tumbled into his bed like a ripe peach, giving up her innocence
with the freedom that comes with blind, trusting love.

She remembered he'd never said the words she wanted to
hear. She'd told herself she had no need for them—words
weren't important. There were unexpected boxes of roses, surprise picnics on the beach with wine in paper cups and lovemaking that was both intense and all consuming. What did

she need with words? When the end had come it had been
swift—but far from painless.

Autumn put his distraction, his moodiness down to trouble
with the novel he was working on. It didn't occur to her that
he'd been bored. It was her habit to fix dinner on Wednesdays
at his home. It was a small, private evening, one she prized
above all others. Her arrival was so natural to her, so routine,
that when she entered his living room and found him dressed
in dinner clothes, she only thought he had decided to add a
more formal atmosphere to their quiet dinner.

"Why, Cat, what are you doing here?" The unexpected
words were spoken so easily, she merely stared. "Ah, it's
Wednesday, isn't it?" There was a slight annoyance in his
tone, as though he had forgotten a dentist appointment. "I
completely forgot. I'm afraid I've made other plans."

"Other plans?" she echoed. Comprehension was still a
long way off.

"I should have phoned you and saved you the trip. Sorry,
Cat, I'm just leaving."

"Leaving?"

"I'm going out." He moved across the room and stared at
her. She shivered. No one's eyes could be as warm—or as
cold—as Lucas McLean's. "Don't be difficult, Autumn, I
don't want to hurt you any more than is necessary."

Feeling the tears of realization rush out, she shook her head
and fought against acceptance. The tears sent him into a fury.

"Stop it! I haven't the time to deal with weeping. Just pack
it in. Chalk it up to experience. God knows you need it."

Swearing, he stomped away to light a cigarette. She had
stood there, weeping without sound.

"Don't make a fool of yourself, Autumn." The calm, rigid
voice was more frightening to her than his anger. At least
anger was an emotion. "When something's over, you forget
it and move on." He turned back with a shrug. "That's life."

"You don't want me anymore?" She stood meekly, like a
dog who waits to feel the lash again. Her vision was too
clouded with tears to see his expression. For a moment, he
was silent.

"Don't worry, Cat," he answered in a careless, brutal voice. "Others will."

She turned and fled. It had taken over a year before he had stopped being the first thing in her mind every morning.

But she had survived, she reminded herself. She slipped into a vivid green dress. And I'll keep right on surviving. She knew she was basically the same person who had fallen in love with Lucas, but now she had a more polished veneer. Innocence was gone, and it would take more than Lucas Mc-Lean to make a fool of her again. She tossed her head, satisfied with the memory of her reception to him. That had given him a bit of a surprise. No, Autumn Gallegher was no one's fool any longer.

Her thoughts drifted to her aunt's odd assortment of guests. She wondered briefly why the rich and famous were gathering here instead of at some exclusive resort. Dismissing the thought with a shrug, she reminded herself it was dinnertime. Aunt Tabby had told her not to be late.

Chapter 2

It was a strange assortment to find clustered in the lounge of a remote Virginia inn: an award-winning writer, an actress, a producer, a wealthy California businessman, a successful cardiovascular surgeon and his wife, an art teacher who wore St. Laurent. Before Autumn's bearings were complete, she found herself enveloped in them. Julia pounced on her possessively and began introductions. Obviously, Julia enjoyed her prior claim and the center-stage position it gave her. Whatever embarrassment Autumn might have felt at being thrust into the limelight was overridden by amusement at the accuracy of Julia's earlier descriptions.

Dr. Robert Spicer was indeed smoothly handsome. He was drifting toward fifty and bursting with health. He wore a casually expensive green cardigan with brown leather patches at the elbows. His wife, Jane, was also as Julia had described: unfortunately dumpy. The small smile she gave Autumn lasted about two seconds before her face slipped back into the dissatisfied grooves that were habitual. She cast dark, bad-tempered glances at her husband while he gave Julia the bulk of his attention.

Watching them, Autumn could find little sympathy for Jane and no disapproval for Julia—no one disapproves of a flower for drawing bees. Julia's attraction was just as natural, and just as potent.

Helen Easterman was attractive in a slick, practiced fashion. The scarlet of her dress suited her, but struck a jarring note in the simply furnished lounge. Her face was perfectly made-up and reminded Autumn of a mask. As a photographer, she knew the tricks and secrets of cosmetics. Instinctively, Autumn avoided her.

In contrast, Steve Anderson was all charm. Good looks, California style, as Julia had said. Autumn liked the crinkles at the corners of his eyes and his careless chic. He wore chinos easily. From his bearing, she knew he would wear black tie with equal aplomb. If he chose a political career, she mused, he should make his way very well.

Julia had offered no description of Jacques LeFarre. What Autumn knew of him came primarily from either the gossip magazines or his films. He was smaller than she had imagined, barely as tall as she, but with a wiry build. His features were strong and he wore his brown hair brushed back from his forehead where three worry lines had been etched. She liked the trim moustache over his mouth, and the way he lifted her hand to kiss it when they were introduced.

"Well, Autumn," Steve began with a smile. "I'm playing bartender in George's absence. What can I fix you?"

"Vodka Collins, easy on the vodka," Lucas answered. Autumn gave up the idea of ignoring him.

"Your memory's improved," she said coolly.

"So's your wardrobe." He ran a finger down the collar of her dress. "I remember when it ran to jeans and old sweaters."

"I grew up." Her eyes were as steady and as measuring as his.

"So I see."

"Ah, you have met before," Jacques put in. "But this is fascinating. You are old friends?"

"Old friends?" Lucas repeated before Autumn could speak. He studied her with infuriating amusement. "Would you say that was an accurate description, Cat?"

"Cat?" Jacques frowned a moment. "Ah, the eyes, *oui*." Pleased, he brushed his index finger over his moustache. "It suits. What do you think, *chérie?*" He turned to Julia, who seemed to be enjoying herself watching the unfolding scene. "She's enchanting, and her voice is quite good."

"I've already warned Autumn about you," Julia drawled, then gave Robert Spicer a glorious smile.

"Ah, Julia," Jacques said mildly, "how wicked of you."

"Autumn works the other side of the camera," Lucas stated. Knowing his eyes had been on her the entire time, Autumn was grateful when Steve returned with her drink. "She's a photographer."

"Again, I'm fascinated." Autumn's free hand was captured in Jacques's. "Tell me why you are behind the camera instead of in front of it? Your hair alone would cause poets to run for their pens."

No woman was immune to flattery with a French accent, and Autumn smiled fully into his eyes. "I doubt I could stand still long enough to begin with."

"Photographers can be quite useful," Helen Easterman stated suddenly. Lifting a hand, she patted her dark, sleek cap of hair. "A good, clear photograph is an invaluable tool…to an artist."

An awkward pause followed the statement. Tension entered the room, so out of place in the comfortable lounge with its chintz curtains that Autumn thought it must be her imagination. Helen smiled into the silence and sipped her drink. Her eyes swept over the others, inclusively, never centering on one.

Autumn knew there was something here which isolated Helen and set her apart from the rest. Messages were being passed without words, though there was no way for Autumn to tell who was communicating what to whom. The mood changed swiftly as Julia engaged Robert Spicer in bright conversation. Jane Spicer's habitual frown became more pronounced.

The easy climate continued as they went in to dinner. Sitting between Jacques and Steve, Autumn was able to add to her education as she observed Julia flirting simultaneously with Lucas and Robert. She was, in Autumn's opinion, magnificent. Even through the discomfort of seeing Lucas casually return the flirtation, she had to admire Julia's talent. Her charm and beauty were insatiable. Jane ate in sullen silence.

Dreary woman, Autumn mused, then wondered what her own reaction would be if it were her husband so enchanted. Action, she decided, not silence. I'd simply claw her eyes out. The image of dumpy Jane wrestling with the elegant Julia made her smile. Even as she enjoyed the notion, she looked up to find Lucas's eyes on her.

His brows were lifted at an angle she knew meant amusement. Autumn turned her attention to Jacques.

"Do you find many differences in the movie industry here in America, Mr. LeFarre?"

"You must call me Jacques." His smile caused the tips of his moustache to rise. "There are differences, yes. I would say that Americans are more…adventurous than Europeans."

Autumn lifted her shoulders and smiled. "Maybe because we're a mixture of nationalities. Not watered down. Just Americanized."

"Americanized." Jacques tried out the word and approved it. His grin was younger than his smile, less urbane. "Yes, I would say I feel Americanized in California."

"Still, California's only one aspect of the country," Steve put in. "And I wouldn't call L.A. or southern California particularly typical." Autumn watched his eyes flick over her hair. His interest brought on a small flutter of response that pleased her. It proved that she was still a woman, open to a man—not just one man. "Have you ever been to California, Autumn?"

"I lived there…once." Her response to Steve, and the need to prove something to herself, urged her to turn her eyes to Lucas. Their gazes locked and held for one brief instant. "I relocated in New York three years ago."

"There was a family here from New York," Steve went on. If he'd noticed the look that had passed, he gave no sign. Yes, a good politician, Autumn thought again. "They just checked out this morning. The woman was one of those robust types with energy pouring out of every cell. She needed it,'' he added with a smile that was for Autumn alone. "She had three boys. Triplets. I think she said they were eleven.''

"Oh, those beastly children!'' Julia switched her attention from Robert and looked across the table. She rolled her summer blue eyes. "Running around like a pack of monkeys. Worse, you could never tell which one of them it was zooming by or leaping down. They did everything in triplicate.'' She shuddered and lifted her water glass. "They ate like elephants.''

"Running and eating are part of childhood,'' Jacques commented with a shake of his head. "Julia,'' he told Autumn with a conspirator's wink, "was born twenty-one and beautiful.''

"Anyone with manners is born twenty-one,'' Julia countered. "Being beautiful was simply a bonus.'' Her eyes were laughing now. "Jacques is crazy about kids,'' she informed Autumn. "He has three specimens of his own.''

Interested, Autumn turned to him. She'd never thought of Jacques LeFarre in terms other than his work. "I'm crazy about them, too,'' she confessed and shot Julia a grin. "What sort of specimens do you have?''

"Boys,'' he answered. Autumn found the fondness in his eyes curiously touching. "They are like a ladder.'' With his hand, he formed imaginary steps. "Seven, eight and nine years. They live in France with my wife—my ex-wife.'' He frowned, then smoothed it away. Autumn realized how the worry lines in his brow had been formed.

"Jacques actually wants custody of the little monsters.'' Julia's look was more tolerant than her words. Here, Autumn saw, affection transcended flirtation. "Even though I hold your sanity suspect, Jacques, I'm forced to admit you make a better father than Claudette makes a mother.''

"Custody suits are sensitive matters,'' Helen announced from the end of the table. She drank from her water glass, peering over the rim with small, sharp eyes. The look that she sent Jacques seemed to brush everyone else out of her line of vision. "It's so important that any...unsuitable information doesn't come to light."

Tension sprang back. Autumn felt the Frenchman stiffen beside her. But there was more. Undercurrents flowed up and down the long pine table. It was impossible not to feel them, though there was nothing tangible, nothing solid. Instinctively, Autumn's eyes sought Lucas's. There was nothing there but the hard, unfathomable mask she had seen too often in the past.

"Your aunt serves such marvelous meals, Miss Gallegher." With a puzzling, satisfied smirk, Helen shifted her attention to Autumn.

"Yes." She blundered into the awful silence. "Aunt Tabby gives food a high rating of importance."

"Aunt Tabby?" Julia's rich laugh warred with the tension, and won. The air was instantly lighter. "What a wonderful name. Did you know Autumn has an Aunt Tabby when you christened her Cat, Lucas?" She stared up at him, her eyes wide and guileless. Autumn was reminded of a movie Julia had been in, in which she played the innocent ingenue to perfection.

"Lucas and I didn't know each other well enough to discuss relatives." Autumn's voice was easy and careless and pleased her very much. So did Lucas's barely perceptible frown.

"Actually," he replied, recovering quickly, "we were too occupied to discuss family trees." He sent her a smile which sneaked through her defenses. Autumn's pulse hammered. "What did we talk about in those days, Cat?"

"I've forgotten," she murmured, knowing she had lost the edge before she'd really held it. "It was a long time ago."

Aunt Tabby bustled in with her prize cobbler.

There was music on the stereo and a muted fire in the hearth when they returned to the lounge. The scene, if Autumn could have captured it on film, was one of relaxed camaraderie. Steve and Robert huddled over a chessboard while Jane made her discontented way through a magazine. Even without a photographer's eye for color, Autumn knew the woman should never wear brown. She felt quite certain that Jane invariably would.

Lucas sprawled on the sofa. Somehow, he always managed to relax in a negligent fashion without seeming sloppy; there was always an alertness about him, energy simmering right under the surface. Autumn knew he watched people without being obvious—not because he cared if he made them uncomfortable, he didn't in the least—it was simply something he was able to do. And in watching them, he was able to learn their secrets. An obsessive writer, he drew his characters from flesh and blood. With no mercy, Autumn recalled.

At the moment, he seemed content with his conversation with Julia and Jacques. They flanked him on the sofa and spoke with the ease that came from familiarity; they shared the same world.

But it's not my world, Autumn reminded herself. I only pretended it was for a little while. I only pretended he was mine for a little while. She had been right when she told Lucas she had grown up. Pretend games were for children.

Yet, Autumn thought as she sat back and observed, there was a game of some sort going on here. There was a faint glistening of unease superimposed over the homey picture. Always attuned to contrasts, she could sense it, feel it. They're not letting me in on the rules, she mused, and found herself grateful. She didn't want to play. Making her excuses to no one in particular, Autumn slipped from the room to find her aunt.

Whatever tension she had felt evaporated the moment Autumn stepped into her aunt's room.

"Oh, Autumn." Aunt Tabby lifted her glasses from her nose and let them dangle from a chain around her neck. "I was just reading a letter from your mother. I'd forgotten it was here until this minute. She says by the time I read this, you'll be here. And here you are." Smiling, she patted Autumn's hand. "Debbie always was so clever. Did you enjoy your pot roast, dear?"

"It was lovely, Aunt Tabby, thank you."

"We'll have to have it once a week while you're with us."
Autumn smiled and thought of how she liked spaghetti. Paul
probably gets spaghetti on his visits, she mused. "I'll just
make a note of that, else it'll slip right through my mind."
Autumn recalled that Aunt Tabby's notes were famous for
their ability to slip into another dimension, and felt more
hopeful. "Where are my glasses?" Aunt Tabby murmured,
puckering her impossibly smooth brow. Standing, she rum-
maged through her desk, lifting papers and peering under
books. "They're never where you leave them."

Autumn lifted the dangling glasses from her aunt's bosom,
then perched them on her nose. After blinking a moment,
Aunt Tabby smiled in her vague fashion.

"Isn't that strange?" she commented. "They were here all
along. You're just as clever as your mother."

Autumn couldn't resist giving her a bone-crushing hug.
"Aunt Tabby, I adore you!"

"You always were such a sweet child." She patted Autumn's cheek, then moved away, leaving the scent of lavender
and talc hanging in the air. "I hope you like your surprise."

"I'm sure I will."

"You haven't seen it yet?" Her small mouth pouted in
thought. "No, I'm quite sure I haven't shown you yet, so you
can't know if you like it. Did you and Miss Bond have a nice
chat? Such a lovely lady. I believe she's in show business."

Autumn's smile was wry. There was no one, she thought,
absolutely no one like Aunt Tabby. "Yes, I believe she is.
I've always admired her."

"Oh, have you met before?" Aunt Tabby asked absently
as she shuffled the papers on her desk back into her own
particular order. "I suppose I'd better show you now while I
have it on my mind."

Autumn tried to keep up with her aunt's thought processes,
but it had been a year since her last visit and she was rusty.
"Show me what, Aunt Tabby?"

"Oh now, it wouldn't be a surprise if I told you, would
it?" Playfully, she shook her finger under Autumn's nose.

"You'll just have to be patient and come along with me."
With this, she bustled from the room.

Autumn followed, deducing they were again discussing the
surprise. She had to shorten her gait to match her aunt's. Autumn usually moved in a loose-limbed stride, a result of lean-
ness and lengthy legs, while her aunt scuttled unrhythmically.
Like a rabbit, Autumn thought, that dashes out in the road
then can't make up its mind which way to run. As they
walked, Aunt Tabby muttered about bed linen. Autumn's
thoughts drifted irresistibly to Lucas.

"Now, here we are." Aunt Tabby stopped. She gave the
door an expectant smile. The door itself, Autumn recalled, led
to a sitting room long since abandoned and converted into a
storage room. It was a convenient place for cleaning supplies,
as it adjoined the kitchen. "Well," Aunt Tabby said, beaming,
"what do you think?"

Searching for the right comment, Autumn realized the surprise must be inside. "Is my surprise in there, Aunt Tabby?"

"Yes, of course, how silly." She clucked her tongue. "You
won't know what it is until I open the door."

With this indisputable logic, she did.

When the lights were switched on, Autumn stood stunned.
Where she had expected to see mops, brooms and buckets
was a fully equipped darkroom. Every detail, every piece of
apparatus stood neat and orderly in front of her. Her voice
had been left outside the door.

"Well, what do you think?" Aunt Tabby repeated. She
moved around the room, stopping now and again to peer at
bottles of developing fluid, tongs and trays. "It all looks so
technical and scientific to me." The enlarger caused her to
frown and tilt her head. "I'm sure I don't understand a thing
about it."

"Oh, Aunt Tabby." Autumn's voice finally joined her
body. "You shouldn't have."

"Oh dear, is something wrong with it? Nelson told me you
developed your own film, and the company that brought in
all these things assured me everything was proper. Of

course..." Her voice wavered in doubt. "I really don't know a thing about it."

Her aunt looked so distressed, Autumn nearly wept with love. "No, Aunt Tabby, it's perfect. It's wonderful." She enveloped the small, soft body in her arms. "I meant that you shouldn't have done this for me. All the trouble and the expense."

"Oh, is that all?" Aunt Tabby interrupted. Her distress dissolved as she beamed around the room again. "Well, it was no trouble at all. These nice young men came in and did all the work. As for the expense, well..." She shrugged her rounded shoulders. "I'd rather see you enjoy my money now than after I'm dead."

Sometimes, Autumn thought, the fuzzy little brain shot straight through to sterling sense. "Aunt Tabby." She framed her aunt's face with her hands. "I've never had a more wonderful surprise. Thank you."

"You just have a good time with it." Aunt Tabby's cheeks grew rosy with pleasure when Autumn kissed them, and she eyed the chemicals and trays again. "I don't suppose you'll blow anything up."

Knowing this wasn't a pun, and that her aunt was concerned about explosions in her vague way, Autumn assured her she would not. Satisfied, Aunt Tabby then bustled off, leaving Autumn to explore on her own.

For more than an hour, Autumn lost herself in what she knew best. Photography, started as a hobby when she had been a child, had become both craft and profession. The chemicals and complicated equipment were no strangers to her. Here, in a darkroom, or with a camera in her hands, she knew exactly who she was and what she wanted. This was where she had learned control—the same control she knew she had to employ over her thoughts of Lucas. She was no longer a dewy-eyed girl, ready to follow the crook of a finger. She was a professional woman with a growing reputation in her field. She had to hang on to that now, as she had for three years. There was no going back to yesterday.

Pleasantly weary after rearranging the darkroom to her own

preference, Autumn wandered into the kitchen to fix herself a solitary cup of tea. The moon was round and white with a thin cloud drifting over it. Unexpectedly, a shudder ran through her, quick and chilling. The odd feeling she had sensed several times that evening came back. She frowned. Imagination? Autumn knew herself well enough to admit she had her share. It was part of her art. But this was different.

Discovering Lucas at the inn had jolted her system, and her emotions had been strained. That, she decided, was all that was wrong. The tension she had felt earlier was her own tension; the strain, her own strain. Dumping the remaining tea into the sink, she decided that what she needed was a good night's sleep. No dreams, she ordered herself firmly. She'd had her fill of dreams three years before.

The house was quiet now. Moonlight filtered in, leaving the corners shadowed. The lounge was dark, but as she passed, Autumn heard muted voices. She hesitated a moment, thinking to stop and say good night, then she detected the subtle signs that told her this wasn't a conversation, but an argument. There was anger in the hushed, sexless voices. The undistinguishable words were quick, staccato and passionate. She walked by quickly, not wanting to overhear a private battle. A brief oath shot out, steeped in temper, elegant in French.

Climbing the stairs, Autumn smothered a grin. Jacques, she concluded, was probably losing patience with Lucas's artistic stubbornness. For entirely malicious reasons, she hoped the Frenchman gave him an earful.

It wasn't until she was halfway down the hall to her room that Autumn saw that she'd been wrong. Even Lucas McLean couldn't be two places at once. And he was definitely in this one. In the doorway of another room, Lucas was locked in a very involved embrace with Julia Bond.

Autumn knew how his arms would feel, how his mouth would taste. She remembered it all, completely, as if no years had come between to dull the sensations. She knew how his hand would trail up the back until he cupped around the neck. And that his fingers wouldn't be gentle. No, there were no gentle caresses from Lucas.

There was no need for her to worry about being seen. Both Lucas and Julia were totally focused on each other. Autumn was certain that the roof could have toppled over their heads, and they would have remained unmoving and entwined. The pain came back, hatefully, in full force.

Hurrying by, she gave vent to hideous and unwelcome jealousy by slamming her door.

Chapter 3

The forest was morning fresh. It held a tranquility that was full of tangy scents and bird song. To the east, the sky was filled with scuttling rags of white clouds. An optimist, Autumn put her hopes in them and ignored the dark, threatening sky in the west. Streaks of red still crowned the peaks of the mountains. Gently, the color faded to pink before it surrendered to blue.

The light was good, filtering through the white clouds and illuminating the forest. The leaves weren't full enough to interfere with the sun, only touching the limbs of trees with dots of green. Sometimes strong, the breeze bent branches and tugged at Autumn's hair. She could smell spring.

Wood violets popped out unexpectedly, the purple dramatic against the moss. She saw her first robin marching importantly on the ground, listening for worms. Squirrels scampered up trees, down trees and over the mulch of last year's leaves.

Autumn had intended to walk to the lake, hoping to catch a deer at early watering, but when her camera insisted on planting itself in front of her face again and again, she didn't resist. She ambled along, happy in the solitude and in tune with nature.

In New York, she never truly felt alone—lonely sometimes, but not solitary. The city intruded. Now, cocooned by mountains and trees, she realized how much she'd needed to feel alone. To recharge. Since leaving California and Lucas, Autumn hadn't permitted herself time alone. There had been a void that had to be filled, and she'd filled it with people, with work, with noise—anything that would keep her mind busy. She'd used the pace of the city. It had been necessary. Now, she wanted the pace of the mountains.

In the distance, the lake shimmered. Reflections of the surrounding mountains and trees were mirrored in the water, reversed and shadowy. There were no deer, but as she drew closer, Autumn noticed two figures circling the far side. The ridge where she stood was some fifty feet above the small valley which held the lake. The view was spectacular.

The lake itself stretched in a wide finger, about a hundred feet in length, forty in width. The breeze that caught at Autumn's hair where she strode didn't reach down to the water; its surface was clear and still. The opaque water gradually darkened towards the center, warning of dangerous depths.

Autumn forgot the people walking around the lake, her mind fully occupied with angles and depths of field and shutter speeds. The distance was too great for her to make them out even if she had been interested.

The sun continued its rise, and Autumn was content. She stopped only to change film. As she replaced the roll, she noted that the lake was now deserted. The light was wrong for the mood she wanted and, turning, she began her leisurely journey back to the inn.

This time, the stillness of the forest seemed different. The sun was brighter, but she felt an odd disquiet she hadn't experienced in the paler light of dawn. Foolishly, she looked back over her shoulder, then told herself she was an idiot. Who would be following her? And why? Yet the feeling persisted.

The serenity had vanished. Autumn forced herself to put aside an impulsive desire to run back to the inn where there would be people and coffee brewing. She wasn't a child to take flight at the thought of ogres or gnomes. To prove to herself that her fantasies hadn't affected her, she forced herself to stop and take the time to perfect a shot of a cooperative squirrel. A faint rustle of dead leaves came from behind her and terror brought her scrambling to her feet.

"Well, Cat, still attached to a camera?"

Blood pounding in her head, Autumn stared at Lucas. His hands were tucked comfortably into the pockets of his jeans as he stood directly in front of her. For a moment, she couldn't speak. The fear had been sharp and real.

"What do you mean by sneaking up behind me that way?" When it returned, her voice was furious. She was annoyed that she'd been foolish enough to be frightened, and angry that he'd been the one to frighten her. She pushed her hair back and glared at him.

"I see you've finally developed the temper to match your hair," he observed in a lazy voice. He crossed the slight distance between them and stood close. Autumn had also developed pride and refused to back away.

"It gets particularly nasty when someone spoils a shot." It was a simple matter to blame her reaction on his interference with her work. Not for a moment would she amuse him by confessing fear.

"You're a bit jumpy, Cat." The devil himself could take lessons on smiling from Lucas McLean, she thought bitterly. "Do I make you nervous?"

His dark hair curled in a confused tangle around his lean face, and his eyes were dark and confident. It was the confidence, she told herself, that she cursed him for. "Don't flatter yourself," she tossed back. "I don't recall you ever being one for morning hikes, Lucas. Have you developed a love of nature?"

"I've always had a fondness for nature." He was studying her with deep, powerful eyes while his mouth curved into a smile. "I've always had a penchant for picnics."

The pain started, a dull ache in her stomach. She could remember the gritty feel of sand under her legs, the tart taste of wine on her tongue and the scent of the ocean everywhere. She forced her gaze to stay level with his. "I lost my taste for them." She turned in dismissal, but he fell into step beside her. "I'm not going straight back," she informed him. The chill in her voice would have discouraged anyone else. Stopping, she took an off-center picture of a blue jay.

"I'm in no hurry," he returned easily. "I've always enjoyed watching you work. It's fascinating how absorbed you become." He watched her back, and let his eyes run down the length of her hair. "I believe you could be snapping a charging rhino and not give an inch until you'd perfected the shot." There was a slight pause as she remained turned away from him. "I saw that photo you took of a burned-out tenement in New York. It was remarkable. Hard, clean and desperate."

Wary of the compliment, Autumn faced him. She knew Lucas wasn't generous with praise. Hard, clean and desperate, she thought. He had chosen the words perfectly. She didn't like discovering that his opinion still mattered. "Thank you." She turned back to focus on a grouping of trees. "Still having trouble with your book?"

"More than I'd anticipated," he muttered. Suddenly, he swooped her hair up into his hands. "I never could resist it, could I?" She continued to give her attention to the trees. Her answer was an absent shrug, but she squeezed her eyes tightly shut a moment. "I've never seen another woman with hair like yours. I've looked, God knows, but the shade is always wrong, or the texture or the length." There was a seductive quality in his voice. Autumn stiffened against it. "It's unique. A fiery waterfall in the sun, deep and vibrant spilling over a pillowcase."

"You always had a gift for description." She adjusted her lens without the vaguest idea of what she was doing. Her voice was detached, faintly bored, while she prayed for him to go. Instead, his grip tightened on her hair. In a swift move, he whirled her around and tore the camera from her hands.

"Damn it, don't use that tone with me. Don't turn your back on me. Don't ever turn your back on me."

She remembered the dark expression and uncertain temper well. There'd been a time when she would have dissolved

when faced with them. But not anymore, she thought fleetingly. Not this time.

"I don't cringe at being sworn at these days, Lucas." She
tossed her head, lifting her chin. "Why don't you save your
attention for Julia? I don't want it."

"So." His smile was light and amused in a rapid-fire
change. "It was you. No need to be jealous, Cat. The lady
made the move, not I."

"Yes, I noticed your mad struggle for release." Even as
she spoke, she regretted the words. Annoyed, Autumn pushed
away, but was only caught closer. His scent teased her senses
and reminded her of things she'd rather forget. "Listen, Lucas," she ground out slowly as both anger and longing rose
inside her. "It took me six months to realize what a bastard
you are, and I've had three years to cement that realization.
I'm a big girl now, and not susceptible to your abundant
charms. Now, take your hands off me and get lost."

"Learned to sink your teeth in, have you, Cat?" To her
mounting fury, his expression was more amused than insulted.
His eyes lowered to her mouth for a moment, lingered then
lifted. "Not malleable anymore, but just as fascinating."

Because his words hurt more than she had thought possible,
she hurled a stream of abuse at him.

His laughter cut off her torrent like a slap. Abandoning
verbal protest, Autumn began to struggle with a wild, furious
rage. Abruptly, he molded her against him. Tasting of punishment and possession, his mouth found hers. The heat was
blinding.

The old, churning need fought its way to the surface. For
three years she had starved, and now all that hunger spilled
out in response. There was no hesitation as her arms found
their way around his neck. Eager for more, her lips parted.
His mouth was urgent and bruising. The pain was like heaven,
and she begged for more. Her blood was flowing again. Lucas
let his mouth roam over her face, then come back to hers with
new demands. Autumn met them and fretted for more. Time
flew backward, then forward again before he lifted his face.

His eyes were incredibly dark, opaque with a passion she

recognized. For the first time she felt the faint throbbing where his hands gripped her and his hold eased to a caress. The taste of him lingered on her lips.

"It's still there, Cat," Lucas murmured. With easy familiarity, he combed his fingers through her hair. "Still there."

All at once, pain and humiliation coursed through her. She pulled away fiercely and swung out a hand. He caught her wrist and, frustrated, she drew back with her other hand. His reflexes were too sharp, and she was denied any satisfaction. With both wrists captured, she could only stand struggling, her breath ragged. Tears burned at her throat, but she refused to acknowledge them. He won't make me cry, she vowed fiercely. He won't see me cry again.

In silence, Lucas watched her battle for control. There was no sound in the forest but Autumn's own jerking breaths. When she could speak, her voice was hard and cold. "There's a difference between love and lust, Lucas. Even you should know one from the other. What's there now may be the same for you, but not for me. I loved you. I *loved* you." The words were an accusation in their repetition. His brows drew together as his gaze grew intense. "You took it all once—my love, my innocence, my pride—then you tossed them back in my face. You can't have them back. The first is dead, the second's gone and the third belongs to me."

For a moment, they both were still. Slowly, without taking his eyes from hers, Lucas released her wrists. He didn't speak, and his expression told her nothing. Refusing to run from him a second time, Autumn turned and walked away. Only when she was certain he wasn't following did she allow her tears their freedom. Her statements about pride and innocence had been true. But her love was far from dead. It was alive, and it hurt.

As the red bricks of the inn came into view, Autumn dashed the drops away. There would be no wallowing in what was over. Loving Lucas changed nothing, any more than it had changed anything three years before. But she'd changed. He wouldn't find her weeping, helpless and—as he had said himself—malleable.

Disillusionment had given her strength. He could still hurt her. She'd learned that quickly. But he could no longer manipulate her as he had once. Still, the encounter with him had left her shaken, and she wasn't pleased when Helen approached from a path to the right.

It was impossible, without being pointedly rude, for Autumn to veer off and avoid her. Instead, she fixed a smile on her face. When Helen turned her head, the livid bruise under her eye became noticeable. Autumn's smile faded into quick concern.

"What happened?" The bruise looked painful and aroused Autumn's sympathy.

"I walked into a branch." Helen gave a careless shrug as she lifted her fingers to stroke the mark. "I'll have to be more careful in the future."

Perhaps it was her turmoil over Lucas that made Autumn detect some hidden shade of meaning in those words, but Helen seemed to mean more than she said. Certainly the eyes which met Autumn's were as hot and angry as the bruise. And the mark itself, Autumn mused, looked more like the result of contact with a violent hand than with any stray branch. She pushed the thought aside. Who would have struck Helen? she asked herself. And why would she cover up the abuse? Her own carelessness made more sense.

"It looks nasty," Autumn commented as they began to walk toward the inn. "You'll have to do something about it. Aunt Tabby should have something to ease the soreness."

"Oh, I intend to do something about it," Helen muttered, then gave Autumn her sharp-eyed smile. "I know just the thing. Out early taking pictures?" she asked while Autumn tried to ignore the unease her words brought. "I've always found people more interesting subjects than trees. I'm especially fond of candid shots." She began to laugh at some private joke. It was the first time Autumn had heard her laugh, and she thought how suited the sound was to Helen's smile. They were both unpleasant.

"Were you down at the lake earlier?" Autumn recalled the

two figures she had spotted. To her surprise, Helen's laughter stopped abruptly. Her eyes grew sharper.

"Did you see someone?"

"No," she began, confused by the harshness of the question. "Not exactly. I saw two people by the lake, but I was too far away to see who they were. I was taking pictures from the ridge."

"Taking pictures," Helen repeated. Her mouth pursed as if she were considering something carefully. She began to laugh again with a harsh burst of sound.

"Well, well, such good humor for such early risers." Julia drifted down the porch steps. Her brow lifted as she studied Helen's cheek. Autumn wondered if the actress's shudder was real or affected. "Good heavens, what have you done to yourself?"

Helen's amusement seemed to have passed. She gave Julia a quick scowl, then fingered the bruise again. "Walked into a branch," she muttered before she stalked up the steps and disappeared inside.

"A fist more likely," Julia commented, and smiled. With a shrug, she dismissed Helen and turned to Autumn. "The call of the wild beckoned to you, too? It seems everyone but me was tramping through forests and over mountains at the cold light of dawn. It's so difficult being sane when one is surrounded by insanity."

Autumn had to smile. Julia looked like a sunbeam. In direct contrast to her own rough jeans and jacket, Julia wore delicate pink slacks and a thin silk blouse flocked with roses. The white sandals she wore wouldn't last fifty yards in the woods. Whatever resentment Autumn had felt for the actress attracting Lucas vanished under her open warmth.

"There are some," Autumn remarked mildly, "who might accuse you of laziness."

"Absolutely," Julia agreed with a nod and a smile. "When I'm not working, I wallow in sloth. If I don't get going again soon, my blood will stop flowing." She gave Autumn a shrewd glance. "Looks like you walked into a rather large branch yourself."

Bewilderment crossed Autumn's face briefly. Julia's eyes, she discovered, were very discerning. The traces of tears hadn't evaporated as completely as Autumn would have liked. Helplessly she moved her shoulders. "I heal quickly."

"Brave child. Come, tell mama all about it." Julia's eyes were sympathetic, balancing the stinging lightness of the words. Linking her arms through Autumn's, she began to walk across the lawn.

"Julia…" Autumn shook her head. Inner feelings were private. She'd broken the rule for Lucas, and wasn't certain she could do so again.

"Autumn." The refusal was firmly interrupted. "You do need to talk. You might not think that you look stricken, but you do." Julia sighed with perfect finesse. "I really don't know why I've become so fond of you; it's totally against my policy. Beautiful women tend to avoid or dislike other beautiful women, especially younger ones."

The statement completely robbed Autumn of speech. The idea of the exquisite, incomparable Julia Bond placing herself on a physical plane anywhere near Autumn's own seemed ludicrous to her. It was one matter to hear the actress speak casually of her own beauty, and quite another for her to speak of Autumn's. Julia's voice flowed over the gaping silence.

"Maybe it's the exposure to those two other females—one so dull and the other so nasty—but I've developed an affection for you." The breeze tugged at her hair, lifting it up so that the sunlight streamed through it. Absently, Julia tucked a strand behind her ear. On the lobe a diamond sparkled. Autumn thought it incongruous that they were walking arm in arm among her aunt's struggling daffodils.

"You're also a kind person," Julia went on. "I don't know a great many kind people." She turned to Autumn so that her exquisite profile became her exquisite full face. "Autumn, darling, I always pry, but I also know how to keep a confidence."

"I'm still in love with him," Autumn blurted out, then followed that rash statement with a deep sigh. Before she knew it, words were tumbling out. She left out nothing, from the beginning to the end, to the new beginning when he had come back into her life the day before. She told Julia everything. Once she'd begun, no effort was needed. She didn't have to think, only feel, and Julia listened. The quality of her listening was so perfect, Autumn all but forgot she was there.

"The monster," Julia said, but with no malice. "You'll find all men, those marvelous creatures, are basically monsters."

Who was Autumn to argue with an expert? As they walked on in silence, she realized that she did feel better. The rawness was gone.

"The main trouble is, of course, that you're still mad about him. Not that I blame you," Julia added when Autumn made a small sound of distress. "Lucas is quite a man. I had a tiny sample last night, and I was impressed." Julia spoke so casually of the passion Autumn had witnessed, it was impossible to be angry. "Lucas is a talented man," Julia went on. By her smile, Autumn knew that Julia was very much aware of the struggle that was going on within Autumn. "He's also arrogant, selfish and used to being obeyed. It's easy for me to see that, because I am, too. We're alike. I doubt very much if we could even enjoy a pleasant affair. We'd be clawing at each other before the bed was turned down."

Autumn found no response to make to the image this produced, and merely walked on.

"Jacques is more my type," Julia mused. "But his attentions are committed elsewhere." She frowned, and Autumn sensed that her thoughts had drifted to something quite different. "Anyway." Julia made an impatient gesture. "You just have to make up your mind what you want. Obviously, Lucas wants you back, at least for as long as it suits him."

Autumn tried to ignore the sting of honesty and just listened.

"Knowing that, you could enjoy a stimulating relationship with him, with your eyes open."

"I can't do that, Julia. The knowing won't stop the hurting. I'm not sure I can survive another...relationship with Lucas. And he'd know I was still in love with him." A flash frame of their parting scene three years before jumped into her mind. "I won't be humiliated again. Pride's the only thing I have left that isn't his already."

"Love and pride don't belong together." Julia patted Autumn's hand. "Well then, you'll have to barricade yourself against the assault. I'll run interference for you."

"How will you do that?"

"Darling!" She lifted her brow as the slow, cat smile drifted to her lips.

Autumn had to laugh. It all seemed so absurd. She lifted her face to the sky. The black clouds were winning after all. For a moment, they blotted out the sun and warmth. "Looks like rain."

Her gaze shifted back to the inn. The windows were black and empty. The struggling light fell gloomily over the bricks and turned the white porch and shutters gray. Behind the building, the sky was like slate. The mountains were colorless and oppressive. She felt a tickle at the back of her neck. To her puzzlement, Autumn found she didn't want to go back inside.

Just as quickly, the clouds shifted, letting the sun pour out through the opening. The windows blinked with light. The shadows vanished. Chiding herself for another flight of fancy, Autumn walked back to the inn with Julia.

Only Jacques joined them for breakfast. Helen was nowhere in sight, and Steve and the Spicers were apparently still hiking. Autumn trained her thoughts away from Lucas. Her appetite, as usual, was unimpaired and outrageous. She put away a healthy portion of bacon, eggs, coffee and muffins while Julia nibbled on a single piece of thin toast and sent her envious scowls.

Jacques seemed preoccupied. His charm was costing him visible effort. Memory of the muffled argument in the lounge came to Autumn's mind. Idly, she began to speculate on who he had been annoyed with. Thinking it over, the entire matter struck her as odd. Jacques LeFarre didn't seem to be the sort of man who would argue with a veritable stranger, yet, as

Autumn knew, both Lucas and Julia had been preoccupied elsewhere.

Appearing totally at ease, Julia rambled on about a mutual friend in the industry. But she's an actress, Autumn reminded herself. A good one. She could easily know the cause of last night's animosity and never show a sign. Jacques, however, wasn't an actor. The distress was there; anger lay just beneath the polished charm. Autumn wondered at it throughout the meal, then dismissed it from her mind as she left to find her aunt. After all, she reflected, it wasn't any of her business.

Aunt Tabby was, as Autumn had known she would be, fussing with Nancy the cook over the day's menu. Keeping silent, Autumn let the story unfold. It seemed that Nancy had planned on chicken while Aunt Tabby was certain they had decided on pork. While the argument raged, Autumn helped herself to another cup of coffee. Through the window, she could see the thick, roiling clouds continue their roll from the west.

"Oh, Autumn, did you have a nice walk?" When she turned, Autumn found her aunt smiling at her. "Such a nice morning, a shame it's going to rain. But that's good for the flowers, isn't it? Sweet little things. Did you sleep well?"

After a moment, Autumn decided to answer only the final question. There was no use confusing her aunt. "Wonderfully, Aunt Tabby. I always sleep well when I visit you."

"It's the air," the woman replied. Her round little face lit with pleasure. "I think I'll make my special chocolate cake for tonight. That should make up for the rain."

"Any hot coffee, Aunt Tabby?" Lucas swept into the kitchen as if he enjoyed the privilege daily. As always, when he came into a room, the air charged. This phenomenon Autumn could accept. The casual use of her aunt's nickname was more perplexing.

"Of course, dear, just help yourself." Aunt Tabby gestured vaguely toward the stove, her mind on chocolate cake. Autumn's confusion grew as Lucas strode directly to the proper cupboard, retrieved a cup and proceeded to fix himself a very homey cup of coffee.

. He drank, leaning against the counter. The eyes that met Autumn's were very cool. All traces of anger and passion were gone, as if they had never existed. His rough black brows lifted as she continued to stare. The damnable devil smile tugged at his mouth.

"Oh, is that your camera, dear?" Aunt Tabby's voice broke into her thoughts. Autumn lowered her eyes.

The camera still hung around her neck, so much a part of her that she'd forgotten it was there.

"My, my, so many numbers. It looks complicated." Aunt Tabby peered at it through narrowed eyes, forgetting the glasses that dangled from her chain. "I have a very nice one, Autumn. You're welcome to use it whenever you like." After giving the Nikon another dubious glance, she beamed up with her misty smile. "You just push a little red button, and the picture pops right out. You can see if you've cut off someone's head or have your thumb in the corner right away, so you can take another picture. And you don't have to grope around in that darkroom either. I don't know how you see what you're doing in there." Her brows drew close, and she tapped a finger against her cheek. "I'm almost certain I can find it."

Autumn grinned. She was compelled to subject her aunt to yet another bear hug. Over the gray-streaked head, Autumn saw that Lucas was grinning as well. It was the warm, natural grin which came to his face so rarely. For a moment, she found she could smile back at him without pain.

Chapter 4

When the rain came, it didn't begin with the slow drip-drop of an April shower. As the sky grew hazy, the light in the lounge became dim. Everyone was back and the inn was again filled with its odd assortment of guests.

Steve, expanding on his role of bartender, had wandered to the kitchen to get coffee. Robert Spicer had trapped Jacques in what seemed to be a technical explanation of open-heart surgery. During the discussion, Julia sat beside him, hanging on every word—or seeming to. Autumn knew better. Occasionally, Julia sent messages across to her with her extraordinary eyes. She was enjoying herself immensely.

Jane sat sullen over a novel Autumn was certain was riddled with explicit sex. She wore dull brown again, slacks and a sweater. Helen, her bruise livid, smoked quietly in long, deep drags. She reminded Autumn eerily of Alice in Wonderland's caterpillar. Once or twice, Autumn found Helen's sharp eyes on her. The speculative smile left her confused and uncomfortable.

Lucas wasn't there. He was upstairs, Autumn knew, hammering away at his typewriter. She hoped it would keep him busy for hours. Perhaps he'd even take his meals in his room.

Abruptly, the dim light outdoors was snuffed out, and the room plunged into gloom. The warmth fled with it. Autumn shuddered with a sharp premonition of dread. The feeling surprised her, as storms had always held a primitive appeal for her. For a heartbeat, there was no sound, then the rain began with a gushing explosion. With instant force, instant fury, it battered against the windows, punctuated by wicked flashes of lightning.

"A spring shower in the mountains," Steve observed. He paused a moment in the doorway with a large tray balanced in his hands. The friendly scent of coffee entered with him.

"More like special effects," Julia returned. With a flutter of her lashes, she cuddled toward Robert. "Storms are so terrifying and moving. I find myself longing to be frightened."

It was straight out of *A Long Summer's Evening,* Autumn noted, amused. But the doctor seemed too overcome with Julia's ingenuous eyes to recognize the line. Autumn wanted to laugh badly. When Julia cuddled even closer and sent her a wink, Autumn's eyes retreated to the ceiling.

Jane wasn't amused. Autumn noticed she was no longer sullen but smoldering. Perhaps she had claws after all, Autumn thought, and felt she would like her better for it. It might be wise, she mused as Steve passed her a cup of coffee, if Julia concentrated on him rather than the doctor.

"Cream, no sugar, right?" Steve smiled down at her with his California blue eyes. Autumn's lips curved in response. He was a man with the rare ability to make a woman feel pampered without being patronizing. She admired him for it.

"Right. You've got a better memory than George." Her eyes smiled at him over the rim of her cup. "You serve with such style, too. Have you been in this line of work long?"

"I'm only here on a trial basis," he told her with a grin. "Please pass your comments on to the management."

Lightning speared through the gloom again. Jacques shifted in his seat as thunder rumbled and echoed through the room. "With such a storm, is it not possible to lose power?" he addressed Autumn.

"We often lose power." Her answer, accompanied by an absent shrug, brought on varying reactions.

Julia found the idea marvelous—candlelight was so wonderfully romantic. At the moment, Robert couldn't have agreed more. Jacques appeared not to care one way or the other. He lifted his hands in a Gallic gesture, indicating his acceptance of fate.

Steve and Helen seemed inordinately put out, though his comments were milder than hers. He mumbled once about inconveniences, then stalked over to the window to stare out at the torrent of wind and rain. Helen was livid.

"I didn't pay good money to grope around in the dark and eat cold meals." Lighting another cigarette with a swift, furious gesture, she glared at Autumn. "It's intolerable that we should have to put up with such inefficiency. Your aunt will certainly have to make the proper adjustments. I for one won't pay these ridiculous prices, then live like a pioneer." She waved her cigarette, preparing to continue, but Autumn cut her off. She aimed the cold, hard stare she had recently developed.

"I'm sure my aunt will give your complaints all the consideration they warrant." Turning pointedly away, she allowed Helen's sharp little darts to bounce off her. "Actually," she told Jacques, noting his smile of approval, "we have a generator. My uncle was as practical as Aunt Tabby is..."

"Charming," Steve supplied, and instantly became her friend.

After she'd finished beaming at him, Autumn continued. "If we lose main power, we switch over to the generator. With that, we can maintain essential power with little inconvenience."

"I believe I'll have candles in my room anyway," Julia decided. She gave Robert an under-the-lashes smile as he lit her cigarette.

"Julia should have been French," Jacques commented. His moustache tilted at the corner. "She's an incurable romantic."

"Too much...romance," Helen murmured, "can be unwise." Her eyes swept the room, then focused on Julia.

Before Autumn's astonished gaze, Julia transformed from mischievous angel to tough lady. "I've always found that only idiots think they're wise." Statement made, she melted back into a celestial being so quickly, Autumn blinked.

Seeing her perform on the screen was nothing compared to a live show. It occurred to Autumn that she had no inkling which woman was the real Julia Bond—if indeed she was either. The notion germinated that she really didn't know any of the people in that room. They were all strangers.

The air was still vibrating with the uncomfortable silence when Lucas entered. He seemed impervious to the swirling tension. Helplessly, Autumn's eyes locked on his. He came to her, ignoring the others in his cavalier fashion. The devil smile was on his face.

She felt a tremor when she couldn't stop the room from receding, leaving only him in her vision. Something of that fear must have been reflected in her face.

"I'm not going to eat you, Cat," Lucas murmured. Against the violent sounds of the storm, his voice was low, only for her. "Do you still like to walk in the rain?" The question was offhand, and didn't require an answer as he searched her face. "I remember when you did." He paused when she said nothing. "Your aunt sent you this." Lucas held out his hand, and Autumn's gaze dropped to it. Tension dissolved into laughter. "I haven't heard that in a long time," Lucas said softly.

She lifted her eyes to his again. He was studying her with a complete, singleminded intensity. "No?" As she accepted Aunt Tabby's famous red-button camera, her shoulders moved in a careless shrug. "Laughing's quite a habit of mine."

"Aunt Tabby says for you to have a good time with it." Dismissively, he turned his back on her and walked to the coffeepot.

"What have you got there, Autumn?" Julia demanded, her eyes following Lucas's progress.

Flourishing the camera, Autumn used a sober, didactic tone. "This, ladies and gentlemen, is the latest technological achievement in photography. At the mere touch of a button, friends and loved ones are beamed inside and spewed out onto a picture which develops before your astonished eyes. No focusing, no need to consult your light meter. The button is faster than the brain. Why, a child of five can operate it while riding his tricycle.''

''It should be known,'' Lucas inserted in a dry voice, ''that Autumn is a photographic snob.'' He stood by the window, carelessly drinking coffee while he spoke to the others. His eyes were on Autumn. ''If it doesn't have interchangeable lenses and filters, multispeed shutters and impossibly complicated operations, it isn't a camera, but a toy.''

''I've noticed her obsession,'' Julia agreed. She sent him a delicious look before she turned to Autumn. ''She wears that black box like other women wear diamonds. She was actually tramping through the forest at the break of dawn, snapping pictures of chipmunks and bunnies.''

With a good-natured grin, Autumn lifted the camera and snapped Julia's lovely face.

''Really, darling,'' Julia said with a professional toss of the head. ''You might have given me the chance to turn my best side.''

''You haven't got a best side,'' Autumn countered.

Julia smiled, obviously torn between amusement and insult while Jacques exploded with laughter. ''And I thought she was such a sweet child,'' she murmured.

''In my profession, Miss Bond,'' Autumn returned gravely, ''I've had occasion to photograph a fair number of women. This one you shoot from the left profile, that one from the right, another straight on. Still another from an upward angle, and so on.'' Pausing a moment, she gave Julia's matchless face a quick, critical survey. ''I could shoot you from any position, any angle, any light, and the result would be equally wonderful.''

''Jacques.'' Julia placed a hand on his arm. ''We really must adopt this girl. She's invaluable for my ego.''

''Professional integrity,'' Autumn claimed before placing the quickly developing snapshot on the table. She aimed Aunt Tabby's prize at Steve.

''You should be warned that with a camera of any sort in

her hands, Autumn becomes a dangerous weapon.'' Lucas moved closer. He lifted the snap of Julia and studied it.

Autumn frowned as she remembered the innumerable photographs she had taken of him. Under the pretext that they were art, she'd never disposed of them. She'd snapped and focused and crouched around him until, exasperated, he'd dislodged the camera from her hands and effectively driven photography from her mind.

Lucas saw the frown. With his eyes dark and unreadable, he reached down to tangle his fingers in her hair. ''You never could teach me how to take a proper picture, could you, Cat?''

''No.'' The battle with the growing ache made her voice brittle. ''I never taught you anything, Lucas. But I learned quite a bit.''

''I've never been able to master anything but a one-button job myself.'' Steve ambled over. Autumn's camera sat on the table beside her. Picking it up, he examined it as if it were a strange contraption from the outer reaches of space. ''How can you remember what all these numbers are for?''

When he perched on the arm of her chair, Autumn grasped at the diversion. She began a lesson in basic photography. Lucas wandered back to the coffeepot, obviously bored. From the corner of her eye, Autumn noticed Julia gliding to join him. Within moments, her hand was tucked into his arm, and he no longer appeared bored. Gritting her teeth, Autumn began to give Steve a more involved lesson.

Lucas and Julia left, arm in arm, ostensibly for Julia to nap and Lucas to work. Autumn's eyes betrayed her by following them.

When she dragged her attention back to Steve, she caught his sympathetic smile. That he understood her feelings was too obvious. Cursing herself, she resumed her explanations of f-stops, grateful that Steve picked up the conversation as if there had been no lull.

The afternoon wore on. It was a long, dreary day with rain beating against windows. Lightning and thunder came and went, but the wind built in force until it was one continuous moan. Robert tended the fire until flames crackled and spit.

The cheery note this might have brought to the room was negated by Jane's sullenness and Helen's pacing. The air was tight.

Evading Steve's suggestion of cards, Autumn sought the peace and activity of her darkroom. As she closed and locked the door behind her, the headache which had started to build behind her temples eased.

This room was without tensions. Her senses picked up no nagging, intangible disturbances here, but were clear and ready to work. Step by step, she took her film through the first stages of development, preparing chemicals, checking temperatures, setting timers. Growing absorbed, she forgot the battering storm.

While it was necessary, Autumn worked in a total absence of light. Her fingers were her eyes at this stage and she worked quickly. Over the muffled sound of the storm, she heard a faint rattle. She ignored it, busy setting the timer for the next stage of developing. When the sound came again, it annoyed her.

Was it the doorknob? she wondered. Had she remembered to lock the door? All she needed at that point was for some layman to blunder in and bring damaging light with him.

"Leave the door alone," she called out just as the radio she had switched on for company went dead. There went the power, she concluded. Standing in the absolute darkness, Autumn sighed as the rattle came again.

Was it someone at the door, or just someone in the kitchen? Curious and annoyed, she walked in the direction of the door to make sure it was locked. Her steps were confident. She knew every inch of the room now. Suddenly, to her astonishment, pain exploded inside her head. Lights flashed and fractured before the darkness again became complete.

"Autumn, Autumn, open your eyes." Though the sound was far off and muffled, she heard the command in the tone. She resisted it. The nearer she came to consciousness, the more hideous grew the throbbing in her head. Oblivion was painless.

"Open your eyes." The voice was clearer now and more insistent. Autumn moaned.

Reluctantly, she opened her eyes as hands brushed the hair from her face. For a moment, she felt them linger against her cheek. Lucas came into focus gradually, dimming and receding until she forced him back, clear and sharp.

"Lucas?" Disoriented, Autumn could not think beyond his name. It seemed to satisfy him.

"That's better," he said with approval. Before any protest could be made, he kissed her hard, with a briefness that spoke of past intimacy. "You had me worried there a minute. What the hell did you do to yourself?"

The accusation was typical of him. She barely noticed it. "Do?" Autumn lifted a hand to touch the spot on her head where the pain was concentrated. "What happened?"

"That's my question, Cat. No, don't touch the lump." He caught her hand in his and held it. "It'll only hurt more if you do. I'm curious as to how you came by it, and why you were lying in a heap on the floor."

It was difficult to keep clear of the mists in her brain. Autumn tried to center in on the last thing she remembered. "How did you get in?" she demanded, remembering the rattling knob. "Hadn't I locked the door?" It came to her slowly that he was cradling her in his arms, holding her close against his chest. She struggled to sit up. "Were you rattling at the door?"

"Take it easy," he ordered as she groaned with the movement.

Autumn squeezed her eyes shut against the pounding in her head. "I must have walked into the door," she murmured, wondering at the quality of her clumsiness.

"You walked into the door and knocked yourself unconscious?" She couldn't tell if Lucas was angry or amused. The ache in her head kept her from caring one way or the other. "Strange, I don't recall you possessing that degree of uncoordination."

"It was dark," she grumbled, coherent enough to feel embarrassed. "If you hadn't been rattling around at the door..."

"I wasn't rattling around at your door," he began, but she cut him off with a startled gasp.

"The lights!" For a second time, she tried to struggle away from him. "You turned on the lights!"

"It was a mad impulse when I saw you crumpled on the floor," he returned dryly. Without any visible effort, he held her still. "I wanted to see the extent of the damage."

"My film!" Her glare was as accusing as her voice, but he responded with laughter.

"The woman's a maniac."

"Let go of me, will you?" Her anger made her less than gracious. Pushing away, she scrambled to her feet. At her movement, the pain grew to a crashing roar. She staggered under it.

"For God's sake, Autumn." Lucas rose and gripped her shoulders, steadying her. "Stop behaving like an imbecile over a few silly pictures."

This statement, under normal conditions, would have been unwise. In her present state of mind, it was a declaration of war. Pain was eclipsed by a pure silver streak of fury. She whirled on him.

"You never could see my work as anything but silly pictures, could you? You never saw me as anything but a silly child, diverting for a while, but eventually boring. You always hated being bored, didn't you, Lucas?" She made a violent swipe at the hair that fell over her eyes. "You sit with your novels and bask in the adulation you get and look down your nose at the rest of us. You're not the only person in the world with talent, Lucas. My abilities are just as creative as yours, and my pictures give me as much fulfillment as your silly little books."

For a moment, he stood in silence, studying her with a frown. When he did speak, his voice was oddly weary. "All right, Autumn, now that you've gotten that out, you'd better get yourself some aspirin."

"Just leave me alone!" She shook off the hand he put on her arm. Turning, she started to take her camera from the shelf she had placed it on before beginning her work. Glancing down at the table, she flared again. "What do you mean by messing around with my equipment? You've exposed an entire roll of film!" Seething with fury, she whirled on him. "It isn't enough to interrupt my work by fooling around at the door, then turn on the lights and ruin what I've started. You have to put your hands into something you know nothing about."

"I told you before, I wasn't fooling around at your door." His eyes were darkening dangerously. "I came back after the power went out and the generator switched on. The door was open, and you were lying in a heap in the middle of the floor. I never touched your damned film."

There was ice in his voice now to go with the heat in his eyes but Autumn was too infuriated to be touched by either. "Foolish as it may seem," he continued, "my concern and attention were on you." Moving toward her, he glanced down at the confusion on her work table. "I don't suppose it occurred to you that in the dark you disturbed the film yourself?"

"Don't be absurd." Her professional ability was again insulted, but he cut off her retort in a voice filled with strained patience. Autumn pondered on it. As she remembered, Lucas had no patience at all.

"Autumn, I don't know what happened to your film. I didn't get any farther into the room than the spot where you were lying. I won't apologize for switching on the lights; I'd do precisely the same thing again." He circled her neck with his fingers and his words took on the old caressing note she remembered. "I happen to think your welfare is more important than your pictures."

Suddenly, her interest in the film waned. She wanted only to escape from him, and the feelings he aroused in her so effortlessly. Programmed response, she told herself. The soft voice and gentle hands tripped the release, and she went under.

"You're pale," Lucas muttered, abruptly dropping his hands and stuffing them into his pockets. "Dr. Spicer can take a look at you."

"No, I don't need—" She got no farther. He grabbed her arms with quicksilver fury.

"Damn it, Cat, must you argue with everything I say? Is there no getting past the hate you've built up for me?" He gave a quick shake. The pain rolled and spun in her head. For an instant, his face went out of focus as dizziness blurred her vision. Swearing with short, precise expertise, he pulled her close against him until the faintness passed. In a swift move, he lifted her into his arms. "You're pale as a ghost," he muttered. "Like it or not, you're going to see the doctor. You can vent your venom on him for a while."

By the time Autumn realized he was carrying her to her room, her temper had ebbed. There was only a dull, wicked ache and the weariness. Flagging, she rested her head against his shoulder and surrendered. This wasn't the time to think about the darkroom door or how it had come to be opened. It wasn't the time to think of how she had managed to walk into it like a perfect fool. This wasn't the time to think at all.

Accepting the fact that she had no choice, Autumn closed her eyes and allowed Lucas to take over. She kept them closed when she felt him lower her to the bed, but she knew he stood looking down at her a moment. She knew too that he was frowning.

The sound of his footsteps told her that he had walked into the adjoining bathroom. The faint splash of water in the sink sounded like a waterfall to her throbbing head. In a moment, there was a cool cloth over the ache in her forehead. Opening her eyes, Autumn looked into his.

"Lie still," he ordered curtly. Lucas brooded down at her with an odd, enigmatic expression. "I'll get Spicer," he muttered abruptly. Turning on his heel, he strode to the door.

"Lucas." Autumn stopped him because the cool cloth had brought back memories of all the gentle things he had ever done. He'd had his gentle moments, though she'd tried hard to pretend he hadn't. It had seemed easier.

When he turned back, impatience was evident in the very air around him. What a man of contradictions he was, she mused. Intemperate, with barely any middle ground at all.

"Thank you," she said, ignoring his obvious desire to be gone. "I'm sorry I shouted at you. You're being very kind."

Lucas leaned against the door and stared back at her. "I've never been kind." His voice was weary again.

Autumn found it necessary to force back the urge to go to him, wipe away his lines of fatigue. He sensed her thoughts, and his eyes softened briefly. On his mouth moved one of his rare, disarming smiles.

"My God, Cat, you always were so incredibly sweet. So terrifyingly warm."

With that, he left her.

Chapter 5

Autumn was staring at the ceiling when Robert entered. Shifting her eyes, she looked at his black bag dubiously. She'd never cared for what doctors carried inside those innocent-looking satchels.

"A house call," she said and managed a smile. "The eighth wonder of the world. I didn't think you'd have your bag with you on vacation."

He was quick enough to note her uneasy glance. "Do you travel without your camera?"

"Touché." She told herself to relax and not to be a baby.

"I don't think we'll need to operate." He sat on the bed and removed the cloth Lucas had placed there. "Mmm, that's going to be colorful. Is your vision blurred?"

"No."

His hands were surprisingly soft and gentle, reminding Autumn of her father's. She relaxed further and answered his questions on dizziness, nausea and so forth while watching his face. He was different, she noted. The competence was still there, but his dapper self-presentation had been replaced by a quiet compassion. His voice was kind, she thought, and so were his eyes. He was well suited to his profession.

"How'd you come by this, Autumn?" As he asked he reached in his bag and her attention switched to his hands.

He removed cotton and a bottle, not the needle she'd worried about.

She wrinkled her nose ruefully. "I walked into a door."

He shook his head with a laugh, and began to bathe the bruise. "A likely story."

"And embarrassingly true. In the darkroom," she added. "I must have misjudged the distance."

His eyes shifted and studied hers a moment before they returned to her forehead. "You struck me as a woman who kept her eyes open," he said a bit grimly, Autumn thought, before he smiled again. "It's just a bump," he told her and held her hand. "Though my diagnosis won't make it hurt any less."

"It's only an agonizing ache now," Autumn returned, trying for lightness. "The cannons have stopped going off."

With a chuckle, he reached into his bag again. "We can do something about smaller artillery."

"Oh." She eyed the bottle of pills he held and frowned. "I was going to take some aspirin."

"You don't put a forest fire out with a water pistol." He smiled at her again and shook out two pills. "They're very mild, Autumn. Take these and rest for an hour or two. You can trust me," he added with exaggerated gravity as her brows stayed lowered. "Even though I am a surgeon."

"Okay." His eyes convinced her and she smiled back, accepting the glass of water and pills. "You're not going to take out my appendix or anything, are you?"

"Not on vacation." He waited until she had swallowed the medication, then pulled a light blanket over her. "Rest," he ordered and left her.

The next time Autumn opened her eyes, the room was in shadows. Rest? she thought and shifted under the blanket. I've been unconscious. How long? She listened. The storm was still raging, whipping against her windows with a fury she'd been oblivious to. Carefully, she pushed herself into a sitting position. Her head didn't pound, but a touch of her fingers assured her she hadn't dreamed up the entire incident. Her next thought was entirely physical—she discovered she was starving.

Rising, she took a quick glance in the mirror, decided she didn't like what she saw and went in search of food and company. She found them both in the dining room. Her timing was perfect.

"Autumn." It was Robert who spotted her first. "Feeling better?"

She hesitated a moment, embarrassed. Hunger was stronger, however, and the scent of Nancy's chicken was too tempting. "Much," she told him. She glanced at Lucas, but he said nothing, only watched her. The gentleness she had glimpsed so briefly before might have been an illusion. His eyes were dark and hard. "I'm starving," she confessed as she took her seat.

"Good sign. Any more pain?"

"Only in my pride." Forging ahead, she began to fill her plate. "Clumsiness isn't a talent I like to brag about, and walking into a door is such a tired cliché. I wish I'd come up with something more original."

"It's odd." Jacques twirled his fork by the stem as he studied her. "It doesn't seem to me that you would have the power enough to knock yourself unconscious."

"An amazon," Autumn explained and let the chicken rest for a delicious moment on her tongue.

"She eats like one," Julia commented. Autumn glanced over in time to catch the speculative look on her face before it vanished into a smile. "I gain weight watching her."

"Metabolism," Autumn claimed and took another forkful of chicken. "The real tragedy is that I lost the two rolls of film I shot on the trip from New York."

"Perhaps we're in for a series of accidents." Helen's voice was as hard as her eyes as they swept the table. "Things come in threes, don't they?" No one answered and she went on, fingering her own bruise. "It's hard to say what might happen next."

Autumn had come to detest the odd little silences that followed Helen's remarks, the fingers of tension that poked holes in the normalcy of the situation. On impulse, she broke her rule and started a conversation with Lucas.

"What would you do with this setting, Lucas?" She turned to him, but found no change in his expression. He's watching all of us, she thought. Just watching. Shaking off her unease, Autumn continued. "Nine people—ten really, counting the cook—isolated in a remote country inn, a storm raging. The main power's already snuffed out. The phone's likely to be next."

"The phone's already out," Steve told her. Autumn drew out a dramatic "Ah."

"And the ford, of course, is probably impassable." Robert winked at her, falling in with the theme.

"What more could you ask for?" Autumn demanded of Lucas. Lightning flashed, as if on cue.

"Murder." Lucas uttered the six-letter word casually, but it hung in the air as all eyes turned to him. Autumn shuddered involuntarily. It was the response she'd expected, yet she felt a chill on hearing it. "But, of course," he continued as the word still whispered in the air, "it's a rather overly obvious setting for my sort of work."

"Life is sometimes obvious, is it not?" Jacques stated. A small smile played on his mouth as he lifted his glass of golden-hued wine.

"I could be very effective," Julia mused. "Gliding down dark passageways in flowing white." She placed her elbows on the table, folded her hands and rested her chin on them. "The flame of my candle flickering into the shadows while the murderer waits with a silk scarf to cut off my life."

"You'd make a lovely corpse," Autumn told her.

"Thank you, darling." She turned to Lucas. "I'd much rather remain among the living, at least until the final scene."

"You die so well." Steve grinned across the table at her. "I was impressed by your Lisa in *Hope Springs*."

"What sort of murder do you see, Lucas?" Steve was eating little, Autumn noted; he preferred the wine. "A crime of passion or revenge? The impulsive act of a discarded lover or the evil workings of a cool, calculating mind?"

"Aunt Tabby could sprinkle an exotic poison over the food and eliminate us one by one," Autumn suggested as she dipped into the mashed potatoes.

"Once someone's dead, they're no more use." Helen brought the group's attention back to her. "Murder is a waste. You gain more by keeping someone alive. Alive and vulnerable." She shot Lucas a look. "Don't you agree, Mr. McLean?"

Autumn didn't like the way she smiled at him. *Cool and calculating.* Jacques's words repeated in her mind. Yes, she mused, this was a cool and calculating woman. In the silence, Autumn shifted her gaze to Lucas.

His face held the faintly bored go-to-hell look she knew so well. "I don't think murder is always a waste." Again, his voice was casual, but Autumn, in tune with him, saw the change in his eyes. They weren't bored, but cold as ice. "The world would gain much by the elimination of some." He smiled, and it was deadly.

They no longer seemed to be speaking hypothetically. Shifting her gaze to Helen, Autumn saw the quick fear. *But it's just a game,* she told herself frantically and looked at Julia. The actress was smiling, but there was none of her summer warmth in it. She was enjoying watching Helen flutter like a moth on a pin. Noting Autumn's expression of dismayed shock, Julia changed the subject without a ripple.

After dinner, the group loitered in the lounge, but the storm, which continued unabated, was wearing on the nerves. Only Julia and Lucas seemed unaffected. Autumn noted how they huddled together in a corner, apparently enthralled with each other's company. Julia's laughter was low and rich over the sound of rain. Once, she watched Lucas pinch a strand of the pale hair between his fingers. Autumn turned away. Julia ran interference expertly, and the knowledge depressed her.

The Spicers, without Julia as a distraction, sat together on the sofa nearest the fire. Though their voices were low, Autumn sensed the strain of a domestic quarrel. She moved farther out of earshot. A bad time, she decided, for Jane to confront Robert on his fascination with Julia when the actress was giving another man the benefit of her attentions. When they left, Jane's face was no longer sullen, but simply miserable. Julia never glanced in their direction, but leaned closer to Lucas and murmured something in his ear that made him laugh. Autumn found she, too, wanted out of the room.

It has nothing to do with Lucas, she told herself as she moved down the hall. I just want to say good night to Aunt Tabby. Julia's doing precisely what I want her to—keeping Lucas entertained. He never even looked at me once Julia stepped in between. Shaking off the hurt, Autumn opened the door to her aunt's room.

"Autumn, dear! Lucas told me you bumped your head." Aunt Tabby stopped clucking over her laundry list and rose to peer at the bruise. "Oh, poor thing. Do you want some aspirin? I have some somewhere."

Though she appreciated Lucas's consideration in giving her aunt a watered-down version, Autumn wondered at the ease of their relationship. It didn't seem quite in character for Lucas McLean to bother overmuch with a vague old woman whose claim to fame was a small inn and a way with chocolate cake.

"No, Aunt Tabby, I'm fine. I've already taken something."

"That's good." She patted Autumn's hand and frowned briefly at the bruise. "You'll have to be more careful, dear."

"I will, Aunt Tabby..."—Autumn poked idly at the papers on her aunt's desk—"how well do you know Lucas? I don't recall you ever calling a roomer by his first name." She knew there was no use in beating around the bush with her aunt. It would produce the same results as reading *War and Peace* in dim light—a headache and confusion.

"Oh, now that depends, Autumn. Yes, that really does depend." Aunt Tabby gently removed her papers from Autumn's reach before she focused on a spot in the ceiling. Autumn knew this meant she was thinking. "There's Mrs. Nollington. She has a corner room every September. I call her Frances and she calls me Tabitha. Such a nice woman. A widow from North Carolina."

"Lucas calls you Aunt Tabby," Autumn pointed out before her aunt could get going on Frances Nollington.

"Yes, dear, quite a number of people do. You do."

"Yes, but—"

"And Paul and Will," Aunt Tabby continued blithely. "And the little boy who brings the eggs. And...oh, several people. Yes, indeed, several people. Did you enjoy your dinner?"

"Yes, very much. Aunt Tabby," Autumn continued, determined that tenacity would prevail. "Lucas seems very much at home here."

"Oh, I am glad!" She beamed at her niece as she took Autumn's hand and patted it. "I do try so hard to make everyone feel at home. It always seems a shame to have to make them pay, but..." She glanced down at her laundry bills and began to mutter.

Give up, Autumn told herself. She kissed her aunt's cheek and left her to her towels and pillowcases.

It was growing late when Autumn finished putting her darkroom back in order. She left the door open this time and kept all the lights on. The echo of rain followed her inside as it beat on the kitchen windows. Other than its angry murmur, the house was silent.

No, Autumn thought, old houses are never silent. They creak and whisper, but the groaning boards and settling didn't disturb her. She liked the humming quality of the silence. Absorbed and content, she emptied trays and replaced bottles. She threw her ruined film into the wastecan with a sigh.

That hurts a bit, she thought, but there's nothing to be done about it. Tomorrow, she decided, she'd develop the film she'd taken that morning—the lake, the early sun, the mirrored trees. It would put her in a better frame of mind. Stretching her back, she lifted her hair from her neck, feeling pleasantly tired.

"I remember you doing that in the mornings."

Autumn whirled, her hair flying out from her shoulders as quick fear brought her heart to her throat. Pushing strands from her face, she stared at Lucas.

He leaned against the open doorway, a cup of coffee in his hand. His eyes locked on hers without effort.

"You'd pull up your hair, then let it fall, tumbling down your back until I ached to get my hands on it." His voice was deep and strangely raw. Autumn couldn't speak at all. "I often wondered if you did it on purpose, just to drive me mad." As he studied her face, he frowned, then lifted the coffee to his lips. "But, of course you didn't. I've never known anyone else who could arouse with such innocence."

"What are you doing here?" The trembling in her voice took some of the power out of the demand.

"Remembering."

Turning, she began to juggle bottles, jumbling them out of their carefully organized state. "You always were clever with words, Lucas." Cooler now that she wasn't facing him, she meticulously studied a bottle of stop bath. "I suppose you have to be in your profession."

"I'm not writing at the moment."

It was easier to deliberately misunderstand him. "Your book still giving trouble?" Turning, Autumn again noticed the signs of strain and fatigue on his face. Sympathy and love flared up, and she struggled to bank them down. His eyes were much too keen. "You might have more success if you'd get a good night's sleep." She gestured toward the cup in his hands. "Coffee's not going to help."

"Perhaps not." He drained the cup. "But it's wiser than bourbon."

"Sleep's better than both." She shrugged her shoulders carelessly. Lucas's habits were no longer her concern. "I'm going up." Autumn walked toward him, but he stayed where he was, barring the door. She pulled up sharply. They were alone. The ground floor was empty but for them and the sound of rain.

"Lucas." She sighed sharply, wanting him to think her impatient rather than vulnerable. "I'm tired. Don't be troublesome."

His eyes smoldered at her tone. Though Autumn remained calm, she could feel her knees turning to water. The dull, throbbing ache was back in her head. When he moved aside, she switched off the lights, then brushed past him. Swiftly, he took her arm, preventing what she had thought was going to be an easy exit.

"There'll come a time, Cat," he murmured, "when you won't walk away so easily."

"Don't threaten me with your overactive masculinity." Her temper rose and she forgot caution. "I'm immune now."

She was jerked against him. All she could see was his fury. "I've had enough of this."

His mouth took hers roughly; she could taste the infuriated desire. When she struggled, he pinned her back against the wall, holding her arms to her sides and battering at her will with his mouth alone. She could feel herself going under and hating herself for it as much, she told herself, as she hated him. His lips didn't soften, even when her struggles ceased. He took and took as the anger vibrated between them.

Her heart was thudding wildly, and she could feel the mad pace of his as they pressed together. Passion was all-encompassing, and her back was to the wall. There's no escape, she thought dimly. There's never been any escape from him. No place to run. No place to hide. She began to tremble with fear and desire.

Abruptly he pulled away. His eyes were so dark, she saw nothing but her own reflection. I'm lost in him, she thought. I've always been lost in him. Then he was shaking her, shocking a gasp out of her.

"Watch how far you push," he told her roughly. "Damn it, you'd better remember I haven't any scruples. I know how to deal with people who pick fights with me." He stopped, but his fingers still dug into her skin. "I'll take you, Cat, take you kicking and screaming if you push me much further."

Too frightened by the rage she saw in his face to think of pride, she twisted away. She flew down the hall and up the stairs.

Chapter 6

Autumn reached her door, out of breath and fighting tears. He shouldn't be allowed to do this to her. She couldn't allow it. Why had he barged back into her life this way? Just when she was beginning to get over him. *Liar.* The voice was clear as crystal inside her head. You've never gotten over him. Never. But I will. She balled her hands into fists as she stood outside her door and caught her breath. I will get over him.

Hearing the sound of his footsteps on the stairs, she fumbled with the doorknob. She didn't want to deal with him again tonight. Tomorrow was soon enough.

Something was wrong. Autumn knew it the moment she opened her door and stumbled into the dark. The scent of perfume was so strong, her head whirled with it. She groped for the light and when it flashed on, she gave a small sound of despair.

The drawers and closet had been turned out and her clothes were tossed and scattered across the room. Some were ripped and torn, others merely lay in heaps. Her jewelry had been dumped from its box and tossed indiscriminately over the mounds of clothes. Bottles of cologne and powder had been emptied out and flung everywhere. Everything—every small object or personal possession—had been abused or destroyed.

She stood frozen in shock and disbelief. The wrong room,

she told herself dumbly. This had to be the wrong room. But the lawn print blouse with its sleeve torn at the shoulder had been a Christmas gift from Will. The sandals, flung into a corner and slashed, she had bought herself in a small shop off Fifth Avenue the summer before.

"No." She shook her head as if that would make it all go away. "It's not possible."

"Good God!" Lucas's voice came from behind her. Autumn turned to see him staring into her room.

"I don't understand." The words were foolish, but they were all she had. Slowly, Lucas shifted his attention to her face. She made a helpless gesture. "Why?"

He came to her, and with his thumb brushed a tear from her cheek. "I don't know, Cat. First we have to find out who."

"But it's—it's so spiteful." She wandered through the rubble of her things, still thinking she must be dreaming. "No one here would have any reason to do this to me. You'd have to hate someone to do this, wouldn't you? No one here has any reason to hate me. No one even knew me before last night."

"Except me."

"This isn't your style." She pressed her fingers to her temple and struggled to understand. "You'd find a more direct way of hurting me."

"Thanks."

Autumn looked over at him and frowned, hardly aware of what was being said. His expression was brooding as he studied her face. She turned away. She wasn't up to discussing Lucas McLean. Then she saw it.

"Oh, *no!*"

Scrambling on all fours, Autumn worked her way over the mangled clothes and began pushing at the tangled sheets of her bed. Her hands shook as she reached for her camera. The lens was shattered, with spiderweb cracks spreading over the surface. The back was broken, hanging drunkenly on one hinge. The film streamed out like the tail of a kite. Exposed.

Ruined. The mirror was crushed. With a moan, she cradled it in her hands and began to weep.

Her clothes and trinkets meant nothing, but the Nikon was more to her than a single-reflex camera. It was as much a part of her as her hands. With it, she had taken her first professional picture. Its mutilation was rape.

Her face was suddenly buried against a hard chest. She made no protest as Lucas's arms came around her, but wept bitterly. He said nothing, offered no comforting words, but his hands were unexpectedly gentle, his arms strong.

"Oh, Lucas." She drew away from him with a sigh. "It's so senseless."

"There's sense to it somewhere, Cat. There always is."

She looked back up at him. "Is there?" His eyes were keeping their secrets so she dropped her own back to her mangled camera. "Well, if someone wanted to hurt me, this was the right way."

Her fingers clenched on the camera. She was suddenly, fiercely angry; it pushed despair and tears out of her mind. Her body flooded with it. She wasn't going to sit and weep any longer. She was going to do something. Pushing her camera into Lucas's hands, Autumn scrambled to her feet.

"Wait a minute." He grabbed her hand before she could rush from the room. "Where are you going?"

"To drag everyone out of bed," she snapped at him, jerking her hand. "And then I'm going to break someone's neck."

He didn't have an easy time subduing her. Ultimately, he pinned her by wrapping his arms around her and holding her against him. "You probably could." There was a touch of surprised admiration in his tone, but it brought her no pleasure.

"Watch me," she challenged.

"Calm down first." He tightened his grip as she squirmed against him.

"I want—"

"I know what you want, Cat, and I don't blame you. But you have to think before you rush in."

"I don't have anything to think about," she tossed back. "Someone's going to pay for this."

"All right, fair enough. Who?"

His logic annoyed her, but succeeded in taking her temper from boil to simmer. "I don't know yet." With an effort, she managed to take a deep breath.

"That's better." He smiled and kissed her lightly. "Though your eyes are still lethal enough." He loosened his grip, but kept a hold on her arm. "Just keep your claws sheathed, Cat, until we find out what's going on. Let's go knock on a few doors."

Julia's room adjoined hers, so Autumn steered there first. Her rage was now packed in ice. Systematic, she told herself, aware of Lucas's grip. All right, we'll be systematic until we find out who did it. And then...

She knocked sharply on Julia's door. After the second knock, Julia answered with a soft, husky slur.

"Get up, Julia," Autumn demanded. "I want to talk to you."

"Autumn, darling." Her voice evoked a picture of Julia snuggling into her pillows. "Even I require beauty sleep. Go away like a good girl."

"Up, Julia," Autumn repeated, barely restraining herself from shouting. "Now."

"Goodness, aren't we grumpy. I'm the one who's being dragged from my bed."

She opened the door, a vision in a white lace negligee, her hair a tousled halo around her face, her eyes dark and heavy with sleep.

"Well, I'm up." Julia gave Lucas a slow, sensual smile and ran a hand through her hair. "Are we going to have a party?"

"Someone tore my room apart," Autumn stated bluntly. She watched Julia's attention switch from the silent flirtation with Lucas to her.

"What?" The catlike expression had melted into a frown of concentration. An actress, Autumn reminded herself. She's an actress and don't forget it.

"My clothes were pulled out and ripped, tossed around the room. My camera's broken." She swallowed on this. It was the most difficult to accept.

"That's crazy." Julia was no longer leaning provocatively against the door, but standing straight. "Let me see." She brushed past them and hurried down the hall. Stopping in the doorway of Autumn's room, she stared. Her eyes, when they turned back, were wide with shock. "Autumn, how awful!" She came back and slipped an arm around Autumn's waist. "How perfectly awful. I'm so sorry."

Sincerity, sympathy, shock. They were all there. Autumn wanted badly to believe them.

"Who would have done that?" she demanded of Lucas. Autumn saw that Julia's eyes were angry now. She was again the tough lady Autumn had glimpsed briefly that afternoon.

"We intend to find out. We're going to wake the others." Something passed between them. Autumn saw it flash briefly, then it was gone.

"All right," Julia said. "Then let's do it." She pushed her hair impatiently behind her ears. "I'll get the Spicers, you get Jacques and Steve. You," she continued to Autumn, "wake up Helen."

Her tone carried enough authority that Autumn found herself turning down the hall to Helen's room. She could hear the pounding, the answering stirs and murmurs from behind her. Reaching Helen's door, Autumn banged against it. This, at least, she thought, was progress. Lucas was right. We need a trial before we can hang someone.

Her knock went unanswered. Annoyed, Autumn rapped again. She wasn't in the mood to be ignored. Now there was more activity behind her as people came out of their rooms to stare at the disaster in hers.

"Helen!" She knocked again with fraying patience. "Come out here." She pushed the door open. It would give her some satisfaction to drag at least one person from bed. Ruthlessly, she switched on the light. "Helen, I—"

Helen wasn't in bed. Autumn stared at her, too shocked to feel horror. She was on the floor, but she wasn't sleeping. She was done with sleeping. Was that blood? Autumn thought in dumb fascination. She took a step forward before the reality struck her.

Horror gripped her throat, denying her the release of screaming. Slowly, she backed away. It was a nightmare. Starting with her room, it was all a nightmare. None of it was real. Lucas's careless voice played back in her head. *Murder.* Autumn shook her head as she backed into a wall. No, that was only a game. She heard a voice shouting in terror for Lucas, not even aware it was her own. Then blessedly, her hands came up to cover her eyes.

"Get her out of here." Lucas's rough command floated through Autumn's brain. She was trapped in a fog of dizziness. Arms came round her and led her from the room.

"Oh my God." Steve's voice was unsteady. When Autumn found the strength to look up at him, his face was ashen. She struggled against the faintness and buried her face in his chest. When was she going to wake up?

Confusion reigned around her. She heard disembodied voices as she drifted from horror to shock. There were Julia's smoky tones, Jane's gravelly voice and Jacques's rapid French-English mixture. Then Lucas's voice joined in—calm, cool, like a splash of cold water.

"She's dead. Stabbed. The phone's out so I'm going into the village to get the police."

"Murdered? She was murdered? Oh God!" Jane's voice rose, then became muffled. Raising her head, Autumn saw Jane being held tightly against her husband.

"I think, as a precaution, Lucas, no one should leave the inn alone." Robert took a deep breath as he cradled his wife. "We have to face the implications."

"I'll go with him." Steve's voice was strained and uneven. "I could use the fresh air."

With a curt nod, Lucas focused on Autumn. His eyes never left hers as he spoke to Robert. "Have you got something to put her out? She can double up with Julia tonight."

"I'm fine." Autumn managed to speak as she drew back from Steve's chest. "I don't want anything." It wasn't a dream, but real, and she had to face it. "Don't worry about me, it's not me. I'm all right." Hysteria was bubbling, and she bit down on her lip to cut it off.

"Come on, darling." Julia's arm replaced Steve's. "We'll go downstairs and sit down for a while. She'll be all right."

"I want—"

"I said she'll be all right," Julia cut off Lucas's protest sharply. "I'll see to her. Do what you have to do." Before he could speak again, she led Autumn down the staircase.

"Sit down," she ordered, nudging Autumn onto the sofa. "You could use a drink."

Looking up, Autumn saw Julia's face hovering over hers. "You're pale," she said stupidly before the brandy burned her throat and brought the world into focus with a jolt.

"I'm not surprised," Julia murmured and sank down on the low table in front of Autumn. "Better?" she asked when Autumn lifted the snifter again.

"Yes, I think so." She took a deep breath and focused on Julia's eyes. "It's really happening, isn't it? She's really lying up there."

"It's happening." Julia drained her own brandy. Color seeped gradually into her cheeks. "The bitch finally pushed someone too far."

Stunned by the hardness of Julia's voice, Autumn could only stare. Calmly, Julia set down her glass.

"Listen." Her tone softened, but her eyes were still cold. "You're a strong lady, Autumn. You've had a shock, a bad one, but you won't fall apart."

"No." Autumn tried to believe it, then said with more strength, "No, I won't fall apart."

"This is a mess, and you have to face it." Julia paused, then leaned closer. "One of us killed her."

Part of her had known it, but the rest had fought against the knowledge, blocking it out. Now that it had been said in cool, simple terms, there was no escape from it. Autumn nodded again and swallowed the remaining brandy in one gulp.

"She got what she deserved."

"Julia!" Jacques strode into the room. His face was covered with horror and disapproval.

"Oh, Jacques, thank God. Give me one of those horrible French cigarettes. Give one to Autumn, too. She could use it."

"Julia." He obeyed her automatically. "You musn't speak so now."

"I'm not a hypocrite." Julia drew deeply on the cigarette, shuddered, then drew again. "I detested her. The police will find out soon enough why we all detested her."

"*Nom de Dieu!* How can you speak so calmly of it?" Jacques exploded in a quick, passionate rage Autumn hadn't thought him capable of. "The woman is dead, murdered. You didn't see the cruelty of it. I wish to God I had not."

Autumn drew hard on her cigarette, trying to block out the picture that flashed back into her mind. She gasped and choked on the power of the smoke.

"Autumn, forgive me." Jacques's anger vanished as he sat down beside her and draped an arm over her shoulders. "I shouldn't have reminded you."

"No." She shook her head, then crushed out the cigarette. It wasn't going to help. "Julia's right. It has to be faced."

Robert entered, but his normally swinging stride was slow and dragging. "I gave Jane a sedative." With a sigh, he too made for the brandy. "It's going to be a long night."

The room grew silent. The rain, so much a part of the night, was no longer noticeable. Jacques paced the room, smoking continually while Robert kindled a fresh fire. The blaze, bright and crackling, brought no warmth. Autumn's skin remained chilled. In defense, she poured herself another brandy but found she couldn't drink it.

Julia remained seated. She smoked in long, slow puffs. The only outward sign of her agitation was the continual tapping of a pink-tipped nail against the arm of her chair. The tapping, the crackling, the hiss of rain, did nothing to diminish the overwhelming power of the silence.

When the front door opened with a click and a thud, all eyes flew toward the sound. Strings of tension tightened and threatened to snap. Autumn waited to see Lucas's face. It would be all right, somehow, as long as she could see his face.

"Couldn't get through the ford," he stated shortly as he came into the room. He peeled off a sopping jacket, then made for the community brandy.

"How bad is it?" Robert looked from Lucas to Steve, then back to Lucas. Already, the line of command had been formed.

"Bad enough to keep us here for a day or two," Lucas informed him. He swallowed a good dose of the brandy, then stared out the window. There was nothing to see but the reflection of the room behind him. "That's if the rain lets up by morning." Turning, he locked onto Autumn, making a long, thorough study. Again he had, in his way, pushed everyone from the room but the two of them.

"The phones," she blurted out, needing to say something, anything. "We could have phone service by tomorrow."

"Don't count on it." Lucas ran a hand through his dripping hair, showering the room with water. "According to the car radio, this little spring shower is the backlash of a tornado. The power's out all over this part of the state." He lit a cigarette with a shrug. "We'll just have to wait and see."

"Days." Steve flopped down beside Autumn, his face still gray. She gave him her unwanted brandy. "It could be days."

"Lovely." Rising, Julia went to Lucas. She plucked the cigarette from his fingers and drew on it. "Well." She stared at him. "What the hell do we do now?"

"First we lock and seal off Helen's room." Lucas lit another cigarette. His eyes stayed on Julia's. "Then we get some sleep."

Chapter 7

Sometime during the first murky light of dawn, Autumn did sleep. She'd passed the night lying wide-eyed, listening to the sound of Julia's gentle breathing beside her. Though she'd envied her ability to sleep, Autumn had fought off the drowsiness. If she closed her eyes, she might see what she'd seen when she opened Helen's door. When her eyes did close, however, the sleep was dreamless—the total oblivion of exhaustion.

It might have been the silence that woke her. Suddenly, she found herself awake and sitting straight up in bed. Confused, she stared around her.

Julia's disorder greeted her. Silk scarves and gold chains were draped here and there. Elegant bottles cluttered the bureau. Small, incredibly high Italian heels littered the floor. Memory returned.

With a sigh, Autumn rose, feeling a bit ridiculous in Julia's black silk nightgown; it neither suited nor fit. After seeing herself in the mirror, Autumn was glad Julia had already awakened and gone. She didn't want to wear any of the clothes that might have survived the attack on her room, and prepared to change back into yesterday's shirt and jeans.

A note lay on them. The elegant, sloping print could only have been Julia's:

Darling, help yourself to some undies and a blouse or sweater. I'm afraid my slacks won't fit you. You're built like a pencil. You don't wear a bra, and in any case, the idea of you filling one of mine is ridiculous.

J.

Autumn laughed, as Julia had intended. It felt so good, so normal, that she laughed again. Julia had known exactly how I'd feel, Autumn realized, and a wave of gratitude swept through her for the simple gesture. She showered, letting the water beat hot against her.

Coming back to the bedroom, Autumn pulled out a pair of cobwebby panties. There was a stack of them in misted pastels that she estimated would cost as much as a wide-angle lens. She tugged on one of Julia's sweaters, then pushed it up to her elbows—it was almost there in any case. Leaving the room, she kept her eyes firmly away from Helen's door.

"Autumn, I was hoping you'd sleep longer."

She paused at the foot of the stairs and waited for Steve to reach her. His face was sleep shadowed and older than it had been the day before. A fragment of his boyish smile touched his lips for her, but his eyes didn't join in.

"You don't look as if you got much," he commented and lifted a finger to her cheek.

"I doubt any of us did."

He draped an arm over her shoulder. "At least the rain's slowed down."

"Oh." Realization slowly seeped in and Autumn gave a weak laugh. "I knew there was something different. The quiet woke me. Where is…" She hesitated as Lucas's name trembled on her tongue. "Everyone?" she amended.

"In the lounge," he told her, but steered her toward the dining room. "Breakfast first. I haven't eaten myself, and you can't afford to drop any weight."

"How charming of you to remind me." She managed a friendly grimace. If he could make the effort to be normal, so could she. "Let's eat in the kitchen, though."

Aunt Tabby was there, as usual, giving instructions to a

much subdued Nancy. She turned as they entered, then enfolded Autumn in her soft, lavender-scented arms.

"Oh, Autumn, what a dreadful tragedy. I don't know what to make of it." Autumn squeezed her. Here was something solid to hold on to. "Lucas said someone killed the poor thing, but that doesn't seem possible, does it?" Drawing back, Aunt Tabby searched Autumn's face. "You didn't sleep well, dear. Only natural. Sit down and have your breakfast. It's the best thing to do."

Aunt Tabby could, Autumn mused, so surprisingly cut through to the quick when she needed to. She began to bustle around the room, murmuring to Nancy as Autumn and Steve sat at the small kitchen table.

There were simple, normal sounds and scents. Bacon, coffee, the quick sizzle of eggs. It was, Autumn had to agree, the best thing to do. The food, the routine, would bring some sense of order. And with the order, she'd be able to think clearly again.

Steve sat across from her, sipping coffee while she toyed with her eggs. She simply couldn't summon her usual appetite, and turned to conversation instead. The questions she asked Steve about himself were general and inane, but he picked up the effort and went with it. She realized, as she nibbled without interest on a piece of toast, that they were supporting each other.

Autumn discovered he was quite well traveled. He'd crisscrossed all over the country performing various tasks in his rôle as troubleshooter for his father's conglomerate. He treated wealth with the casual indifference of one who has always had it, but she sensed a knowledge and a dedication toward the company which had provided him with it. He spoke of his father with respect and admiration.

"He's sort of a symbol of success and ingenuity," Steve said, pushing his own half-eaten breakfast around his plate. "He worked his way up the proverbial ladder. He's tough." He grinned and shrugged. "He's earned it."

"How does he feel about you going into politics?"

"He's all for it." Steve glanced down at her plate and sent

her a meaningful look. Autumn only smiled and shook her head. "Anyway, he's always encouraged me to 'go for what I want and I better be good at it.'" He grinned again. "He's tough, but since I am good at it and intend to keep it that way, we'll both be satisfied. I like paperwork." He gestured with both hands. "Organizing. Refining the system from within the system."

"That can't be as easy as it sounds," Autumn commented, encouraging his enthusiasm.

"No, but—" He shook his head. "Don't get me started. I'll make a speech." He finished off his second cup of coffee. "I'll be making enough of those when I get back to California and my campaign officially starts."

"It just occurs to me that you, Lucas, Julia and Jacques are all from California." Autumn pushed her hair behind her back and considered the oddity. "It's strange that so many people from the coast would be here at one time."

"The Spicers, too," Aunt Tabby added from across the room, deeply involved in positioning pies in the oven. "Yes, I'm almost sure Dr. Spicer told me they were from California. So warm and sunny there. Well"—she patted the range as if to give it the confidence it needed to handle her pies—"I must see to the rooms now. I moved you next door to Lucas, Autumn. Such a terrible thing about your clothes. I'll have them cleaned for you."

"I'll help you, Aunt Tabby." Pushing away her plate, Autumn rose.

"Oh no, dear, the cleaners will do it."

Smiling wasn't as difficult as Autumn had thought. "I meant with the rooms."

"Oh..." Aunt Tabby trailed off and clucked her tongue. "I do appreciate it, Autumn, I really do, but..." She looked up with a touch of distress in her eyes. "I have my own system, you see. You'd just confuse me. It's all done with numbers."

Leaving Autumn to digest this, she gave her an apologetic touch on the cheek and bustled out.

There seemed nothing to do but join the others in the lounge.

The rain, though it was little more than a mist now, seemed to Autumn like prison bars. Standing at the window in the lounge, she wished desperately for sun. Conversation did not sparkle. When anyone spoke, it was around or over or under Helen Easterman. Perhaps it would have been better if they'd closeted themselves in their rooms, but human nature had them bound together.

Julia and Lucas sat on the sofa, speaking occasionally in undertones. Autumn found his eyes on her too often. Her defenses were too low to deal with what one of his probing looks could do to her, so she kept her back to him and watched the rain.

"I really think it's time we talked about this," Julia announced suddenly.

"Julia." Jacques's voice was both strained and weary.

"We can't go on like this," Julia stated practically. "We'll all go crazy. Steve's wearing out the floor, Robert's running out of wood to fetch and if you smoke another cigarette, you'll keel over." Contrarily, she lit another herself. "Unless we want to pretend that Helen stabbed herself, we've got to deal with the fact that one of us killed her."

Into the penetrating silence, Lucas's voice flowed, calm and detached. "I think we can rule out suicide." He watched as Autumn pressed her forehead to the glass. "And conveniently, we all had the opportunity to do it. Ruling out Autumn and her aunt, that leaves the six of us."

Autumn turned from the window and found every eye in the room on her. "Why should I be ruled out?" She shuddered and lifted her arms to hug herself. "You said we all had the opportunity."

"Motive, Cat," he said simply. "You're the only one in the room without a motive."

"Motive?" It was becoming too much like one of his screenplays. She needed to cling to reality. "What possible motive could any of us have had?"

"Blackmail." Lucas lit a cigarette as she gaped at him.

"Helen was a professional leech. She thought she had quite a little goldmine in the six of us." He glanced up and caught Autumn with one of his looks. "She miscalculated."

"Blackmail." Autumn could only mumble the word as she stared at him. "You're—you're making this up. This is just one of your scenarios."

He waited a beat, his eyes locked on hers. "No."

"How do you know so much?" Steve demanded. Slowly, Lucas's eyes swerved from Autumn. "If she were blackmailing you, it doesn't necessarily follow that she was blackmailing all of us."

"How clever of you, Lucas," Julia interjected, running a hand down his arm, then letting it rest on his. "I had no idea she was sticking her fangs in anyone other than the three of us." Glancing at Jacques, she gave him a careless shrug. "It seems we're in good company."

Autumn made a small sound, and Julia's attention drifted over to her. Her expression was both sympathetic and amused. "Don't look so shocked, darling. Most of us have things we don't particularly want made public. I might have paid her off if she'd threatened me with something more interesting." Leaning back, she pouted effectively. "An affair with a married senator..." She sent a lightning smile to Autumn. "I believe I mentioned him before. That hardly had me quaking in my shoes at the thought of exposure. I'm not squeamish about my indiscretions. I told her to go to hell. Of course," she added, smiling slowly, "there's only my word for that, isn't there?"

"Julia, don't make jokes." Jacques lifted a hand to rub his eyes.

"I'm sorry." Julia rose to perch on the arm of his chair. Her hand slipped to his shoulder.

"This is crazy." Unable to comprehend what was happening, Autumn searched the faces that surrounded her. They were strangers again, holding secrets. "What are you all doing here? Why did you come?"

"It's very simple." Lucas rose and crossed over to her, but unlike Julia, he didn't touch to comfort. "I made plans to come here for my own reasons. Helen found out. She was very good at finding things out—too good. She learned that Julia and Jacques were to join me.'' He turned, half blocking Autumn from the rest with his body. Was it protection, she wondered, or defense? ''She must have contacted the rest of you, and made arrangements to have all her…clients here at once.''

''You seem to know quite a bit,'' Robert muttered. He poked unnecessarily at the fire.

''It isn't difficult to figure out,'' Lucas returned. ''I knew she was holding nasty little threats over three of us; we'd discussed it. When I noticed her attention to Anderson, and you and your wife, I knew she was sucking elsewhere, too.''

Jane began to cry in dry, harsh sobs that racked her body. Instinctively, Autumn moved past Lucas to offer comfort. Before she was halfway across the room, Jane stopped her with a look that was like a fist to the jaw.

''You could have done it just as easily as anyone else. You've been spying on us, taking that camera everywhere.'' Jane's voice rose dramatically as Autumn froze. ''You were working for her, you could have done it. You can't prove you didn't. I was with Robert.'' There was nothing bland or dull about her now. Her eyes were wild. ''I was with Robert. He'll tell you.''

Robert's arm came around her. His voice was quiet and soothing as she sobbed against his chest. Autumn didn't move. There seemed no place to go.

''She was going to tell you I was gambling again, tell you about all the money I'd lost.'' She clung to him, a sad sight in a dirt-brown dress. Robert continued to murmur and stroke her hair. ''But I told you last night, I told you myself. I couldn't pay her anymore, and I told you. I didn't kill her, Robert. Tell them I didn't kill her.''

''Of course you didn't, Jane. Everyone knows that. Come with me now, you're tired. We'll go upstairs.''

He was leading her across the room as he spoke. His eyes met Autumn's half in apology, half in a plea for understanding. She saw, quite suddenly, that he loved his wife very much.

Autumn turned away, humiliated for Jane, sorry for Robert. The faint trembling in her hands indicated she'd been dealt one more shock. When Steve's arm came around her, she turned into it and drew the comfort offered.

"I think we could all use a drink," Julia announced. Moving to the bar, she poured a hefty glass of sherry, then took it to Autumn. "You first," she ordered, pressing the glass into her hand. "Autumn seems to be getting the worst of this. Hardly seems fair, does it, Lucas?" Her eyes lifted to his and held briefly before she turned back to the bar. He made no answer. "She's probably the only one of us here who's even remotely sorry that Helen's dead."

Autumn drank, wishing the liquor would soften the words.

"She was a vulture," Jacques murmured. Autumn saw the message pass between him and Julia. "But even a vulture doesn't deserve to be murdered." Leaning back, he accepted the glass Julia brought him. He clasped her hand as she once again sat on the arm of his chair.

"Perhaps my motive is the strongest," Jacques said and drank once, deeply. "When the police come, all will be opened and studied. Like something under a microscope." He looked at Autumn, as if to direct his explanation to her. "She threatened the happiness of the two things most important to me—the woman I love and my children." Autumn's eyes skipped quickly to Julia's. "The information she had on my relationship with this woman could have damaged my suit for custody. The beauty of that love meant nothing to Helen. She would turn it into something sordid and ugly."

Autumn cradled her drink in both hands. She wanted to tell Jacques to stop, that she didn't want to hear, didn't want to be involved. But it was too late. She was already involved.

"I was furious when she arrived here with her smug smile and evil eyes." He looked down into his glass. "There were times, many times, I wanted my hands around her throat, wanted to bruise her face as someone else had done."

"Yes, I wonder who." Julia caught her bottom lip between

her teeth in thought. "Whoever did that was angry, perhaps angry enough to kill." Her eyes swept up, across Steve and Autumn and Lucas.

"You were at the inn that morning," Autumn stated. Her voice sounded odd, thready, and she swallowed.

"So I was." Julia smiled at her. "Or so I said. Being alone in bed is hardly an airtight alibi. No..." She leaned back on the wing of the chair. "I think the police will want to know who socked Helen. You came in with her, Autumn. Did you see anyone?"

"No." Her eyes flew instantly to Lucas. His were dark, already locked on her face. There were warning signals of anger and impatience she could read too easily. She dropped her gaze to her drink. "No, I..." How could she say it? How could she think it?

"Autumn's had enough for a while." Steve tightened his arm protectively around her. "Our problems don't concern her. She doesn't deserve to be in the middle."

"Poor child." Jacques studied her pale, strained face. "You've walked into a viper's nest, *oui?* Go sleep, forget us for a while."

"Come on, Autumn, I'll take you up." Steve slipped the glass from her hand and set it on the table. With one final glance at Lucas, Autumn went with him.

Chapter 8

They didn't speak as they mounted the steps. Autumn was too busy trying to force the numbness from her brain. She hadn't been able to fully absorb everything she'd been told. Steve hurried her by Helen's door before stopping at the one beside Lucas's.

"Is this the room your aunt meant?"

"Yes." She lifted both hands to her hair, pushing its weight away from her face. "Steve." She searched his face and found herself faltering. "Is all this true? Everything Lucas said? Was Helen really blackmailing all of you?" She noted the discomfort in his eyes and shook her head. "I don't mean to pry, but—"

"No," he cut her off, then let out a long breath. "No, it's hardly prying at this point. You're not involved, but you're caught, aren't you?"

The word was so apt, so close to her own thinking, that she nearly laughed. Caught. Yes, that was it exactly.

"It seems McLean is right on target. Helen had information concerning a deal I made for the company—perfectly within the circle of the law, but…" He gave a rueful smile and lifted his shoulders. "Maybe not quite as perfectly as it should have been. There was an ethical question, and it wouldn't look so good on paper. The technicalities are too complicated to explain, but the gist of it is I didn't want any shadows on my career. These days, when you're heading into politics, you have to cover all the angles.''

"Angles," Autumn repeated and pressed her fingers to her temple. "Yes, I suppose you do."

"She threatened me, Autumn, and I didn't care for it—but it wasn't enough to provoke murder." He drew a quick breath and shook his head. "But that doesn't help much, does it? None of us are likely to admit it."

"I appreciate you telling me anyway," Autumn said. Steve's eyes were gentle on her face, but the lines and strain of tension still showed. "It can't be pleasant for you to have to explain."

"I'll have to explain to the police before long," he said grimly, then noted her expression. "I don't mind telling you, Autumn, if you feel better knowing. Julia's right." His fingers strayed absently to her hair. "It's much healthier to get it out in the open. But you've had enough for now." He smiled at her, then realized his hands were in her hair. "I suppose you're used to this. Your hair's not easy to resist. I've wanted to touch it since the first time I saw it. Do you mind?"

"No." She wasn't surprised to find herself in his arms, his mouth on hers. It was an easy kiss, one that comforted rather than stirred. Autumn relaxed with it, and gave back what she could.

"You'll get some rest?" Steve murmured, holding her to his chest a moment.

"Yes. Yes, I will. Thank you." She pulled back to look up at him, but her eyes were drawn past him. Lucas stood at the doorway of his room, watching them both. Without speaking, he disappeared inside.

When she was alone, Autumn lay down on the white heirloom bedspread, but sleep wouldn't come. Her mind ached with fatigue. Her body was numb from it, but sleep, like a spiteful lover, stayed away. Time drifted as her thoughts ran over each member of the group.

She could feel nothing but sympathy for Jacques and the Spicers. She remembered the Frenchman's eyes when he spoke of his children and could still see Robert protecting his wife as she sobbed. Julia, on the other hand, needed no sympathy. Autumn felt certain the actress could take care of herself; she'd need no supporting arm or soothing words. Steve had also seemed more annoyed than upset by Helen's threats. He, too, could handle himself, she felt. There was a streak of street sense under the California gloss; he didn't need Autumn to worry for him.

Lucas was a different matter. Though he had nudged admissions from the rest of them, whatever threat Helen had held over him was still his secret. He had seemed very cool, very composed when he'd spoken of blackmail—but Autumn knew him. He was fully capable of concealing his emotions when there was a purpose to it. He was a hard man. Who knew better than she?

Cruel? Yes, she mused. Lucas could be cruel. She still had the scars attesting to it. But murder? No. Autumn couldn't picture Lucas plunging something sharp into Helen Easterman. Scissors, she remembered, though she tried hard not to. The scissors that had lain on the floor beside Helen. No, she couldn't believe him capable of that. She wouldn't believe him capable of it.

Neither could she rationally believe it of any of the others. Could they all conceal such hate, such ugliness behind their shocked faces and shadowed eyes?

But, of course, one of them was the killer.

Autumn blanked it from her mind. She couldn't think of it anymore. Not just then. Steve's prescription was valid—she needed to rest. Yet she rose and walked to the window to stare out at the slow, hateful rain.

The knock at her door vibrated like an explosion. Whirling, she wrapped her arms protectively around her body. Her heart pounded while her throat dried up with fear. Stop it! she ordered herself. No one has any cause to hurt you.

"Yes, come in." The calmness of her own voice brought her relief. She was hanging on.

Robert entered. He looked so horribly weary and stricken,

Autumn automatically reached out to him. She thought no more of fear. He clasped her hands and squeezed once, hard.

"You need food," he stated as he searched her face. "It shows in the face first."

"Yes, I know. My delicate hollows become craters very quickly." She made her own search. "You could use some yourself."

He sighed. "I believe you're one of those rare creatures who is inherently kind. I apologize for my wife."

"No, don't." His sigh had been long and broken. "She didn't mean it. We're all upset. This is a nightmare."

"She's been under a lot of strain. Before..." He broke off and shook his head. "She's sleeping now. Your head"—he brushed the hair from her forehead to examine the colorful bruise—"is it giving you any trouble?"

"No, none. I'm fine." The mishap seemed like some ridiculous comic relief in the midst of a melodrama now. "Can I help you, Robert?"

His eyes met hers, once, desperately, then moved away. "That woman put Jane through hell. If I'd just known, I would have put a stop to it long ago." Anger overpowered his weariness and he turned to prowl the room. "She tormented her, drained every drop of money Jane could raise. She played on a sickness, encouraging Jane to gamble to meet the payments. I knew nothing about it! I should have. Yesterday, Jane told me herself and I was going to enjoy dealing with the Easterman woman this morning." Autumn saw the soft, gentle hands clench into fists. "God help me, that's the only reason I'm sorry she's dead."

"Robert..." She wasn't certain what to say, how to deal with this side of his character. "Anyone would feel the same way," she said carefully. "She was an evil woman. She hurt someone you love." Autumn watched the fingers in his left hand relax, one at a time. "It isn't kind, but none of us will mourn her. Perhaps no one will. I think that's very sad."

He turned back and focused on her again. After a moment, he seemed to pull himself back under control. "I'm sorry you're caught up in this." With the anger gone from his eyes, they were vulnerable. "I'm going to go check on Jane. Will you be all right?"

"Yes."

She watched him go, then sank down into a chair. Each different crisis drained her. If possible, she was wearier now than before. When did the madness start? Only a few days ago she'd been safe in her apartment in Manhattan. She'd never met any of these people who were tugging at her now. Except one.

Even as she thought of him, Lucas strode in through the door. He stalked over to her, stared down and frowned.

"You need to eat," he said abruptly. Autumn thought of how tired she was of hearing that diagnosis. "I've been watching the pounds drop off you all day. You're already too thin."

"I adore flattery." His arrogant entrance and words boosted her flagging energy. She didn't have to take abuse from Lucas McLean anymore. "Don't you know how to knock?"

"I've always appreciated the understatedness of your body, Cat. You remember." He pulled her to her feet, then molded her against him. Her eyes flashed with quick temper. "Anderson seems to have discovered the charm as well. Did it occur to you that you might have been kissing a murderer?"

He spoke softly while his hand caressed her back. His eyes were mocking her. Her temper snapped at the strain of fighting her need for him.

"One might be holding me now."

He tightened his fingers on her hair so that she cried out in surprise. The mockery was replaced by a burning, terrifying rage. "You'd like to believe that, wouldn't you? You'd like to see me languishing in prison or, better yet, dangling from the end of a rope." She would have shaken her head, but his grip on her hair made movement impossible. "Would that be suitable punishment for my rejecting you, Cat? How deep is the hate? Deep enough to pull the lever yourself?"

"No, Lucas. Please, I didn't mean—"

"The hell you didn't." He cut off her protest. "The thought of me with blood on my hands comes easily to you. You can cast me in the role of murderer, can't you? Standing over Helen with the scissors in my hand.''

"No!" In defense, she closed her eyes. "Stop it! Please stop it." He was hurting her now, but not with his hands. The words cut deeper.

He lowered his voice in a swift change of mood. Ice ran down Autumn's back. "I could have used my hands and been more tidy." A strong, lean-fingered hand closed around her throat. Her eyes flew open.

"Lucas—"

"Very simple and no mess," he went on, watching her eyes widen. "Quick enough, too, if you know what to do. More my style. More—as you put it—direct. Isn't that right?"

"You're only doing this to frighten me." Her breath was trembling in and out of her lungs. It was as if he were forcing her to think the worst of him, wanting her to think him capable of something monstrous. She'd never seen him like this. His eyes were black with fury while his voice was cold, so cold. She shivered. "I want you to leave, Lucas. Leave right now."

"Leave?" He slid his hand from her throat to the back of her neck. "I don't think so, Cat." His face inched closer. "If I'm going to hang for murder, I'd best take what consolation I can while I have the chance."

His mouth closed fast over hers. She struggled against him, more frightened than she'd been when she'd turned on the light in Helen's room. She could only moan; movement was impossible when he held her this close. He slipped a hand under her sweater to claim her breast with the swift expertise of experience. Heart thudded madly against heart.

"How can anyone so skinny be so soft?" he murmured against her mouth. The words he'd spoken so often in the past brought more agony than she could bear. The hunger from him was thunderous; he was like a man who had finally broken free of his tether. "My God, how I want you." The words were torn from him as he ravaged her neck. "I'll be damned if I'll wait any longer."

They sank onto the bed. With all the strength that remained, she flailed out against him. Pinning her arms to her sides,

Lucas stared down at her with a wild kind of fury. "Bite and scratch all you want, Cat. I've reached my limit."

"I'll scream, Lucas." The words shuddered out of her. "If you touch me again, I'll scream."

"No, you won't."

His mouth was on hers, proving him right and her wrong. His body molded to hers with bittersweet accuracy. She arched once in defense, in desperation, but his hands were roaming, finding all the secret places he'd discovered over three years before. There was no resisting him. The wild, reckless demand that had always flavored his lovemaking left her weak. He knew too much of her. Autumn knew, before his fingers reached the snap of her jeans, that she couldn't prevent her struggles from becoming demands. When his mouth left hers to roam her neck, she didn't scream, but moaned with the need he had always incited in her.

He was going to win again, and she would do nothing to stop him. Tears welled, then spilled from her eyes as she knew he'd soon discover her pitiful, abiding love. Even her pride, it seemed, again belonged to him.

Lucas stopped abruptly. All movement ceased when he drew back his head to stare down at her. She thought, through her blurred vision, that she saw some flash of pain cross his face before it became still and emotionless. Lifting a hand, he caught a teardrop on his fingertip. With a swift oath, he lifted his weight from her.

"No, I won't be responsible for this again." Turning, he stalked to the window and stared out.

Sitting up, Autumn lowered her face to her knees and fought against the tears. She'd promised herself he'd never see her cry again. Not over him. Never over him. The silence stretched on for what seemed an eternity.

"I won't touch you like this again," he said quietly. "You have my word, for what it's worth."

Autumn thought she heard him sigh, long and deep, before his footsteps crossed to her. She didn't look up, but only squeezed her eyes closed.

"Autumn, I...oh, sweet God." He touched her arm, but she only curled herself tighter into a ball in defense.

The room fell silent again. The dripping rain seemed to echo into it. When Lucas spoke again, his voice was harsh and strained. "When you've rested, get something to eat. I'll have your aunt send up a tray if you're not down for dinner. I'll see that no one disturbs you."

She heard him leave, heard the quiet click of her door. Alone, she kept curled in her ball as she lay down. Ultimately, the storm of tears induced sleep.

Chapter 9

It was dark when Autumn awoke, but she was not refreshed. The sleep had been only a temporary relief. Nothing had changed while she had slept. But no, she thought as she glanced around the room. She was wrong. Something had changed. It was quiet. Really quiet. Rising, she walked to the window. She could see the moon and a light scattering of stars. The rain had stopped.

In the dim light, she moved to the bathroom and washed her face. She wasn't certain she had the courage to look in the mirror. She let the cold cloth rest against her eyes for a long time, hoping the swelling wasn't as bad as it felt. She felt something else as well. Hunger. It was a healthy sign, she decided. A normal sign. The rain had stopped and the nightmare was going to end. And now she was going to eat.

Her bare feet didn't disturb the silence that hung over the inn. She was glad of it. She wanted food now, not company. But when she passed the lounge, she heard the murmur of voices. She wasn't alone after all. Julia and Jacques were silhouetted by the window. Their conversation was low and urgent. Before she could melt back into the shadows, Julia turned and spotted her. The conversation ceased abruptly.

"Oh, Autumn, you've surfaced. We thought we'd seen the last of you until morning." She glided to her, then slipped a friendly arm around her waist. "Lucas wanted to send up a tray, but Robert outranked him. Doctor's orders were to let you sleep until you woke up. You must be famished. Let's see what your Aunt Tabby left for you."

Julia was doing all the talking, and quite purposefully leading Autumn away. A glance showed her that Jacques was still standing by the window, unmoving. Autumn let it go, too hungry to object.

"Sit down, darling," Julia ordered as she steered Autumn into the kitchen. "I'm going to fix you a feast."

"Julia, you don't have to fix me anything. I appreciate it, but—"

"Now let me play mother," Julia interrupted, pressing down on Autumn's shoulder until she sat. "You're past the sticky-finger stage, so I really quite enjoy it."

Sitting back, Autumn managed a smile. "You're not going to tell me you can cook."

Julia aimed an arched glance. "I don't suppose you should eat anything too heavy at this time of night," she said mildly. "There's some marvelous soup left from dinner, and I'll fix you my specialty. A cheese omelette."

Autumn decided that watching Julia Bond bustle around a kitchen was worth the market price of an ounce of gold. She seemed competent enough and kept up a bouncy conversation that took no brainpower to follow. With a flourish, she plopped a glass of milk in front of Autumn.

"I'm not really very fond of milk," Autumn began and glanced toward the coffeepot.

"Now, drink up," Julia instructed. "You need roses in your cheeks. You look terrible."

"Thanks."

Steaming chicken soup joined the milk, and Autumn attacked it with singleminded intensity. Some of the weakness drained from her limbs.

"Good girl," Julia approved as she dished up the omelette. "You look nearly human again."

Glancing over, Autumn smiled. "Julia, you're marvelous."

"Yes, I know. I was born that way." She sipped coffee

and watched Autumn start on the eggs. "I'm glad you were able to rest. This day has been a century."

For the first time, Autumn noticed the mauve shadows under the blue eyes and felt a tug of guilt. "I'm sorry. You should be in bed, not waiting on me."

"Lord, but you're sweet." Julia pulled out a cigarette. "I haven't any desire to go up to my room until exhaustion takes over. I'm quite selfishly prepared to keep you with me until it does. Actually, Autumn," she added, watching through a mist of smoke, "I wonder if it's very wise for you to be wandering about on your own."

"What?" Autumn looked up again and frowned. "What do you mean?"

"It was your room that was broken into," Julia pointed out.

"Yes, but..." She was surprised to realize she'd almost overlooked the ransacking of her room with everything else that had happened. "It must have been Helen," she ventured.

"Oh, I doubt that," Julia returned and continued to sip contemplatively. "I very much doubt that. If Helen had broken into your room, it would have been to look for something she could use on you. She'd have been tidy. We've given this some thought."

"We?"

"Well, I've given it some thought," Julia amended smoothly. "I think whoever tore up your things was looking for something, then covered the search with overdone destruction."

"Looking for what?" Autumn demanded. "I don't have anything anyone here could be interested in."

"Don't you?" Julia ran the tip of her tongue over her teeth. "I've been thinking about what happened in your darkroom."

"You mean when the power went off?" Autumn shook her head and touched the bruise on her forehead. "I walked into the door."

"Did you?" Julia sat back and studied the harsh ceiling light. "I wonder. Lucas told me that you said you heard someone rattling at the knob and walked over. What if..." She brought her eyes back to Autumn's. "What if someone swung the door open and hit you with it?"

"It was locked," Autumn insisted, then remembered that it had been open when Lucas found her.

"There are keys, darling." She watched Autumn's face closely. "What are you thinking?"

"The door was open when Lucas—" She cut herself off and shook her head. "No, Julia, it's ridiculous. Why would anyone want to do that to me?"

Julia lifted a brow. "Interesting question. What about your ruined film?"

"The film?" Autumn felt herself being pulled in deeper. "It must have been an accident."

"You didn't spoil it, Autumn, you're too competent." She waited while Autumn spread her hands on the table and looked down at them. "I've watched you. Your movements are very fluid, very assured. And you're a professional. You wouldn't botch up a roll of film without being aware of it."

"No," Autumn agreed and looked back up. Her eyes were steady again. "What are you trying to tell me?"

"What if someone's worried that you took a picture they don't want developed? The film in your room was ruined, too."

"I can follow your logic that far, Julia." Autumn pushed aside the remaining omelette. "But then it's a dead end. I haven't taken any pictures anyone could worry about. I was shooting scenery. Trees, animals, the lake."

"Maybe someone isn't certain about that." She crushed out her cigarette in a quick motion and leaned forward. "Whoever is worried enough about a picture to risk destroying your room and knocking you unconscious is dangerous. Dangerous enough to murder. Dangerous enough to hurt you again if necessary."

Staring back, Autumn controlled a tremor. "Jane? Jane accused me of spying, but she couldn't—"

"Oh yes, she could." Julia's voice was hard again, and definite. "Face it, Autumn, anyone pushed hard enough is capable of murder. Anyone."

Autumn's thoughts flicked back to Lucas and the look on his face when he had slipped his hand around her throat.

"Jane was desperate," Julia continued. "She claims to have made a full confession to Robert, but what proof is there? Or Robert, furious at what Helen had put his wife through, could have done it himself. He loves Jane quite a lot."

"Yes, I know." The sudden, sweeping anger in Robert's eyes flashed through her mind.

"Or there's Steve." Julia's finger began to tap on the table. "He tells me that Helen found out about some unwise deal he put through, something potentially damaging to his political career. He's very ambitious."

"But, Julia—"

"Then there's Lucas." Julia went on as if Autumn hadn't spoken. "There's a matter of a delicate divorce suit. Helen held information she claimed would interest a certain estranged husband." She lit another cigarette and let the smile float up and away. "Lucas is known for his temper. He's a very physical man."

Autumn met the look steadily. "Lucas is a lot of things, not all of them admirable, but he wouldn't kill."

Julia smiled and said nothing as she brought the cigarette to her lips. "Then there's me." The smile widened. "Of course, I claim I didn't care about Helen's threats, but I'm an actress. A good one. I've got an Oscar to prove it. Like Lucas, my temper is no secret. I could give you a list of directors who would tell you I'm capable of anything." Idly she tapped her cigarette in the ashtray. "But then, if I had killed her, I would have set the scene differently. I would have discovered the body myself, screamed, then fainted magnificently. As it was, you stole the show."

"That's not funny, Julia."

"No," she agreed and rubbed her temple. "It's not. But the fact remains that I could have killed Helen, and you're far too trusting."

"If you'd killed her," Autumn countered, "why would you warn me?"

"Bluff and double bluff," Julia answered with a new smile that made Autumn's skin crawl. "Don't trust anyone, not even me."

Autumn wasn't going to let Julia frighten her, though she seemed determined to do so. She kept her eyes level. "You haven't included Jacques."

To Autumn's surprise, Julia's eyes flickered, then dropped. The smooth, tapering fingers crushed out her cigarette with enough force to break the filter. "No, I haven't. I suppose he must be viewed through your eyes like the rest of us, but I know..." She looked up again, and Autumn saw the vulnerability. "I know he isn't capable of hurting anyone."

"You're in love with him."

Julia smiled, quite beautifully. "I love Jacques very much, but not the way you mean." She rose then and, getting another cup, poured them both coffee. "I've known Jacques for ten years. He's the only person in the world I care about more than myself. We're friends, real friends, probably because we've never been lovers."

Autumn drank the coffee black. She wanted the kick of it. *She'd protect him,* she thought. *She'd protect him any way she could.*

"I have a weakness for men," Julia continued, "and I indulge it. With Jacques, the time or place was never right. Ultimately, the friendship was too important to risk messing it up in the bedroom. He's a good, gentle man. The biggest mistake he ever made was in marrying Claudette."

Julia's voice hardened. Her nails began to tap on the table again, quicker than before. "She did her best to eat him alive. For a long time, he tried to keep the marriage together for the children. It simply wasn't possible. I won't go into details; they'd shock you." Tilting her head, Julia gave Autumn a smile that put her squarely into adolescence. "And, in any case, it's Jacques's miserable secret. He didn't divorce her, on the numerous grounds he could have, but allowed her to file."

"And Claudette got the children."

"That's right. It nearly killed him when she was awarded

custody. He adores them. And, I must admit, they are rather sweet little monsters.'' The nails stopped tapping as she reached for her coffee. ''Anyway, skipping over this and that, Jacques filed a custody suit about a year ago. He met someone shortly after. I can't tell you her name—you'd recognize it, and I have Jacques's confidence. But I can tell you she's perfect for him. Then Helen crawled her slimy way in.''

Autumn shook her head. ''Why don't they just get married?''

Julia leaned back with an amused sigh. ''If life were only so simple. Jacques is free, but his lady won't be for another few months. They want nothing more than to marry, bring Jacques's little monsters to America and raise as many more as possible. They're crazy about each other.''

Julia sipped her cooling coffee. ''They can't live together openly until the custody thing is resolved so they rented this little place in the country. Helen found out. You can figure out the rest. Jacques paid her, for his children and because his lady's divorce isn't as cut-and-dried as it might be, but when Helen turned up here, he'd reached his limit. They argued about it one night in the lounge. He told her she wouldn't get another cent. I'm sure, no matter how much Jacques had already paid her, Helen would still have turned her information over to Claudette—for a price.''

Autumn stared at her, unable to speak. She had never seen Julia look so cold. She saw the ruthlessness cover the exquisite face. Julia looked over, then laughed with genuine amusement.

''Oh, Autumn, you're like an open book!'' The hard mask had melted away, leaving her warm and lovely again. ''Now you're thinking I could have murdered Helen after all. Not for myself, but for Jacques.''

Autumn fell into a fitful sleep sometime after dawn. This was no deep, empty sleep brought on by medication or exhaustion, but was confused and dream riddled.

At first, there were only vague shadows and murmured voices floating through her mind, taunting her to try to see and hear more clearly. She fought to focus on them. Shadows moved, shapes began to sharpen, then became fuzzy and disordered again. She pitted all her determination against them, wanting more than hints and whispers. Abruptly, the shadows evaporated. The voices grew to a roar in her ears.

Wild-eyed, Jane crushed Autumn's camera underfoot. She screamed, pointing a pair of scissors to keep Autumn at bay. "Spy!" she shouted as the cracking of the camera's glass echoed like gunfire. "Spy!"

Wanting to escape the madness and accusations, Autumn turned. Colors whirled around her, then there was Robert.

"She tormented my wife." His arm held Autumn firmly, then slowly tightened, cutting off her breath. "You need some food," he said softly. "It shows in the face first." He was smiling, but the smile was a travesty. Breaking away, Autumn found herself in the corridor.

Jacques came toward her. There was blood on his hands. His eyes were sad and terrifying as he held them out to her. "My children." There was a tremor in his voice as he gestured to her. Turning, she fell into Steve.

"Politics," he said with a bright, boyish smile. "Nothing personal, just politics." Taking her hair, he wrapped it around her throat. "You got caught in the middle, Autumn." The smile turned into a leer as he tightened the noose. "Too bad."

Pushing away, she fell through a door. Julia's back was to her. She wore the lovely, white lace negligee. "Julia!" In the dream, the urgency in Autumn's voice came at a snail's pace. "Julia, help me."

When Julia turned, the slow, cat smile was on her face and the lace was splattered with scarlet. "Bluff and double bluff, darling." Throwing back her head, she laughed her smoky laugh. With the sound still spinning in her head, Autumn pressed her hands to her ears and ran.

"Come back to mother!" Julia called, still laughing as Autumn stumbled into the corridor.

There was a door blocking her path. Throwing it open, Autumn dashed inside. She knew only a desperate need for escape. But it was Helen's room. Terrified, Autumn turned, only to find the door closed behind her. She battered on it, but the sound was dull and flat. Fear was raw now, a primitive fear of the dead. She couldn't stay there. Wouldn't stay. She turned, thinking to escape through the window.

It wasn't Helen's room, but her own. There were bars at the windows, gray liquid bars of rain, but when she ran to them, they solidified, holding her in. She pulled and tugged, but they were cold and unyielding in her hands. Suddenly, Lucas was behind her, drawing her away. He laughed as he turned her into his arms.

"Bite and scratch all you want, Cat."

"Lucas, please!" There was hysteria in her voice that even the dream couldn't muffle. "I love you. I love you. Help me get out. Help me get away!"

"Too late, Cat." His eyes were dark and fierce and amused. "I warned you not to push me too far."

"No, Lucas, not you." She clung to him. He was kissing her hard, passionately. "I love you. I've always loved you." She surrendered to his arms, to his mouth. Here was her escape, her safety.

Then she saw the scissors in his hand.

Chapter 10

Autumn sat straight up in bed. The film of cold sweat had her shivering. During the nightmare, she had kicked off the sheets and blankets and lay now with only a damp nightgown for cover. Needing the warmth, she pulled the tangled blanket around her and huddled into it.

Only a dream, she told herself, waiting for the clarity of it to fade. It was only a dream. It was natural enough after the late-night conversation with Julia. Dreams couldn't hurt you. Autumn wanted to hang on to that.

It was morning. She trembled still as she watched the sunlight pour into her window. No bars. That was over now, just as the night was over. The phones would soon be repaired. The water in the ford would go down. The police would come. Autumn sat, cocooned by the blanket, and waited for her breathing to even.

By the end of the day, or tomorrow at the latest, everything would be organized and official. Questions would be answered, notes would be taken, the wheels of investigation would start to turn, settling everything into facts and reality. Slowly her muscles began to relax and she loosened her desperate grip on the blanket.

Julia's imagination had gotten out of hand, Autumn decided. She was so used to the drama of her profession that she had built up the scenario. Helen's death was a hard, cold fact. None of them could avoid that. But Autumn was certain her two misfortunes had been unconnected. If I'm going to stay sane until the police come, she amended, I *have* to believe it.

Calmer now, she allowed herself to think. Yes, there had been a murder. There was no glossing over that. Murder was a violent act, and in this case, it had been a personal one. She had no involvement in it. There wasn't any correlation. What had happened in the darkroom had been simple clumsiness. That was the cleanest and the most reasonable explanation. As for the invasion of her room… Autumn shrugged. It had been Helen. She'd been a vicious, evil woman. The destruction of Autumn's clothes and personal belongings had been a vicious, evil act. For some reason of her own, Helen had taken a dislike to her. There was no one else at the inn who would have any reason to feel hostility toward her.

Except Lucas. Autumn shook her head firmly, but the thought remained. Except Lucas. She huddled the blanket closer, cold again.

No, even that made no sense. Lucas had rejected her, not the other way around. She had loved him. And he, very simply, hadn't loved her. *Would that matter to him?* The voice in her brain argued with the voice from her heart. Ignoring the queaziness in her stomach, Autumn forced herself to consider, dispassionately, Lucas in the role of murderer.

It had been obvious from the beginning that he was under strain. He hadn't been sleeping well and he'd been tense. Autumn had known him to struggle over a stage of a book for a week on little sleep and coffee, but he'd never shown the effects. All that stored energy he had was just waiting to take over whenever he needed it. No, in all her memory, she had never seen Lucas McLean tired. Until now.

Helen's blackmail must have disturbed him deeply. Autumn couldn't imagine Lucas concerning himself over publicity, adverse or otherwise. The woman involved in divorce must mean a great deal to him. She shut her eyes on a flash of pain and forced herself to continue.

Why had he come to the Pine View Inn? Why would he choose a remote place nearly a continent away from his home? To work? Autumn shook her head. It just didn't follow. She knew Lucas never traveled when he was writing. He'd do his research first, extensively if necessary, before he began. Once he had a plot between his teeth, he'd dig into his beachside home for the duration. Come to Virginia to write in peace? No. Lucas McLean could write on the 5:15 subway if he chose to. She knew no one else with a greater ability to block people out.

So, his reason for coming to the inn was quite different. Autumn began to wonder if Helen had been a pawn as well as a manipulator. Had Lucas lured her to this remote spot and surrounded her with people with reasons to hate her? He was clever enough to have done it, and calculating enough. How difficult was it going to be to prove which one of the six had killed her? Motive and opportunity he'd said—six people had both. Why should one be examined any closer than the others?

The setting would appeal to him, she thought as she looked out at mountains and pines. Obvious, Lucas had called it. An obvious setting for murder. But then, as Jacques had pointed out, life was often obvious.

She wouldn't dwell on it. It brought the nightmare too close again. Pushing herself from the bed, Autumn began to dress in her very tired jeans and a sweater Julia had given her the night before. She wasn't going to spend another day picking at her doubts and fears. It would be better to hang on to the knowledge that the police would be there soon. It wasn't up to her to decide who had killed Helen.

When she started down the stairs, she felt better. She'd take a long, solitary walk after breakfast and clear the cobwebs from her mind. The thought of getting out of the inn lifted her spirits.

But her confidence dropped away when she saw Lucas at the foot of the stairs. He was watching her closely, silently. Their eyes met for one brief, devastating moment before he turned to walk away.

"Lucas." She heard herself call out before she could stop

herself. Stopping, he turned to face her again. Autumn gathered all her courage and hurried down the rest of the stairs. She had questions, and she had to ask them. He still mattered much too much to her. She stood on the bottom step so that their eyes would be level. His told her nothing. They seemed to look through her, bored and impatient.

"Why did you come here?" Autumn asked him quickly. "Here, to the Pine View Inn?" She wanted him to give her any reason. She wanted to accept it.

Lucas focused on her intensely for a moment. There was something in his face for her to read, but it was gone before she could decipher it. "Let's just say I came to write, Autumn. Any other reason has been eliminated."

There was no expression in his voice, but the words chilled her. *Eliminated.* Would he choose such a clean word for murder? Something of her horror showed in her face. She watched his brows draw together in a frown.

"Cat—"

"No." Before he could speak again, she darted away from him. He'd given her an answer, but it wasn't one she wanted to accept.

The others were already at the table. The sun had superficially lightened the mood, and by unspoken agreement, the conversation was general, with no mention of Helen. They all needed an island of normalcy before the police came.

Julia, looking fresh and lovely, chattered away. Her attitude was so easy, even cheerful, that Autumn wondered if their conversation in the kitchen was as insubstantial as her nightmare. She was flirting again, with every man at the table. Two days of horror hadn't dulled her style.

"Your aunt," Jacques told Autumn, "has an amazing cuisine." He speared a fluffy, light pancake. "It surprises me at times because she has such a charming, drifting way about her. Yet, she remembers small details. This morning, she tells me she has saved me a piece of her apple pie to enjoy with my lunch. She doesn't forget I have a fondness for it. Then when I kiss her hand because I find her so enchanting, she smiled and wandered away, and I heard her say something about towels and chocolate pudding.''

The laughter that followed was so normal, Autumn wanted to hug it to her. ''She has a better memory about the guests' appetites than her family's,'' Autumn countered, smiling at him. ''She's decided that pot roast is my favorite and has promised to provide it weekly, but it's actually my brother Paul's favorite. I haven't figured out how to move her toward spaghetti.''

She gripped her fork tightly at a sudden flash of pain. Very clearly, Autumn could see herself stirring spaghetti sauce in Lucas's kitchen while he did his best to distract her. Would she never pry herself loose from the memories? Quickly, she plunged into conversation again.

''Aunt Tabby sort of floats around the rest of the world,'' she continued. ''I remember once, when we were kids, Paul smuggled some formaldehyde frog legs out of his biology class. He brought them with him when we came on vacation and gave them to Aunt Tabby, hoping for a few screams. She took them, smiled and told him she'd eat them later.''

''Oh, God.'' Julia lifted her hand to her throat. ''She didn't actually eat them, did she?''

''No.'' Autumn grinned. ''I distracted her, which of course is the easiest thing in the world to do, and Paul disposed of his biology project. She never missed them.''

''I must remember to thank my parents for making me an only child,'' Julia murmured.

''I can't imagine growing up without Paul and Will.'' Autumn shook her head as old memories ran through her mind. ''The three of us were always very close, even when we tormented each other.''

Jacques chuckled, obviously thinking of his own children. ''Does your family spend much time here?''

''Not as much as we used to.'' Autumn lifted her shoulders. ''When I was a girl, we'd all come for a month during the summer.''

''To tramp through the woods?'' Julia asked with a wicked gleam in her eyes.

"That," Autumn returned mildly, and imitated the actress's arched-brow look, "and some camping." She went on, amused by Julia's rolling eyes. "Boating and swimming in the lake."

"Boating," Robert spoke up, cutting off a small, nagging memory. Autumn looked over at him, unable to hang on to it. "That's my one true vice. Nothing I like better than sailing. Right, Jane?" He patted her hand. "Jane's quite a sailor herself. Best first mate I've ever had." He glanced over at Steve. "I suppose you've done your share of sailing."

Steve answered with a rueful shake of his head. "I'm afraid I'm a miserable sailor. I can't even swim."

"You're joking!" This came from Julia. She stared at him in disbelief. Her eyes skimmed approvingly over his shoulders. "You look like you could handle the English Channel."

"I can't even handle a wading pool," he confessed, more amused than embarrassed. He grinned and gestured with his fork. "I make up for it in land sports. If we had a tennis court here, I'd redeem myself."

"Ah well." Jacques gave his French shrug. "You'll have to content yourself with hiking. The mountains here are beautiful. I hope to bring my children one day." He frowned, then stared into his coffee.

"Nature lovers!" Julia's smiling taunt kept the room from sliding into gloom. "Give me smog-filled L.A. anytime. I'll look at your mountains and squirrels in Autumn's photographs."

"You'll have to wait until I add to my supply." She kept her voice light, trying not to be depressed over the loss of her film. She couldn't yet bring herself to think of the loss of her camera. "Losing that film is like losing a limb, but I'm trying to be brave about it." Taking a bite of pancake, she shrugged. "And I could have lost all four rolls instead of three. The shots I took of the lake were the best, so I can comfort myself with that. The light was perfect that morning, and the shadows..."

She trailed off as the memory seeped through. She could see herself, standing on the ridge looking down at the glistening water, the mirrored trees. And the two figures that walked the far side. That was the morning she had met Lucas in the woods, then Helen. Helen with an angry bruise under her eye.

"Autumn?"

Hearing Jacques's voice, she snapped herself back. "I'm sorry, what?"

"Is something wrong?"

"No, I..." She met his curious eyes. "No."

"I would think light and shadow are the very essence of photography," Julia commented, flowing over the awkward silence. "But I've always concerned myself with looking into the lens rather than through. Remember that horrible little man, Jacques, who used to pop up at the most extraordinary times and stick a camera in my face. What was his name? I really became quite fond of him."

Julia had centered the attention on herself so smoothly that Autumn doubted anyone had noticed her own confusion. She stared down at the pancakes and syrup on her plate as if the solution to the mysteries of the universe were written there. But she could feel Lucas's eyes boring into her averted head. She could feel them, but she couldn't look at him.

She wanted to be alone, to think, to reason out what was whirling in her head. She forced down the rest of her breakfast and let the conversation buzz around her.

"I have to see Aunt Tabby," Autumn murmured, at last thinking she could leave without causing curiosity. "Excuse me." She had reached the kitchen door before Julia waylaid her.

"Autumn, I want to talk to you." The grip of the slender fingers was quite firm. "Come up to my room."

From the expression on the enviable face, Autumn could see arguing was useless. "All right, right after I see Aunt Tabby. She'll be worried because I didn't say good night to her yesterday. I'll be up in a few minutes." She kept her voice reasonable and friendly, and managed a smile. Autumn decided she was becoming quite an actress herself.

For a small stretch of silence, Julia studied Autumn's face, then loosened her grip. "All right, come up as soon as you've finished."

"Yes, I will." Autumn slipped into the kitchen with the promise still on her lips. It wasn't difficult to go through the kitchen to the mud room without being noticed. Aunt Tabby and Nancy were deep in their morning argument. Taking down her jacket from the hook where she had placed it the morning of the storm, Autumn checked the pocket. Her fingers closed over the roll of film. For a moment, she simply held it in the palm of her hand.

Moving quickly, she changed from shoes to boots, transferred the film to the pocket of Julia's sweater, grabbed her jacket and went out the back door.

Chapter 11

The air was sharp. The rain had washed it clean. Budded leaves Autumn had photographed only days before were fuller, thicker, but still tenderly green. Her mind was no longer on the freedom she had longed for all the previous day. Now, Autumn was only intent on reaching the cover of the forest without being seen. She ran for the trees, not stopping until she was surrounded. Silence was deep and it cradled her.

The ground sucked and skidded under her feet, spongy with rain. There was some wind damage here and there that she noticed when she forced herself to move more carefully. Broken limbs littered the ground. The sun was warm, and she shed her jacket, tossing it over a branch. She made herself concentrate on the sights and sounds of the forest until her thoughts could calm.

The mountain laurel hinted at blooms. A bird circled overhead, then darted deeper into the trees with a sharp cry. A squirrel scurried up a tree trunk and peered down at her. Autumn reached in her pocket and closed her hand over the roll of film. The conversation in the kitchen with Julia now made horrible sense.

Helen must have been at the lake that morning. From the evidence of the bruise, she had argued violently with someone. And that someone had seen Autumn on the ridge. That someone wanted the pictures destroyed badly enough to risk breaking into both her darkroom and her bedroom. The film had to be potentially damaging for anyone to risk knocking her unconscious and ransacking her room. Who else but the killer would care enough to take such dangerous actions? Who else? At every turn, logic pointed its finger toward Lucas.

It had been his plans that brought the group together in the first place. Lucas was the person Autumn had met just before coming across Helen. Lucas had bent over her as she lay on the darkroom floor. Lucas had been up, fully dressed, the night of Helen's murder. Autumn shook her head, wanting to shatter the logic. But the film was solid in her hand.

He must have seen her as she stood on the ridge. She would have been in clear view. When he intercepted her, he had tried to rekindle their relationship. He would have known better than to have attempted to remove the film from her camera. She would have caused a commotion that would have been heard in two counties. Yes, he knew her well enough to use subtler means. But he wouldn't have known she had already switched to a fresh roll.

He had played on her old weakness for him. If she had submitted, he would have found ample time and opportunity to destroy the film. Autumn admitted, painfully, that she would have been too involved with him to have noticed the loss. But she hadn't submitted. This time, she had rejected him. He would have been forced to employ more extreme measures.

He only pretended to want me, she realized. That, more than anything else, hurt. He had held her, kissed her, while his mind had been busy calculating how best to protect himself. Autumn forced herself to face facts. Lucas had stopped wanting her a long time ago, and his needs had never been the same as hers. Two facts were very clear. She had never stopped loving him, and he had never begun to love her.

Still, she balked at the idea of Lucas as a cold-blooded killer. She could remember his sudden spurts of gentleness, his humor, the careless bouts of generosity. That was part of him, too—part of the reason she had been able to love him so easily. Part of the reason she had never stopped.

A hand gripped her shoulder. With a quick cry of alarm, she whirled and found herself face-to-face with Lucas. When she shrank from him, he dropped his hands and stuffed them into his pockets. His eyes were dark and his voice was icy.

"Where's the film, Autumn?"

Whatever color left in her face drained. She hadn't wanted to believe it. Part of her had refused to believe it. Now, her heart shattered. He was leaving her no choice.

"Film?" She shook her head as she took another step back. "What film?"

"You know very well what film." Impatience pulled at the words. He narrowed his eyes, watching her retreat. "I want the fourth roll. Don't back away from me!"

Autumn stopped at the curt command. "Why?"

"Don't play stupid." His impatience was quickly becoming fury. She recognized all the signs. "I want the film. What I do with it is my business."

She ran, thinking only to escape from his words. It had been easier to live with the doubt than the certainty. He caught her arm before she had dashed three yards. Spinning her around, he studied her face.

"You're terrified." He looked stunned, then angry. "You're terrified of me." With his hands gripping hard on her arms he brought her closer. "We've run the gamut, haven't we, Cat? Yesterday's gone." There was a finality in his voice that brought more pain than his hands or his temper.

"Lucas." Autumn was trembling, emotionally spent. "Please don't hurt me anymore." The pain she spoke of had nothing to do with the physical, but he released her with a violent jerk. The struggle for control was visible on his face.

"I won't lay a hand on you now, or ever again. Just tell me where that film is. I'll get out of your life as quickly as possible."

She had to reach him. She had to try one last time. "Lucas, please, it's senseless. You must see that. Can't you—"

"Don't push me!" The words exploded at her, rocking her

back on her heels. "You stupid fool, do you have any idea how dangerous that film is? Do you think for one minute I'm going to let you keep it?" He took a step toward her. "Tell me where it is. Tell me now, or by God, I'll throttle it out of you."

"In the darkroom." The lie came quickly and without calculation. Perhaps that was why he accepted it so readily.

"All right. Where?" She watched his features relax slightly. His voice was calmer.

"On the bottom shelf. On the wet side."

"That's hardly illuminating to a layman, Cat." There was a touch of his old mockery as he reached for her arm. "Let's go get it."

"No!" She jerked away wildly. "I won't go with you. There's only one roll; you'll find it. You found the others. Leave me alone, Lucas. For God's sake, leave me alone!"

She ran again, skidding on the mud. This time he didn't stop her.

Autumn had no idea how far she ran or even the direction she took. Ultimately, her feet slowed to a walk. She stopped to stare up at a sky that had no clouds. What was she going to do?

She could go back. She could go back and try to get to the darkroom first, lock herself in. She could develop the film, blow up the two figures beside the lake and see the truth for herself. Her hand reached for the hated film again. She didn't want to see the truth. With absolute certainty, she knew she could never hand the film over to the police. No matter what Lucas had done or would do, she couldn't betray him. He'd been wrong, she thought. She could never pull the lever.

Withdrawing the film from her pocket, she stared down at it. It looked so innocent. She had felt so innocent that day, up on the ridge with the sun coming up. But when she had done what she had to do, she would never feel innocent again. She would expose the film herself.

Lucas, she thought and nearly laughed. Lucas McLean was the only man on earth who could make her turn her back on her own conscience. And when it was done, only the two of them would know. She would be as guilty as he.

Do it quickly, she told herself. Do it fast and think about it later. Her palm was damp where the film was cradled in it. You're going to have a whole lifetime to think about it. Taking a deep breath, Autumn started to uncap the plastic capsule she used to protect her undeveloped film. A movement on the path behind her had her stuffing the roll back into her pocket and whirling around.

Could Lucas have searched the darkroom so quickly? What would he do now that he knew she had lied to him? Foolishly, Autumn wanted to run again. Instead, she straightened and waited. The final encounter would have to come sooner or later.

Autumn's relief when she saw Steve approaching quickly became irritation. She wanted to be alone, not to make small talk and useless conversation while the film burned in her pocket.

"Hi!" Steve's lightning smile did nothing to decrease her annoyance, but Autumn pasted on one of her own. If she were going to be playing a game for the rest of her life, she might as well start now.

"Hello. Taking Jacques up on the hiking?" God, how normal and shallow her voice sounded! Was she going to be able to live like this?

"Yeah. I see you needed to get away from the inn, too." Taking a deep breath of the freshened air, he flexed his shoulders. "Lord, it feels good to be outside again."

"I know what you mean." Autumn eased the tension from her own shoulders. This was a reprieve, she told herself. Accept it. When it's over, nothing's ever going to be the same again.

"And Jacques is right," Steve went on, staring out through the thin leaves. "The mountains are beautiful. It reminds you that life goes on."

"I suppose we all need to remember that now." Unconsciously, Autumn dipped her hand in her pocket.

"Your hair glows in the sunlight." Steve caught at the ends

and moved them between his fingertips. Autumn saw, with some alarm, that warmth had crept into his eyes. A romantic interlude was more than she could handle.

"People often seem to think more about my hair than me." She smiled and kept her voice light. "Sometimes I'm tempted to hack it off."

"Oh no." He took a more generous handful. "It's very special, very unique." His eyes lifted to hers. "And I've been thinking quite a lot about you the last few days. You're very special, too."

"Steve…" Autumn turned and would have walked on, but his hand was still in her hair.

"I want you, Autumn."

The words, so gentle, almost humble, nearly broke her heart. She turned back with apology in her eyes. "I'm sorry, Steve. I really am."

"Don't be sorry." He lowered his head to brush her lips. "If you let me, I could make you happy."

"Steve, please." Autumn lifted her hands to his chest. If only he were Lucas, she thought as she stared up at him. If only it were Lucas looking at me like this. "I can't."

He let out a long breath, but didn't release her. "McLean? Autumn, he only makes you unhappy. Why won't you let go?"

"I can't tell you how many times I've asked myself the same question." She sighed, and he watched the sun shoot into her eyes. "I don't have the answer—except that I love him."

"Yes, it shows." Frowning, he brushed a strand of hair from her cheek. "I'd hoped you'd be able to get over him, but I don't suppose you will."

"No, I don't suppose I will. I've given up trying."

"Now I'm sorry, Autumn. It makes things difficult."

Autumn dropped her eyes to stare at the ground. She didn't want pity. "Steve, I appreciate it, but I really need to be alone."

"I want the film, Autumn."

Astonished, she jerked her head up. Without consciously

making the step, she aligned herself with Lucas. "Film? I don't know what you mean."

"Oh yes, I'm afraid you do." He was still speaking gently, one hand stroking her hair. "The pictures you took of the lake the morning Helen and I were down there. I have to have them."

"You?" For a moment, the implication eluded her. "You and Helen?" Confusion turned into shock. She could only stare at him.

"We were having quite a row that morning. You see, she had decided she wanted a lump-sum payment from me. Her other sources were drying up fast. Julia wouldn't give her a penny, just laughed at her. Helen was furious about that." His face changed with a grim smile. "Jacques had finished with her, too. She never had anything worthwhile on Lucas in the first place. She counted on intimidating him. Instead, he told her to go to hell and threatened to press charges. That threw her off balance for a while. She must have realized Jane was on the edge. So...she concentrated on me."

He had been staring off into the distance as he spoke. Now, his attention came back to Autumn. The first hint of anger swept into his eyes. "She wanted two hundred and fifty thousand dollars in two weeks. A quarter of a million, or she'd hand over the information she had on me to my father."

"But you said what she knew wasn't important." Autumn let her eyes dart past his for a moment. The path behind them was empty. She was alone.

"She knew a bit more than I told you." Steve gave her an apologetic smile. "I could hardly tell you everything then. I've covered my tracks well enough now so that I don't think the police will ever know. It was actually a matter of extortion."

"Extortion?" The hand on her hair was becoming more terrifying with each passing moment. Keep him talking, she told herself frantically. Keep him talking and someone will come.

"Borrowing, really. The money will be mine sooner or later." He shrugged it off. "I just took some a little early.

Unfortunately, my father wouldn't see it that way. I told you, remember? He's a tough man. He wouldn't think twice about booting me out the door and cutting off my income. I can't have that, Autumn.'' He flashed her a smile. ''I have very expensive tastes.''

''So you killed her.'' Autumn said it flatly. She was finished with horror.

''I didn't have a choice. I couldn't possibly get my hands on that much cash in two weeks.'' He said it so calmly, Autumn could almost see the rationale behind it. ''I nearly killed her that morning down by the lake. She just wouldn't listen to me. I lost my temper and hit her. Knocked her cold. When I saw her lying there on the ground, I realized how much I wanted her dead.''

Autumn didn't interrupt. She could see he was far from finished. Let him talk it out, she ordered herself, controlling the urge to break from him and run. Someone's going to come.

''I bent over her,'' he continued. ''My hands were almost around her throat when I saw you standing up on the ridge. I knew it was you because the sun was shining on your hair. I didn't think you could recognize me from that distance, but I had to be sure. Of course, I found out later that you weren't paying attention to us at all.''

''No, I barely noticed.'' Her knees were starting to shake. He was telling her too much. Far too much.

''I left Helen and circled around, thinking to intercept you. Lucas got to you first. Quite a touching little scene.''

''You watched us?'' She felt a stir of anger edge through the fear.

''You were too involved in each other to notice.'' He smiled again. ''In any case, that's when I learned you'd been taking pictures. I had to get rid of that film; it was too chancy. I hated to hurt you, Autumn. I found you very attractive right from the first.''

A rabbit darted down the path, veering off and bounding into the woods. She heard the call of a quail, faint with distance. The simple, natural texture of her surroundings gave his words a sense of unreality. "The darkroom."

"Yes. I was glad the blow with the door knocked you out. I didn't want to have to hit you with the flashlight. I didn't see your camera, but found a roll of film. I was so certain I had things taken care of. You can imagine how I felt when you said you'd lost two rolls, and that they were shots of your trip down from New York. I didn't know how the other roll had been ruined."

"Lucas. Lucas turned on the lights when he found me." Suddenly, through the horror came a bright flash of realization. *It hadn't been Lucas.* He'd done nothing but simply be who he was. She felt overwhelming relief at his innocence, then guilt at ever having believed what she had of him. "Lucas," she said again, almost giddy with the onslaught of sensations.

"Well, it hardly matters now," Steve said practically. Autumn snapped back. She had to keep alert, had to keep a step ahead of him. "I knew if I just took the film from your camera, you'd begin to wonder. You might start thinking too closely about the pictures you'd taken. I hated doing that to your things, breaking your camera. I know it was important to you."

"I have another at home." It was a weak attempt to sound unconcerned. Steve only smiled.

"I went to Helen's room right after I'd finished with yours. I knew I was going to have to kill her. She stood there pointing to the bruise and telling me it was going to cost me another hundred thousand. I didn't know what I was going to do...I thought I was going to strangle her. Then I saw the scissors. That was better—anyone could have used scissors. Even little Jane. I stopped thinking when I picked them up until it was over."

He shuddered, and Autumn thought, *Run! Run now!* But his hand tightened on her hair. "I've never been through anything like that. It was terrible. I almost folded. I knew I had to think, had to be careful, or I'd lose everything. Staying in that room was the hardest thing I've ever done. I wiped the handles of the scissors clean and tore up my shirt. Her blood was on it. I flushed the pieces down the toilet. When I got back to my room, I showered and went to bed. I remember being surprised that the whole thing took less than twenty minutes. It seemed like years.''

''It must have been dreadful for you,'' Autumn murmured, but he was oblivious to the edge in her voice.

''Yes, but it was all working out. No one could prove where they were when Helen was killed. The storm—the phones, the power—that was all a bonus. Every one of us had a reason to want Helen out of the way. I really think Julia and I will be the least likely suspects when the time comes. The police should look to Jacques because he had more cause, and Lucas because he has the temper.''

''Lucas couldn't kill anyone,'' Autumn said evenly. ''The police will know that.''

''I wouldn't bank on it.'' He gave her a crooked smile. ''You haven't been so sure of that yourself.''

She could say nothing when struck with the truth. *Why wasn't someone coming?*

''This morning, you started talking about four rolls of film, and the pictures you took of the lake. I could tell the moment when you remembered.''

So much for my talent at acting, she thought grimly. ''I only remembered there'd been people down by the lake that morning.''

''You were putting it all together quickly.'' He traced a finger down her cheek and Autumn forced herself not to jerk away. ''I had hoped to distract you, gain your affection. It was obvious you were hurting over McLean. If I could have moved in, I might have gotten my hands on that film without having to hurt you.''

Autumn kept her eyes and voice steady. He'd finished talking now; she could sense it. ''What are you going to do?''

''Damn it, Autumn. I'm going to have to kill you.''

He said it in much the same way her father had said, *''Damn it, Autumn, I'm going to have to spank you.''* She nearly broke into hysterical giggles.

"They'll know this time, Steve." Her body was beginning to shake, but she spoke calmly. If she could reason with him...

"No, I don't think so." He spoke practically, as if he considered she might have a viable point. "I was careful to get out without being seen. Everyone's spread out again. I doubt anyone even knows you went outside. I wouldn't have known myself if I hadn't found your jacket and boots missing. Then again, if I hadn't found the jacket hanging on a branch and been able to follow your tracks from there, I wouldn't have found you so easily."

He shrugged, as if showing her why his reasoning was better than hers. "When you're found missing, I'll make certain I come this way when we look for you. I can do a lot of damage to the tracks and no one will know any better. Now, Autumn, I need the film. Tell me where you've put it."

"I'm not going to tell you." She tossed back her head. As long as she had the film, he had to keep her alive. "They'll find it. When they do, they'll know it was you."

He made a quick sound of impatience. "You'll tell me Autumn, eventually. It would be easier for you if you told me now. I don't want to hurt you any more than I have to. I can make it quick, or I can make it painful."

His hand shot out so swiftly, Autumn had no time to dodge the blow. The force of it knocked her back into a tree. The pain welled inside her head and rolled through, leaving dizziness. She clutched at the rough bark to keep her balance as she saw him coming toward her.

Oh no, she wasn't going to stand and be hit again. He'd gotten away with it twice, and twice was enough. With as much force as she could muster, she kicked, aiming well below the waist. He went down on his knees like a shot. Autumn turned and fled.

Chapter 12

She ran blindly. *Escape!* It was the only coherent thought in her brain. It wasn't until the first wave of panic had ebbed that Autumn realized she had run not only away from Steve, but away from the inn. It was too late to double back. She could only concentrate as much effort as possible into putting distance between them. She veered off the path and into thicker undergrowth.

When she heard him coming after her, Autumn didn't look back, but increased her pace. His breathing was labored, but close. Too close. She swerved again and plunged on. The ground sucked and pulled at her boots, but she told herself she wouldn't slip. If she slipped, he would be on top of her in a moment. His hands would be at her throat. *She would not slip.*

Her heart was pounding and her lungs were screaming in agony for more air. A branch whipped back, stinging her cheek. But she told herself she wouldn't stop. She would run and run and run until she no longer heard him coming after her.

A tree had fallen and lay drunkenly in her path. Without breaking stride, Autumn vaulted it, sliding for a moment when her boots hit the mud, then pounding on. He slipped. She heard the slick sound of his boots as they lost traction, then his muffled curse. She kept up her wild pace, nearly giddy at the few seconds his fall had given her.

Time and direction ceased to exist. For her, the pursuit had no beginning, no end. It was only the race. Her thoughts were no longer rational. She knew only that she had to keep running though she'd almost forgotten why. Her breath was coming in harsh gasps, her legs were like rubber. She knew only the mindless flight of the hunted—the naked fear of the hunter.

Suddenly, she saw the lake. It glistened as the sun hit its surface. With some last vestige of lucidity, Autumn remembered Steve's admission that morning. He couldn't swim. The race had a goal now, and she dashed for it.

Her crazed approach through the woods had taken her away from the ridge where the incline graduated for easy descent. Instead, she came to the edge of a cliff that fell forty feet in a sheer drop. Without hesitation, Autumn plunged down at full speed. She scrambled and slid, her fingers clawing to keep herself from overbalancing. Like a lizard, she clung to the mountain. Her body scraped on jagged rocks and slid on mud. Julia's designer sweater shredded. Autumn realized, as the pain grew hot, that her skin suffered equally. Fear pushed her beyond the pain. The lake beckoned below. Safety. Victory.

Still, he came after her. She could hear his boots clatter on the rocks above her head, jarring pebbles that rained down on her. Autumn leaped the last ten feet. The force of the fall shot up her legs, folding them under her until she rolled into a heap. Then she was scrambling and streaking for the lake.

She heard him cry out for her. With a final mad impetus, she flung herself into the water, slicing through its surface. Its sharp frigidity shocked her system and gave her strength. Clawing through it, she headed for depth. She was going to win.

Like a light switched off, the momentum which had driven her so wildly, sapped. The weight of her boots pulled her down. The water closed over her head. Thrashing and choking, Autumn fought for the surface. Her lungs burned as she tried to pull in air. Her arms were heavy, and her feeble strokes had her bobbing up and down. Mists gathered in front

of her eyes. Still, she resisted, fighting as the water sucked at
her. It was now as deadly an enemy as the one she had sought
to escape.

She heard someone sobbing, and realized dimly it was her
own voice calling for help. But she knew there would be none.
The fight was gone out of her. Was it music she heard? She
thought it came from below her, deep, beckoning. Slowly,
surrendering, she let the water take her like a lover.

Someone was hurting her. Autumn didn't protest. Darkness
blanketed her mind and numbed the pain. The pushing and
prodding were no more irritating to her than a faint itch. Air
forced its way into her lungs, and she moaned gently in annoyance.

Lucas's voice touched the edges of her mind. He was calling her back in a strange, unnatural voice. Panic? Yes, even
through the darkness she could detect a note of panic. What
an odd thing to hear in Lucas's voice. Her eyelids were heavy,
and the darkness was so tempting. The need to tell him was
stronger. Autumn forced her eyes open. Blackness receded to
a verge of mist.

His face loomed over her, water streaming from it and his
hair. It splattered cold on her cheeks. Yet her mouth felt
warm, as if his had just left it. Autumn stared at him, groping
for the power of speech.

"Oh God, Autumn." Lucas brushed the water from her
cheeks even as it fell on them again from his own hair. "Oh
God. Listen to me. It's all right, you're going to be all right,
do you hear? You're going to be all right. I'm going to take
you back to the inn. Can you understand me?"

His voice was desperate, as were his eyes. She'd never
heard that tone or seen that expression. Not from Lucas. Autumn wanted to say something that would comfort him, but
lacked the strength. The mists were closing in again, and she
welcomed them. For a moment, she held them off and dug
deep for her voice.

"I thought you killed her, Lucas. I'm sorry."

"Oh, Cat." His voice was intolerably weary. She felt his mouth touch hers. Then she felt nothing.

Voices, vague and without texture, floated down a long tunnel. Autumn didn't welcome them. She wanted her peace. She tried to plunge deeper into the darkness again, but Lucas had no respect for what anyone else wanted. His voice broke into her solitude, suddenly clear and, as always, demanding.

"I'm staying with her until she wakes up. I'm not leaving her."

"Lucas, you're dead on your feet." Robert's voice was low and soothing, in direct contrast to Lucas's. "I'll stay with Autumn. It's part of my job. She's probably going to be floating in and out all night. You wouldn't know what to do for her."

"Then you'll tell me what to do. I'm staying with her."

"Of course you are, dear." Aunt Tabby's voice surprised Autumn even in the dim, drifting darkness. It was so firm and strong. "Lucas will stay, Dr. Spicer. You've already said it's mainly a matter of rest, and waiting until she wakes naturally. Lucas can take care of her."

"I'll sit with you, Lucas, if you'd like…all right, but you've only to call me." Julia's voice rolled over Autumn, as smoky as the mists.

Suddenly, she wanted to ask them what was happening. What they were doing in her own private world. She struggled for words and formed a moan. A cool hand fell on her brow.

"Is she in pain?" Was that Lucas's voice? Autumn thought. Trembling? "Damn it, give her something for the pain!"

The darkness was whirling again, jumbling the sounds. Autumn let it swallow her.

She dreamed. The deep black curtain took on a velvet, moonlight texture. Lucas stared down at her. His face seemed oddly vivid for a dream. His hand felt real and cool on her cheek. "Cat, can you hear me?"

Autumn stared at him, then drew together all her scraps and

rags of concentration. "Yes." She closed her eyes and let the darkness swirl.

When her eyes reopened, he was still there. Autumn swallowed. Her throat was burning dry. "Am I dead?"

"No. No, Cat, you're not dead." Lucas poured something cool down her throat. Her eyes drooped again as she tried to patch together her memory. It was too hard, and she let it go.

Pain shot through her. Unexpected and sharp, it rocketed down her arms and legs. Autumn heard someone moan pitifully. Lucas loomed over her again, his face pale in a shaft of moonlight. "It hurts," she complained.

"I know." He sat beside her and brought a cup to her lips. "Try to drink."

Floating, like a bright red balloon, Autumn felt herself drift through space. The pain had eased as she stumbled back into consciousness. "Julia's sweater," she murmured as she opened her eyes again. "It's torn. I think I tore it. I'll have to buy her another."

"Don't worry about it, Cat. Rest." Lucas's hand was on her hair and she turned her face to it, seeking reassurance. She floated again.

"I'm sure it was valuable," she murmured, nearly an hour later. "But I don't really need that new tripod. Julia lent me that sweater. I should have been more careful."

"Julia has dozens of sweaters, Cat. Don't worry."

Autumn closed her eyes, comforted. But she knew her tripod would have to wait.

"Lucas." She pulled herself back, but now the moonlight was the gray light of dawn.

"Yes, I'm here."

"Why?"

"Why what, Cat?"

"Why are you here?"

But he moved out of focus again. She never heard his answer.

Chapter 13

The sunlight was strong. Used to darkness, Autumn blinked in protest.

"Ah, are you with us to stay this time, Autumn, or is this another quick visit?" Julia bent over her and patted her cheek. "There's a bit of color coming back, and you're cool. How do you feel?"

Autumn lay still for a moment and tried to find out. "Hollow," she decided, and Julia laughed.

"Trust you to think of your stomach."

"Hollow all over," Autumn countered. "Especially my head." She glanced confusedly around the room. "Have I been sick?"

"You gave us quite a scare." Julia eased down on the bed and studied her. "Don't you remember?"

"I was...dreaming?" Autumn's search for her memory found only bits and pieces. "Lucas was here. I was talking to him."

"Yes, he said you were drifting in and out through the night. Managed to say a word or two now and again. Did you really think I'd let you sacrifice your new tripod?" She kissed Autumn's cheek, then held her a moment. "God, when Lucas carried you in, we thought..." Shaking her head briskly, she sat up. Autumn saw that her eyes were damp.

"Julia." Autumn squeezed her eyes a moment, but nothing came clear. "I was supposed to come to your room, but I didn't."

"No, you didn't. I should have dragged you with me then and there. None of this would have happened." She stood up again. "It appears Lucas and I were both taken in by those big green eyes. I don't know how much time we wasted searching for that damn film before he went back to find you."

"I don't understand. Why..." As she reached up to brush at her hair, Autumn noticed the bandages on her hands. "What are these for? Did I hurt myself?"

"It's all right now." Julia brushed away the question. "I'd better let Lucas explain. He'll be furious that I chased him downstairs for some coffee, and you woke up."

'Julia—''

"No more questions now." She cut Autumn off as she plucked a robe from a chair. "Why don't you slip this on. You'll feel better." She eased the silk over Autumn's arms and covered more bandages. The sight of them brought added confusion, more juggled memories. "Just lie still and relax," Julia ordered. "Aunt Tabby already has some soup simmering, just waiting for you. I'll tell her to pour it into an enormous bowl."

She kissed Autumn again, then glided to the door. "Listen, Autumn." Julia turned back with a slow, cat smile. "He's been through hell these past twenty-four hours, but don't make it too easy for him."

Autumn frowned at the door when Julia had gone and wondered what the devil she was talking about.

Deciding she wouldn't find any answers lying in bed, Autumn dragged herself out. Every joint, every muscle revolted. She nearly succumbed to the desire to crawl back in, but curiosity was stronger. Her legs wobbled as she went to the mirror.

"Good God!" She looked, Autumn decided, even worse than she felt. The bruise on her temple had company. There was a light discoloration along her cheekbone and a few odd scratches. There was a sudden, clear memory of rough bark scraping against her hands. Lifting them, Autumn stared at the bandages. ''What have I done to myself?'' she asked aloud, then belted the robe to disguise the worst of the damage.

The door opened, and in the reflection she watched Lucas enter the room. He looked as though he hadn't slept in days. The lines of strain were deeper now and his chin was shadowed and unshaven. Only his eyes were the same. Dark and intense.

''You look like hell,'' she told him without turning. ''You need some sleep.''

He laughed. In a gesture of weariness she had never seen in him, he lifted his hands to run them down his face. ''I might have expected it,'' he murmured. He sighed, then gave her a smile from the past. ''You shouldn't be out of bed, Cat. You're liable to topple over any minute.''

''I'm all right. At least I was before I looked in the mirror.'' Turning, she faced him directly. ''I nearly fainted from shock.''

''You are,'' he began in quiet, serious tones, ''the most beautiful thing I've ever seen.''

''Kindness to the invalid,'' she said, looking away. That had hurt, and she wasn't certain she could deal with any more pain. ''I could use some explanations. My mind's a little fuddled.''

''Robert said that was to be expected after...'' He trailed off and jammed clenched fists into his pockets. ''After everything that's happened.''

Autumn looked again at her bandaged hands. ''What did happen? I can't quite remember. I was running...'' She lifted her eyes to his and searched. ''In the woods, down the cliff. I...'' She shook her head. There were only bits and pieces. ''I tore Julia's sweater.''

''God! You would latch on to a damn sweater!'' His explosion had Autumn's eyes widening. ''You almost drowned, and all you think about is Julia's sweater.''

Her mouth trembled open. ''The lake.'' Memory flooded

back in a tidal wave. She leaned back against the dresser.
"Steve. It was Steve. He killed Helen. He was chasing me.
The film, I wouldn't give it to him." She swallowed, trying
to keep calm. "I lied to you. I had it in my pocket. I kept
running, but he was right behind me."

"Cat." She backed away, but he wrapped his arms around
her. "Don't. Don't think about it. Damn it, I shouldn't have
told you that way." He pressed his cheek against her hair. "I
can't seem to do anything properly with you."

"No. No, let me think it through." Autumn pushed away.
She wanted the details. Once she had them all, the fear would
ease. "He found me in the woods after you'd gone in. He'd
been with Helen down by the lake the morning I was taking
pictures. He told me he had killed her. He told me everything."

"We know all of it," Lucas cut her off sharply. "He let
out with everything once we got him back here. We got
through to the police this morning." He whipped out a cigarette and lit it swiftly. "He's already in custody. They've got
your film, too, for whatever it's worth. Jacques found it on
the path."

"It must have fallen out of my pocket. Lucas, it was so
strange." Her brow knitted as she remembered the timeless
incident with Steve. "He apologized for having to kill me.
Then when I told him I wouldn't give him the film, he slugged
me so hard I saw stars."

Face thunderous, Lucas spun around and stalked to the window. He stared out without speaking.

"When he came at me again, I kicked him, hard, where I
knew it would do the most damage."

She heard Lucas mutter something so uncharacteristically
vulgar she thought she misunderstood. For a time she rambled
about her flight through the woods, talking more to herself
than to him.

"I saw you when you started your suicidal plunge down
the cliff." His back was still to her, his voice still rough.
"How in God's name you managed to get to the bottom without cracking your skull..." Lucas turned when Autumn re-

mained silent. "I'd been tracking you through the woods. When I saw you were making for the lake, I veered off and started for the ridge. I hoped to cut Anderson off." He pulled on his cigarette, then took a long, shuddering breath. "I saw you flying down those rocks. You never should have made it down alive. I called you, but you just kept tearing for the lake. I was on him before you hit the water."

"I heard someone call. I thought it was Steve." She pushed a bandaged hand against her temple. "All I could think about was getting into the water before he caught me. I remembered he couldn't swim. Then when I had trouble keeping myself up, I panicked and forgot all those nifty rules you learn in lifeguard class."

Very slowly, very deliberately, Lucas crushed out his cigarette. "By the time I finished kicking his head in, you were already floundering. How you got out so far after the run you'd had, and with boots that must weigh twenty pounds, I'll never know. I was a good ten yards from you when you went under the last time. You sank like a stone."

He turned away again to stare out the window. "I thought..." He shook his head a moment, then continued. "I thought you were dead when I dragged you out. You were dead white and you weren't breathing. At least not enough that I could tell." He took out another cigarette and this time had to fight with his lighter to get flame. He cursed and drew deeply.

"I remember you dripping on me," Autumn murmured into the silence. "Then I thought I died."

"You damn near did." The smoke came out of his lungs in a violent stream. "I must have pumped two gallons of water out of you. You came around just long enough to apologize for thinking I killed Helen."

"I'm sorry, Lucas."

"Don't!" His tone was curt as he swung around again.

"But I should never have—"

"No?" He cut her off with one angry word. "Why? It's easy enough to see how you reached your conclusions, culminating with my last attack about the film."

After a moment, Autumn trusted herself to speak. "There were so many things you said that made me think...and you were so angry. When you asked me for the film, I wanted you to tell me anything."

"But instead of explanations, I bullied you. Typical of me, though, isn't it?" He drew a breath, but his body remained tense. "That's another apology I owe you. I seem to have chalked up quite a few. Would you like them in a group, Cat, or one at a time?"

Autumn turned away from that. It wasn't an apology she wanted, but an explanation. "Why did you want it, Lucas? How did you know?"

"It might be difficult for you to believe at this point, but I'm not completely inhuman. I wanted the film because I hoped, if I had it and made it known that I did, that you'd be safe. And..." She turned back as a shadow crossed his face. "I thought you knew, or had remembered what was on the film, and that you were protecting Anderson."

"Protecting him?" Astonishment reflected in her voice. "Why would I do that?"

He moved his shoulders in a shrug. "You seemed fond of him."

"I thought he was nice," Autumn said slowly. "I imagine we all did. But I hardly knew him. As it turns out, I didn't know him at all."

"I misinterpreted your natural friendliness for something else. Then compounded the mistake by overreacting. I was furious that you gave him what you wouldn't give me. Trust, companionship. Affection."

"Dog in the manger, Lucas?" The words shot out icily.

A muscle twitched at the corner of his mouth in contrast to another negligent shrug. "If you like."

"I'm sorry." With a sigh, Autumn pushed wearily at her hair. "That was uncalled for."

"Was it?" he countered and crushed out his cigarette. "I doubt that. You're entitled to launch a few shafts, Cat. You've taken enough of them from me."

"We're getting off the point." She moved away. Julia's

silk robe whispered around her. "You thought I was protecting Steve. I'll accept that. But how did you know he needed protecting?"

"Julia and I had already pieced together a number of things. We were almost certain he was the one who had killed Helen."

"You and Julia." Now she turned to him, curious. Autumn gestured with her hands, then stopped as the pain throbbed in them. "You're going to have to clear things up, Lucas. I might still be a little dim."

"Julia and I had discussed Helen's blackmail thoroughly. Until her murder, we centered on Jacques's problem. Neither Julia nor I were concerned with the petty threats Helen held over us. After she was killed and your room broken into, we tossed around the idea that they were connected. Autumn, why don't you get back in bed. You're so pale."

"No." She shook her head, warding off the creeping warmth the concern in his voice brought her. "I'm fine. Please, don't stop now."

He seemed about to argue, then changed his mind. "I'd never believed you'd ruin your own film, or knock youself senseless. So, Julia and I began a process of elimination. I hadn't killed Helen, and I knew that Julia hadn't. I'd been in her room that night receiving a heated lecture on my technique with women until I came down to see you. And I'd passed Helen in the hall right before I'd gone into Julia's room, so even if Julia'd had the inclination to kill Helen, it's doubtful that she would have had two identical white negligees. There'd have been blood." He shrugged again. "In any case, if Julia had killed her, she probably would have admitted it."

"Yes." Autumn gave a murmured agreement and wondered what Julia's lace-clad lecture had included.

"I've known Jacques for years," Lucas continued. "He's simply not capable of killing. Julia and I all but eliminated the Spicers. Robert is entirely too dedicated to life to take one, and Jane would dissolve into tears."

Lucas began to pace. "Anderson fit the bill. And, for reasons of my own, I wanted it to be him. Our intrepid Julia copped the spare key from Aunt Tabby and searched his room for the shirt he had worn the night of the murder. I nearly strangled her when she told me she'd done it. She's quite a woman.''

"Yes.'' Jealousy warred with affection. Affection won. "She's wonderful.''

"The shirt wasn't there. Julia claims to have an unerring eye for wardrobe, and I wanted to believe her. We decided you should be put on guard without going into specifics. I thought it best if you were wary of everyone. We decided that Julia would talk to you because you'd trust her more quickly than you'd trust me. I hadn't done anything to warrant your trust.''

"She frightened me pretty successfully,'' Autumn recalled. "I had nightmares.''

"I'm sorry. It seemed the best way at the time. We thought the film had been destroyed, but we didn't want to take any chances.''

"She was telling Jacques that night, wasn't she?''

"Yeah.'' Lucas noted the faint annoyance in her tone. "That way there would have been three of us to look out for you.''

"I might have looked out for myself if I'd been told.''

"No, I don't think so. Your face is a dead giveaway. That morning at breakfast when you started rambling about a fourth roll and remembered, everything showed in your eyes.''

"If I'd been prepared—''

"If you hadn't been a damn fool and had gone with Julia, we could have kept you safe.''

"I wanted to think,'' she began, angry at being kept in the dark.

"It was my fault.'' Lucas held up a hand to stop her. "The whole thing's been my doing. I should have handled things differently. You'd never have been hurt if I had.''

"No, Lucas.'' Guilt swamped her when she remembered the look on his face after he had dragged her from the lake. "I'd be dead if it weren't for you.''

"Good God, Cat, don't look at me like that. I can't cope

with it.'' He turned away. ''I'm doing my best to keep my word. I'll get Robert; he'll want to examine you.''

''Lucas.'' She wasn't going to let him walk out that door until he told her everything. ''Why did you come here? And don't tell me you came to Virginia to write. I know—I remember your habits.''

Lucas turned, but kept his hand on the knob. ''I told you before, the other reason no longer exists. Leave it.''

He had retreated behind the cool, detached manner he used so well, but Autumn wasn't going to be shoved aside. ''This is my aunt's inn, Lucas. Your coming here, however indirectly, started this chain of events. I have a right to know why you came.''

For several seconds, he stared at her, then his hands sought his pockets again. ''All right,'' he agreed. ''I don't suppose I have any right to pride after this, and you deserve to get in a few licks after the way I've treated you.'' He came no closer, but his eyes locked hard on hers. ''I came here because of you. Because I had to get you back or go crazy.''

''Me?'' The pain was so sharp, Autumn laughed. She would not cry again. ''Oh Lucas, please, do better.'' She saw him flinch before he walked again to the window. ''You tossed me out, remember? You didn't want me then. You don't want me now.''

''Didn't want you!'' He whirled, knocking over a vase and sending it crashing. The anger surrounding him was fierce and vivid. ''You can't even comprehend how much I wanted you, have wanted you all these years. I thought I'd lose my mind from wanting you.''

''No, I won't listen to this.'' Autumn turned away to lean against the bedpost. ''I won't listen.''

''You asked for it. Now you'll listen.''

''You told me you didn't want me,'' she flung at him. ''I never meant anything to you. You told me it was finished and shrugged your shoulders like it had been nothing all along. Nothing, *nothing's* ever hurt me like the way you brushed me aside.''

''I know what I did.'' The anger was gone from his voice

to be replaced by strain. "I know the things I said to you while you stood there staring at me. I hated myself. I wanted you to scream, to rage, to make it easy for me to push you out. But you just stood there with tears falling down your face. I've never forgotten how you looked."

Autumn pulled herself together and faced him again. "You said you didn't want me. Why would you have said it if it weren't true?"

"Because you terrified me."

He said it so simply, she slumped down on the bed to stare at him. "Terrified you? *I* terrified *you?*"

"You don't know what you did to me—all that sweetness, all that generosity. You never asked anything of me, and yet you asked everything." He began to pace again. Autumn watched him in bewilderment. "You were an obsession, that's what I told myself. If I sent you away, hurt you badly enough to make you go, I'd be cured. The more I had of you, the more I needed. I'd wake up in the middle of the night and curse you for not being there. Then I'd curse myself for needing you there. I had to get away from you. I couldn't admit, not even to myself, that I loved you."

"Loved me?" Autumn repeated the words dumbly. "You loved me?"

"Loved then, love now and for the rest of my life." Lucas drew in a deep breath as if the words had left him shaken. "I wasn't able to tell you. I wasn't able to believe it." He stopped pacing and looked at her. "I've kept close tabs on you these past three years. I found all sorts of excuses to do so. When I found out about the inn, and your connection with it, I began to fly out here off and on. Finally, I admitted to myself that I wasn't going to make it without you. I mapped out a plan. I had it all worked out." He gave her an ironic smile.

"Plan?" Autumn repeated. Her mind was still whirling.

"It was easy to plant the idea in Aunt Tabby's head to write you and ask you to visit. Knowing you, I was sure you'd come without question. That was all I needed. I was so sure of myself. I thought all I'd have to do would be to issue the invitation, and you'd fall right back into my arms. Just like old times. I'd have you back, marry you before you sorted things out and pat myself on the back for being so damn clever."

"Marry me?" Autumn's brows flew up in astonishment.

"Once we were married," Lucas went on as if she hadn't interrupted, "I'd never have to worry about losing you again. I'd simply never give you a divorce no matter how you struggled. I deserved a good kick in the teeth, Cat, and you gave it to me. Instead of falling into my arms, you turned up your nose and told me to get lost. But that didn't throw me off for long. No, you'd loved me once, and I'd make you love me again. I could deal with the anger, but the ice...

"I didn't know I could be hurt that way. It was quite a shock. Seeing you again..." He paused and seemed to struggle for words. "It was torture, pure and simple, to be so close and not be able to have you. I wanted to tell you what you meant to me, then every time I got near you I'd behave like a maniac. The way you cringed from me yesterday, telling me not to hurt you again, I can't tell you what that did to me."

"Lucas—"

"You'd better let me finish," he told her. "I'll never be able to manage this again." He reached for a cigarette, changed his mind, then continued. "Julia roasted me, but I couldn't seem to stop myself. The more you resisted, the worse I treated you. Every time I approached you, I ended up doing the wrong thing. That day, up in your room..." He stopped and Autumn watched the struggle on his face. "I nearly raped you. I was crazy with jealousy after seeing you and Anderson. When I saw you cry—I swore I'd never be responsible for putting that look on your face again.

"I'd come up that day, ready to beg, crawl, plead, whatever it took. When I saw you kissing him, something snapped. I started thinking about the men you'd been with these past three years. The men who'd have you again when I couldn't."

"I've never been with any man but you," Autumn interrupted quietly.

Lucas's expression changed from barely suppressed fury to confusion before he studied her face with his familiar intensity. "Why?"

"Because every time I started to, I remembered he wasn't you."

As if in pain, Lucas shut his eyes, then turned from her. "Cat, I've never done anything in my life to deserve you."

"No, you probably haven't." She rose from the bed to stand behind him. "Lucas, if you want me, tell me so, and tell me why. Ask me, Lucas. I want it spelled out."

"All right." He moved his shoulders as he turned back, but his eyes weren't casual. "Cat..." He reached up to touch her cheek, then thrust the hand in his pocket. "I want you, desperately, because life isn't even tolerable without you. I need you because you are, and always were, the best part of my life. I love you for reasons it would take hours to tell you. Take me back, please. Marry me."

She wanted to throw herself into his arms, but held back. *Don't make it too easy on him.* Julia's words played back in her head. No, Lucas had had too much come too easily to him. Autumn smiled at him, but didn't reach out.

"All right," she said simply.

"All right?" He frowned, uncertain. "All right what?"

"I'll marry you. That's what you want, isn't it?"

"Yes, damn it, but—"

"The least you could do is kiss me, Lucas. It's traditional."

Lightly, he rested his hands on her shoulders. "Cat, I want you to be sure, because I'll never be able to let go. If it's gratitude, I'm desperate enough to take it. But I want you to think about what you're doing."

She tilted her head. "You did know I thought it was you with Helen on that film?"

"Cat, for God's sake—"

"I went into the woods," she continued mildly. "I was just about to expose that film when Steve found me. Lucas." She inched closer. "Do you know how I feel about the sanctity of film?"

His breath came out in a small huff of relief as he lifted a hand to either side of her face. He grinned. "Yes. Yes, I do. Something about the eleventh commandment."

"Thou shalt not expose unprocessed film. Now,"—she slid her arms up his back—"are you going to kiss me, or do I have to make you?"

*   *   *   *   *

THE WELCOMING

For my friend Catherine Coulter,
because she's always good for a laugh.

Chapter 1

Everything he needed was in the backpack slung over his shoulders. Including his .38. If things went well he would have no use for it.

Roman drew a cigarette out of the crumpled pack in his breast pocket and turned away from the wind to light it. A boy of about eight raced along the rail of the ferry, cheerfully ignoring his mother's calls. Roman felt a tug of empathy for the kid. It was cold, certainly. The biting wind off Puget Sound was anything but springlike. But it was one hell of a view. Sitting in the glass-walled lounge would be cozier, but it was bound to take something away from the experience.

The kid was snatched by a blond woman with pink cheeks and a rapidly reddening nose. Roman listened to them grumble at each other as she dragged the boy back inside. Families, he thought, rarely agreed on anything. Turning away, he leaned over the rail, lazily smoking as the ferry steamed by clumpy islands.

They had left the Seattle skyline behind, though the mountains of mainland Washington still rose up to amaze and impress the viewer. There was an aloneness here, despite the smattering of hardy passengers walking the slanting deck or bundling up in the patches of sunlight along wooden benches. He preferred the city, with its pace, its crowds, its energy. Its anonymity. He always had. For the life of him, he couldn't understand where this restless discontent he felt had come from, or why it was weighing so heavily on him.

The job. For the past year he'd been blaming it on the job. The pressure was something he'd always accepted, even courted. He'd always thought life without it would be bland and pointless. But just lately it hadn't been enough. He moved from place to place, taking little away, leaving less behind.

Time to get out, he thought as he watched a fishing boat chug by. Time to move on. And do what? he wondered in disgust, blowing out a stream of smoke. He could go into business for himself. He'd toyed with that notion a time or two. He could travel. He'd already been around the world, but it might be different to do it as a tourist.

Some brave soul came out on deck with a video camera. Roman turned, shifted, eased out of range. It was in all likelihood an unnecessary precaution; the move was instinctive. So was the watchfulness, and so was the casual stance, which hid a wiry readiness.

No one paid much attention to him, though a few of the women looked twice.

He was just over average height, with the taut, solid build of a lightweight boxer. The slouchy jacket and worn jeans hid well-tuned muscles. He wore no hat and his thick black hair flew freely away from his tanned, hollow-cheeked face. It was unshaven, tough-featured. The eyes, a pale, clear green, might have softened the go-to-hell appearance, but they were intense, direct and, at the moment, bored.

It promised to be a slow, routine assignment.

Roman heard the docking call and shifted his pack. Routine or not, the job was his. He would get it done, file his report, then take a few weeks to figure out what he wanted to do with the rest of his life.

He disembarked with the smattering of other walking passengers. There was a wild, sweet scent of flowers now that competed with the darker scent of the water. The flowers grew in free, romantic splendor, many with blossoms as big as his fist. Some part of him appreciated their color and their charm, but he rarely took the time to stop and smell the roses.

Cars rolled off the ramp and cruised toward home or a day of sightseeing. Once the car decks were unloaded, the new passengers would board and set off for one of the other islands or for the longer, colder trip to British Columbia.

Roman pulled out another cigarette, lit it and took a casual look around—at the pretty, colorful gardens, the charming white hotel and restaurant, the signs that gave information on ferries and parking. It was all a matter of timing now. He ignored the patio café, though he would have dearly loved a cup of coffee, and wound his way to the parking area.

He spotted the van easily enough, the white-and-blue American model with Whale Watch Inn painted on the side. It was his job to talk himself onto the van and into the inn. If the details had been taken care of on this end, it would be routine. If not, he would find another way.

Stalling, he bent down to tie his shoe. The waiting cars were being loaded, and the foot passengers were already on deck. There were no more than a dozen vehicles in the parking area now, including the van. He was taking another moment to unbutton his jacket when he saw the woman.

Her hair was pulled back in a braid, not loose as it had been in the file picture. It seemed to be a deeper, richer blonde in the sunlight. She wore tinted glasses, big-framed amber lenses that obscured half of her face, but he knew he wasn't mistaken. He could see the delicate line of her jaw, the small, straight nose, the full, shapely mouth.

His information was accurate. She was five-five, a hundred and ten pounds, with a small, athletic build. Her dress was casual—jeans, a chunky cream-colored cableknit sweater over a blue shirt. The shirt would match her eyes. The jeans were tucked into suede ankle boots, and a pair of slim crystal earrings dangled at her ears.

She walked with a sense of purpose, keys jingling in one hand, a big canvas bag slung over her other shoulder. There was nothing flirtatious about the walk, but a man would notice it. Long, limber strides, a subtle swing at the hips, head up, eyes ahead.

Yeah, a man would notice, Roman thought as he flicked the cigarette away. He figured she knew it.

He waited until she reached the van before he started toward her.

Charity stopped humming the finale of Beethoven's *Ninth*, looked down at her right front tire and swore. Because she didn't think anyone was watching, she kicked it, then moved around to the back of the van to get the jack.

"Got a problem?"

She jolted, nearly dropped the jack on her foot, then whirled around.

A tough customer. That was Charity's first thought as she stared at Roman. His eyes were narrowed against the sun. He had one hand hooked around the strap of his backpack and the other tucked in his pocket. She put her own hand on her heart, made certain it was still beating, then smiled.

"Yes. I have a flat. I just dropped a family of four off for the ferry, two of whom were under six and candidates for reform school. My nerves are shot, the plumbing's on the fritz in unit 6, and my handyman just won the lottery. How are you?"

The file hadn't mentioned that she had a voice like café au lait, the rich, dark kind you drank in New Orleans. He noted that, filed it away, then nodded toward the flat. "Want me to change it?"

Charity could have done it herself, but she wasn't one to refuse help when it was offered. Besides, he could probably do it faster, and he looked as though he could use the five dollars she would give him.

"Thanks." She handed him the jack, then dug a lemon drop out of her bag. The flat was bound to eat up the time she'd scheduled for lunch. "Did you just come in on the ferry?"

"Yeah." He didn't care for small talk, but he used it, and her friendliness, as handily as he used the jack. "I've been doing some traveling. Thought I'd spend some time on Orcas, see if I can spot some whales."

"You've come to the right place. I saw a pod yesterday from my window." She leaned against the van, enjoying the sunlight. As he worked, she watched his hands. Strong, competent, quick. She appreciated someone who could do a simple job well. "Are you on vacation?"

"Just traveling. I pick up odd jobs here and there. Know anyone looking for help?"

"Maybe." Lips pursed, she studied him as he pulled off the flat. He straightened, keeping one hand on the tire. "What kind of work?"

"This and that. Where's the spare?"

"Spare?" Looking into his eyes for more than ten seconds was like being hypnotized.

"Tire." The corner of his mouth quirked slightly in a reluctant smile. "You need one that isn't flat."

"Right. The spare." Shaking her head at her own foolishness, she went to get it. "It's in the back." She turned and bumped into him. "Sorry."

He put one hand on her arm to steady her. They stood for a moment in the sunlight, frowning at each other. "It's all right. I'll get it."

When he climbed into the van, Charity blew out a long, steadying breath. Her nerves were more ragged than she'd have believed possible. "Oh, watch out for the—" She grimaced as Roman sat back on his heels and peeled the remains of a cherry lollipop from his knee. Her laugh was spontaneous and as rich as her voice. "Sorry. A souvenir of Orcas Island from Jimmy 'The Destroyer' MacCarthy, a five-year-old delinquent."

"I'd rather have a T-shirt."

"Yes, well, who wouldn't?" Charity took the sticky mess from him, wrapped it in a tattered tissue and dropped it into her bag. "We're a family establishment," she explained as he climbed out with the spare. "Mostly everyone enjoys having children around, but once in a while you get a pair like Jimmy and Judy, the twin ghouls from Walla Walla, and you think about turning the place into a service station. Do you like children?"

He glanced up as he slipped the tire into place. "From a safe distance."

She laughed appreciatively at his answer. "Where are you from?"

"St. Louis." He could have chosen a dozen places. He couldn't have said why he'd chosen to tell the truth. "But I don't get back much."

"Family?"

"No."

The way he said it made her stifle her innate curiosity. She wouldn't invade anyone's privacy any more than she would drop the lint-covered lollipop on the ground. "I was born right here on Orcas. Every year I tell myself I'm going to take six months and travel. Anywhere." She shrugged as he tightened the last of the lug nuts. "I never seem to manage it. Anyway, it's beautiful here. If you don't have a deadline, you may find yourself staying longer than you planned."

"Maybe." He stood up to replace the jack. "If I can find some work, and a place to stay."

Charity didn't consider it an impulse. She had studied, measured and considered him for nearly fifteen minutes. Most job interviews took little more. He had a strong back and intelligent—if disconcerting—eyes, and if the state of his pack and his shoes was any indication he was down on his luck. As her name implied, she had been taught to offer people a helping hand. And if she could solve one of her more immediate and pressing problems at the same time...

"You any good with your hands?" she asked him.

He looked at her unable to prevent his mind from taking a slight detour. "Yeah. Pretty good."

Her brow—and her blood pressure—rose a little when she saw his quick survey. "I mean with tools. Hammer, saw, screwdriver. Can you do any carpentry, household repairs?"

"Sure." It was going to be easy, almost too easy. He wondered why he felt the small, unaccustomed tug of guilt.

"Like I said, my handyman won the lottery, a big one. He's gone to Hawaii to study bikinis and eat poi. I'd wish him well, except we were in the middle of renovating the west

wing. Of the inn,'' she added, pointing to the logo on the van.
"If you know your way around two-by-fours and drywall I
can give you room and board and five an hour.''

"Sounds like we've solved both our problems.''

"Great.'' She offered a hand. "I'm Charity Ford.''

"DeWinter.'' He clasped her hand. "Roman DeWinter.''

"Okay, Roman.'' She swung her door open. "Climb
aboard.''

She didn't look gullible, Roman thought as he settled into
the seat beside her. But then, he knew—better than most—
that looks were deceiving. He was exactly where he wanted
to be, and he hadn't had to resort to a song and dance. He lit
a cigarette as she pulled out of the parking lot.

"My grandfather built the inn in 1938,'' she said, rolling
down her window. "He added on to it a couple of times over
the years, but it's still really an inn. We can't bring ourselves
to call it a resort, even in the brochures. I hope you're looking
for remote.''

"That suits me.''

"Me too. Most of the time.'' Talkative guy, she mused with
a half smile. But that was all right. She could talk enough for
both of them. "It's early in the season yet, so we're a long
way from full.'' She cocked her elbow on the opened window
and cheerfully took over the bulk of the conversation. The
sunlight played on her earrings and refracted into brilliant colors. "You should have plenty of free time to knock around.
The view from Mount Constitution's really spectacular. Or, if
you're into it, the hiking trails are great.''

"I thought I might spend some time in B.C.''

"That's easy enough. Take the ferry to Sidney. We do
pretty well with tour groups going back and forth.''

"We?''

"The inn. Pop—my grandfather—built a half-dozen cabins
in the sixties. We give a special package rate to tour groups.
They can rent the cabins and have breakfast and dinner included. They're a little rustic, but the tourists really go for
them. We get a group about once a week. During the season
we can triple that.''

She turned onto a narrow, winding road and kept the speed at fifty.

Roman already knew the answers, but he knew it might seem odd if he didn't ask the questions. "Do you run the inn?"

"Yeah. I've worked there on and off for as long as I can remember. When my grandfather died a couple of years ago I took over." She paused a moment. It still hurt; she supposed it always would. "He loved it. Not just the place, but the whole idea of meeting new people every day, making them comfortable, finding out about them."

"I guess it does pretty well."

She shrugged. "We get by." They rounded a bend where the forest gave way to a wide expanse of blue water. The curve of the island was clear, jutting out and tucking back in contrasting shades of deep green and brown. A few houses were tucked high in the cliffs beyond. A boat with billowing white sails ran with the wind, rippling the glassy water. "There are views like this all around the island. Even when you live here they dazzle you."

"And scenery's good for business."

She frowned a little. "It doesn't hurt," she said, and glanced back at him. "Are you really interested in seeing whales?"

"It seemed like a good idea since I was here."

She stopped the van and pointed to the cliffs. "If you've got patience and a good set of binoculars, up there's a good bet. We've spotted them from the inn, as I said. Still, if you want a close look, your best bet's out on a boat." When he didn't comment, she started the van again. He was making her jittery, she realized. He seemed to be looking not at the water or the forest but at her.

Roman glanced at her hands. Strong, competent, no-nonsense hands, he decided, though the fingers were beginning to tap a bit nervously on the wheel. She continued to drive fast, steering the van easily through the switchbacks. Another car approached. Without slackening speed, Charity lifted a hand in a salute.

"That was Lori, one of our waitresses. She works an early shift so she can be home when her kids get back from school. We usually run with a staff of ten, then add on five or six part-time during the summer."

They rounded the next curve, and the inn came into view. It was exactly what he'd expected, and yet it was more charming than the pictures he'd been shown. It was white clapboard, with weathered blue trim around arched and oval windows. There were fanciful turrets, narrow walkways and a wide skirting porch. A sweep of lawn led directly to the water, where a narrow, rickety dock jutted out. Tied to it was a small motorboat that swung lazily in the current.

A mill wheel turned in a shallow pond at the side of the inn, slapping the water musically. To the west, where the trees began to thicken, he could make out one of the cabins she had spoken of. Flowers were everywhere.

"There's a bigger pond out back." Charity drove around the side and pulled into a small graveled lot that was already half full. "We keep the trout there. The trail takes you to cabins 1, 2 and 3. Then it forks off to 4, 5 and 6." She stepped out and waited for him to join her. "Most everyone uses the back entrance. I can show you around the grounds later, if you like, but we'll get you settled in first."

"It's a nice place." He said it almost without thinking, and he meant it. There were two rockers on the square back porch, and an adirondack chair that needed its white paint freshened. Roman turned to study the view a guest would overlook from the empty seat. Part forest, part water, and very appealing. Restful. Welcoming. He thought of the pistol in his backpack. Appearances, he thought again, were deceiving.

With a slight frown, Charity watched him. He didn't seem to be looking so much as absorbing. It was an odd thought, but she would have sworn if anyone were to ask him to describe the inn six months later he would be able to, right down to the last pinecone.

Then he turned to her, and the feeling remained, more personal now, more intense. The breeze picked up, jingling the wind chimes that hung from the eaves.

"Are you an artist?" she asked abruptly.

"No." He smiled, and the change in his face was quick and charming. "Why?"

"Just wondering." You'd have to be careful of that smile, Charity decided. It made you relax, and she doubted he was a man it was wise to relax around.

The double glass doors opened up into a large, airy room that smelled of lavender and woodsmoke. There were two long, cushiony sofas and a pair of overstuffed chairs near a huge stone fireplace where logs crackled. Antiques were scattered throughout the room—a desk and chair with a trio of old inkwells, an oak hatrack, a buffet with glossy carved doors. Tucked into a corner was a spinet with yellowing keys and the pair of wide arched windows that dominated the far wall made the water seem part of the room's decor. At a table near them, two women were playing a leisurely game of Scrabble.

"Who's winning today?" Charity asked.

Both looked up. And beamed. "It's neck and neck." The woman on the right fluffed her hair when she spotted Roman. She was old enough to be his grandmother, but she slipped her glasses off and straightened her thin shoulders. "I didn't realize you were bringing back another guest, dear."

"Neither did I." Charity moved over to add another log to the fire. "Roman DeWinter, Miss Lucy and Miss Millie."

His smile came again, smoothly. "Ladies."

"DeWinter." Miss Lucy put on her glasses to get a better look. "Didn't we know a DeWinter once, Millie?"

"Not that I recall." Millie, always ready to flirt, continued to beam at Roman, though he was hardly more than a myopic blur. "Have you been to the inn before, Mr. DeWinter?"

"No, ma'am. This is my first time in the San Juans."

"You're in for a treat." Millie let out a little sigh. It was really too bad what the years did. It seemed only yesterday that handsome young men had kissed her hand and asked her to go for a walk. Today they called her ma'am. She went wistfully back to her game.

"The ladies have been coming to the inn longer than I can

remember,'' Charity told Roman as she led the way down a hall. ''They're lovely, but I should warn you about Miss Millie. I'm told she had quite a reputation in her day, and she still has an eye for an attractive man.''

''I'll watch my step.''

''I get the impression you usually do.'' She took out a set of keys and unlocked the door. ''This leads to the west wing.'' She started down another hall, brisk, businesslike. ''As you can see, renovations were well under way before George hit the jackpot. The trim's been stripped.'' She gestured to the neat piles of wood along the freshly painted wall. ''The doors need to be refinished yet, and the original hardware's in that box.''

After taking off her sunglasses, she dropped them into her bag. He'd been right. The collar of her shirt matched her eyes almost exactly. He looked into them as she examined George's handiwork.

''How many rooms?''

''There are two singles, a double and a family suite in this wing, all in varying stages of disorder.'' She skirted a door that was propped against a wall, then walked into a room. ''You can take this one. It's as close to being finished as I have in this section.''

It was a small, bright room. Its window was bordered with stained glass and looked out over the mill wheel. The bed was stripped, and the floors were bare and in need of sanding. Wallpaper that was obviously new covered the walls from the ceiling down to a white chair rail. Below that was bare drywall.

''It doesn't look like much now,'' Charity commented.

''It's fine.'' He'd spent time in places that made the little room look like a suite at the Waldorf.

Automatically she checked the closet and the adjoining bath, making a mental list of what was needed. ''You can start in here, if it'll make you more comfortable. I'm not particular. George had his own system. I never understood it, but he usually managed to get things done.''

He hooked his thumbs in the front pockets of his jeans. "You got a game plan?"

"Absolutely."

Charity spent the next thirty minutes taking him through the wing and explaining exactly what she wanted. Roman listened, commenting little, and studied the setup. He knew from the blueprints he'd studied that the floor plan of this section mirrored that of the east wing. His position in it would give him easy access to the main floor and the rest of the inn.

He'd have to work, he mused as he looked at the half-finished walls and the paint tarps. He considered it a small bonus. Working with his hands was something he enjoyed and something he'd had little time for in the past.

She was very precise in her instructions. A woman who knew what she wanted and intended to have it. He appreciated that. He had no doubt that she was very good at what she did, whether it was running an inn...or something else.

"What's up there?" He pointed to a set of stairs at the end of the hallway.

"My rooms. We'll worry about them after the guest quarters are done." She jingled the keys as her thoughts went off in a dozen directions. "So, what do you think?"

"About what?"

"About the work."

"Do you have tools?"

"In the shed, the other side of the parking area."

"I can handle it."

"Yes." Charity tossed the keys to him. She was certain he could. They were standing in the octagonal parlor of the family suite. It was empty but for stacks of material and tarps. And it was quiet. She noticed all at once that they were standing quite close together and that she couldn't hear a sound. Feeling foolish, she took a key off her ring.

"You'll need this."

"Thanks." He tucked it in his pocket.

She drew a deep breath, wondering why she felt as though she'd just taken a long step with her eyes closed. "Have you had lunch?"

"No."

"I'll show you down to the kitchen. Mae'll fix you up." She started out, a little too quickly. She wanted to escape from the sensation that she was completely alone with him. And helpless. Charity moved her shoulders restlessly. A stupid thought, she told herself. She'd never been helpless. Still, she felt a breath of relief when she closed the door behind them.

She took him downstairs, through the empty lobby and into a large dining room decorated in pastels. There were small milk-glass vases on each table, with a handful of fresh flowers in each. Big windows opened onto a view of the water, and as if carrying through the theme, an aquarium was built into the south wall.

She stopped there for a moment, hardly breaking stride, scanning the room until she was satisfied that the tables were properly set for dinner. Then she pushed through a swinging door into the kitchen.

"And I say it needs more basil."

"I say it don't."

"Whatever you do," Charity murmured under her breath, "don't agree with either of them. Ladies," she said, using her best smile. "I brought you a hungry man."

The woman guarding the pot held up a dripping spoon. The best way to describe her was wide—face, hips, hands. She gave Roman a quick, squint-eyed survey. "Sit down, then," she told him, jerking a thumb in the direction of a long wooden table.

"Mae Jenkins, Roman DeWinter."

"Ma'am."

"And Dolores Rumsey." The other woman was holding a jar of herbs. She was as narrow as Mae was wide. After giving Roman a nod, she began to ease her way toward the pot.

"Keep away from that," Mae ordered, "and get the man some fried chicken."

Muttering, Dolores stalked off to find a plate.

"Roman's going to pick up where George left off," Charity explained. "He'll be staying in the west wing."

"Not from around here." Mae looked at him again, the way he imagined a nanny would look at a small, grubby child. "No."

With a sniff, she poured him some coffee. "Looks like you could use a couple of decent meals."

"You'll get them here," Charity put in, playing peace-maker. She winced only a little when Dolores slapped a plate of cold chicken and potato salad in front of Roman.

"Needed more dill." Dolores glared at him, as if she were daring him to disagree. "She wouldn't listen."

Roman figured the best option was to grin at her and keep his mouth full. Before Mae could respond, the door swung open again.

"Can a guy get a cup of coffee in here?" The man stopped and sent Roman a curious look.

"Bob Mullins, Roman DeWinter. I hired him to finish the west wing. Bob's one of my many right hands."

"Welcome aboard." He moved to the stove to pour himself a cup of coffee, adding three lumps of sugar as Mae clucked her tongue at him. The sweet tooth didn't seem to have an effect on him. He was tall, perhaps six-two, and he couldn't weigh more than 160. His light brown hair was cut short around his ears and swept back from his high forehead.

"You from back east?" Bob asked between sips of coffee.

"East of here."

"Easy to do." He grinned when Mae flapped a hand to move him away from her stove.

"Did you get that invoice business straightened out with the greengrocer?" Charity asked.

"All taken care of. You got a couple of calls while you were out. And there's some papers you need to sign."

"I'll get to it." She checked her watch. "Now." She glanced over at Roman. "I'll be in the office off the lobby if there's anything you need to know."

"I'll be fine."

"Okay." She studied him for another moment. She couldn't quite figure out how he could be in a room with four other people and seem so alone. "See you later."

* * *

Roman took a long, casual tour of the inn before he began to haul tools into the west wing. He saw a young couple who had to be newlyweds locked in an embrace near the pond. A man and a young boy played one-on-one on a small concrete basketball court. The ladies, as he had come to think of them, had left their game to sit on the porch and discuss the garden. Looking exhausted, a family of four pulled up in a station wagon, then trooped toward the cabins. A man in a fielder's cap walked down the pier with a video camera on his shoulder.

There were birds trilling in the trees, and there was the distant sound of a motorboat. He heard a baby crying half-heartedly, and the strains of a Mozart piano sonata.

If he hadn't pored over the data himself he would have sworn he was in the wrong place.

He chose the family suite and went to work, wondering how long it would take him to get into Charity's rooms.

There was something soothing about working with his hands. Two hours passed, and he relaxed a little. A check of his watch had him deciding to take another, unnecessary trip to the shed. Charity had mentioned that wine was served in what she called the gathering room every evening at five. It wouldn't hurt for him to get another, closer look at the inn's guests.

He started out, then stopped by the doorway to his room. He'd heard something, a movement. Cautious, he eased inside the door and scanned the empty room.

Humming under her breath, Charity came out of the bath, where she'd just placed fresh towels. She unfolded linens and began to make the bed.

"What are you doing?"

Muffling a scream, she stumbled backward, then eased down on the bed to catch her breath. "My God, Roman, don't do that."

He stepped into the room, watching her with narrowed eyes. "I asked what you were doing."

"That should be obvious." She patted the pile of linens with her hand.

"You do the housekeeping, too?"

"From time to time." Recovered, she stood up and smoothed the bottom sheet on the bed. "There's soap and towels in the bath," she told him, then tilted her head. "Looks like you can use them." She unfolded the top sheet with an expert flick. "Been busy?"

"That was the deal."

With a murmur of agreement, she tucked up the corners at the foot of the bed the way he remembered his grandmother doing. "I put an extra pillow and blanket in the closet." She moved from one side of the bed to the other in a way that had him watching her with simple male appreciation. He couldn't remember the last time he'd seen anyone make a bed. It stirred thoughts in him that he couldn't afford. Thoughts of what it might be like to mess it up again—with her.

"Do you ever stop?"

"I've been known to." She spread a white wedding-ring quilt on the bed. "We're expecting a tour tomorrow, so everyone's a bit busy."

"Tomorrow?"

"Mmm. On the first ferry from Sidney." She fluffed his pillows, satisfied. "Did you—"

She broke off when she turned and all but fell against him. His hands went to her hips instinctively as hers braced against his shoulders. An embrace—unplanned, unwanted and shockingly intimate.

She was slender beneath the long, chunky sweater, he realized, even more slender than a man might expect. And her eyes were bluer than they had any right to be, bigger, softer. She smelled like the inn, smelled of that welcoming combination of lavender and woodsmoke. Drawn to it, he continued to hold her, though he knew he shouldn't.

"Did I what?" His fingers spread over her hips, drawing her just a fraction closer. He saw the dazed confusion in her eyes; her reaction tugged at him.

She'd forgotten everything. She could only stare, almost stupefied by the sensations that spiked through her. Involuntarily her fingers curled into his shirt. She got an impression of strength, a ruthless strength with the potential for violence. The fact that it excited her left her speechless.

"Do you want something?" he murmured.

"What?"

He thought about kissing her, about pressing his mouth hard on hers and plunging into her. He would enjoy the taste, the momentary passion. "I·asked if you wanted something." Slowly he ran his hands up under her sweater to her waist.

The shock of heat, the press of fingers, brought her back. "No." She started to back away, found herself held still, and fought her rising panic. Before she could speak again, he had released her. Disappointment. That was an odd reaction, she thought, when you'd just missed getting burned.

"I was—" She took a deep breath and waited for her scattered nerves to settle. "I was going to ask if you'd found everything you needed."

His eyes never left hers. "It looks like it."

She pressed her lips together to moisten them. "Good. I've got a lot to do, so I'll let you get back."

He took her arm before she could step away. Maybe it wasn't smart, but he wanted to touch her again. "Thanks for the towels."

"Sure."

He watched her hurry out, knowing her nerves were as jangled as his own. Thoughtfully he pulled out a cigarette. He couldn't remember ever having been thrown off balance so easily. Certainly not by a woman who'd done nothing more than look at him. Still, he made a habit of landing on his feet.

It might be to his advantage to get close to her, to play on the response he'd felt from her. Ignoring a wave of self-disgust, he struck a match.

He had a job to do. He couldn't afford to think about Charity Ford as anything more than a means to an end.

He drew smoke in, cursing the dull ache in his belly.

Chapter 2

It was barely dawn, and the sky to the east was fantastic. Roman stood near the edge of the narrow road, his hands tucked in his back pockets. Though he rarely had time for them, he enjoyed mornings such as this, when the air was cool and sparkling clear. A man could breathe here, and if he could afford the luxury he could empty his mind and simply experience.

He'd promised himself thirty minutes, thirty solitary, soothing minutes. The blooming sunlight pushed through the cloud formations, turning them into wild, vivid colors and shapes. Dream shapes. He considered lighting a cigarette, then rejected it. For the moment he wanted only the taste of morning air flavored by the sea.

There was a dog barking in the distance, a faint yap, yap, yap that only added to the ambience. Gulls, out for an early feeding, swooped low over the water, slicing the silence with their lonely cries. The fragrance of flowers, a celebration of spring, carried delicately on the quiet breeze.

He wondered why he'd been so certain he preferred the rush and noise of cities.

As he stood there he saw a deer come out of the trees and raise her head to scent the air. That was freedom, he thought abruptly. To know your place and to be content with it. The doe cleared the trees, picking her way delicately toward the high grass. Behind her came a gangly fawn. Staying upwind, Roman watched them graze.

He was restless. Even as he tried to absorb and accept the peace around him he felt the impatience struggling through. This wasn't his place. He had no place. That was one of the things that made him so perfect for his job. No roots, no family, no woman waiting for his return. That was the way he wanted it.

But he'd felt enormous satisfaction in doing the carpentry the day before, in leaving his mark on something that would last. All the better for his cover, he told himself. If he showed some skill and some care in the work he would be accepted more easily.

He was already accepted.

She trusted him. She'd given him a roof and a meal and a job, thinking he needed all three. She seemed to have no guile in her. Something had simmered between them the evening before, yet she had done nothing to provoke or prolong it. She hadn't—though he knew all females were capable of it from birth—issued a silent invitation that she might or might not have intended to keep.

She'd simply looked at him, and everything she felt had been almost ridiculously clear in her eyes.

He couldn't think of her as a woman. He couldn't think of her as ever being *his* woman.

He felt the urge for a cigarette again, and this time he deliberately suppressed it. If there was something you wanted that badly, it was best to pass it by. Once you gave in, you surrendered control.

He'd wanted Charity. For one brief, blinding instant the day before, he had craved her. A very serious error. He'd blocked the need, but it had continued to surface—when he'd heard her come into the wing for the night, when he'd listened to the sound of Chopin drifting softly down the stairway from her rooms. And again in the middle of the night, when he'd awakened to the deep country silence, thinking of her, imagining her.

He didn't have time for desires. In another place, at another time, they might have met and enjoyed each other for as long as enjoyments lasted. But now she was part of an assignment—nothing less, nothing more.

He heard the sound of running footsteps and tensed instinctively. The deer, as alert as he, lifted her head, then sprinted back into the trees with her young. His weapon was strapped just above his ankle, more out of habit than necessity, but he didn't reach for it. If he needed it it could be in his hand in under a second. Instead he waited, braced, to see who was running down the deserted road at dawn.

Charity was breathing fast, more from the effort of keeping pace with her dog than from the three-mile run. Ludwig bounded ahead, tugged to the right, jerked to the left, tangled and untangled in the leash. It was a daily routine, one that both of them were accustomed to. She could have controlled the little golden cocker, but she didn't want to spoil his fun. Instead, she swerved with him, adjusting her pace from a flat-out run to an easy jog and back again.

She hesitated briefly when she saw Roman. Then, because Ludwig sprinted ahead, she tightened her grip on the leash and kept pace.

"Good morning," she called out, then skidded to a halt when Ludwig decided to jump on Roman's shins and bark at him. "He doesn't bite."

"That's what they all say." But he grinned and crouched down to scratch between the dog's ears. Ludwig immediately collapsed, rolled over and exposed his belly for rubbing. "Nice dog."

"A nice spoiled dog," Charity added. "I have to keep him fenced because of the guests, but he eats like a king. You're up early."

"So are you."

"I figure Ludwig deserves a good run every morning, since he's so understanding about being fenced."

To show his appreciation, Ludwig raced once around Roman, tangling his lead around his legs.

"Now if I could only get him to understand the concept of

a leash.'' She stooped to untangle Roman and to control the now-prancing dog.

Her light jacket was unzipped, exposing a snug T-shirt darkened with sweat between her breasts. Her hair, pulled straight, almost severely, back from her face, accented her bone structure. Her skin seemed almost translucent as it glowed from her run. He had an urge to touch it, to see how it felt under his fingertips. And to see if that instant reaction would rush out again.

''Ludwig, be still a minute.'' She laughed and tugged at his collar.

In response, the dog jumped up and lapped at her face. ''He listens well,'' Roman commented.

''You can see why I need the fence. He thinks he can play with everyone.'' Her hand brushed Roman's leg as she struggled with the leash.

When he took her wrist, both of them froze.

He could feel her pulse skip, then sprint. It was a quick, vulnerable response that was unbearably arousing. Though it cost him, he kept his fingers loose. He had only meant to stop her before she inadvertently found his weapon. Now they crouched, knee to knee, in the center of the deserted road, with the dog trying to nuzzle between them.

''You're trembling.'' He said it warily, but he didn't release her. ''Do you always react that way when a man touches you?''

''No.'' Because it baffled her, she kept still and waited to see what would happen next. ''I'm pretty sure this is a first.''

It pleased him to hear it, and it annoyed him, because he wanted to believe it. ''Then we'll have to be careful, won't we?'' He released her, then stood up.

More slowly, because she wasn't sure of her balance, she rose. He was angry. Though he was holding on to his temper, it was clear enough to see in his eyes. ''I'm not very good at being careful.''

His gaze whipped back to hers. There was a fire in it, a fire that raged and then was quickly and completely suppressed. ''I am.''

"Yes." The brief, heated glance had alarmed her, but Charity had always held her own. She tilted her head to study him. "I think you'd have to be, with that streak of violence you have to contend with. Who are you mad at, Roman?"

He didn't like to be read that easily. Watching her, he lowered a hand to pet Ludwig, who was resting his front paws on his knees. "Nobody at the moment," he told her, but it was a lie. He was furious—with himself.

She only shook her head. "You're entitled to your secrets, but I can't help wondering why you'd be angry with yourself for responding to me."

He took a lazy scan of the road, up, then down. They might have been alone on the island. "Would you like me to do something about it, here and now?"

He could, she realized. And he would. If he was pushed too far he would do exactly what he wanted, when he wanted. The frisson of excitement that passed through her annoyed her. Macho types were for other women, different women—not Charity Ford. Deliberately she looked at her watch.

"Thanks. I'm sure that's a delightful offer, but I have to get back and set up for breakfast." Struggling with the dog, she started off at what she hoped was a dignified walk. "I'll let you know if I can squeeze in, say, fifteen minutes later."

"Charity?"

She turned her head and aimed a cool look. "Yes?"

"Your shoe's untied."

She just lifted her chin and continued on.

Roman grinned at her back and tucked his thumbs in his pockets. Yes, indeed, the woman had one hell of a walk. It was too damn bad all around that he was beginning to like her.

He was interested in the tour group. It was a simple matter for Roman to loiter on the first floor, lingering over a second cup of coffee in the kitchen, passing idle conversation with the thick-armed Mae and the skinny Dolores. He hadn't expected to be put to work, but when he'd found himself with an armful of table linens he had made the best of it.

Charity, wearing a bright red sweatshirt with the inn's logo across the chest, meticulously arranged a folded napkin in a water glass. Roman waited a moment, watching her busy fingers smoothing and tapering the cloth.

"Where do you want these?"

She glanced over, wondering if she should still be annoyed with him, then decided against it. At the moment she needed every extra hand she could get. "On the tables would be a good start. White on the bottom, apricot on top, slanted. Okay?" She indicated a table that was already set.

"Sure." He began to spread the cloths. "How many are you expecting?"

"Fifteen on the tour." She held a glass up to the light and placed it on the table only after a critical inspection. "Their breakfast is included. Plus the guests already registered. We serve between seven-thirty and ten." She checked her watch, satisfied, then moved to another table. "We get some drop-ins, as well." After setting a chipped bread plate aside, she reached for another. "But it's lunch and dinner that really get hectic."

Dolores swooped in with a stack of china, then dashed out again when Mae squawked at her. Before the door had swung closed, the waitress they had passed on the road the day before rushed out with a tray of clanging silverware.

"Right," Roman murmured.

Charity rattled off instructions to the waitress, finished setting yet another table, then rushed over to a blackboard near the doorway and began to copy out the morning menu in a flowing, elegant hand.

Dolores, whose spiky red hair and pursed lips made Roman think of a scrawny chicken, shoved through the swinging door and set her fists on her skinny hips. "I don't have to take this, Charity."

Charity calmly continued to write. "Take what?"

"I'm doing the best that I can, and you know I told you I was feeling poorly."

Dolores was always feeling poorly, Charity thought as she

added a ham-and-cheese omelet to the list. Especially when she didn't get her way. "Yes, Dolores."

"My chest's so tight that I can hardly take a breath."

"Um-hmm."

"Was up half the night, but I come in, just like always."

"And I appreciate it, Dolores. You know how much I depend on you."

"Well." Slightly mollified, Dolores tugged at her apron. "I guess I can be counted on to do my job, but you can just tell that woman in there—" She jerked a thumb toward the kitchen. "Just tell her to get off my back."

"I'll speak to her, Dolores. Just try to be patient. We're all a little frazzled this morning, with Mary Alice out sick again."

"Sick." Dolores sniffed. "Is that what they're calling it these days?"

Listening with only half an ear, Charity continued to write. "What do you mean?"

"Don't know why her car was in Bill Perkin's driveway all night again if she's sick. Now, with my condition—"

Charity stopped writing. Roman's brow lifted when he heard the sudden thread of steel in her voice. "We'll talk about this later, Dolores."

Deflated, Dolores poked out her lower lip and stalked back into the kitchen.

Storing her anger away, Charity turned to the waitress. "Lori?"

"Almost ready."

"Good. If you can handle the registered guests, I'll be back to give you a hand after I check the tour group in."

"No problem."

"I'll be at the front desk with Bob." Absently she pushed her braid behind her back. "If it gets too busy, send for me. Roman—"

"Want me to bus tables?"

She gave him a quick, grateful smile. "Do you know how?"

"I can figure it out."

"Thanks." She checked her watch, then rushed out.

He hadn't expected to enjoy himself, but it was hard not to, with Miss Millie flirting with him over her raspberry preserves. The scent of baking—something rich, with apples and cinnamon—the quiet strains of classical music and the murmur of conversation made it almost impossible not to relax. He carried trays to and from the kitchen. The muttered exchanges between Mae and Dolores were more amusing than annoying.

So he enjoyed himself. And took advantage of his position by doing his job.

As he cleared the tables by the windows, he watched a tour van pull up to the front entrance. He counted heads and studied the faces of the group. The guide was a big man in a white shirt that strained across his shoulders. He had a round, ruddy, cheerful face that smiled continually as he piloted his passengers inside. Roman moved across the room to watch them mill around in the lobby.

They were a mix of couples and families with small children. The guide—Roman already knew his name was Block—greeted Charity with a hearty smile and then handed her a list of names.

Did she know that Block had done a stretch in Leavenworth for fraud? he wondered. Was she aware that the man she was joking with had escaped a second term only because of some fancy legal footwork?

Roman's jaw tensed as Block reached over and flicked a finger at Charity's dangling gold earring.

As she assigned cabins and dealt out keys, two of the group approached the desk to exchange money. Fifty for one, sixty for the other, Roman noted as Canadian bills were passed to Charity's assistant and American currency passed back.

Within ten minutes the entire group was seated in the dining room, contemplating breakfast. Charity breezed in behind them, putting on an apron. She flipped open a pad and began to take orders.

She didn't look as if she were in a hurry, Roman noted. The way she chatted and smiled and answered questions, it was as though she had all the time in the world. But she moved like lightning. She carried three plates on her right arm, served coffee with her left hand and cooed over a baby, all at the same time.

Something was eating at her, Roman mused. It hardly showed…just a faint frown between her eyes. Had something gone wrong that morning that he'd missed? If there was a glitch in the system, it was up to him to find it and exploit it. That was the reason he was here on the inside.

Charity poured another round of coffee for a table of four, joked with a bald man wearing a paisley tie, then made her way over to Roman.

"I think the crisis has passed." She smiled at him, but again he caught something…. Anger? Disappointment?

"Is there anything you don't do around here?"

"I try to stay out of the kitchen. The restaurant has a three-star rating." She glanced longingly at the coffeepot. There would be time for that later. "I want to thank you for pitching in this morning."

"That's okay." He discovered he wanted to see her smile. Really smile. "The tips were good. Miss Millie slipped me a five."

She obliged him. Her lips curved quickly, and whatever had clouded her eyes cleared for a moment. "She likes the way you look in a tool belt. Why don't you take a break before you start on the west wing?"

"All right."

She grimaced at the sound of glass breaking. "I didn't think the Snyder kid wanted that orange juice." She hurried off to clean up the mess and listen to the parents' apologies.

The front desk was deserted. Roman decided that Charity's assistant was either shut up in the side office or out hauling luggage to the cabins. He considered slipping behind the desk and taking a quick look at the books but decided it could wait. Some work was better done in the dark.

An hour later Charity let herself into the west wing. She'd managed to hold on to her temper as she'd passed the guests on the first floor. She'd smiled and chatted with an elderly couple playing Parcheesi in the gathering room. But when the door closed behind her she let loose with a series of furious, pent-up oaths. She wanted to kick something.

Roman stepped into a doorway and watched her stride down the hall. Anger had made her eyes dark and brilliant.

"Problem?"

"Yes," she snapped. She stalked half a dozen steps past him, then whirled around. "I can take incompetence, and even some degree of stupidity. I can even tolerate an occasional bout of laziness. But I won't be lied to."

Roman waited a beat. Her anger was ripe and rich, but it wasn't directed at him. "All right," he said, and waited.

"She could have told me she wanted time off, or a different shift. I might have been able to work it out. Instead she lies, calling in sick at the last minute five days out of the last two weeks. I was worried about her." She turned again, then gave in and kicked a door. "I hate being made a fool of. And I *hate* being lied to."

It was a simple matter to put two and two together. "You're talking about the waitress…Mary Alice?"

"Of course." She spun around. "She came begging me for a job three months ago. That's our slowest time, but I felt sorry for her. Now she's sleeping with Bill Perkin—or I guess it's more accurate to say she's not getting any sleep, so she calls in sick. I had to fire her." She let out a breath with a sound like an engine letting off steam. "I get a headache whenever I have to fire anybody."

"Is that what was bothering you all morning?"

"As soon as Dolores mentioned Bill, I knew." Calmer now, she rubbed at the insistent ache between her eyes. "Then I had to get through the check-in and the breakfast shift before I could call and deal with her. She cried." She gave Roman a long, miserable look. "I knew she was going to cry."

"Listen, baby, the best thing for you to do is take some aspirin and forget about it."

"I've already taken some."

"Give it a chance to kick in." Before he realized what he was doing, he lifted his hands and framed her face. Moving his thumbs in slow circles, he massaged her temples. "You've got too much going on in there."

"Where?"

"In your head."

She felt her eyes getting heavy and her blood growing warm. "Not at the moment." She tilted her head back and let her eyes close. Moving on instinct, she stepped forward. "Roman…" She sighed a little as the ache melted out of her head and stirred in the very center of her. "I like the way you look in a tool belt, too."

"Do you know what you're asking for?"

She studied his mouth. It was full and firm, and it would certainly be ruthless on a woman's. "Not exactly." Perhaps that was the appeal, she thought as she stared up at him. She didn't know. But she felt, and what she felt was new and thrilling. "Maybe it's better that way."

"No." Though he knew it was a mistake, he couldn't resist skimming his fingers down to trace her jaw, then her lips. "It's always better to know the consequences before you take the action."

"So we're being careful again."

He dropped his hands. "Yeah."

She should have been grateful. Instead of taking advantage of her confused emotions he was backing off, giving her room. She wanted to be grateful, but she felt only the sting of rejection. He had started it, she thought. Again. And he had stopped it. Again. She was sick and tired of being jolted along according to his whims.

"You miss a lot that way, don't you, Roman? A lot of warmth, a lot of joy."

"A lot of disappointment."

"Maybe. I guess it's harder for some of us to live our lives aloof from others. But if that's your choice, fine." She drew in a deep breath. Her headache was coming back, doubled. "Don't touch me again. I make it a habit to finish whatever I start." She glanced into the room behind them. "You're doing a nice job here," she said briskly. "I'll let you get back to it."

He cursed her as he sanded the wood for the window trim. She had no right to make him feel guilty just because he wanted to keep his distance. Noninvolvement wasn't just a habit with him; it was a matter of survival. It was self-indulgent and dangerous to move forward every time you were attracted to a woman.

But it was more than attraction, and it was certainly different from anything he'd felt before. Whenever he was near her, his purpose became clouded with fantasies of what it would be like to be with her, to hold her, to make love with her.

And fantasies were all they were, he reminded himself. If things went well he would be gone in a matter of days. Before he was done he might very well destroy her life.

It was his job, he reminded himself.

He saw her, walking out to the van with those long, purposeful strides of hers, the keys jingling in her hand. Behind her were the newlyweds, holding hands, even though each was carrying a suitcase.

She would be taking them to the ferry, he thought. That would give him an hour to search her rooms.

He knew how to go through every inch of a room without leaving a trace. He concentrated first on the obvious—the desk in the small parlor. It was common for people to be careless in the privacy of their own homes. A slip of paper, a scribbled note, a name in an address book, were often left behind for the trained eye to spot.

It was an old desk, solid mahogany with a few rings and scratches. Two of the brass pulls were loose. Like the rest of the room, it was neat and well organized. Her personal papers—insurance documents, bills, correspondence—were filed on the left. Inn business took up the three drawers on the right.

He could see from a quick scan that the inn made a reasonable profit, most of which she funneled directly back into it. New linens, bathroom fixtures, paint. The stove Mae was so territorial about had been purchased only six months earlier.

She took a salary for herself, a surprisingly modest one. He didn't find, even after a more critical study, any evidence of her using any of the inn's finances to ease her own way.

An honest woman, Roman mused. At least on the surface.

There was a bowl of potpourri on the desk, as there was in every room in the inn. Beside it was a framed picture of Charity standing in front of the mill wheel with a fragile-looking man with white hair.

The grandfather, Roman decided, but it was Charity's image he studied. Her hair was pulled back in a ponytail, and her baggy overalls were stained at the knees. From gardening, Roman guessed. She was holding an armful of summer flowers. She looked as if she didn't have a care in the world, but he noted that her free arm was around the old man, supporting him.

He wondered what she had been thinking at that moment, what she had done the moment after the picture had been snapped. He swore at himself and looked away from the picture.

She left notes to herself: Return wallpaper samples. New blocks for toy chest. Call piano tuner. Get flat repaired.

He found nothing that touched on his reason for coming to the inn. Leaving the desk, he meticulously searched the rest of the parlor.

Then he went into the adjoining bedroom. The bed, a four-poster, was covered with a lacy white spread and plumped with petit-point pillows. Beside it was a beautiful old rocker, its arms worn smooth as glass. In it sat a big purple teddy bear wearing yellow suspenders.

The curtains were romantic priscillas. She'd left the windows open, and the breeze came through billowing them. A woman's room, Roman thought, unrelentingly feminine with its lace and pillows, its fragile scents and pale colors. Yet somehow it welcomed a man, made him wish, made him want. It made him want one hour, one night, in that softness, that comfort.

He crossed the faded handhooked rug and, burying his self-disgust, went through her dresser.

He found a few pieces of jewelry he took to be heirlooms.

They belonged in a safe, he thought, annoyed with her. There was a bottle of perfume. He knew exactly how it would smell. It would smell the way her skin did. He nearly reached for it before he caught himself. Perfume wasn't of any interest to him. Evidence was.

A packet of letters caught his eye. From a lover? he wondered, dismissing the sudden pang of jealousy he felt as ridiculous.

The room was making him crazy, he thought as he carefully untied the slender satin ribbon. It was impossible not to imagine her there, curled on the bed, wearing something white and thin, her hair loose and the candles lit.

He shook himself as he unfolded the first letter. A room with a purple teddy bear wasn't seductive, he told himself.

The date showed him that they had been written when she had attended college in Seattle. From her grandfather, Roman realized as he scanned them. Every one. They were written with affection and humor, and they contained dozens of little stories about daily life at the inn. Roman put them back the way he'd found them.

Her clothes were casual, except for a few dresses hanging in the closet. There were sturdy boots, sneakers spotted with what looked like grass stains, and two pairs of elegant heels on either side of fuzzy slippers in the shape of elephants. Like the rest of her rooms, they were meticulously arranged. Even in the closet he didn't find a trace of dust.

Besides an alarm clock and a pot of hand cream she had two books on her nightstand. One was a collection of poetry, the other a murder mystery with a gruesome cover. She had a cache of chocolate in the drawer and Chopin on her small portable stereo. There were candles, dozens of them, burned down to various heights. On one wall hung a seascape in deep, stormy blues and grays. On another was a collection of photos, most taken at the inn, many of her grandfather. Roman searched behind each one. He discovered that her paint was fading, nothing more.

Her rooms were clean. Roman stood in the center of the bedroom, taking in the scents of candle wax, potpourri and perfume. They couldn't have been cleaner if she'd known they were going to be searched. All he knew after an hour was that she was an organized woman who liked comfortable clothes and Chopin and had a weakness for chocolate and lurid paperback novels.

Why did that make her fascinating?

He scowled and shoved his hands in his pockets, struggling for objectivity as he had never had to struggle before. All the evidence pointed to her being involved in some very shady business. Everything he'd discovered in the last twenty-four hours indicated that she was an open, honest and hardworking woman.

Which did he believe?

He walked toward the door at the far end of the room. It opened onto a postage-stamp size porch with a long set of stairs that led down to the pond. He wanted to open the door, to step out and breathe in the air, but he turned his back on it and went out the way he had come in.

The scent of her bedroom stayed with him for hours.

Chapter 3

"**I** told you that girl was no good."

"I know, Mae."

"I told you you were making a mistake taking her on like you did."

"Yes, Mae." Charity bit back a sigh. "You told me."

"You keep taking in strays, you're bound to get bit."

Charity resisted—just barely—the urge to scream. "So you've told me."

With a satisfied grunt, Mae finished wiping off her pride and joy, the eight-burner gas range. Charity might run the inn, but Mae had her own ideas about who was in charge. "You're too softhearted, Charity."

"I thought you said it was hardheaded."

"That too." Because she had a warm spot for her young employer, Mae poured a glass of milk and cut a generous slab from the remains of her double chocolate cake. Keeping her voice brisk, she set both on the table. "You eat this now. My baking always made you feel better as a girl."

Charity took a seat and poked a finger into the icing. "I would have given her some time off."

"I know." Mae rubbed her wide-palmed hand on Charity's shoulder. "That's the trouble with you. You take your name too seriously."

"I hate being made a fool of." Scowling, Charity took a huge bite of cake. Chocolate, she was sure, would be a better cure for her headache than an entire bottle of aspirin. Her guilt was a different matter. "Do you think she'll get another job? I know she's got rent to pay."

"Types like Mary Alice always land on their feet. Wouldn't surprise me if she moved in lock, stock and barrel with that Perkin boy, so don't you be worrying about the likes of her. Didn't I tell you she wouldn't last six months?"

Charity pushed more cake into her mouth. "You told me," she mumbled around it.

"Now then, what about this man you brought home?"

Charity took a gulp of her milk. "Roman DeWinter."

"Screwy name." Mae glanced around the kitchen, surprised and a little disappointed that there was nothing left to do. "What do you know about him?"

"He needed a job."

Mae wiped her reddened hands on the skirt of her apron. "I expect there's a whole slew of pickpockets, cat burglars and mass murderers who need jobs."

"He's not a mass murderer," Charity stated. She thought she had better reserve judgment on the other occupations.

"Maybe, maybe not."

"He's a drifter." She shrugged and took another bite of the cake. "But I wouldn't say aimless. He knows where he's going. In any case, with George off doing the hula, I needed someone. He does good work, Mae."

Mae had determined that for herself with a quick trip into the west wing. But she had other things on her mind. "He looks at you."

Stalling, Charity ran a fingertip up and down the side of her glass. "Everyone looks at me. I'm always here."

"Don't play stupid with me, young lady. I powdered your bottom."

"Whatever that has to do with anything," Charity answered with a grin. "So he looks?" She moved her shoulders again. "I look back." When Mae arched her brows, Charity just smiled. "Aren't you always telling me I need a man in my life?"

"There's men and there's men," Mae said sagely. "This one's not bad on the eyes, and he ain't afraid of working. But he's got a hard streak in him. That one's been around, my girl, and no mistake."

"I guess you'd rather I spent time with Jimmy Logger-man."

"Spineless worm."

After a burst of laughter, Charity cupped her chin in her hands. "You were right, Mae. I do feel better."

Pleased, Mae untied the apron from around her ample girth. She didn't doubt that Charity was a sensible girl, but she intended to keep an eye on Roman herself. "Good. Don't cut any more of that cake or you'll be up all night with a belly-ache."

"Yes'm."

"And don't leave a mess in my kitchen," she added as she tugged on a practical brown coat.

"No, ma'am. Good night, Mae."

Charity sighed as the door rattled shut. Mae's leaving usu-ally signaled the end of the day. The guests would be tucked into their beds or finishing up a late card game. Barring an emergency, there was nothing left for Charity to do until sun-rise.

Nothing to do but think.

Lately she'd been toying with the idea of putting in a whirl-pool. That might lure a small percentage of the resortgoers. She'd priced a few solarium kits, and in her mind she could already see the sun room on the inn's south side. In the winter guests could come back from hiking to a hot, bubbling tub and top off the day with rum punch by the fire.

She would enjoy it herself, especially on those rare winter days when the inn was empty and there was nothing for her to do but rattle around alone.

Then there was her long-range plan to add on a gift shop supplied by local artists and craftsmen. Nothing too elaborate, she thought. She wanted to keep things simple, in keeping with the spirit of the inn.

She wondered if Roman would stay around long enough to work on it.

It wasn't wise to think of him in connection with any of her plans. It probably wasn't wise to think of him at all. He was, as she had said herself, a drifter. Men like Roman didn't light in one spot for long.

She couldn't seem to stop thinking about him. Almost from the first moment she'd felt something. Attraction was one thing. He was, after all, an attractive man, in a tough, dangerous kind of way. But there was more. Something in his eyes? she wondered. In his voice? In the way he moved? She toyed with the rest of her cake, wishing she could pin it down. It might simply be that he was so different from herself. Taciturn, suspicious, solitary.

And yet…was it her imagination, or was part of him waiting, to reach out, to grab hold? He needed someone, she thought, though he was probably unaware of it.

Mae was right, she mused. She had always had a weakness for strays and a hard-luck story. But this was different. She closed her eyes for a moment, wishing she could explain, even to herself, why it was so very different.

She'd never experienced anything like the sensations that had rammed into her because of Roman. It was more than physical. She could admit that now. Still it made no sense. Then again, Charity had always thought that feelings weren't required to make sense.

For a moment out on the deserted road this morning she'd felt emotions pour out of him. They had been almost frightening in their speed and power. Emotions like that could hurt…the one who felt them, the one who received them. They had left her dazed and aching—and wishing, she admitted.

She thought she knew what his mouth would taste like. Not soft, not sweet, but pungent and powerful. When he was ready, he wouldn't ask, he'd take. It worried her that she didn't resent that. She had grown up knowing her own mind, making her own choices. A man like Roman would have little respect for a woman's wishes.

It would be better, much better, for them to keep their relationship—their short-term relationship, she added—on a purely business level. Friendly but careful. She let her chin sink into her hands again. It was a pity she had such a difficult time combining the two.

He watched her toy with the crumbs on her plate. Her hair was loose now and tousled, as if she had pulled it out of the braid and ran impatient fingers through it. Her bare feet were crossed at the ankles, resting on the chair across from her.

Relaxed. Roman wasn't sure he'd ever seen anyone so fully relaxed except in sleep. It was a sharp contrast to the churning energy that drove her during the day.

He wished she were in her rooms, tucked into bed and sleeping deeply. He'd wanted to avoid coming across her at all. That was personal. He needed her out of his way so that he could go through the office off the lobby. That was business.

He knew he should step back and keep out of sight until she retired for the night.

What was it about this quiet scene that was so appealing, so irresistible? The kitchen was warm and the scents of cooking were lingering, pleasantly overlaying those of pine and lemon from Mae's cleaning. There was a hanging basket over the sink that was almost choked with some leafy green plant. Every surface was scrubbed, clean and shiny. The huge refrigerator hummed.

She looked so comfortable, as if she were waiting for him to come in and sit with her, to talk of small, inconsequential things.

That was crazy. He didn't want any woman waiting for him, and especially not her.

But he didn't step back into the shadows of the dining room, though he could easily have done so. He stepped toward her, into the light.

"I thought people kept early hours in the country."

She jumped but recovered quickly. She was almost used to

the silent way he moved. "Mostly. Mae was giving me choc-olate and a pep talk. Want some cake?"

"No."

"Just as well. If you had I'd have taken another piece and made myself sick. No willpower. How about a beer?"

"Yeah. Thanks."

She got up lazily and moved to the refrigerator to rattle off a list of brands. He chose one and watched her pour it into a pilsner glass. She wasn't angry, he noted, though she had certainly been the last time they were together. So Charity didn't hold grudges. She wouldn't, Roman decided as he took the glass from her. She would forgive almost anything, would trust everyone and would give more than was asked.

"Why do you look at me that way?" she murmured.

He caught himself, then took a long, thirsty pull on the beer. "You have a beautiful face."

She lifted a brow when he sat down and pulled out a cig-arette. After taking an ashtray from a drawer, she sat beside him. "I like to accept compliments whenever I get them, but I don't think that's the reason."

"It's reason enough for a man to look at a woman." He sipped his beer. "You had a busy night."

Let it go, Charity told herself. "Busy enough that I need to hire another waitress fast. I didn't get a chance to thank you for helping out with the dinner crowd."

"No problem. Lose the headache?"

She glanced up sharply. But, no, he wasn't making fun of her. It seemed, though she couldn't be sure why the impres-sion was so strong, that his question was a kind of apology. She decided to accept it.

"Yes, thanks. Getting mad at you took my mind off Mary Alice, and Mae's chocolate cake did the rest." She thought about brewing some tea, then decided she was too lazy to bother. "So, how was your day?"

She smiled at him in an easy offer of friendship that he found difficult to resist and impossible to accept. "Okay. Miss Millie said the door to her room was sticking, so I pretended to sand it."

"And made her day."

He couldn't prevent the smile. "I don't think I've ever been ogled quite so completely before."

"Oh, I imagine you have." She tilted her head to study him from a new angle. "But, with apologies to your ego, in Miss Millie's case it's more a matter of nearsightedness than lust. She's too vain to wear her glasses in front of any male over twenty."

"I'd rather go on thinking she's leering at me," he said. "She said she's been coming here twice a year since '52." He thought that over for a moment, amazed that anyone could return time after time to the same spot.

"She and Miss Lucy are fixtures here. When I was young I thought we were related."

"You been running this place long?"

"Off and on for all of my twenty-seven years." Smiling, she tipped back in her chair. She was a woman who relaxed easily and enjoyed seeing others relaxed. He seemed so now, she thought, with his legs stretched out under the table and a glass in his hand. "You don't really want to hear the story of my life, do you, Roman?"

He blew out a stream of smoke. "I've got nothing to do." And he wanted to hear her version of what he'd read in her file.

"Okay. I was born here. My mother had fallen in love a bit later in life than most. She was nearly forty when she had me, and fragile. There were complications. After she died, my grandfather raised me, so I grew up here at the inn, except for the periods of time when he sent me away to school. I loved this place." She glanced around the kitchen. "In school I pined for it, and for Pop. Even in college I missed it so much I'd ferry home every weekend. But he wanted me to see something else before I settled down here. I was going to travel some, get new ideas for the inn. See New York, New Orleans, Venice. I don't know...." Her words trailed off wistfully.

"Why didn't you?"

"My grandfather was ill. I was in my last year of college

when I found out *how* ill. I wanted to quit, come home, but the idea upset him so much I thought it was better to graduate. He hung on for another three years, but it was…difficult." She didn't want to talk about the tears and the terror, or about the exhaustion of running the inn while caring for a near-invalid. "He was the bravest, kindest man I've ever known. He was so much a part of this place that there are still times when I expect to walk into a room and see him checking for dust on the furniture."

He was silent for a moment, thinking as much about what she'd left out as about what she'd told him. He knew her father was listed as unknown—a difficult obstacle anywhere, but especially in a small town. In the last six months of her grandfather's life his medical expenses had nearly driven the inn under. But she didn't speak of those things; nor did he detect any sign of bitterness.

"Do you ever think about selling the place, moving on?"

"No. Oh, I still think about Venice occasionally. There are dozens of places I'd like to go, as long as I had the inn to come back to." She rose to get him another beer. "When you run a place like this, you get to meet people from all over. There's always a story about a new place."

"Vicarious traveling?"

It stung, perhaps because it was too close to her own thoughts. "Maybe." She set the bottle at his elbow, then took her dishes to the sink. Even knowing that she was overly sensitive on this point didn't stop her from bristling. "Some of us are meant to be boring."

"I didn't say you were boring."

"No? Well, I suppose I am to someone who picks up and goes whenever and wherever he chooses. Simple, settled and naive."

"You're putting words in my mouth, baby."

"It's easy to do, *baby*, since you rarely put any there yourself. Turn off the lights when you leave."

He took her arm as she started by in a reflexive movement that he regretted almost before it was done. But it was done, and the sulky, defiant look she sent him began a chain reaction that raced through his system. There were things he could do with her, things he burned to do, that neither of them would ever forget.

"Why are you angry?"

"I don't know. I can't seem to talk to you for more than ten minutes without getting edgy. Since I normally get along with everyone, I figure it's you."

"You're probably right."

She calmed a little. It was hardly his fault that she had never been anywhere. "You've been around a little less than forty-eight hours and I've nearly fought with you three times. That's a record for me."

"I don't keep score."

"Oh, I think you do. I doubt you forget anything. Were you a cop?"

He had to make a deliberate effort to keep his face bland and fingers from tensing. "Why?"

"You said you weren't an artist. That was my first guess." She relaxed, though he hadn't removed his hand from her arm. Anger was something she enjoyed only in fast, brief spurts. "It's the way you look at people, as if you were filing away descriptions and any distinguishing marks. And sometimes when I'm with you I feel as though I should get ready for an interrogation. A writer, then? When you're in the hotel business you get pretty good at matching people with professions."

"You're off this time."

"Well, what are you, then?"

"Right now I'm a handyman."

She shrugged, making herself let it go. "Another trait of hotel people is respecting privacy, but if you turn out to be a mass murderer Mae's never going to let me hear the end of it."

"Generally I only kill one person at a time."

"That's good news." She ignored the suddenly very real anxiety that he was speaking the simple truth. "You're still holding my arm."

"I know."

So this was it, she thought, and struggled to keep her voice. "Should I ask you to let go?"

"I wouldn't bother."

She drew a deep, steadying breath. "All right. What do you want, Roman?"

"To get this out of the way, for both of us."

He rose. Her step backward was instinctive, and much more surprising to her than to him. "I don't think that's a good idea."

"Neither do I." With his free hand, he gathered up her hair. It was soft, as he'd known it would be. Thick and full and so soft that his fingers dived in and were lost. "But I'd rather regret something I did than something I didn't do."

"I'd rather not regret at all."

"Too late." He heard her suck in her breath as he yanked her against him. "One way or the other, we'll both have plenty to regret."

He was deliberately rough. He knew how to be gentle, though he rarely put the knowledge into practice. With her, he could have been. Perhaps because he knew that, he shoved aside any desire for tenderness. He wanted to frighten her, to make certain that when he let her go she would run, run away from him, because he wanted so badly for her to run to him.

Buried deep in his mind was the hope that he could make her afraid enough, repelled enough, to send him packing. If she did, she would be safe from him, and he from her. He thought he could accomplish it quickly. Then, suddenly, it was impossible to think at all.

She tasted like heaven. He'd never believed in heaven, but the flavor was on her lips, pure and sweet and promising. Her hand had gone to his chest in an automatic defensive movement. Yet she wasn't fighting him, as he'd been certain she would. She met his hard, almost brutal kiss with passion laced with trust.

His mind emptied. It was a terrifying experience for a man who kept his thoughts under such stringent control. Then it filled with her, her scent, her touch, her taste.

He broke away—for his sake now, not for hers. He was

and had always been a survivor. His breath came fast and raw. One hand was still tangled in her hair, and his other was clamped tight on her arm. He couldn't let go. No matter how he chided himself to release her, to step back and walk away, he couldn't move. Staring at her, he saw his own reflection in her eyes.

He cursed her—it was a last quick denial—before he crushed his mouth to hers again. It wasn't heaven he was heading for, he told himself. It was hell.

She wanted to soothe him, but he never gave her the chance. As before, he sent her rushing into some hot, airless place where there was room only for sensation.

She'd been right. His mouth wasn't soft, it was hard and ruthless and irresistible. Without hesitation, without thought of self-preservation, she opened for him, greedily taking what was offered, selflessly giving what was demanded.

Her back was pressed against the smooth, cool surface of the refrigerator, trapped there by the firm, taut lines of his body. If it had been possible, she would have brought him closer.

His face was rough as it scraped against hers, and she trembled at the thrill of pleasure even that brought her. Desperate now, she nipped at his lower lip, and felt a new rush of excitement as he groaned and deepened an already bottomless kiss.

She wanted to be touched. She tried to murmur this new, compelling need against his mouth, but she managed only a moan. Her body ached. Just the anticipation of his hands running over her was making her shudder.

For a moment their hearts beat against each other in the same wild rhythm.

He tore away, aware that he had come perilously close to a line he didn't dare cross. He could hardly breathe, much less think. Until he was certain he could do both, he was silent.

"Go to bed, Charity."

She stayed where she was, certain that if she took a step her legs would give away. He was still close enough for her to feel the heat radiating from his body. But she looked into his eyes and knew he was already out of reach.

"Just like that?"

Hurt. He could hear it in her voice, and he wished he could make himself believe she had brought it on herself. He reached for his beer but changed his mind when he saw that his hand was unsteady. Only one thing was clear. He had to get rid of her, quickly, before he touched her again.

"You're not the type for quick sex on the kitchen floor."

The color that passion had brought to her cheeks faded. "No. At least I never have been." After taking a deep breath, she stepped forward. She believed in facing facts, even unpleasant ones. "Is that all this would have been, Roman?"

His hand curled into a fist. "Yes," he said. "What else?"

"I see." She kept her eyes on his, wishing she could hate him. "I'm sorry for you."

"Don't be."

"You're in charge of your feelings, Roman, not mine. And I am sorry for you. Some people lose a leg or a hand or an eye. They either deal with that loss or become bitter. I can't see what piece of you is missing, Roman, but it's just as tragic." He didn't answer; she hadn't expected him to. "Don't forget the lights."

He waited until she was gone before he fumbled for a match. He needed time to gain control of his head—and his hands—before he searched the office. What worried him was that it was going to take a great deal longer to gain control of his heart.

Nearly two hours later he hiked a mile and a half to use the pay phone at the nearest gas station. The road was quiet, the tiny village dark. The wind had come up, and it tasted of rain. Roman hoped dispassionately that it would hold off until he was back at the inn.

He placed the call, waited for the connection.

"Conby."

"DeWinter."

"You're late."

Roman didn't bother to check his watch. He knew it was just shy of 3:00 a.m. on the East Coast. "Get you up?"

"Am I to assume that you've established yourself?"

"Yeah, I'm in. Rigging the handyman's lottery ticket cleared the way. Arranging the flat gave me the opening. Miss Ford is...trusting."

"So we were led to believe. Trusting doesn't mean she's not ambitious. What have you got?"

A bad case of guilt, Roman thought as he lit a match. A very bad case. "Her rooms are clean." He paused and held the flame to the tip of his cigarette. "There's a tour group in now, mostly Canadians. A few exchanged money. Nothing over a hundred."

The pause was very brief. "That's hardly enough to make the business worthwhile."

"I got a list out of the office. The names and addresses of the registered guests."

There was another, longer pause, and a rustling sound that told Roman that his contact was searching for writing materials. "Let me have it."

He read them off from the copy he'd made. "Block's the tour guide. He's the regular, comes in once a week for a one- or two-night stay, depending on the package."

"Vision Tours."

"Right."

"We've got a man on that end. You concentrate on Ford and her staff." Roman heard the faint *tap-tap-tap* of Conby's pencil against his pad. "There's no way they can be pulling this off without someone on the inside. She's the obvious answer."

"It doesn't fit."

"I beg your pardon?"

Roman crushed the cigarette under his boot heel. "I said it doesn't fit. I've watched her. I've gone through her personal accounts, damn it. She's got under three thousand in fluid cash. Everything else goes into the place for new sheets and soap."

"I see." The pause again. It was maddening. "I suppose our Miss Ford hasn't heard of Swiss bank accounts."

"I said she's not the type, Conby. It's the wrong angle."

"I'll worry about the angles, DeWinter. You worry about doing your job. I shouldn't have to remind you that it's taken us nearly a year to come close to pinning this thing down. The Bureau wants this wrapped quickly, and that's what I expect from you. If you have a personal problem with this, you'd better let me know now."

"No." He knew personal problems weren't permitted. "You want to waste time, and the taxpayers' money, it's all the same to me. I'll get back to you."

"Do that."

Roman hung up. It made him feel a little better to scowl at the phone and imagine Conby losing a good night's sleep. Then again, his kind rarely did. He'd wake some hapless clerk up at six and have the list run through the computer. Conby would drink his coffee, watch the *Today* show and wait in his comfortable house in the D.C. suburbs for the results.

Grunt work and dirty work were left to others.

That was the way the game was played, Roman reminded himself as he started the long walk back to the inn. But lately, just lately, he was getting very tired of the rules.

Charity heard him come in. Curious, she glanced at the clock after she heard the door close below. It was after one, and the rain had started nearly thirty minutes before with a gentle hissing that promised to gain strength through the night.

She wondered where he had been.

His business, she reminded herself as she rolled over and tried to let the rain lull her to sleep. As long as he did his job, Roman DeWinter was free to come and go as he pleased. If he wanted to walk in the rain, that was fine by her.

How could he have kissed her like that and felt nothing?

Charity squeezed her eyes shut and swore at herself. It was her feelings she had to worry about, not Roman's. The trouble was, she always felt too much. This was one time she couldn't afford that luxury.

Something had happened to her when he'd kissed her. Something thrilling, something that had reached deep inside her and opened up endless possibilities. No, not possibilities, fantasies, she thought, shaking her head. If she were wise she would take that one moment of excitement and stop wanting more. Drifters made poor risks emotionally. She had the perfect example before her.

Her mother had turned to a drifter and had given him her heart, her trust, her body. She had ended up pregnant and alone. She had, Charity knew, pined for him for months. She'd died in the same hospital where her baby had been born, only days later. Betrayed, rejected and ashamed.

Charity had only discovered the extent of the shame after her grandfather's death. He'd kept the diary her mother had written. Charity had burned it, not out of shame but out of pity. She would always think of her mother as a tragic woman who had looked for love and had never found it.

But she wasn't her mother, Charity reminded herself as she lay awake listening to the rain. She was far, far less fragile. Love was what she had been named for, and she had felt its warmth all her life.

Now a drifter had come into her life.

He had spoken of regrets, she remembered. She was afraid that whatever happened—or didn't happen—between them, she would have them.

Chapter 4

The rain continued all morning, soft, slow, steady. It brought a chill, and a gloom that was no less appealing than the sunshine. Clouds hung over the water, turning everything to different shades of gray. Raindrops hissed on the roof and at the windows, making the inn seem all the more remote. Occasionally the wind gusted, rattling the panes.

At dawn Roman had watched Charity, bundled in a hooded windbreaker, take Ludwig out for his morning run. And he had watched her come back, dripping, forty minutes later. He'd heard the music begin to play in her room after she had come in the back entrance. She had chosen something quiet and floating with lots of violins this time. He'd been sorry when it had stopped and she had hurried down the hallway on her way to the dining room.

From his position on the second floor he couldn't hear the bustle in the kitchen below, but he could imagine it. Mae and Dolores would be bickering as waffle or muffin batter was whipped up. Charity would have grabbed a quick cup of coffee before rushing out to help the waitress set up tables and write the morning's menu.

Her hair would be damp, her voice calm as she smoothed over Dolores's daily complaints. She'd smell of the rain. When the early risers wandered down she would smile, greet them by name and make them feel as though they were sharing a meal at an old friend's house.

That was her greatest skill, Roman mused. Making a stranger feel at home.

Could she be as uncomplicated as she seemed? A part of him wanted badly to believe that. Another part of him found it impossible. Everyone had an angle, from the mailroom clerk dreaming of a desk job to the CEO wheeling another deal. She couldn't be any different.

He wouldn't have called the kiss they'd shared uncomplicated. There had been layers to it he couldn't have begun to peel away. It seemed contradictory that such a calm-eyed, smooth-voiced woman could explode with such towering passion. Yet she had. Perhaps her passion was as much a part of the act as her serenity.

It annoyed him. Just remembering his helpless response to her infuriated him. So he made himself dissect it further. If he was attracted to what she seemed to be, that was reasonable enough. He'd lived a solitary and often turbulent life. Though he had chosen to live that way, and certainly preferred it, it wasn't unusual that at some point he would find himself pulled toward a woman who represented everything he had never had. And had never wanted, Roman reminded himself as he tacked up a strip of molding.

He wasn't going to pretend he'd found any answers in Charity. The only answers he was looking for pertained to the job.

For now he would wait until the morning rush was over. When Charity was busy in her office, he would go down and charm some breakfast out of Mae. There was a woman who didn't trust him, Roman thought with a grin. There wasn't a naive bone in her sturdy body. And except for Charity there was no one, he was sure, who knew the workings of the inn better.

Yes, he'd put some effort into charming Mae. And he'd keep some distance between himself and Charity. For the time being.

"You're looking peaked this morning."

"Thank you very much." Charity swallowed a yawn as she poured her second cup of coffee. Peaked wasn't the word, she thought. She was exhausted right down to the bone. Her body wasn't used to functioning on three hours' sleep. She had Roman to thank for that, she thought, and shoved the just-filled cup aside.

"Sit." Mae pointed to the table. "I'll fix you some eggs."

"I haven't got time. I—"

"Sit," Mae repeated, waving a wooden spoon. "You need fuel."

"Mae's right," Dolores put in. "A body can't run on coffee. You need protein and carbohydrates." She set a blueberry muffin on the table. "Why, if I don't watch my protein intake I get weak as a lamb. 'Course, the doctor don't say, but I think I'm hydroglycemic."

"Hypoglycemic," Charity murmured.

"That's what I said." Dolores decided she liked the sound of it. At the moment, however, it was just as much fun to worry about Charity as it was to worry about herself. "She could use some nice crisp bacon with those eggs, Mae. That's what I think."

"I'm putting it on."

Outnumbered, Charity sat down. The two women could scrap for days, but when they had common cause they stuck together like glue.

"I'm not peaked," she said in her own defense. "I just didn't sleep well last night."

"A warm bath before bed," Mae told her as the bacon sizzled. "Not hot, mind you. Lukewarm."

"With bath salts. Not bubbles or oils," Dolores added as she plunked down a glass of juice. "Good old-fashioned bath salts. Ain't that right, Mae?"

"Couldn't hurt," Mae mumbled, too concerned about Charity to think of an argument. "You've been working too hard, girl."

"I agree," Charity said, because it was easiest that way. "The reason I don't have time for a long, leisurely breakfast is that I have to see about hiring a new waitress so I don't have to work so hard. I put an ad in this morning's paper, so the calls should be coming in.''

''Told Bob to cancel the ad,'' Mae announced, cracking an egg into the pan.

''What? Why?'' Charity started to rise. ''Damn it, Mae, if you think I'm going to take Mary Alice back after she—''

''No such thing, and don't you swear at me, young lady.''

''Testy.'' Dolores clucked her tongue. ''Happens when you work too hard.''

''I'm sorry,'' Charity mumbled, managing not to grind her teeth. ''But, Mae, I was counting on setting up interviews over the next couple of days. I want someone in by the end of the week.''

''My brother's girl left that worthless husband of hers in Toledo and came home.'' Keeping her back to Charity, Mae set the bacon to drain, then poked at the eggs. ''She's a good girl, Bonnie is. Worked here a couple of summers while she was in school.''

''Yes, I remember. She married a musician who was playing at one of the resorts in Eastsound.''

Mae scowled and began to scoop up the eggs. ''Saxophone player,'' she said, as if that explained it all. ''She got tired of living out of a van and came home a couple weeks back. Been looking for work.''

With a sigh, Charity pushed a hand through her bangs. ''Why didn't you tell me before?''

''You didn't need anyone before.'' Mae set the eggs in front of her. ''You need someone now.''

Charity glanced over as Mae began wiping off the stove. The cook's heart was as big as the rest of her. ''When can she start?''

Mae's lips curved, and she cleared her throat and wiped at a spill with more energy. ''Told her to come in this afternoon so's you could have a look at her. Don't expect you to hire her unless she measures up.''

''Well, then.'' Charity picked up her fork. Pleased at the thought of having one job settled, she stretched out her legs and rested her feet on an empty chair. "I guess I've got time for breakfast after all."

Roman pushed through the door and almost swore out loud. The dining room was all but empty. He'd been certain Charity would be off doing one of the dozens of chores she took on. Instead, she was sitting in the warm, fragrant kitchen, much as she had been the night before. With one telling difference, Roman reflected. She wasn't relaxed now.

Her easy smile faded the moment he walked in. Slowly she slipped her feet off the chair and straightened her back. He could see her body tense, almost muscle by muscle. Her fork stopped halfway to her lips. Then she turned slightly away from him and continued to eat. It was, he supposed, as close to a slap in the face as she could manage.

He rearranged his idea about breakfast and gossip in the kitchen. For now he'd make do with coffee.

"Wondered where you'd got to," Mae said as she pulled bacon out of the refrigerator again.

"I didn't want to get in your way." He nodded toward the coffeepot. "I thought I'd take a cup up with me."

"You need fuel." Dolores busied herself arranging a place setting across from Charity. "Isn't that right, Mae? Man can't work unless he has a proper breakfast."

Mae poured a cup. "He looks like he could run on empty well enough."

It was quite true, Charity thought. She knew what time he'd come in the night before, and he'd been up and working when she'd left the wing to oversee the breakfast shift. He couldn't have gotten much more sleep than she had herself, but he didn't look any the worse for wear.

"Meals are part of your pay, Roman." Though her appetite had fled, Charity nipped off a bite of bacon. "I believe Mae has some pancake batter left over, if you'd prefer that to eggs."

It was a cool invitation, so cool that Dolores opened her mouth to comment. Mae gave her a quick poke and a scowl. He accepted the coffee Mae shoved at him and drank it black.

"Eggs are fine." But he didn't sit down. The welcoming

feel that was usually so much a part of the kitchen was not evident. Roman leaned against the counter and sipped while Mae cooked beside him.

She wasn't going to feel guilty, Charity told herself, ignoring a chastising look from Dolores. After all, she was the boss, and her business with Roman was…well, just business. But she couldn't bear the long, strained silence.

"Mae, I'd like some petits fours and tea sandwiches this afternoon. The rain's supposed to last all day, so we'll have music and dancing in the gathering room." Because breakfast seemed less and less appealing, Charity pulled a notepad out of her shirt pocket. "Fifty sandwiches should do if we have a cheese tray. We'll set up an urn of tea, and one of hot chocolate."

"What time?"

"At three, I think. Then we can bring out the wine at five for anyone who wants to linger. You can have your niece help out."

She began making notes on the pad.

She looked tired, Roman thought. Pale and heavy-eyed and surprisingly fragile. She'd apparently pulled her hair back in a hasty ponytail when it had still been damp. Little tendrils had escaped as they'd dried. They seemed lighter than the rest, their color more delicate than rich. He wanted to brush them away from her temples and watch the color come back into her cheeks.

"Finish your eggs," Mae told her. Then she nodded at Roman. "Yours are ready."

"Thanks." He sat down, wishing no more fervently than Charity that he was ten miles away.

Dolores began to complain that the rain was making her sinuses swell.

"Pass the salt," Roman murmured.

Charity pushed it in his direction. Their fingers brushed briefly, and she snatched hers away.

"Thanks."

"You're welcome." Charity poked her fork into her eggs. She knew from experience that it would be difficult to escape from the kitchen without cleaning her plate, and she intended to do it quickly.

"Nice day," he said, because he wanted her to look at him again. She did, and pent-up anger was simmering in her eyes. He preferred it, he discovered, to the cool politeness that had been there.

"I like the rain."

"Like I said—" he broke open his muffin "—it's a nice day."

Dolores blew her nose heartily. Amusement curved the corners of Charity's mouth before she managed to suppress it. "You'll find the paint you need—wall, ceiling, trim—in the storage cellar. It's marked for the proper rooms."

"All right."

"The brushes and pans and rollers are down there, too. Everything's on the workbench on the right as you come down the stairs."

"I'll find them."

"Good. Cabin 4 has a dripping faucet."

"I'll look at it."

She didn't want him to be so damn agreeable, Charity thought. She wanted him to be as tense and out of sorts as she was. "The window sticks in unit 2 in the east wing."

He sent her an even look. "I'll unstick it."

"Fine." Suddenly she noticed that Dolores had stopped complaining and was gawking at her. Even Mae was frowning over her mixing bowl. The hell with it, Charity thought as she shoved her plate away. So she was issuing orders like Captain Bligh. She damn well felt like Captain Bligh.

She took a ring of keys out of her pocket. She'd just put them on that morning, having intended to see to the minor chores herself. "Make sure to bring these back to the office when you've finished. They're tagged for the proper doors."

"Yes, ma'am." Keeping his eyes on hers, he dropped the ring into his breast pocket. "Anything else?"

"I'll let you know." She rose, took her plate to the sink and stalked out.

"What got into her?" Dolores wanted to know. "She looked like she wanted to chew somebody's head off."

"She just didn't sleep well." More concerned than she wanted to let on, Mae set down the mixing bowl in which she'd been creaming butter and sugar. Because she felt like the mother of an ill-mannered child, she picked up the coffeepot and carried it over to Roman. "Charity's not feeling quite herself this morning," she told him as she poured him a second cup. "She's been overworked lately."

"I've got thick skin." But he'd felt the sting. "Maybe she should delegate more."

"Ha! That girl?" Pleased that he hadn't complained, she became more expansive. "It ain't in her. Feels responsible if a guest stubs his toe. Just like her grandpa." Mae added a stream of vanilla to the bowl and went back to her mixing. "Not a thing goes on around here she don't have a finger— more likely her whole hand—in. Except my cooking." Mae's wide face creased in a smile. "I shooed her out of here when she was a girl, and I can shoo her out of here today if need be."

"Girl can't boil water without scorching the pan," Dolores put in.

"She could if she wanted to," Mae said defensively, turning back to Roman with a sniff. "There's no need for her to cook when she's got me, and she's smart enough to know it. Everything else, though, from painting the porch to keeping the books, has to have her stamp on it. She's one who takes her responsibilities to heart."

Roman played out the lead she had offered him. "That's an admirable quality. You've worked for her a long time."

"Between Charity and her grandfather, I've worked at the inn for twenty-eight years come June." She jerked her head in Dolores's direction. "She's been here eight."

"Nine," Dolores said. "Nine years this month."

"It sounds like when people come to work here they stay."

"You got that right," Mae told him.

"It seems the inn has a loyal, hardworking staff."

"Charity makes it easy." Competently Mae measured out baking powder. "She was just feeling moody this morning."

"She did look a little tired," Roman said slowly, ignoring a pang of guilt. "Maybe she'll rest for a while today."

"Not likely."

"The housekeeping staff seems tight."

"She'll still find a bed to make."

"Bob handles the accounts."

"She'll poke her nose in the books and check every column." There was simple pride in her voice as she sifted flour into the bowl. "Not that she don't trust those who work for her," Mae added. "It would just make her heart stop dead to have a bill paid late or an order mixed up. Thing is, she'd rather blame herself than somebody else if a mistake's made."

"I guess nothing much gets by her."

"By Charity?" With a snicker, Mae plugged in her electric mixer. "She'd know if a napkin came back from the laundry with a stain on it. Watch where you sneeze," she added as Dolores covered her face with a tissue. "Drink some hot water with a squeeze of lemon."

"Hot tea with honey," Dolores said.

"Lemon. Honey'll clog your throat."

"My mother always gave me hot tea with honey," Dolores told her.

They were still arguing about it when Roman slipped out of the kitchen.

He spent most of his time closed off in the west wing. Working helped him think. Though he heard Charity pass in and out a few times, neither of them sought the other's company. He could be more objective, Roman realized, when he wasn't around her.

Mae's comments had cemented his observations and the information that had been made available to him. Charity Ford ran the inn from top to bottom. Whatever went on in it or passed through it was directly under her eye. Logically that meant that she was fully involved with, perhaps in charge of, the operation he had come to destroy.

And yet…what he had said to Conby the night before still held true. It didn't fit.

The woman worked almost around the clock to make the inn a success. He'd seen her do everything from potting geraniums to hauling firewood. And, unless she was an astounding actress, she enjoyed it all.

She didn't seem the type who would want to make money the easy way. Nor did she seem the type who craved all the things easy money could buy. But that was instinct, not fact.

The problem was, Conby ran on facts. Roman had always relied heavily on instinct. His job was to prove her guilt, not her innocence. Yet, in less than two days, his priorities had changed.

It wasn't just a matter of finding her attractive. He had found other women attractive and had brought them down without a qualm. That was justice. One of the few things he believed in without reservation was justice.

With Charity he needed to be certain that his conclusions about her were based on more than the emotions she dragged out of him. Feelings and instincts were different. If a man in his position allowed himself to be swayed by feelings, he was useless.

Then what was it? No matter how long or how hard he thought it through, he couldn't pinpoint one specific reason why he was certain of her innocence. Because it was the whole of it, Roman realized. Her, the inn, the atmosphere that surrounded her. It made him want to believe that such people, such places, existed. And existed untainted.

He was getting soft. A pretty woman, big blue eyes, and he started to think in fairy tales. In disgust, he took the brushes and the paint pans to the sink to clean them. He was going to take a break, from work and from his own rambling thoughts.

In the gathering room, Charity was thinking just as reluctantly of him as she set a stack of records on the table between Miss Millie and Miss Lucy.

"What a lovely idea." Miss Lucy adjusted her glasses and

peered at the labels. "A nice old-fashioned tea dance." From one of the units in the east wing came the unrelenting whine of a toddler. Miss Lucy sent a sympathetic glance in the direction of the noise. "I'm sure this will keep everyone entertained."

"It's hard for young people to know what to do with themselves on a rainy day. It makes them cross. Oh, look." Miss Millie held up a 45. "Rosemary Clooney. Isn't this delightful?"

"Pick out your favorites." Charity gave the room a distracted glance. How could she prepare for a party when all she could think of was the way Roman had looked at her across the breakfast table? "I'm depending on you."

The long buffet and a small server had been cleared off to hold the refreshments. If she could count on Mae—and she always had—they should be coming up from the kitchen shortly.

Would Roman come in? she wondered. Would he hear the music and slip silently into the room? Would he look at her until her heart started to hammer and she forgot there was anything or anyone but him?

She was going crazy, Charity decided. She glanced at her watch. It was a quarter to three. Word had been passed to all the guests, and with luck she would be ready for them when they began to arrive. The ladies were deep in a discussion of Perry Como. Leaving them to it, Charity began to tug on the sofa.

"What are you doing?"

A squeal escaped her, and she cursed Roman in the next breath. "If you keep sneaking around I'm going to take Mae's idea of you being a cat burglar more seriously."

"I wasn't sneaking around. You were so busy huffing and puffing you didn't hear me."

"I wasn't huffing or puffing." She tossed her hair over her shoulder and glared at him. "But I am busy, so if you'd get out of my way—"

She waved a hand at him, and he caught it and held it. "I asked what you were doing."

She tugged, then tugged harder, struggling to control her temper. If he wanted to fight, she thought, she'd be happy to oblige him. "I'm knitting an afghan," she snapped. "What does it look like I'm doing? I'm moving the sofa."

"No, you're not."

She could, when the occasion called for, succeed in being haughty. "I beg your pardon?"

"I said you're not moving the sofa. It's too heavy."

"Thank you for your opinion, but I've moved it before." She lowered her voice when she noticed the interested glances the ladies were giving her. "And if you'd get the hell out of my way I'd move it again."

He stood where he was, blocking her. "You really do have to do everything yourself, don't you?"

"Meaning?"

"Where's your assistant?"

"The computer sprang a leak. Since Bob's better equipped to deal with that, he's playing with components and I'm moving furniture. Now—"

"Where do you want it?"

"I didn't ask you to—" But he'd already moved to the other end of the sofa.

"I said, where do you want it?"

"Against the side wall." Charity hefted her end and tried not to be grateful.

"What else?"

She smoothed down the skirt of her dress. "I've already given you a list of chores."

He hooked a thumb in his pocket as they stood on either side of the sofa. He had an urge to put his hand over her angry face and give it a nice hard shove. "I've finished them."

"The faucet in cabin 4?"

"It needed a new washer."

"The window in unit 2?"

"A little sanding."

She was running out of steam. "The painting?"

"The first coat's drying." He angled his head. "Want to check it out?"

She blew out a breath. It was difficult to be annoyed when he'd done everything she'd asked. "Efficient, aren't you, DeWinter?"

"That's right. Got your second wind?"

"What do you mean?"

"You looked a little tired this morning." He skimmed a glance over her. The dark plum-colored dress swirled down her legs. Little silver buttons ranged down from the high neck to the hem, making him wonder how long it would take him to unfasten them. There was silver at her ears, as well, a fanciful trio of columns he remembered having seen in her drawer. "You don't now," he added, bringing his eyes back to hers.

She started to breathe again, suddenly aware that she'd been holding her breath since he'd started his survey. Charity reminded herself that she didn't have time to let him—or her feelings for him—distract her.

"I'm too busy to be tired." Relieved, she signaled to a waitress who was climbing the steps with a laden tray. "Just set it on the buffet, Lori."

"Second load's right behind me."

"Great. I just need to—" She broke off when the first damp guests came through the back door. Giving up, she turned to Roman. If he was going to be in the way anyway, he might as well make himself useful. "I'd appreciate it if you'd roll up the rug and store it in the west wing. Then you're welcome to stay and enjoy yourself."

"Thanks. Maybe I will."

Charity greeted the guests, hung up their jackets, offered them refreshments and switched on the music almost before Roman could store the rug out of sight. Within fifteen minutes she had the group mixing and mingling.

She was made for this, he thought as he watched her. She was made for being in the center of things, for making people feel good. His place had always been on the fringe.

"Oh, Mr. DeWinter." Smelling of lilacs, Miss Millie offered him a cup and saucer. "You must have some tea. Nothing like tea to chase the blues away on a rainy day."

He smiled into her blurred eyes. If even she could see that he was brooding, he'd better watch his step. "Thanks."

"I love a party," she said wistfully as she watched a few couples dance to a bluesy Clooney ballad. "Why, when I was a girl, I hardly thought of anything else. I met my husband at a tea like this. That was almost fifty years ago. We danced for hours."

He would never have considered himself gallant, but she was hard to resist. "Would you like to dance now?"

The faintest of blushes tinted her cheeks. "I'd love to, Mr. DeWinter."

Charity watched Roman lead Miss Millie onto the floor. Her heart softened. She tried to harden it again but found it was a lost cause. It was a sweet thing to do, she thought, particularly since he was anything but a sweet man. She doubted that teas and dreamy little old ladies were Roman's style, but Miss Millie would remember this day for a long time.

What woman wouldn't? Charity mused. To dance with a strong, mysterious man on a rainy afternoon was a memory to be pressed in a book like a red rose. It was undoubtedly fortunate he hadn't asked her. She had already stored away too many memories of Roman. With a sigh, she herded a group of children into the television room and pushed a Disney movie into the VCR.

Roman saw her leave. And he saw her come back.

"That was lovely," Miss Millie told him when the music had stopped.

"What?" Quickly he brought himself back. "My pleasure." Then he made her pleasure complete by kissing her hand. By the time she had walked over to sigh with her sister he had forgotten her and was thinking of Charity.

She was laughing as an older man led her onto the floor. The music had changed. It was up-tempo now, something brisk and Latin. A mambo, he thought. Or a merengue. He wouldn't know the difference. Apparently Charity knew well enough. She moved through the complicated, flashy number as if she'd been dancing all her life.

Her skirt flared, wrapped around her legs, then flared again as she turned. She laughed, her face level and close to her partner's as they matched steps. The first prick of jealousy infuriated Roman and made him feel like a fool. The man Charity was matching steps with was easily old enough to be her father.

By the time the music ended he had managed to suppress the uncomfortable emotion but another had sprung up to take its place. Desire. He wanted her, wanted to take her by the hand and pull her out of that crowded room into someplace dim and quiet where all they would hear was the rain. He wanted to see her eyes go big and unfocused the way they had when he'd kissed her. He wanted to feel the incredible sensation of her mouth softening and heating under his.

"It's an education to watch her, isn't it?"

Roman jerked himself back as Bob eased over to pluck a sandwich from the tray. "What?"

"Charity. Watching her dance is an education." He popped the tiny sandwich into his mouth. "She tried to teach me once, hoping I'd be able to entertain some of the ladies on occasions like this. Trouble is, I not only have two left feet, I have two left legs." He gave a cheerful shrug and reached for another sandwich.

"Did you get the computer fixed?"

"Yeah. Just a couple of minor glitches." The little triangle of bread disappeared. Roman caught a hint of nerves in the way Bob's knuckle tapped against the server. "I can't teach Charity about circuit boards and software any more than she can teach me the samba. How's the work going?"

"Well enough." He watched as Bob poured a cup of tea and added three sugars to it. "I should be done in two or three weeks."

"She'll find something else for you to do." He glanced over to where Charity and a new partner were dancing a fox-trot. "She's always got a new idea for this place. Lately she's been making noises about adding on a sun room and putting in one of those whirlpool tubs.''

Roman lit a cigarette. He was watching the guests now, making mental notes to pass on to Conby. There were two men who seemed to be alone, though they were chatting with other members of the tour group. Block stood by the doors, holding a plate full of sandwiches that he was dispatching with amazing ease and grinning at no one in particular.

''The inn must be doing well.''

''Oh, it's stable.'' Bob turned his attention to the petits fours. ''A couple of years ago things were a little rocky, but Charity would always find a way to keep the ship afloat. Nothing's more important to her.''

Roman was silent for a moment. ''I don't know much about the hotel business, but she seems to know what she's doing.''

''Inside and out.'' Bob chose a cake with pink frosting. ''Charity *is* the inn.''

''Have you worked for her long?''

''About two and a half years. She couldn't really afford me, but she wanted to turn things around, modernize the bookkeeping. Pump new life into the place, was what she said.'' Someone put on a jitterbug, and he grinned. ''She did just that.''

''Apparently.''

''So you're from back east.'' Bob paused for a moment, then continued when Roman made no comment. ''How long are you planning to stay?''

''As long as it takes.''

He took a long sip of tea. ''As long as what takes?''

''The job.'' Roman glanced idly toward the west wing. ''I like to finish what I start.''

''Yeah. Well...'' He arranged several petits fours on a plate. ''I'm going to go offer these to the ladies and hope they let me eat them.''

Roman watched him pass Block and exchange a quick word with him before he crossed the room. Wanting time to think, Roman slipped back into the west wing.

It was still raining when he came back hours later. Music

was playing, some slow, melodic ballad from the fifties. The room was dimmer now, lit only by the fire and a glass-globed lamp. It was empty, too, except for Charity, who was busy tidying up, humming along with the music.

"Party over?"

She glanced around, then went hurriedly back to stacking cups and plates. "Yes. You didn't stay long."

"I had work to do."

Because she wanted to keep moving, she switched to emptying ashtrays. She'd held on to her guilt long enough. "I was tired this morning, but that's no excuse for being rude to you. I'm sorry if I gave you the impression that you couldn't enjoy yourself for a few hours."

He didn't want to accept an apology that he knew he didn't deserve. "I enjoy the work."

That only made her feel worse. "Be that as it may, I don't usually go around barking orders. I was angry with you."

"Was?"

She looked up, and her eyes were clear and direct. "Am. But that's my problem. If it helps, I'm every bit as angry with myself for acting like a child because you didn't let things get out of hand last night."

Uncomfortable, he picked up the wine decanter and poured a glass. "You didn't act like a child."

"A woman scorned, then, or something equally dramatic. Try not to contradict me when I'm apologizing."

Despite his best efforts, his lips curved against the rim of his glass. If he didn't watch himself he could find he was crazy about her. "All right. Is there more?"

"Just a little." She picked up one of the few petits fours that were left over, debated with herself, then popped it into her mouth. "I shouldn't let my personal feelings interfere with my running of the inn. The problem is, almost everything I think or feel connects with the inn."

"Neither of us were thinking of the inn last night. Maybe that's the problem."

"Maybe."

"Do you want the couch moved back?"

''Yes.'' Business as usual, Charity told herself as she walked over to lift her end. The moment it was in place she scooted around to plump the pillows. ''I saw you dancing with Miss Millie. It thrilled her.''

''I like her.''

''I think you do,'' Charity said slowly, straightening and studying him. ''You're not the kind of man who likes easily.''

''No.''

She wanted to go to him, to lift a hand to his cheek. That was ridiculous, she told herself. Apology notwithstanding, she was still angry with him for last night. ''Has life been so hard?'' she murmured.

''No.''

With a little laugh, she shook her head. ''Then again, you wouldn't tell me if it had been. I have to learn not to ask you questions. Why don't we call a truce, Roman? Life's too short for bad feelings.''

''I don't have any bad feelings toward you, Charity.''

She smiled a little. ''It's tempting, but I'm not going to ask what kind of feelings you do have.''

''I wouldn't be able to tell you, because I haven't figured it out.'' He was amazed that the words had come out. After draining the wine, he set the empty glass aside.

''Well.'' Nonplussed, she pushed her hair back with both hands. ''That's the first thing you've told me I can really understand. Looks like we're in the same boat. Do I take it we have a truce?''

''Sure.''

She glanced back as another record dropped onto the turntable. ''This is one of my favorites. 'Smoke Gets in Your Eyes.''' She was smiling again when she looked back at him. ''You never asked me to dance.''

''No, I didn't.''

''Miss Millie claims you're very smooth.'' She held out a hand in a gesture that was as much a peace offering as an invitation. Unable to resist, he took it in his. Their eyes stayed locked as he drew her slowly toward him.

Chapter 5

A fire simmered in the grate. Rain pattered against the windows. The record was old and scratchy, the tune hauntingly sad. Whether they wanted it or not, their bodies fitted. Her hand slid gently over his shoulder, his around her waist. With their faces close, they began to dance.

The added height from her heels brought her eyes level with his. He could smell the light fragrance that seemed so much a part of her. Seduced by it, he brought her closer, slowly. Their thighs brushed. Still closer. Her body melted against his.

It was so quiet. There was only the music, the rain, the hissing of the fire. Gloomy light swirled into the room. He could feel her heart beating against his, quick now, and not too steady.

His wasn't any too steady now, either.

Was that all it took? he wondered. Did he only have to touch her to think that she was the beginning and the end of everything? And to wish… His hand slid up her back, fingers spreading until they tangled in her hair. To wish she could belong to him.

He wasn't sure when that thought had sunk its roots in him. Perhaps it had begun the first moment he had seen her. She was—should have been—unattainable for him. But when she was in his arms, warm, just bordering on pliant, dozens of possibilities flashed through his head.

She wanted to smile, to make some light, easy comment. But she couldn't push the words out. Her throat was locked. The way he was looking at her now, as if she were the only woman he had ever seen or ever wanted to see, made her forget that the dance was supposed to be a gesture of friendship.

She might never be his friend, she knew, no matter how hard she tried. But with his eyes on hers she understood how easily she could be his lover.

Maybe it was wrong, but it didn't seem to matter as they glided across the floor. The song spoke of love betrayed, but she heard only poetry. She felt her will ebb away even as the music swelled inside her head. No, it didn't seem to matter. Nothing seemed to matter as long as she went on swaying in his arms.

She didn't even try to think, never attempted to reason. Following her heart, she pressed her lips to his.

Instant. Irresistible. Irrevocable. Emotions funneled from one to the other, then merged in a torrent of need. She didn't expect him to be gentle, though her kiss had offered comfort, as well as passion. He dived into it, into her, with a speed and force that left her reeling, then fretting for more.

So this was what drove people to do mad, desperate acts, she thought as their tongues tangled. This wild, painful pleasure, once tasted, would never be forgotten, would always be craved. She wrapped her arms around his neck as she gave herself to it.

With quick, rough kisses he drove them both to the edge. It was more than desire, he knew. Desire had never hurt, not deeply. It was like a scratch, soon forgotten, easily healed. This was a raw, deep wound.

Lust had never erased every coherent thought from his mind. Still, he could only think of her. Those thoughts were jumbled, and all of them were forbidden. Desperate, he ran his lips over her face, while wild fantasies of touching, of tasting every inch of her whirled in his head. It wouldn't be enough. It would never be enough. No matter how much he took from her, she would draw him back. And she could make him beg. The certainty of it terrified him.

She was trembling again, even as she strained against him. Her soft gasps and sighs pushed him toward the brink of reason. He found her mouth again and feasted on it.

He hardly recognized the change, could find no reason for it. All at once she was like glass in his arms, something precious, something fragile, something he needed to protect and defend. He lifted his hands to her face, his fingers light and cautiously caressing. His mouth, ravenous only a moment before, gentled.

Stunned, she swayed. New, vibrant emotions poured into her. Weak from the onslaught, she let her head fall back. Her arms slipped, boneless, to her sides. There was beauty here, a soft, shimmering beauty she had never known existed. Tenderness did what passion had not yet accomplished. As freely as a bird taking wing, her heart flew out to him.

Love, first experienced, was devastating. She felt tears burn the back of her eyes, heard her own quiet moan of surrender. And she tasted the glory of it as his lips played gently with hers.

She would always remember that one instant when the world changed—the music, the rain, the scent of fresh flowers. Nothing would ever be quite the same again. Nor would she ever want it to be.

Shaken, she drew back to lift a hand to her spinning head. "Roman—"

"Come with me." Unwilling to think, he pulled her against him again. "I want to know what it's like to be with you, to undress you, to touch you."

With a moan, she surrendered to his mouth again.

"Charity, Mae wants to—" Lori stopped on a dime at the top of the stairs. After clearing her throat, she stared at the painting on the opposite wall as if it fascinated her. "Excuse me. I didn't mean to…"

Charity had jerked back like a spring and was searching for composure. "It's all right. What is it, Lori?"

"It's, well...Mae and Dolores... Maybe you could come down to the kitchen when you get a minute." She rushed down the stairs, grinning to herself.

"I should..." Charity paused to draw in a steadying breath but managed only a shaky one. "I should go down." She retreated a step. "Once they get started, they need—" She broke off when Roman took her arm. He waited until she lifted her head and looked at him again.

"Things have changed."

It sounded so simple when he said it. "Yes. Yes, they have."

"Right or wrong, Charity, we'll finish this."

"No." She was far from calm, but she was very determined. "If it's right, we'll finish it. I'm not going to pretend I don't want you, but you're right when you say things have changed, Roman. You see, I know what I'm feeling now, and I have to get used to it."

He tightened his grip when she turned to go. "What are you feeling?"

She couldn't have lied if she'd wanted to. Dishonesty was abhorrent to her. When it came to feelings, she had neither the ability nor the desire to suppress them. "I'm in love with you."

His fingers uncurled from her arm. Very slowly, very carefully, as if he were retreating from some dangerous beast, he released her.

She read the shock on his face. That was understandable. And she read the distrust. That was painful. She gave him a last unsmiling look before she turned away.

"Apparently we both have to get used to it."

She was lying. Roman told himself that over and over as he paced the floor in his room. If not to him, then certainly to herself. People seemed to find love easy to lie about.

He stopped by the window and stared out into the dark. The rain had stopped, and the moon was cruising in and out of the clouds. He jerked the window open and breathed in the damp, cool air. He needed something to clear his head.

She was working on him. Annoyed, he turned away from the view of trees and flowers and started pacing again. The easy smiles, the openhanded welcome, the casual friendliness...then the passion, the uninhibited response, the seduction. He wanted to believe it was a trap, even though his well-trained mind found the idea absurd.

She had no reason to suspect him. His cover was solid. Charity thought of him as a drifter, passing through long enough to take in some sights and pick up a little loose change. It was he who was setting the trap.

He dropped down on the bed and lit a cigarette, more out of habit than because he wanted one. Lies were part of his job, a part he was very good at. She hadn't lied to him, he reflected as he inhaled. But she was mistaken. He had made her want, and she had justified her desire for a relative stranger by telling herself she was in love.

But if it was true...

He couldn't allow himself to think that way. Leaning back against the headboard, he stared at the blank wall. He couldn't allow himself the luxury of wondering what it would be like to be loved, and especially not what it would be like to be loved by a woman to whom love would mean a lifetime. He couldn't afford any daydreams about belonging, about having someone belong to him. Even if she hadn't been part of his assignment he would have to sidestep Charity Ford.

She would think of love, then of white picket fences, Sunday dinners and evenings by the fire. He was no good for her. He would never be any good for her. Roman DeWinter, he thought with a mirthless smile. Always on the wrong side of the tracks. A questionable past, an uncertain future. There was nothing he could offer a woman like Charity.

But God, he wanted her. The need was eating away at his insides. He knew she was upstairs now. He imagined her curled up in the big four-poster, under white blankets, perhaps with a white candle burning low on the table.

He had only to climb the stairs and walk through the door. She wouldn't send him away. If she tried, it would take him only moments to break down her resistance. Believing herself in love, she would yield, then open her arms to him. He ached to be in them, to sink into that bed, into her, and let oblivion take them both.

But she had asked for time. He wasn't going to deny her what he needed himself. In the time he gave her he would use all his skill to do the one thing he knew how to do for her. He would prove her innocence.

Roman watched the tour group check out the following morning. Perched on a stepladder in the center of the lobby, he took his time changing bulbs in the ceiling fixture. The sun was out now, full and bright, bathing the lobby in light as a few members of the tour loitered after breakfast.

At the front desk, Charity was chatting with Block. He was wearing a fresh white shirt and his perpetual smile. Taking a calculator from his briefcase, he checked to see if Charity's tallies matched his own.

Bob poked his head out of the office and handed her a computer printout. Roman didn't miss the quick, uncertain look Bob sent in his direction before he shut himself away again.

Charity and Block compared lists. Still smiling, he took a stack of bills out of his briefcase. He paid in Canadian, cash. Having already adjusted the bill to take the exchange rate into account, Charity locked the cash away in a drawer, then handed Block his receipt.

"Always a pleasure, Roger."

"Your little party saved the day," he told her. "My people consider this the highlight of the tour."

Pleased, she smiled at him. "They haven't seen Mount Rainier yet."

"You're going to get some repeaters out of this." He patted her hand, then checked his watch. "Time to move them out. See you next week."

"Safe trip, Roger." She turned to make change for a departing guest, then sold a few postcards and a few souvenir key chains with miniature whales on them.

Roman replaced the globe on the ceiling fixture, taking his

time until the lobby was clear again. "Isn't it strange for a company like that to pay cash?"

Distracted from her reservations list, Charity glanced up at him. "We never turn down cash." She smiled at him as she had promised herself she would. Her feelings, her problem, she reminded herself as he climbed down from the ladder. She only wished the hours she'd spent soul-searching the night before had resulted in a solution.

"It seems like they'd charge, or pay by check."

"It's their company policy. Believe me, with a small, independent hotel, a cash-paying customer like Vision can make all the difference."

"I'll bet. You've been dealing with them for a while?"

"A couple of years. Why?"

"Just curious. Block doesn't look much like a tour guide."

"Roger? No, I guess he looks more like a wrestler." She went back to her papers. It was difficult to make small talk when her feelings were so close to the surface. "He does a good job."

"Yeah. I'll be upstairs."

"Roman." There was so much she wanted to say, but she could feel, though they were standing only a few feet apart, that he had distanced himself from her. "We never discussed a day off," she began. "You're welcome to take Sunday, if you like."

"Maybe I will."

"And if you'd give Bob your hours at the end of the week, he generally takes care of payroll."

"All right. Thanks."

A young couple with a toddler walked out of the dining room. Roman left her to answer their questions on renting a boat.

It wasn't going to be easy to talk to him, Charity decided later. But she had to do it. She'd spent all morning on business, she'd double-checked the housekeeping in the cabins, she'd made every phone call on her list, and if Mae's comments were anything to go on she'd made a nuisance of herself in the kitchen.

She was stalling.

That wasn't like her. All her life she'd made a habit of facing her problems head-on and plowing through them. Not only with business, she thought now. Personal problems had always been given the same kind of direct approach. She had handled being parentless. Even as a child she had never evaded the sometimes painful questions about her background.

But then, she'd had her grandfather. He'd been so solid, so loving. He'd helped her understand that she was her own person. Just as he'd helped her through her first high-school crush, Charity remembered.

He wasn't here now, and she wasn't a fifteen-year-old mooning over the captain of the debating team. But if he had taught her anything, it was that honest feelings were nothing to be ashamed of.

Armed with a thermos full of coffee, she walked into the west wing. She wished it didn't feel so much like bearding the lion in his den.

He'd finished the parlor. The scent of fresh paint was strong, though he'd left a window open to air it out. The doors still had to be hung and the floors varnished, but she could already imagine the room with sheer, billowy curtains and the faded floral-print rug she'd stored in the attic.

From the bedroom beyond, she could hear the buzz of an electric saw. A good, constructive sound, she thought as she pushed the door open to peek inside.

His eyes were narrowed in concentration as he bent over the wood he had laid across a pair of sawhorses. Wood dust flew, dancing gold in the sunlight. His hands, and his arms where he'd rolled his sleeves up past the elbow, were covered with it. He'd used a bandanna to keep the hair out of his eyes. He didn't hum while he worked, as she did. Or talk to himself, she mused, as George had. But, watching him, she thought she detected a simple pleasure in doing a job and doing it well.

He could do things, she thought as she watched him measure the wood for the next cut. Good things, even important things. She was sure of it. Not just because she loved him, she realized. Because it was in him. When a woman spent all her life entertaining strangers in her home, she learned to judge, and to see.

She waited until he put the saw down before she pushed the door open. Before she could speak he whirled around. Her step backward was instinctive, defensive. It was ridiculous, she told herself, but she thought that if he'd had a weapon he'd have drawn it.

"I'm sorry." The nerves she had managed to get under control were shot to hell. "I should have realized I'd startle you."

"It's all right." He settled quickly, though it annoyed him to have been caught off guard. Perhaps if he hadn't been thinking of her he would have sensed her.

"I needed to do some things upstairs, so I thought I'd bring you some coffee on my way." She set the thermos on the stepladder, then wished she'd kept it, as her empty hands made her feel foolish. "And I wanted to check how things were going. The parlor looks great."

"It's coming along. Did you label the paint?"

"Yes. Why?"

"Because it was all done in this tidy printing on the lid of each can in the color of the paint. That seemed like something you'd do."

"Obsessively organized?" She made a face. "I can't seem to help it."

"I liked the way you had the paintbrushes arranged according to size."

She lifted a brow. "Are you making fun of me?"

"Yeah."

"Well, as long as I know." Her nerves were calmer now. "Want some of this coffee?"

"Yeah. I'll get it."

"You've got sawdust all over your hands." Waving him aside, she unscrewed the top. "I take it our truce is back on."

"I didn't realize it had been off."

She glanced back over her shoulder, then looked around

and poured the coffee into the plastic cup. "I made you uncomfortable yesterday. I'm sorry."

He accepted the cup and sat down on a sawhorse. "You're putting words in my mouth again, Charity."

"I don't have to this time. You looked as if I'd hit you with a brick." Restless, she moved her shoulders. "I suppose I might have reacted the same way if someone had said they loved me out of the blue like that. It must have been pretty startling, seeing as we haven't known each other for long."

Finding he had no taste for it, he set the coffee aside. "You were reacting to the moment."

"No." She turned back to him, knowing it was important to talk face-to-face. "I thought you might think that. In fact, I even considered playing it safe and letting you. I'm lousy at deception. It seemed more fair to tell you that I'm not in the habit of...what I mean is, I don't throw myself at men as a rule. The truth is, you're the first."

"Charity." He dragged a hand through his hair, pulling out the bandanna and sending more wood dust scattering. "I don't know what to say to you."

"You don't have to say anything. The fact is, I came in here with my little speech all worked out. It was a pretty good one, too...calm, understanding, a couple of dashes of humor to keep it light. I'm screwing it up."

She kicked a scrap of wood into the corner before she paced to the window. Columbine and bluebells grew just below in a bed where poppies were waiting to burst into color. On impulse, she pushed up the window to breathe in their faint, fragile scents.

"The point is," she began, hating herself for keeping her back to him, "we can't pretend I didn't say it. I can't pretend I don't feel it. That doesn't mean I expect you to feel the same way, because I don't."

"What do you expect?"

He was right behind her. She jumped when his hand gripped her shoulder. Gathering her courage, she turned around. "For you to be honest with me." She was speaking quickly now, and she didn't notice his slight, automatic retreat. "I appreciate the fact that you don't pretend to love me. I may be simple, Roman, but I'm not stupid. I know it might be easier to lie, to say what you think I want to hear."

"You're not simple," he murmured, lifting a hand and brushing it against her cheek. "I've never met a more confusing, complicated woman."

Shock came first, then pleasure. "That's the nicest thing you've ever said to me. No one's ever accused me of being complicated."

He'd meant to lower his hand, but she had already lifted hers and clasped it. "I didn't mean it as a compliment."

That made her grin. Relaxed again, she sat back on the windowsill. "Even better. I hope this means we're finished feeling awkward around each other."

"I don't know what I feel around you." He ran his hands up her arms to her shoulders, then down to the elbows again. "But awkward isn't the word for it."

Touched—much too deeply—she rose. "I have to go."

"Why?"

"Because it's the middle of the day, and if you kiss me I might forget that."

Already aroused, he eased her forward. "Always organized."

"Yes." She put a hand to his chest to keep some distance between them. "I have some invoices I have to go over upstairs." Holding her breath, she backed toward the door. "I do want you, Roman. I'm just not sure I can handle that part of it."

Neither was he, he thought after she shut the door. With another woman he would have been certain that physical release would end the tension. With Charity he knew that making love with her would only add another layer to the hold she had on him.

And she did have a hold on him. It was time to admit that, and to deal with it.

Perhaps he'd reacted so strongly to her declaration of love because he was afraid, as he'd never been afraid of anything in his life, that he was falling in love with her.

"Roman!" He heard the delight in Charity's voice when she called to him. He swung open the door and saw her standing on the landing at the top of the stairs. "Come up. Hurry. I want you to see them."

She disappeared, leaving him wishing she'd called him anyplace but that innocently seductive bedroom.

When he walked into her sitting room, she called again, impatience in her tone now. "Hurry. I don't know how long they'll stay."

She was sitting on the windowsill, her upper body out the opening, her long legs hooked just above the ankles. There was music playing, something vibrant, passionate. How was it he had never thought of classical music as passionate?

"Damn it, Roman, you're going to miss them. Don't just stand in the doorway. I didn't call you up to tie you to the bedposts."

Because he felt like a fool, he crossed to her. "There goes my night."

"Very funny. Look." She was holding a brass spy glass, and she pointed with it now, out to sea. "Orcas."

He leaned out the window and followed her guiding hand. He could see a pair of shapes in the distance, rippling the water as they swam. Fascinated, he took the spyglass from Charity's hand.

"There are three of them," he said. Delighted, he joined her on the windowsill. Their legs were aligned now, and he rested his hand absently on her knee. This time, instead of fire, there was simple warmth.

"Yes, there's a calf. I think it might be the same pod I spotted a few days ago." She closed a hand over his as they both stared out to sea. "Great, aren't they?"

"Yeah, they are." He focused on the calf, which was just visible between the two larger whales. "I never really expected to see any."

"Why? The island's named after them." She narrowed her eyes, trying to follow their path. She didn't have the heart to ask Roman for the glass. "My first clear memory of seeing one was when I was about four. Pop had me out on this little excuse for a fishing boat. One shot up out of the water no more than eight or ten yards away. I screamed my lungs out.'' Laughing, she leaned back against the windowframe. ''I thought it was going to swallow us whole, like Jonah or maybe Pinocchio.''

Roman lowered the glass for a moment. ''Pinocchio?''

''Yes, you know the puppet who wanted to be a real boy. Jiminy Cricket, the Blue Fairy. Anyway, Pop finally calmed me down. It followed us for ten or fifteen minutes. After that, I nagged him mercilessly to take me out again.''

''Did he?''

''Every Monday afternoon that summer. We didn't always see something, but they were great days, the best days. I guess we were a pod, too, Pop and I.'' She turned her face into the breeze. ''I was lucky to have him as long as I did, but there are times—like this—when I can't help wishing he were here.''

''Like this?''

''He loved to watch them,'' she said quietly. ''Even when he was ill, really ill, he would sit for hours at the window. One afternoon I found him sitting there with the spyglass on his lap. I thought he'd fallen asleep, but he was gone.'' There was a catch in her breath when she slowly let it out. ''He would have wanted that, to just slip away while watching for his whales. I haven't been able to take the boat out since he died.'' She shook her head. ''Stupid.''

''No.'' He reached for her hand for the first time and linked his fingers with hers. ''It's not.''

She turned her face to his again. ''You can be a nice man.'' The phone rang, and she groaned but slipped dutifully from the windowsill to answer it.

''Hello. Yes, Bob. What does he mean he won't deliver them? New management be damned, we've been dealing with that company for ten years. Yes, all right. I'll be right there. Oh, wait.'' She glanced up from the phone. ''Roman, are they still there?''

''Yes. Heading south. I don't know if they're feeding or just taking an afternoon stroll.''

She laughed and put the receiver at her ear again. "Bob—What? Yes, that was Roman." Her brow lifted. "That's right. We're in my room. I called Roman up here because I spotted a pod out my bedroom window. You might want to tell any of the guests you see around. No, there's no reason for you to be concerned. Why should there be? I'll be right down."

She hung up, shaking her head. "It's like having a houseful of chaperons," she muttered.

"Problem?"

"No. Bob realized that you were in my bedroom—or rather that we were alone in my bedroom—and got very big-brotherly. Typical." She opened a drawer and pulled out a fabric-covered band. In a few quick movements she had her hair caught back from her face. "Last year Mae threatened to poison a guest who made a pass at me. You'd think I was fifteen."

He turned to study her. She was wearing jeans and a sweat-shirt with a silk-screened map of the island. "Yes, you would."

"I don't take that as a compliment." But she didn't have time to argue. "I have to deal with a small crisis downstairs. You're welcome to stay and watch the whales." She started toward the door, but then she stopped. "Oh, I nearly forgot. Can you build shelves?"

"Probably."

"Great. I think the parlor in the family suite could use them. We'll talk about it."

He heard her jog down the stairs. Whatever crisis there might be at the other end of the inn, he was sure she would handle it. In the meantime, she had left him alone in her room. It would be a simple matter to go through her desk again, to see if she'd left anything that would help him move his investigation forward.

It should be simple, anyway. Roman looked out to sea again. It should be something he could do without hesitation. But he couldn't. She trusted him. Sometime during the past twenty-four hours he reached the point where he couldn't violate that trust.

That made him useless. Swearing, Roman leaned back
against the windowframe. She had, without even being aware
of it, totally undermined his ability to do his job. It would be
best for him to call Conby and have himself taken off the
case. It would simply be a matter of him turning in his resignation now, rather than at the end of the assignment. It was
a question of duty.

He wasn't going to do that, either.

He needed to stay. It had nothing to do with being loved,
with feeling at home. He needed to believe that. He also
needed to finish his job and prove, beyond a shadow of a
doubt, Charity's innocence. That was a question of loyalty.

Conby would have said that his loyalty belonged to the
Bureau, not to a woman he had known for less than a week.
And Conby would have been wrong, Roman thought as he
set aside the spyglass. There were times, rare times, when you
had a chance to do something good, something right. Something that proved you gave a damn. That had never mattered
to him before, but it mattered now.

If the only thing he could give Charity was a clear name,
he intended to give it to her. And then get out of her life.

Rising, he looked around the room. He wished he were
nothing more than the out-of-work drifter Charity had taken
into her home. If he were maybe he would have the right to
love her. As it was, all he could do was save her.

Chapter 6

The weather was warming. Spring was busting loose, full of glory and color and scent. The island was a treasure trove of wildflowers, leafy trees and birdsong. At dawn, with thin fingers of fog over the water, it was a mystical, timeless place.

Roman stood at the side of the road and watched the sun come up as he had only days before. He didn't know the names of the flowers that grew in tangles on the roadside. He didn't know the song of a jay from that of a sparrow. But he knew Charity was out running with her dog and that she would pass the place he stood on her return.

He needed to see her, to talk to her, to be with her.

The night before, he had broken into her cash drawer and examined the bills she had neatly stacked and marked for today's deposit. There had been over two thousand dollars in counterfeit Canadian currency. His first impulse had been to tell her, to lay everything he knew and needed to know out in front of her. But he had quashed that. Telling her wouldn't prove her innocence to men like Conby.

He had enough to get Block. And nearly enough, he thought, to hang Bob along with him. But he couldn't get them without casting shadows on Charity. By her own admission, and according to the statements of her loyal staff, a pin couldn't drop in the inn without her knowing it.

If that was so, how could he prove that there had been a counterfeiting and smuggling ring going on under her nose for nearly two years?

He believed it, as firmly as he had ever believed anything. Conby and the others at the Bureau wanted facts. Roman drew on his cigarette and watched the fog melt away with the rising of the sun. He had to give them facts. Until he could, he would give them nothing.

He could wait and make sure Conby dropped the ax on Block on the guide's next trip to the inn. That would give Roman time. Time enough, he promised himself, to make certain Charity wasn't caught in the middle. When it went down, she would be stunned and hurt. She'd get over it. When it was over, and she knew his part in it, she would hate him. He would get over that. He would have to.

He heard a car and glanced over, then returned his gaze to the water. He wondered if he could come back someday and stand in this same spot and wait for Charity to run down the road toward him.

Fantasies, he told himself, pitching his half-finished cigarette into the dirt. He was wasting too much time on fantasies.

The car was coming fast, its engine protesting, its muffler rattling. He looked over again, annoyed at having his morning and his thoughts disturbed.

His annoyance saved his life.

It took him only an instant to realize what was happening, and a heartbeat more to evade it. As the car barreled toward him, he leaped aside, tucking and rolling into the brush. A wave of displaced air flattened the grass before the car's rear tires gripped the roadbed again. Roman's gun was in his hand even as he scrambled to his feet. He caught a glimpse of the car's rear end as it sped around a curve. There wasn't even time to swear before he heard Charity's scream.

He ran, unaware of the fire in his thigh where the car had grazed him and the blood on his arm where he had rolled into a rock. He had faced death. He had killed. But he had never understood terror until this moment, with her scream still echoing in his head. He hadn't understood agony until he'd seen Charity sprawled beside the road.

The dog was curled beside her, whimpering, nuzzling her face with her nose. He turned at Roman's approach and began to growl, then stood, barking.

"Charity." Roman crouched beside her, and felt for a pulse, his hand shaking. "Okay, baby. You're going to be okay," he murmured to her as he checked for broken bones.

Had she been hit? A sickening vision of her being tossed into the air as the car slammed into her pulsed through his head. Using every ounce of control he possessed, he blocked it out. She was breathing. He held on to that. The dog whined as he turned her head and examined the gash on her temple. It was the only spot of color on her face. He stanched the blood with his bandanna, cursing when he felt its warmth on his fingers.

Grimly he replaced his weapon, then lifted her into his arms. Her body seemed boneless. Roman tightened his grip, half afraid she might melt through his arms. He talked to her throughout the half-mile walk back to the inn, though she remained pale and still.

Bob raced out the front door of the inn. "My God! What happened? What the hell did you do to her?"

Roman paused just long enough to aim a dark, furious look at him. "I think you know better. Get me the keys to the van. She needs a hospital."

"What's all this?" Mae came through the door, wiping her hands on her apron. "Lori said she saw—" She went pale, but then she began to move with surprising speed, elbowing Bob aside to reach Charity. "Get her upstairs."

"I'm taking her to the hospital."

"Upstairs," Mae repeated, moving back to open the door for him. "We'll call Dr. Mertens. It'll be faster. Come on, boy. Call the doctor, Bob. Tell him to hurry."

Roman passed through the door, the dog at his heels. "And call the police," he added. "Tell them they've got a hit-and-run."

Wasting no time on words, Mae led the way upstairs. She

was puffing a bit by the time she reached the second floor, but she never slowed down. When they moved into Charity's room, her color had returned.

"Set her on the bed, and be careful about it." She yanked the lacy coverlet aside and then just as efficiently, brushed Roman aside. "There, little girl, you'll be just fine. Go in the bathroom," she told Roman. "Get me a fresh towel." Easing a hip onto the bed, she cupped Charity's face with a broad hand and examined her head wound. "Looks worse than it is." She let out a long breath. After taking the towel Roman offered, she pressed it against Charity's temple. "Head wounds bleed heavy, make a mess. But it's not too deep."

He only knew that her blood was still on his hands. "She should be coming around."

"Give her time. I want you to tell me what happened later, but I'm going to undress her now, see if she's hurt anywhere else. You go on and wait downstairs."

"I'm not leaving her."

Mae glanced up. Her lips were pursed, and lines of worry fanned out from her eyes. After a moment, she simply nodded. "All right, then, but you'll be of some use. Get me the scissors out of her desk. I want to cut this shirt off."

So that was the way of it, Mae mused as she untied Charity's shoes. She knew a man who was scared to death and fighting his heart when she saw one. Well, she'd just have to get her girl back on her feet. She didn't doubt for a moment that Charity could deal with the likes of Roman DeWinter.

"You can stay," she told him when he handed her the scissors. "But whatever's been going on between the two of you, you'll turn your back till I make her decent."

He balled his hands into impotent fists and shoved them into his pockets as he spun around. "I want to know where she's hurt."

"Just hold your horses." Mae peeled the shirt away and put her emotions on hold as she examined the scrapes and bruises. "Look in that top right-hand drawer and get me out a nightshirt. One with buttons. And keep your eyes to yourself," she added, "or I'll throw you out of here."

In answer, he tossed a thin white nightshirt onto the bed. "I don't care what she's wearing. I want to know how badly she's hurt."

"I know, boy." Mae's voice softened as she slipped Charity's limp arm into a sleeve. "She's got some bruises and scrapes, that's all. Nothing broken. The cut on her head's going to need some tending, but cuts heal. Why, she hurt herself worse when she fell out of a tree some time back. There's my girl. She's coming around."

He turned to look then, shirt or no shirt. But Mae had already done up the buttons. He controlled the urge to go to her—barely—and, keeping his distance, watched Charity's lashes flutter. The sinking in his stomach was pure relief. When she moaned, he wiped his clammy hands on his thighs.

"Mae?" As she struggled to focus her eyes, Charity reached out a hand. She could see the solid bulk of her cook, but little else. "What— Oh, God, my head."

"Thumping pretty good, is it?" Mae's voice was brisk, but she cradled Charity's hand in hers. She would have kissed it if she'd thought no one would notice. "The doc'll fix that up."

"Doctor?" Baffled, Charity tried to sit up, but the pain exploded in her head. "I don't want the doctor."

"Never did, but you're having him just the same."

"I'm not going to..." Arguing took too much effort. Instead, she closed her eyes and concentrated on clearing her mind. It was fairly obvious that she was in bed—but how the devil had she gotten there?

She'd been walking the dog, she remembered, and Ludwig had found a tree beside the road irresistible. Then...

"There was a car," she said, opening her eyes again. "They must have been drunk or crazy. It seemed like they came right at me. If Ludwig hadn't already been pulling me off the road, I—" She wasn't quite ready to consider that. "I stumbled, I think. I don't know."

"It doesn't matter now," Mae assured her. "We'll figure it all out later."

After a brisk knock, the outside door opened. A short, spry

little man with a shock of white hair hustled in. He carried a black bag and was wearing grubby overalls and muddy boots. Charity took one look, then closed her eyes again.

"Go away, Dr. Mertens. I'm not feeling well."

"She never changes." Mertens nodded to Roman, then walked over to examine his patient.

Roman slipped quietly out into the sitting room. He needed a moment to pull himself together, to quiet the rage that was building now that he knew she would be all right. He had lost his parents, he had buried his best friend, but he had never, never felt the kind of panic he had experienced when he had seen Charity bleeding and unconscious beside the road.

Taking out a cigarette, he went to the open window. He thought about the driver of the old, rusted Chevy that had run her down. Even as his rage cooled, Roman understood one thing with perfect clarity. It would be his pleasure to kill whoever had hurt her.

"Excuse me." Lori was standing in the hall doorway, wringing her hands. "The sheriff's here. He wants to talk to you, so I brought him up." She tugged at her apron and stared at the closed door on the other side of the room. "Charity?"

"The doctor's with her," Roman said. "She'll be fine."

Lori closed her eyes and took a deep breath. "I'll tell the others. Go on in, sheriff."

Roman studied the paunchy man, who had obviously been called out of bed. His shirttail was only partially tucked into his pants, and he was sipping a cup of coffee as he came into the room.

"You Roman DeWinter?"

"That's right."

"Sheriff Royce." He sat, with a sigh, on the arm of Charity's rose-colored Queen Anne chair. "What's this about a hit-and-run?"

"About twenty minutes ago somebody tried to run down Miss Ford."

Royce turned to stare at the closed door just the way Lori had done. "How is she?"

"Banged up. She's got a gash on her head and some bruises."

"Were you with her?" He pulled out a pad and a stubby pencil.

"No. I was about a quarter mile away. The car swerved at me, then kept going. I heard Charity scream. When I got to her, she was unconscious."

"Don't suppose you got a good look at the car?"

"Dark blue Chevy. Sedan, '67, '68. Muffler was bad. Right front fender was rusted through. Washington plates Alpha Foxtrot Juliet 847."

Royce lifted both brows as he took down the description. "You got a good eye."

"That's right."

"Good enough for you to guess if he ran you down on purpose?"

"I don't have to guess. He was aiming."

Without a flicker of an eye, Royce continued taking notes. He added a reminder to himself to do a routine check on Roman DeWinter. "He? Did you see the driver?"

"No," Roman said shortly. He was still cursing himself for that.

"How long have you been on the island, Mr. DeWinter?"

"Almost a week."

"A short time to make enemies."

"I don't have any—here—that I know of."

"That makes your theory pretty strange." Still scribbling, Royce glanced up. "There's nobody on the island who knows Charity and has a thing against her. If what you're saying's true, we'd be talking attempted murder."

Roman pitched his cigarette out the window. "That's just what we're talking about. I want to know who owns that car."

"I'll check it out."

"You already know."

Royce tapped his pad on his knee. "Yes, sir, you do have a good eye. I'll say this. Maybe I do know somebody who owns a car that fits your description. If I do, I know that that person wouldn't run over a rabbit on purpose, much less a woman. Then again, there's no saying you have to own a car to drive it.''

Mae opened the connecting door, and he glanced up. ''Well, now, Maeflower.''

Mae's lips twitched slightly before she thinned them. ''If you can't sit in a chair proper you can stand on your feet, Jack Royce.''

Royce rose, grinning. ''Mae and I went to school together,'' he explained. ''She liked to bully me then, too. I don't suppose you've got any waffles on the menu today, Maeflower.''

''Maybe I do. You find out who hurt my girl and I'll see you get some.''

''I'm working on it.'' His face sobered again as he nodded toward the door. ''Is she up to talking to me?''

''Done nothing but talk since she came around.'' Mae blinked back a flood of relieved tears. ''Go ahead in.''

Royce turned to Roman. ''I'll be in touch.''

''Doc said she could have some tea and toast.'' Mae sniffled, then made a production out of blowing her nose. ''Hay fever,'' she said roughly. ''I'm grateful you were close by when she was hurt.''

''If I'd been closer she wouldn't have been hurt.''

''And if she hadn't been walking that dog she'd have been in bed.'' She paused and gave Roman a level look. ''I guess we could shoot him.''

She surprised a little laugh out of him. ''Charity might object to that.''

''She wouldn't care to know you're out here brooding, either. Your arm's bleeding, boy.''

He looked down dispassionately at the torn, bloodstained sleeve of his shirt. ''Some.''

''Can't have you bleeding all over the floor.'' She walked to the door, waving a hand. ''Well, come on downstairs. I'll clean you up. Then you can bring the girl up some breakfast. I haven't got time to run up and down these steps all morning.''

After the doctor had finished his poking and the sheriff had finished his questioning, Charity stared at the ceiling. She hurt everywhere there was to hurt. Her head especially, but the rest of her was throbbing right along in time.

The medication would take the edge off, but she wanted to keep her mind clear until she'd worked everything out. That was why she had tucked the pill Dr. Mertens had given her under her tongue until she'd been alone. As soon as she'd organized her thoughts she would swallow it and check into oblivion for a few hours.

She'd only caught a flash of the car, but it had seemed familiar. While she'd spoken with the sheriff she'd remembered. The car that had nearly run her over belonged to Mrs. Norton, a sweet, flighty lady who crocheted doilies and doll clothes for the local craft shops. Charity didn't think Mrs. Norton had ever driven over twenty-five miles an hour. That was a great deal less than the car had been doing when it had swerved at her that morning.

She hadn't seen the driver, not really, but she had the definite impression it had been a man. Mrs. Norton had been widowed for six years.

Then it was simple, Charity decided. Someone had gotten drunk, stolen Mrs. Norton's car, and taken it for a wild joyride around the island. They probably hadn't even seen her at the side of the road.

Satisfied, she eased herself up in the bed. The rest was for the sheriff to worry about. She had problems of her own.

The breakfast shift was probably in chaos. She thought she could rely on Lori to keep everyone calm. Then there was the butcher. She still had her list to complete for tomorrow's order. And she had yet to choose the photographs she wanted to use for the ad in the travel brochure. The deposit hadn't been paid, and the fireplace in cabin 3 was smoking.

What she needed was a pad, a pencil and a telephone. That was simple enough. She'd find all three at the desk in the sitting room. Carefully she eased her legs over the side of the bed. Not too bad, she decided, but she gave herself a moment to adjust before she tried to stand.

Annoyed with herself, she braced a hand on one of the

bedposts. Her legs felt as though they were filled with Mae's whipped cream rather than muscle and bone.

"What the hell are you doing?"

She winced at the sound of Roman's voice, then gingerly turned her head toward the doorway. "Nothing," she said, and tried to smile.

"Get back in bed."

"I just have a few things to do."

She was swaying on her feet, as pale as the nightshirt that buttoned modestly high at the neck and skimmed seductively high on her thighs. Without a word, he set down the tray he was carrying, crossed to her and scooped her up in his arms.

"Roman, don't: I—"

"Shut up."

"I was going to lie back down in a minute," she began. "Right after—"

"Shut up," he repeated. He laid her on the bed, then gave up. Keeping his arms around her, he buried his face against her throat. "Oh, God, baby."

"It's all right." She stroked a hand through his hair. "Don't worry."

"I thought you were dead. When I found you I thought you were dead."

"Oh, I'm sorry." She rubbed at the tension at the back of his neck, trying to imagine how he must have felt. "It must have been awful, Roman. But it's only some bumps and bruises. In a couple of days they'll be gone and we'll forget all about it."

"I won't forget." He pulled himself away from her. "Ever."

The violence she saw in his eyes had her heart fluttering. "Roman, it was an accident. Sheriff Royce will take care of it."

He bit back the words he wanted to say. It was best that she believe it had been an accident. For now. He got up to get her tray. "Mae said you could eat."

She thought of the lists she had to make and decided she

had a better chance getting around him if she cooperated. "I'll try. How's Ludwig?"

"Okay. Mae put him out and gave him a hambone."

"Ah, his favorite." She bit into the toast and pretended she had an appetite.

"How's your head?"

"Not too bad." It wasn't really a lie, she thought. She was sure a blow with a sledgehammer would have been worse. "No stitches." She pulled back her hair to show him a pair of butterfly bandages. A bruise was darkening around them. "You want to hold up some fingers and ask me how many I see?"

"No." He turned away, afraid he would explode. The last thing she needed was another outburst from him, he reminded himself. He wasn't the kind to fall apart—at least he hadn't been until he'd met her.

He began fiddling with bottles and bowls set around the room. She loved useless little things, he thought as he picked up a wand-shaped amethyst crystal. Feeling clumsy, he set it down again.

"The sheriff said the car swerved at you." She drank the soothing chamomile tea, feeling almost human again. "I'm glad you weren't hurt."

"Damn it, Charity." He whirled, then made an effort to get a handle on his temper. "No, I wasn't hurt." And he was going to see to it that *she* wasn't hurt again. "I'm sorry. This whole business has made me edgy."

"I know what you mean. Want some tea? Mae sent up two cups."

He glanced at the pretty flowered pot. "Not unless you've got some whiskey to go in it."

"Sorry, fresh out." Smiling again, she patted the bed. "Why don't you come sit down?"

"Because I'm trying to keep my hands off you."

"Oh." Her smile curved wider. It pleased her that she was resilient enough to feel a quick curl of desire. "I like your hands on me, Roman."

"Bad timing." Because he couldn't resist, he crossed to

the bed to take her hand in his. "I care about you, Charity. I want you to believe that."

"I do."

"No." His fingers tightened insistently on hers. He knew he wasn't clever with words, but he needed her to understand. "It's different with you than it's ever been with anyone." Fighting a fresh wave of frustration, he relaxed his grip. "I can't give you anything else."

She felt her heart rise up in her throat. "If I had known I could get that much out of you I might have bashed my head on a rock before."

"You deserve more." He sat down and ran a gentle finger under the bruise on her temple.

"I agree." She brought his hand to her lips and watched his eyes darken. "I'm patient."

Something was moving inside him, and he was helpless to prevent it. "You don't know enough about me. You don't know anything about me."

"I know I love you. I figured you'd tell me the rest eventually."

"Don't trust me, Charity. Not so much."

There was trouble here. She wanted to smooth it from his face, but she didn't know how. "Have you done something so unforgivable, Roman?"

"I hope not. You should rest." Knowing he'd already said too much, he set her tray aside.

"I was going to, really. Right after I take care of a few things."

"The only thing you have to take care of today is yourself."

"That's very sweet of you, and as soon as I—"

"You're not getting out of bed for at least twenty-four hours."

"That's the most ridiculous thing I've ever heard. What possible difference does it make whether I'm lying down or sitting down?"

"According to the doctor, quite a bit." He picked up a

tablet from the nightstand. "Is this the medication he gave you?"

"Yes."

"The same medication that you were supposed to take before he left?"

She struggled to keep from pouting. "I'm going to take it after I make a few phone calls."

"No phone calls today."

"Now listen, Roman, I appreciate your concern, but I don't take orders from you."

"I know. You give them to me."

Before she could respond, he lowered his lips to hers. Here was gentleness again, whisper-soft, achingly warm. With a little sound of pleasure, she sank into it.

He'd thought it would be easy to take one, only one, fleeting taste. But his hand curled into a fist as he fought the need to demand more. She was so fragile now. He wanted to soothe, not arouse...to comfort, not seduce. But in seconds he was both aroused and seduced.

When he started to pull back, she gave a murmur of protest and pressed him close again. She needed this sweetness from him, needed it more than any medication.

"Easy," he told her, clawing for his self-control. "I'm a little low on willpower, and you need rest."

"I'd rather have you."

She smiled at him, and his stomach twisted into knots. "Do you drive all men crazy?"

"I don't think so." Feeling on top of the world, she brushed his hair back from his brow. "Anyway, you're the first to ask."

"We'll talk about it later." Determined to do his best for her, he held out the pill. "Take this."

"Later."

"Uh-uh. Now."

With a sound of disgust, she popped the pill into her mouth, then picked up her cooling tea and sipped it. "There. Satisfied?"

He had to grin. "I've been a long way from satisfied since I first laid eyes on you, baby. Lift up your tongue."

"I beg your pardon?"

"You heard me. You're pretty good." He put a hand under her chin. "But I'm better. Let's have the pill."

She knew she was beaten. She took the pill out of her mouth, then made a production out of swallowing it. She touched the tip of her tongue to her lips. "It might still be in there. Want to search me for it?"

"What I want—" he kissed her lightly "—is for you to stay in bed." He shifted his lips to her throat. "No calls, no paperwork, no sneaking downstairs." He caught her earlobe between his teeth and felt her shudder, and his own. "Promise."

"Yes." Her lips parted as his brushed over them. "I promise."

"Good." He sat back and picked up the tray. "I'll see you later."

"But—" She set her teeth as he walked to the door. "You play dirty, DeWinter."

"Yeah." He glanced back at her. "And to win."

He left her, knowing she would no more break her word than she would fly out of the window. He had business of his own to attend to.

Chapter 7

An important part of Roman's training had been learning how to pursue an assignment in a thorough and objective manner. He had always found it second nature to do both. Until now. Still, for very personal reasons, he fully intended to be thorough.

When he left Charity, Roman expected to find Bob in the office, and he hoped to find him alone. He wasn't disappointed. Bob had the phone receiver at his ear and the computer monitor blinking above his fingers. After waving a distracted hand in Roman's direction, he went on with his conversation.

"I'll be happy to set that up for you and your wife, Mr. Parkington. That's a double room for the nights of the fifteenth and sixteenth of July."

"Hang up," Roman told him. Bob merely held up a finger, signaling a short wait.

"Yes, that's available with a private bath and includes breakfast. We'd be happy to help you arrange the rentals of kayaks during your stay. Your confirmation number is—"

Roman slammed a hand down on the phone, breaking the connection.

"What the hell are you doing?"

"Wondering if I should bother to talk to you or just kill you."

Bob sprang out of his chair and managed to put the desk between him and Roman. "Look, I know you've had an upsetting morning—"

"Do you?" Roman didn't bother to try to outmaneuver. He simply stood where he was and watched Bob sweat. "Upsetting. That's a nice, polite word for it. But you're a nice, polite man, aren't you, Bob?"

Bob glanced at the door and wondered if he had a chance of getting that far. "We're all a bit edgy because of Charity's accident. You could probably use a drink."

Roman moved over to a stack of computer manuals and unearthed a small silver flask. "Yours?" he said. Bob stared at him. "I imagine you keep this in here for those long nights when you're working late—and alone. Wondering how I knew where to find it?" He set it aside. "I came across it when I broke in here a couple of nights ago and went through the books."

"You broke in?" Bob wiped the back of his hand over suddenly dry lips. "That's a hell of a way to pay Charity back for giving you a job."

"Yeah, you're right about that. Almost as bad as using her inn to pass counterfeit bills and slip undesirables in and out of the country."

"I don't know what you're talking about." Bob took one cautious sideways step toward the door. "I want you out of here, DeWinter. When I tell Charity what you've done—"

"But you're not going to tell her. You're not going to tell her a damn thing—yet. But you're going to tell me." One look stopped Bob's careful movement cold. "Try for the door and I'll break your leg." Roman tapped a cigarette out of his pack. "Sit down."

"I don't have to take this." But he took a step back, away from the door, and away from Roman. "I'll call the police."

"Go ahead." Roman lit the cigarette and watched him through a veil of smoke. It was a pity Bob was so easily cowed. He'd have liked an excuse to damage him. "I was tempted to tell Royce everything I knew this morning. The problem with that was that it would have spoiled the satisfaction of dealing with you and the people you're with personally. But go ahead and call him.'' Roman shoved the phone across the desk in Bob's direction. ''I can find a way of finishing my business with you once you're inside.''

Bob didn't ask him to explain. He had heard the cell door slam the moment Roman had walked into the room. ''Listen, I know you're upset....''

''Do I look upset?'' Roman murmured.

No, Bob thought, his stomach clenched. He looked cold— cold enough to kill. Or worse. But there had to be a way out. There always was. ''You said something about counterfeiting. Why don't you tell me what this is all about, and we'll try to settle this calm—?'' Before he got the last word out he was choking as Roman hauled him out of the chair by the collar.

''Do you want to die?''

''No.'' Bob's fingers slid helplessly off Roman's wrists.

''Then cut the crap.'' Disgusted, Roman tossed him back into the chair. ''There are two things Charity doesn't do around here. Only two. She doesn't cook, and she doesn't work the computer. *Can't* would be a better word. She can't cook because Mae didn't teach her. Pretty easy to figure why. Mae wanted to rule in the kitchen, and Charity wanted to let her.''

He moved to the window and casually lowered the shades so that the room was dim and private. ''It's just as simple to figure why she can't work a basic office computer. You didn't teach her, or you made the lessons so complicated and contradictory she never caught on. You want me to tell you why you did that?''

''She was never really interested.'' Bob swallowed, his throat raw. ''She can do the basics when she has to, but you know Charity—she's more interested in people than machines. I show her all the printouts.''

''All? You and I know you haven't shown her all of them. Should I tell you what I think is on those disks you've got hidden in the file drawer?''

Bob pulled out a handkerchief with fumbling fingers and mopped at his brow. "I don't know what you're talking about."

"You keep the books for the inn, and for the little business you and your friends have on the side. I figure a man like you would keep backups, a little insurance in case the people you work for decided to cut you out." He opened a file drawer and dug out a disk. "We'll take a look at this later," he said, and tossed it onto the desk. "Two to three thousand a week washes through this place. Fifty-two weeks a year makes that a pretty good haul. Add that to the fee you charge to get someone back and forth across the border mixed with the tour group and you've got a nice, tidy sum."

"That's crazy." Barely breathing, Bob tugged at his collar. "You've got to know that's crazy."

"Did you know your references were still on file here?" Roman asked conversationally. "The problem is, they don't check out. You never worked for a hotel back in Ft. Worth, or in San Francisco."

"So I padded my chances a bit. That doesn't prove anything."

"I think we'll turn up something more interesting when we run your prints."

Bob stared down at the disk. Sometimes you could bluff, and sometimes you had to fold. "Can I have a drink?"

Roman picked up the flask, tossed it to him and waited while he twisted off the cap. "You made me for a cop, didn't you? Or you were worried enough to keep your ear to the ground. You heard me asking the wrong questions, were afraid I'd told Charity about the operation and passed it along to your friends."

"It didn't feel right." Bob wiped the vodka from his lips, then drank again. "I know a scam when I see one, and you made me nervous the minute I saw you."

"Why?"

"When you're in my business you get so you can spot cops. In the supermarket, on the street, buying underwear at a department store. It doesn't matter where, you get so you can make them.''

Roman thought of himself and of the years he'd spent on the other side of the street. He'd made his share of cops, and he still could. "Okay. So what did you do?''

"I told Block I thought you were a plant, but he figured I was going loopy. I wanted to back off until you'd gone, but he wouldn't listen. Last night, when you went down for dinner, I looked through your room. I found a box of shells. No gun, just the shells. That meant you were wearing it. I called Block and told him I was sure you were a cop. You'd been spending a lot of time with Charity, so I figured she was working with you on it.''

"So you tried to kill her.''

"No, not me.'' Panicked, Bob pressed back in his chair. "I swear. I'm not a violent man, DeWinter. Hell, I like Charity. I wanted to pull out, take a breather. We'd already set up another place, in the Olympic Mountains. I figured we could take a few weeks, run legit, then move on it. Block just said he'd take care of it, and I thought he meant we'd handle next week's tour on the level. That would give me time to fix everything here and get out. If I'd known what he was planning…''

"What? Would you have warned her?''

"I don't know.'' Bob drained the flask, but the liquor did little to calm his nerves. "Look, I do scams, I do cons. I don't kill people.''

"Who was driving the car?''

"I don't know. I swear it,'' he said. Roman took a step toward him, and he gripped the arms of his chair. "Listen, I got in touch with Block the minute this happened. He said he'd hired somebody. He couldn't have done it himself, because he was on the mainland. He said the guy wasn't trying to kill her. Block just wanted her out of the way for a few days. We've got a big shipment coming in and—'' He broke off, knowing he was digging himself in deeper.

Roman merely nodded. "You're going to find out who was driving the car.''

"Okay, sure." He made the promise without knowing if he could keep it. "I'll find out."

"You and I are going to work together for the next few days, Bob."

"But...aren't you going to call Royce?"

"Let me worry about Royce. You're going to go on doing what you do best. Lying. Only now you're going to lie to Block. You do exactly what you're told and you'll stay alive. If you do a good job I'll put in a word for you with my superior. Maybe you can make a deal, turn state's evidence."

After resting a hip on the desk, Roman leaned closer. "If you try to check out, I'll hunt you down. I'll find you wherever you hide, and when I'm finished you'll wish I'd killed you."

Bob looked into Roman's eyes. He believed him. "What do you want me to do?"

"Tell me about the next shipment."

Charity was sick of it. It was bad enough that she'd given her word to Roman and had to stay in bed all day. She couldn't even use the phone to call the office and see what was going on in the world.

She'd tried to be good-humored about it, poking through the books and magazines that Lori had brought up to her. She'd even admitted—to herself—that there had been times, when things had gotten crazy at the inn, that she'd imagined having the luxury of an idle day in bed.

Now she had it, and she hated it.

The pill Roman had insisted she swallow had made her groggy. She drifted off periodically, only to wake later, annoyed that she didn't have enough control to stay awake and be bored. Because reading made her headache worse, she tried to work up some interest in the small portable television perched on the shelf across the room.

When she'd found *The Maltese Falcon* flickering in black and white she'd felt both pleasure and relief. If she had to be trapped in bed, it might as well be with Bogart. Even as Sam Spade succumbed to the Fat Man's drug, Charity's own medication sent her under. She awoke in a very poor temper to a rerun of a sitcom.

He'd made her promise to stay in bed, she thought, jabbing an elbow at her pillow. And he didn't even have the decency to spend five minutes keeping her company. Apparently he was too busy to fit a sickroom call into his schedule. That was fine for him, she decided, running around doing something useful while she was moldering between the sheets. It wasn't in her nature to do nothing, and if she had to do it for five minutes longer she was going to scream.

Charity smiled a bit as she considered that. Just what would he do if she let out one long bloodcurdling scream? It might be interesting to find out. Certainly more interesting, she decided, than watching a blond airhead jiggle around a set to the beat of a laugh track. Nodding, she sucked in her breath.

"What are you doing?"

She let it out again in a long huff as Roman pushed open the door. Pleasure came first, but she quickly buried it in resentment. "You're always asking me that."

"Am I?" He was carrying another tray. Charity distinctly caught the scent of Mae's prize chicken soup and her biscuits. "Well, what were you doing?"

"Dying of boredom. I think I'd rather be shot." After eyeing the tray, she decided to be marginally friendly. But not because she was glad to see him, she thought. It was dusk, and she hadn't eaten for hours. "Is that for me?"

"Possibly." He set the tray over her lap, then stayed close and took a long, hard look at her. There was no way for him to describe the fury he felt when he saw the bruises and the bandages. Just as there was no way for him to describe the sense of pleasure and relief he experienced when he saw the annoyance in her eyes and the color in her cheeks.

"I think you're wrong, Charity. You're going to live."

"No thanks to you." She dived into the soup. "First you trick a promise out of me, then you leave me to rot for the next twelve hours. You might have come up for a minute to see if I had lapsed into a coma."

He *had* come up, about the time Sam Spade had been unwrapping the mysterious bird, but she'd been sleeping. Nonetheless, he'd stayed for nearly half an hour, just watching her.

"I've been a little busy," he told her, and broke off half of her biscuit for himself.

"I'll bet." Feeling far from generous, she snatched it back. "Well, since you're here, you might tell me how things are going downstairs."

"They're under control," he murmured, thinking of Bob and the phone calls that had already been made.

"It's only Bonnie's second day. She hasn't—"

"She's doing fine," he said, interrupting her. "Mae's watching her like a hawk. Where'd all these come from?" He gestured toward half a dozen vases of fresh flowers.

"Oh, Lori brought up the daisies with the magazines. Then the ladies came up. They really shouldn't have climbed all those stairs. They brought the wood violets." She rattled off more names of people who had brought or sent flowers.

He should have brought her some, Roman thought, rising and thrusting his hands into his pockets. It had never crossed his mind. Things like that didn't, he admitted. Not the small, romantic things a woman like Charity was entitled to.

"Roman?"

"What?"

"Did you come all the way up here to scowl at my peonies?"

"No." He hadn't even known the name for them. He turned away from the fat pink blossoms. "Do you want any more to eat?"

"No." She tapped the spoon against the side of her empty bowl. "I don't want any more to eat, I don't want any more magazines, and I don't want anyone else to come in here, pat my hand and tell me to get plenty of rest. So if that's what you've got in mind you can leave."

"You're a charming patient, Charity." Checking his own temper, he removed the tray.

"No, I'm a miserable patient." Furiously, she tossed aside her self-control, and just as furiously tossed a paperback at his head. Fortunately for them both, her aim was off. "And

I'm tired of being stuck in here as though I had some communicable disease. I have a bump on the head, damn it, not a brain tumor.''

"I don't think a brain tumor's contagious."

"Don't be clever with me." Glaring at him, she folded her arms and dropped them over her chest. "I'm sick of being here, and sicker yet of being told what to do."

"You don't take that well, do you? No matter how good it is for you?"

When she was being unreasonable there was nothing she wanted to hear less than the truth. "I have an inn to run, and I can't do it from bed."

"Not tonight you don't."

"It's my inn, just like it's my body and my head." She tossed the covers aside. Even as she started to scramble out of bed her promise weighed on her like a chain. Swinging her legs up again, she fell back against the pillows.

Thumbs hooked in his pockets, he measured her. "Why don't you get up?"

"Because I promised. Now get out, damn it. Just get out and leave me alone."

"Fine. I'll tell Mae and the rest that you're feeling more like yourself. They've been worried about you."

She threw another book—harder—but had only the small satisfaction of hearing it slap against the closing door.

The hell with him, she thought as she dropped her chin on her knees. The hell with everything.

The hell with her. He hadn't gone up there to pick a fight, and he didn't have to tolerate a bad-tempered woman throwing things at him, especially when he couldn't throw them back. Roman got halfway down the stairs, turned around and stalked back up again.

Charity was moping when he pushed open the door. She knew it, she hated it, and she wished everyone would leave her in peace to get on with it.

"What now?"

"Get up."

Charity straightened her spine against the headboard. "Why?"

"Get up," Roman repeated. "Get dressed. There must be a floor to mop or a trash can to empty around here."

"I said I wouldn't get up—" she set her chin "—and I won't."

"You can get out of bed on your own, or I can drag you out."

Temper had her eyes darkening and her chin thrusting out even farther. "You wouldn't dare." She regretted the words even as she spoke them. She'd already decided he was a man who would dare anything.

She was right. Roman crossed to the bed and grabbed her arm. Charity gripped one of the posts. Despite her hold, he managed to pull her up on her knees before she dug in. Before the tug-of-war could get much further she began to giggle.

"This is stupid." She felt her grip slipping and hooked her arm around the bedpost. "Really stupid. Roman, stop. I'm going to end up falling on my face and putting another hole in my head."

"You wanted to get up. So get up."

"No, I wanted to feel sorry for myself. And I was doing a pretty good job of it, too. Roman, you're about to dislocate my shoulder."

"You're the most stubborn, hardheaded, unreasonable woman I've ever met," he said. But he released her.

"I have to go along with the first two, but I'm not usually unreasonable." Offering him a smile, she folded her legs Indian-style. The storm was over. At least hers was, she thought. She recognized the anger that was still darkening his eyes. She let out a long sigh. "I guess you could say I was having a really terrific pity party for myself when you came in. I'm sorry I took it out on you."

"I don't need an apology."

"Yes, you do." She would have offered him a hand, but he didn't look ready to sign any peace treaties. "I'm not used to being cut off from what's going on. I'm hardly ever sick, so I haven't had much practice in taking it like a good little soldier.'' She idly pleated the sheet between her fingers as she slanted a look at him. "I really am sorry, Roman. Are you going to stay mad at me?''

"That might be the best solution." Anger had nothing to do with what he was feeling at the moment. She looked so appealing with that half smile on her face, her hair tousled, the nightshirt buttoned to her chin and skimming her thighs.

"Want to slug me?''

"Maybe." It was hopeless. He smiled and sat down beside her. He balled his hand into a fist and skimmed it lightly over her chin. "When you're back on your feet again I'll take another shot.''

"It was nice of you to bring me dinner. I didn't even thank you.''

"No, you didn't.''

She leaned forward to kiss his cheek. "Thanks.''

"You're welcome.''

After blowing the hair out of her eyes, she decided to start over. "Did we have a good crowd tonight?''

"I bused thirty tables.''

"I'm going to have to give you a raise. I guess Mae made her chocolate mousse torte.''

"Yeah." Roman found his lips twitching again.

"I don't suppose there was any left over.''

"Not a crumb. It was great.''

"You had some?''

"Meals are part of my pay.''

Feeling deprived, Charity leaned back against the pillows. "Right.''

"Are you going to sulk again?''

"Just for a minute. I wanted to ask you if the sheriff had any news about the car.''

"Not much. He found it about ten miles from here, abandoned." He reached over to smooth away a line between her brows. "Don't worry about it.''

"I'm not. Not really. I'm just glad the driver didn't hurt anyone else. Lori said you'd cut your arm.''

"A little." Their hands were linked. He didn't know whether he had taken hers or she had taken his.

"Were you taking a walk?"

"I was waiting for you."

"Oh." She smiled again.

"You'd better get some rest." He was feeling awkward again, awkward and clumsy. No other woman had ever drawn either reaction from him.

Reluctantly she released his hand. "Are we friends again?"

"I guess you could say that. Good night, Charity."

"Good night."

He crossed to the door and opened it. But he couldn't step across the threshold. He stood there, struggling with himself. Though it was only a matter of seconds, it seemed like hours to both of them.

"I can't." He turned back, shutting the door quietly behind him.

"Can't what?"

"I can't leave."

Her smile bloomed, in her eyes, on her lips. She opened her arms to him, as he had known she would. Walking back to her was nearly as difficult as walking away. He took her hands and held them hard in his.

"I'm no good for you, Charity."

"I think you're very good for me." She brought their joined hands to her cheek. "That means one of us is wrong."

"If I could, I'd walk out the door and keep going."

She felt the sting and accepted it. She'd never expected loving Roman to be painless. "Why?"

"For reasons I can't begin to explain to you." He stared down at their linked hands. "But I can't walk away. Sooner or later you're going to wish I had."

"No." She drew him down onto the bed. "Whatever happens, I'll always be glad you stayed." This time she smoothed the lines from his brow. "I told you before that this wouldn't happen unless it was right. I meant that." Lifting her hands, she linked them behind his neck. "I love you, Roman. Tonight is something I want, something I've chosen."

Kissing her was like sinking into a dream. Soft, drugging, and too impossibly beautiful to be real. He wanted to take care, such complete, such tender care, not to hurt her now, knowing that he would have no choice but to hurt her eventually.

But tonight, for a few precious hours, there would be no future. With her he could be what he had never tried to be before. Gentle, loving, kind. With her he could believe it was possible for love to be enough.

He loved her. Though he'd never known he was capable of that strong and fragile emotion, he felt it with her. It streamed through him, painless and sweet, healing wounds he'd forgotten he had, soothing aches he'd lived with forever. How could he have known when he'd walked into her life that she would be his salvation? In the short time he had left he would show her. And in showing her he would give himself something he had never expected to have.

He made her feel beautiful. And delicate, Charity thought as his mouth whispered over hers. It was as though he knew that this first time together was to be savored and remembered. She heard her own sigh, then his, as her hands slid up his back. Whatever she had wished they could have together was nothing compared to this.

He laid her back gently, barely touching her, as the kiss lengthened. Even loving him as she did, she hadn't known he'd possessed such tenderness. Nor could she know that he had just discovered it in himself.

The lamplight glowed amber. He hadn't thought to light the candles. But he could see her in the brilliance of it, her eyes dark and on his, her lips curved as he brought his to meet them. He hadn't thought to set the music. But her nightshirt whispered as she brought her arms around him. It was a sound he would remember always. Air drifted in through the open window, stirring the scent of the flowers others had brought to her. But it was the fragrance of her skin that filled his head. It was the taste of it that he yearned for.

Lightly, almost afraid he might bruise her with a touch, he cupped her breasts in his hands. Her breath caught, then released on a moan against the side of his neck. He knew that nothing had ever excited him more.

Then her hands were on his shirt, her fingers undoing his buttons as her eyes remained on his. They were as dark, as deep, as vibrant, as the water that surrounded her home. He could read everything she felt in them.

"I want to touch you," she said as she drew the shirt from his shoulders. Her heart began to sprint as she looked at him, the taut muscles, the taut skin.

There was a strength in him that excited, perhaps because she understood that he could be ruthless. There was a toughness to his body, a toughness that made her realize he was a man who had fought, a man who would fight. But his hands were gentle on her now, almost hesitant. Her excitement leaped higher, and there was no fear in it.

"It seems I've wanted to touch you like this all my life." She ran her fingertips lightly over the bandage on his arm. "Does it hurt?"

"No." Every muscle in his body tensed when she trailed her hands from his waist to his chest. It was impossible for him to understand how anyone could bring him peace and torment at the same time. "Charity…"

"Just kiss me again, Roman," she murmured.

He was helpless to refuse. He wondered what she would ask him for if she knew that he was powerless to deny her anything at this moment. Fighting back a flood of desperation, he kept his hands easy, sliding and stroking them over her until he felt the tremors begin.

He knew he could give her pleasure. The need to do so pulsed heavily inside him. He could ignite her passions. The drive to fan them roared through him like a brushfire. As he touched her he knew he could make her weak or strong, wild or limp. But it wasn't power that filled him at the knowledge. It was awe.

She would give him whatever he asked, without questions, without restrictions. This strong, beautiful, exciting woman was his. This wasn't a dream that would awaken him to frustration in the middle of the night. This wasn't a wish that he'd have to pretend he'd never made. It was real. She was real, and she was waiting for him. '

He could have torn the nightshirt from her with one pull of his hand. Instead he released button after tiny button, hearing her breath quicken, following the narrow path with soft, lingering kisses. Her fingers dug into his back, then went limp as her system churned. She could only groan as his tongue moistened her flesh, teasing and heating it. The night air whispered over her as he undressed her. Then he was lifting her, cradling her in his arms.

She was twined around him, her heart thudding frantically against his lips. He needed a moment to drag himself back, to find the control he wanted so that he could take her up, take her over. Murmuring to her, he used what skills he had to drive her past the edge of reason.

Her body was rigid against his. He watched her dazed eyes fly open. She gasped his name, and then he covered her mouth with his to capture her long, low moan as her body went limp.

She seemed to slide like water through his hands when he laid her down again. To his delight, her arousal burst free again at his lightest touch.

It was impossible. It was impossible to feel so much and still need more. Blindly she reached for him. Fresh pleasure poured into her until her arms felt too heavy to move. She was a prisoner, a gloriously willing prisoner, of the frantic sensations he sent tearing through her. She wanted to lock herself around him, to keep him there, always there. He was taking her on a long, slow journey to places she had never seen, places she never wanted to leave.

When he slid inside her she heard his low, breathless moan. So he was as much a captive as she.

With his face pressed against her neck, he fought the need to sprint toward release. He was trapped between heaven and hell, and he gloried in it. In her. In them. He heard her sob out his name, felt the strength pour into her. She was with him as no one had ever been.

*   *   *

Charity wrapped her arms around Roman to keep him from shifting away. "Don't move."

"I'm hurting you."

"No." She let out a long, long sigh. "No, you're not."

"I'm too heavy," he insisted, and compromised by gathering her close and rolling so that their positions were reversed.

"Okay." Satisfied, she rested her head on his shoulder. "You are," she said, "the most incredible lover."

He didn't even try to prevent the smile. "Thanks." He stroked a possessive hand down to her hip. "Have you had many?"

It was her turn to smile. The little trace of jealousy in his voice was a tremendous addition to an already-glorious night. "Define *many*."

Ignoring the quick tug of annoyance he felt, he played the game. "More than three. Three is a few. Anything more than three is many."

"Ah. Well, in that case." She almost wished she could lie and invent a horde. "I guess I've had less than a few. That doesn't mean I don't know an incredible one when I find him."

He lifted her head to stare at her. "I've done nothing in my life to deserve you."

"Don't be stupid." She inched up to kiss him briefly. "And don't change the subject."

"What subject?"

"You're clever, DeWinter, but not that clever." She lifted a brow and studied him in the lamplight. "It's my turn to ask you if you've had many lovers."

He didn't smile this time. "Too many. But only one who's meant anything."

The amusement faded from her eyes before she closed them. "You'll make me cry," she murmured, lowering her head to his chest again.

Not yet, he thought, stroking her hair. Soon enough, but

not yet. "Why haven't you ever gotten married?" he wondered aloud. "Had babies?"

"What a strange question. I haven't loved anyone enough before." She winced at her own words, then made herself smile as she lifted her head. "That wasn't a hint."

But it was exactly what he'd wanted to hear. He knew he was crazy to let himself think that way, even for a few hours, but he wanted to imagine her loving him enough to forgive, to accept and to promise.

"How about the traveling you said you wanted to do? Shouldn't that come first?"

She shrugged and settled against him again. "Maybe I haven't traveled because I know deep down I'd hate to go all those places alone. What good is Venice if you don't have someone to ride in a gondola with? Or Paris if there's no one to hold hands with?"

"You could go with me."

Already half asleep, she laughed. She imagined Roman had little more than the price of a ferry ticket to his name. "Okay. Let me know when to pack."

"Would you?" He lifted her chin to look into her drowsy eyes.

"Of course." She kissed him, snuggled her head against his shoulder and went to sleep.

Roman switched off the lamp beside the bed. For a long time he held her and stared into the dark.

Chapter 8

Charity opened her eyes slowly, wondering why she couldn't move. Groggy, she stared into Roman's face. It was only inches from hers. He had pulled her close in his sleep, effectively pinning her arms and legs with his. Though his grip on her was somewhat guardlike, she found it unbearably sweet.

Ignoring the discomfort, she lay still and took advantage of the moment by looking her fill.

She'd always thought that people looked softer, more vulnerable, in sleep. Not Roman. He had the body of a fighter and the eyes of a man accustomed to facing trouble head-on. His eyes were closed now, and his body was relaxed. Almost.

Still, studying him, she decided that, asleep or awake, he looked tough as nails. Had he always been? she wondered. Had he had to be? It was true that smiling lent a certain charm to his face. It lightened the wariness in his eyes. In Charity's opinion, Roman smiled much too seldom.

She would fix that. Her own lips curved as she watched him. In time she would, gently, teach him to relax, to enjoy, to trust. She would make him happy. It wasn't possible to love as she had loved and not have it returned. And it wasn't possible to share what they had shared during the night without his heart being as lost as hers.

Sooner or later—sooner, if she had her way—he would

come to accept how good they were together. And how much better they would become in all the years to follow. Then there would be time for promises and families and futures.

I'm not letting you go, she told him silently. You don't realize it yet, but I've got a hold on you, and it's going to be mighty hard to break it.

He had such a capacity for giving, she thought. Not just physically, though she wasn't ashamed to admit that his skill there had dazed and delighted her. He was a man full of emotions, too many of them strapped down. What had happened to him, she wondered, that had made him so wary of love, and so afraid to give it?

She loved him too much to demand an answer. It was a question he had to answer on his own...a question she knew he would answer as soon as he trusted her enough. When he did, all she had to do was show him that none of it mattered. All that counted, from this moment on, was what they felt for each other.

Inching over, she brushed a light kiss on his mouth. His eyes opened instantly. It took only a heartbeat longer for them to clear. Fascinated, Charity watched their expression change from one of suspicion to one of desire.

"You're a light sleeper," she began. "I just—"

Before she could complete the thought, his mouth, hungry and insistent, was on hers. She managed a quiet moan as she melted into his kiss.

It was the only way he knew to tell her what it meant to him to wake and find her close and warm and willing. Too many mornings he had woken alone in strange beds in empty rooms.

That was what he expected. For years he had deliberately separated himself from anyone who had tried to get close. The job. He'd told himself it was because of the job. But that was a lie, one of many. He'd chosen to remain alone because he hadn't wanted to risk losing again. Grieving again. Now, overnight, everything had changed.

He would remember it all, the pale fingers of light creeping into the room, the high echoing sound of the first birds calling to the rising sun, the scent of her skin as it heated against his. And her mouth…he would remember the taste of her mouth as it opened eagerly under his.

There were such deep, dark needs in him. She felt them, understood them, and met them unquestioningly. As dawn swept the night aside, he stirred her own until their needs mirrored each other's.

Slowly, easily, while his lips cruised over her face, he slipped inside her. With a sigh and a murmur, she welcomed him.

She felt as strong as an ox and as content as a cat with cream on its whiskers. With her eyes closed, Charity stretched her arms to the ceiling.

"And to think I used to consider jogging the best way to start the day." Laughing, she curled over against him again. "I have to thank you for showing me how very wrong I was."

"My pleasure." He could still feel his own heart thudding like a jackhammer against his ribs. "Give me a minute and I'll show you the best reason for staying in bed in the morning."

Lord, it was tempting. Before her blood could begin to heat she shook her head. She took a quick nip at his chin before she sat up. "Maybe if you've got some time when I get back."

He took her wrist but kept his fingers light. "From where?"

"From taking Ludwig for his run."

"No."

The hand that had lifted to push back her hair paused. Deliberately she continued to lift it to finger-comb the hair away from her face. "No, what?"

He recognized that tone. She was the boss again, despite the fact that her face was still glowing from lovemaking and she was naked to where the sheets pooled at her waist. This was the woman who didn't take orders. Roman decided he would have to show her again that she was wrong.

"No, you're not taking the dog out for a run."

Because she wanted to be reasonable, she added a smile.

"Of course I am. I kept my promise and stayed in bed all day yesterday. And all night, for that matter. Now I'm going to get back to work."

Around the inn, that was fine. In fact, the sooner everything got back to normal the better it would be. But there was no way he was having her walking down a deserted road by herself. "You're in no shape to go for a mile hike."

"Three miles, and yes, I am."

"Three?" Lifting a brow, he stroked a hand over her thigh. "No wonder you've got such great muscle tone."

"That's not the point." She shifted away before his touch could weaken her.

"You have the most incredible body."

She shoved at his seeking hands. "Roman... I do?"

His lips curved. This was the way he liked them best. "Absolutely. Let me show you."

"No, I..." She caught his hands as they stroked her thighs. "We'll probably kill each other if we try this again."

"I'll risk it."

"Roman, I mean it." Her head fell back and she gasped when he scraped his teeth over her skin. It was impossible, she thought, impossible, for this deep, dark craving to take over again. "Roman—"

"Fabulous legs," he murmured, skimming his tongue behind her knee. "I didn't pay nearly enough attention to them last night."

"Yes, you—" She braced a hand against the mattress as she swayed. "You're trying to distract me."

"Yeah."

"You can't." She closed her eyes. He could, and he was. "Ludwig needs the run," she managed. "He enjoys it."

"Fine." He sat up and circled her waist with his hands. "I'll take him."

"You?" Wanting to catch her breath, she turned her head to avoid his kiss, then shuddered as his lips trailed down her throat. "It's not necessary. I'm perfectly... Roman." She said his name weakly as his thumbs circled her breasts.

"Yes, a truly incredible body," he murmured. "Long and lean and incredibly responsive. I can't seem to touch you and not want you."

She came up on her knees as he dragged another gasp out of her. "You're trying to seduce me."

"Nothing gets by you, does it?"

She was losing, weakening shamelessly. She knew it would infuriate her later, but for now all she could do was cling to him and let him have his way. "Is this your answer for everything?"

"No." He lifted her hips and brought her to him. "But it'll do."

Unable to resist, she wrapped her limbs around him and let passion take them both. When it was spent, she slid bonelessly down in the bed. She didn't argue when he drew the sheets over her shoulders.

"Stay here," he told her, kissing her hair. "I'll be back."

"His leash is on a hook under the steps," Charity murmured. "He gets two scoops of dog food when he gets back. And fresh water."

"I think I can handle a dog, Charity."

She yawned and tugged the blankets higher. "He likes to chase the Fitzsimmonses' cat. But don't worry, he can't catch her."

"That makes me breathe easier." He laced up his shoes. "Anything else I should know?"

"Mmm." She snuggled into the pillow. "I love you."

As always, it knocked him backward to hear her say it, to know she meant it. In silence, he stepped outside.

She wasn't tired, Charity thought as she stretched under the sheets. But Roman was right. Sleep wasn't the best reason for staying in bed in the morning. Despite her bumps and bruises, she knew she'd never felt better in her life.

Still, she indulged herself, lingering in bed, half dreaming, until guilt finally prodded her out.

Moving automatically, she turned on the stereo, then tidied the bed. In the parlor she glanced over the notes she'd left for herself, made a few more. Then she headed for the shower.

She was humming along to Tchaikovsky's violin concerto when the curtain swished open.

"Roman!" She pressed both hands to her heart and leaned back against the tile. "You might as well shoot me as scare me to death. Didn't you ever hear of the Bates Motel?"

"I left my butcher knife in my other pants." She had her hair piled on top of her head and a cake of some feminine scented soap in her hand. Her skin was gleaming wet and already soapy. He pulled off his shirt and tossed it aside. "Did you ever consider teaching that dog to heel?"

"No." She grinned as she watched Roman unfasten his jeans. "I guess you could use a shower." Saying nothing, he tossed his jeans on top of his shirt. Charity took a moment to make a long, thorough survey. "Well, apparently that run didn't...tire you out." She was laughing when he stepped in with her.

It was nearly an hour later when Charity made it down to the lobby. "I could eat one of everything." She pressed a hand to her stomach. "Good morning, Bob." She paused at the front desk to smile at him.

"Charity." Bob felt the sweat spring onto his palms when he spotted Roman behind her. "How are you feeling? It's awfully soon for you to be up and around."

"I'm fine." Idly she glanced at the papers on the desk. "Sorry I left you in the lurch yesterday."

"Don't be silly." Fear ground in his stomach as he eyed the wound on her temple. "We were worried about you."

"I appreciate that, but there's no need to worry anymore." She slanted a smile at Roman. "I've never felt better in my life."

Bob caught the look, and his stomach sank. If the cop was in love with her, he thought, things were going to be even stickier. "Glad to hear it. But—"

She stopped his protest by raising a hand. "Is there anything urgent?"

"No." He glanced at Roman again. "No, nothing."

"Good." After setting the papers aside again, Charity studied his face. "What's wrong, Bob?"

"Nothing. What could be wrong?"

"You look a little pale. You're not coming down with anything, are you?"

"No, everything's fine. Just fine. We got some new reservations. July's almost booked solid."

"Great. I'll look things over after breakfast. Get yourself some coffee." She patted his hand and walked into the dining room.

Three tables were already occupied, the patrons enjoying Mae's coffee cake before their meal was served. Bonnie was busy taking orders. The breakfast menu was neatly listed on the board, and music was playing in the background, soft and soothing. The flowers were fresh, and the coffee was hot.

"Something wrong?" Roman asked her.

"No." Charity smoothed down the collar of her shirt. "What could be wrong? It looks like everything's just dandy." Feeling useless, she walked into the kitchen.

There was no bickering to referee. Mae and Dolores were working side by side, and Lori loaded up a tray with her first order.

"We need more butter for the French toast," Mae called out.

"Coming right up." Cheerful as a bird, Dolores began to scoop up neat balls of butter. As she offered the newly filled bowl to Lori, she spotted Charity standing inside the door. "Well, good morning." Her thin face creased with a smile. "Didn't expect to see you up."

"I'm fine."

"Sit down, girl." Hardly glancing around, Mae continued to sprinkle shredded cheese into an omelet. "Dolores will get you some tea."

Charity smiled with clenched teeth. "I don't want any tea."

"Want and need's two different things."

"Glad to see you're feeling better," Lori said as she rushed out with her tray.

Bonnie came in, pad in hand. "Oh, hi, Charity, we thought you'd rest another day. Feeling better?"

"I'm fine," Charity said tightly. "Just fine."

"Great. Two omelets with bacon, Mae. And an order of French toast with sausage. Two herb teas, an English muffin—crisp. And we're running low on coffee." After punching her order sheet on a hook by the stove, she took the fresh pot Dolores handed her and hurried out.

Charity walked over to get an apron, only to have Mae smack her hand away. "I told you to sit."

"And I told you I'm fine. That's *f-i-n-e*. I'm going to help take orders."

"The only orders you're taking today are from me. Now sit." She ran a hand up and down Charity's arm. Nobody recognized or knew how to deal with that stubborn look better than Mae. "Be a good girl, now. I won't worry so much if I know you've had a good breakfast. You don't want me to worry, do you?"

"No, of course not, but—"

"That's right. Now take a seat. I'll fix you some French toast. It's your favorite."

She sat down. Dolores set a cup of tea in front of her and patted her head. "You sure did give us all a fright yesterday. Have a seat, Roman. I'll get your coffee."

"Thanks. You're sulking," he murmured to Charity.

"I am not."

"Doc's coming by this morning to take another look at you."

"Oh, for heaven's sake, Mae—"

"You're not doing nothing till he gives the okay." With a nod, she began preparing Bonnie's order. "Fat lot of good you'll do if you're not a hundred percent. Things were hard enough yesterday."

Charity stopped staring into her tea and looked up. "Were they?"

"Everybody asking questions nobody had the answer to. Whole stacks of linens lost."

"Lost? But—"

"Found them." Mae made room at the stove for Dolores. "But it sure was confusing for a while. Then the dinner shift... Could have used an extra pair of hands for sure." Mae winked at Roman over Charity's head. "We'll all be mighty glad when the doc gives you his okay. Let that bacon crisp, Dolores."

"It is crisp."

"Not enough."

"Want me to burn it?"

Charity smiled and sipped her tea. It was good to be back.

It was midafternoon before she saw Roman again. She had a pencil behind her ear, a pad in one pocket and a dustcloth in another, and she was dashing down the hallway toward her rooms.

"In a hurry?"

"Oh." She stopped long enough to smile at him. "Yes. I have some papers up in my room that should be in the office."

"What's this?" He tugged at the dustcloth.

"One of the housekeepers came down with a virus. I sent her home." She looked at her watch and frowned. She thought she could spare about two minutes for conversation. "I really hope that's not what's wrong with Bob."

"What's wrong with Bob?"

"I don't know. He just doesn't look well." She tossed her hair back, causing the slender gold spirals in her ears to dance. "Anyway, we're short a housekeeper, and we've got guests checking into units 3 and 5 today. The Garsons checked out of 5 this morning. They won't win any awards for neatness."

"The doctor said you were supposed to rest an hour this afternoon."

"Yes, but— How did you know?"

"I asked him." Roman pulled the dustcloth out of her pocket. "I'll clean 5."

"Don't be ridiculous. It's not your job."

"My job's to fix things. I'll fix 5." He took her chin in his hand before she could protest. "When I'm finished I'm going to go upstairs. If you aren't in bed I'm coming after you."

"Sounds like a threat."

He bent down and kissed her, hard. "It is."

"I'm terrified," she said, and dashed up the stairs.

* * *

It wasn't that she meant to ignore the doctor's orders. Not really. It was only that a nap came far down on her list of things to be done. Every phone call she made had to include a five-minute explanation of her injuries.

No, she was really quite well. Yes, it was terrible that someone had stolen poor Mrs. Norton's car and driven it so recklessly. Yes, she was sure the sheriff would get to the bottom of it. No, she had not broken her legs...her arm...her shoulder.... Yes, she intended to take good care of herself, thank you very much.

The goodwill and concern would have warmed her if she hadn't been so far behind in her work. To make it worse, Bob was distracted and disorganized. Worried that he was ill or dealing with a personal problem, Charity took on the brunt of his work.

Twice she'd fully intended to take a break and go up to her rooms, and twice she'd been delayed by guests checking in. Taking it on faith that Roman had spruced up unit 5, she showed a young pair of newlyweds inside.

"You have a lovely view of the garden from here," Charity said as a cover while she made sure there were fresh towels. Roman had hung them on the rack, exactly where they belonged. The bed, with its heart-shaped white wicker headboard, was made up with a military precision she couldn't have faulted. It cost her, but she resisted the temptation to turn up the coverlet and check sheets.

"We serve complimentary wine in the gathering room every evening at five. We recommend that you make a reservation for dinner if you plan to join us, particularly since it's Saturday night. Breakfast is served between seven-thirty and ten. If you'd like to—" She broke off when Roman stepped into the room. "I'll be with you in a minute," she told him, and started to turn back to the newlyweds.

"Excuse me." Roman gave them both a friendly nod before he scooped Charity up in his arms. "Miss Ford is needed elsewhere. Enjoy your stay."

As the first shock wore off she began to struggle. "Are you out of your mind? Put me down."

"I intend to—when I get you to bed."

"You can't just..." The words trailed off into a groan as he carried her through the gathering room.

Two men sitting on the sofa stopped telling fish stories. A family coming in from a hike gawked from the doorway. Miss Millie and Miss Lucy halted their daily game of Scrabble by the window.

"Isn't that the most romantic thing?" Miss Millie said when they disappeared into the west wing.

"You have totally embarrassed me."

Roman shifted her weight in his arms and carried her upstairs. "You're lucky that's all I did."

"You had no right interrupting me when I was welcoming guests. Then, to make matters worse, you decide to play Rhett Butler."

"As I recall, he had something entirely different in mind when he carried another stubborn woman up to bed." He dropped her, none too gently, on the mattress. "You're going to rest."

"I'm tempted to tell you to go to hell."

He leaned down to cage her head between his hands. "Be my guest."

She'd be damned if she'd smile. "My manners are too ingrained to permit it."

"Aren't I the lucky one?" He leaned a little closer. There was amusement in his eyes now, enough of it so she had to bite her lip to keep from laughing. "I don't want you to get out of this bed for sixty minutes."

"Or?"

"Or...I'll sic Mae on you."

"A low blow, DeWinter."

He brushed a kiss just below the fresh bandage on her temple. "Tune out for an hour, baby. It won't kill you."

She reached up to toy with the top button of his shirt. "I'd like it better if you got in with me."

"I said tuned out, not turned on." When the phone in the parlor rang, he held her down with one hand. "Not a chance. Stay here and I'll get it."

She rolled her eyes behind his back as he walked into the adjoining room.

"Yes? She's resting. Tell him she'll get back to him in an hour. Hold her calls until four. That's right." He glanced down idly at a catalog she'd left open on her desk. She had circled a carved gold bracelet with a square-cut purple stone. "You handle whatever needs to be handled for the next hour. That's right."

"What was it?" Charity called from the next room.

"I'll tell you in an hour."

"Damn it, Roman."

He stopped in the doorway. "You want the message, I'll give it to you in an hour."

"But if it's important—"

"It's not."

She sent him a smoldering look. "How do you know?"

"I know it's not more important than you. Nothing is." He closed the door on her astonished expression.

He needed to keep Bob on a tight leash, he thought as he headed downstairs. As long as he was more afraid of him than of Block, things would be fine. He only had to keep the pressure on for a few more days. Block and Vision Tours would be checking in on Tuesday. When they checked out on Thursday morning he would lock the cage.

Roman pushed open the door of the office to find Bob staring at the computer screen and gulping coffee. "For somebody who's made his living from scams you're a mess."

Bob gulped more coffee. "I never worked with a cop looking over my shoulder before."

"Just think of me as your new partner," Roman advised him. He took the mug out of his hand and sniffed at it. "And lay off the booze."

"Give me a break."

"I'm giving you more of one than you deserve. Charity's worried that you're coming down with something—something other than a stretch in federal prison. I don't want her worrying."

"Look, you want me to carry on like it's business as usual.

I'm lying to Block, setting him up.'' His hand shook as he passed it over his hair. ''You don't know what he's capable of. *I* don't know what he's capable of.'' He looked at the mug, which Roman had set out of reach. ''I need a little something to help me through the next few days.''

''Let this get you through.'' Roman calmly lit a cigarette. ''You pull this off and I'll go to bat for you. Screw up and I'll see to it that you're in a cage for a long time. Now take a break.''

''What?''

''I said, take a break, go for a walk, get some real coffee.'' Roman tapped the ash from his cigarette into a little mosaic bowl.

''Sure.'' As he rose, Bob rubbed his palms on his thighs. ''Look, DeWinter, I'm playing it straight with you. When this goes down, I expect you to keep Block off me.''

''I'll take care of Block.'' That was a promise he intended to keep. When the door closed behind Bob, he picked up the phone. ''DeWinter,'' he said when the connection was made.

''Make it quick,'' Conby told him. ''I'm entertaining friends.''

''I'll try not to let your martini get warm. I want to know if you've located the driver.''

''DeWinter, an underling is hardly important at this point.''

''It's important to me. Have you found him?''

''A man answering the description your informant gave you was detained in Tacoma this morning. He's being held for questioning by the local police.'' Conby put his hand over the receiver. Roman heard him murmur something that was answered by light laughter.

''We're using our influence to lengthen the procedure,'' Conby continued. ''I'll be flying out there on Monday. By Tuesday afternoon I should be checked into the inn. I'm told I'll have a room overlooking a fish pond. It sounds very quaint.''

''I want your word that Charity will be left out of this.''

''As I explained before, if she's innocent she has nothing to worry about.''

"It's not a matter of *if*." Struggling to hold his temper, Roman crushed out his cigarette. "She is innocent. We've got it on record."

"On the word of a whimpering little bookkeeper."

"She was damn near killed, and she doesn't even know why."

"Then keep a closer eye on her. We have no desire to see Miss Ford harmed, or to involve her any more deeply than necessary. There's a police officer out there who shares the same passionate opinion of Miss Ford as you do. Sheriff Royce managed to trace you to us."

"How?"

"He's a smart cop with connections. He has a cousin or brother-in-law or some such thing with the Bureau. He wasn't at all pleased at being left in the dark."

"I'll bet."

"I imagine he'll be paying you a visit before long. Handle him carefully, DeWinter, but handle him."

Just as Roman heard the phone click in his ear the office door opened. For once, Roman thought, Conby was right on target. He replaced the receiver before settling back in his chair.

"Sheriff."

"I want to know what the hell's going on around here, Agent DeWinter."

"Close the door." Roman pushed back in the chair and considered half a dozen different ways of handling Royce. "I'd appreciate it if you'd drop the 'Agent' for now."

Royce just laid both palms on the surface of the desk. "I want to know what a federal agent is doing undercover in my territory."

"Following orders. Sit down?" He indicated a chair.

"I want to know what case you're working on."

"What did they tell you?"

Royce snorted disgustedly. "It got to the point where even my cousin started giving me the runaround, DeWinter, but I've got to figure that your being here had something to do with Charity being damn near run down yesterday."

"I'm here because I was assigned here." Roman waited a moment, sending Royce a long, direct look. "But my first priority is keeping Charity safe."

Royce hadn't been in law enforcement for nearly twenty years without being able to take the measure of a man. He took Roman's now, and was satisfied. "I got a load of bull from Washington about her being under investigation."

"She was. Now she's not. But she could be in trouble. Are you willing to help?"

"I've known that girl all her life." Royce took off his hat and ran his fingers through his hair. "Why don't you stop asking fool questions and tell me what's going on?"

Roman briefed him, pausing only once or twice to allow Royce to ask questions. "I don't have time to get into any more specifics. I want to know how many of your men you can spare Thursday morning."

"All of them," Royce said immediately.

"I only want your most experienced. I have information that Block will not only be bringing the counterfeit money, but also a man who'll register as Jack Marshall. His real name is Vincent Dupont. A week ago he robbed two banks in Ontario, killed a guard and wounded a civilian. Block will smuggle him out of Canada in the tour group, keep him here for a couple of days, then send him by short routes to South America. For his travel service to men like Dupont he takes a nice stiff fee. Both Dupont and Block are dangerous men. We'll have agents here at the inn, but we also have civilians. There's no way we can clear the place without tipping them off."

"It's a chancy game you're playing."

"I know." He thought of Charity dozing upstairs. "It's the only way I know how to play it."

Chapter 9

Charity drove back to the inn after dropping a trio of guests at the ferry. She was certain it was the most beautiful morning she'd ever seen. After the most wonderful night of her life, she thought. No, two of the most wonderful nights of her life.

Though she'd never considered herself terribly romantic, she'd always imagined what it would be like to really be in love. Her daydreams hadn't come close to what she was feeling now. This was solid and bewildering. It was simple and staggering. He filled her thoughts just as completely as he filled her heart. She couldn't wait to walk back into the inn, just knowing Roman would be there.

It seemed that every hour they spent together brought them closer. Gradually, step by step, she could feel the barriers he had placed around him lowering. She wanted to be there when they finally dropped completely.

He was in love with her. She was sure he was, whether he knew it or not. She could tell by the way he looked at her, by the way he touched her hair when he thought she was sleeping. By the way he held her so tightly all through the night, as if he were afraid she might somehow slip away from him. In time she would show him that she wasn't going any-where—and that he wasn't going anywhere, either.

Something was troubling him. That was another thing she

was sure of. Her eyes clouded as she drove along the water. There were times when she could feel the tension pulsing in him even when he was across the room. He seemed to be watching, waiting. But for what?

Since the accident he'd barely let her out of his sight. It was sweet, she mused. But it had to stop. She might love him, but she wouldn't be pampered. She was certain that if he had known she planned to drive to the ferry that morning he would have found a way to stop her.

She was right again. It had taken Roman some time to calm down after he had learned Charity wasn't in the office or the kitchen or anywhere else in the inn.

"She's driven up to drop some guests at the ferry," Mae told him, then watched in fascination as he let his temper loose.

"My, my," she said when the air was clear again. "You've got it bad, boy."

"Why did you let her go?"

"Let her go?" Mae let out a rich, appreciative laugh. "I haven't *let* that girl do anything since she could walk. She just does it." She stopped stirring custard to study him. "Any reason she shouldn't drive to the ferry?"

"No."

"All right, then. Just cool your britches. She'll be back in half an hour."

He sweated and paced, nearly the whole time she was away. Mae and Dolores exchanged glances across the room. There would be plenty of gossip to pass around once they had the kitchen to themselves.

Mae thought of the way Charity had been smiling that morning. Why, the girl had practically danced into the kitchen. She kept her eye on Roman as he brooded over a cup of coffee and watched the clock. Yes, indeed, she thought, the boy had it bad.

"You got today off, don't you?" Mae asked him.

"What?"

"It's Sunday," she said patiently. "You got the day off?"

"Yeah, I guess."

"Nice day, too. Good weather for a picnic." She began slicing roast beef for sandwiches. "Got any plans?"

"No."

"Charity loves picnics. Yes, sir, she's mighty partial to them. You know, I don't think that girl's had a day away from this place in better than a month."

"Got any dynamite?"

Dolores piped up. "What's that?"

"I figure it would take dynamite to blast Charity out of the inn for a day."

It took her a minute, but Dolores finally got the joke. She chuckled. "Hear that, Mae? He wants dynamite."

"Pair of fools," Mae muttered as she cut generous pieces of chocolate cheesecake. "You don't move that girl with dynamite or threats or orders. Might as well bash your head against a brick wall all day." She tried not to sound pleased about it, and failed. "You want her to do something, you make her think she's doing you a favor. Make her think it's important to you. Dolores, you go on in that back room and get me the big wicker hamper. Boy, if you keep walking back and forth you're going to wear out my floor."

"She should have been back by now."

"She'll be back when she's back. You know how to run a boat?"

"Yes, why?"

"Charity always loved to picnic on the water. She hasn't been out in a boat in a long time. Too long."

"I know. She told me."

Mae turned around. Her face was set. "Do you want to make my girl happy?"

He tried to shrug it off, but he couldn't. "Yes. Yes, I do."

"Then you take her out on the boat for the day. Don't let her say no."

"All right."

Satisfied, she turned around again. "Go down in the cellar and get a bottle of wine. French. She likes the French stuff."

"She's lucky to have you."

Her wide face colored a bit, but she kept her voice brisk.

"Around here, we got each other. You're all right," she added. "I wasn't sure of it when you first came around, but you're all right."

He was ready for her when she came back. Even as she stepped out of the van he was walking across the gravel lot, the wicker hamper in his hand.

"Hi."

"Hi." She greeted him with a smile and a quick kiss. Despite the two teenagers shooting hoops on the nearby court, Roman wrapped an arm around her and brought her hard against him for a longer, more satisfying embrace. "Well..." She had to take a deep breath and steady herself against the van. "Hello again." She noted then that he had pulled a loose black sweater over his jeans and was carrying a hamper. "What's this?"

"It's a basket," he told her. "Mae put a few things in it for me. It's my day off."

"Oh." She tossed her braid behind her back. "That's right. Where are you off to?"

"Out on the water, if I can use the boat."

"Sure." She glanced up at the sky, a bit wistfully. "It's a great day for it. Light wind, hardly a cloud."

"Then let's go."

"Let's?" He was already pulling her toward the pier. "Oh, Roman, I can't. I have dozens of things to do this afternoon. And I..." She didn't want to admit she wasn't ready to go out on the water again. "I can't."

"I'll have you back before the dinner shift." He laid a hand on her cheek. "I need you with me, Charity. I need to spend some time with you, alone."

"Maybe we could go for a drive. You haven't seen the mountains."

"Please." He set the hamper down to take both of her arms. "Do this for me."

Had he ever said "Please" before? she wondered. She didn't think so. With a sigh, she looked out at the boat rocking gently against the pier. "All right. Maybe for an hour. I'll go in and change."

The red sweater and jeans would keep her warm enough on the water, he decided. She would know that, too. She was stalling. "You look fine." He kept her hand in his as they walked down the pier. "This could use a little maintenance."

"I know. I keep meaning to." She waited until Roman stepped down into the boat. When he held up a hand, she hesitated, then forced herself to join him. "I have a key on my ring."

"Mae already gave me one."

"Oh." Charity sat down in the stern. "I see. A conspiracy."

It took him only two pulls to start the engine. Mae had told him Charity kept the boat for the staff to use. "From what you said to me the other day, I don't think he'd want you to grieve forever."

"No." As her eyes filled, she looked back toward the inn. "No, he wouldn't. But I loved him so much." She took a deep breath. "I'll cast off."

Before he sent the boat forward, Roman took her hand and drew her down beside him. After a moment she rested her head on his shoulder.

"Have you done much boating?"

"From time to time. When I was a kid we used to rent a boat a couple times each summer and take it on the river."

"Who's we?" She watched the shutters come down over his face. "What river?" she asked instead.

"The Mississippi." He smiled and slipped an arm over her shoulders. "I come from St. Louis, remember?"

"The Mississippi." Her mind was immediately filled with visions of steamboats and boys on wooden rafts. "I'd love to see it. You know what would be great? Taking a cruise all the way down, from St. Louis to New Orleans. I'll have to put that in my file."

"Your file?"

"The file I'm going to make on things I want to do." With

a laugh, she waved to a passing sailboat before leaning over
to kiss Roman's cheek. "Thanks."

"For what?"

"For talking me into this. I've always loved spending an
afternoon out here, watching the other boats, looking at the
houses. I've missed it."

"Have you ever considered that you give too much to the
inn?"

"No. You can't give too much to something you love."
She turned. If she shielded her eyes with her hand she could
just see it in the distance. "If I didn't have such strong feelings for it, I would have sold it, taken a job in some modern
hotel in Seattle or Miami or…or anywhere. Eight hours a day,
sick leave, two weeks paid vacation." Just the idea made her
laugh. "I'd wear a nice neat business suit and sensible shoes,
have my own office and quietly go out of my mind." She
dug into her bag for her sunglasses. "You should understand
that. You have good hands and a sharp mind. Why aren't you
head carpenter for some big construction firm?"

"Maybe when the time came I made the wrong choices."

With her head tilted, she studied him, her eyes narrowed
and thoughtful behind the tinted lenses. "No, I don't think so.
Not for you."

"You don't know enough about me, Charity."

"Of course I do. I've lived with you for a week. That
probably compares with knowing someone on a casual basis
for six months. I know you're very intense and internal. You
have a wicked temper that you seldom lose. You're an excellent carpenter who likes to finish the job he starts. You can
be gallant with little old ladies." She laughed a little and
turned her face into the wind. "You like your coffee black,
you're not afraid of hard work…and you're a wonderful
lover."

"And that's enough for you?"

She lifted her shoulders. "I don't imagine you know too
much more about me. I'm starving," she said abruptly. "Do
you want to eat?"

"Pick a spot."

"Head over that way," she told him. "See that little jut of land? We can anchor the boat there."

The land she'd indicated was hardly more than a jumble of big, smooth rocks that fell into the water. As they neared it he could see a narrow stretch of sand crowded by trees. Cutting back the engine, he maneuvered toward the beach, Charity guiding him in with hand signals. As the current lapped at the sides of the boat, she pulled off her shoes and began to roll up her jeans.

"You'll have to give me a hand." As she said it she plunged into the knee-high water. "God, it's cold!" Then she was laughing and securing the line. "Come on."

The water was icy on his bare calves. Together they pulled the boat up onto a narrow spit of sand.

"I don't suppose you brought a blanket."

He reached into the boat and took out the faded red blanket Mae had given him. "This do?"

"Great. Grab the basket." She splashed through the shallows and onto the shore. After spreading the blanket at the base of the sheltering rocks she rolled down the damp legs of her jeans. "Lori and I used to come here when we were kids. To eat peanut butter sandwiches and talk about boys." Kneeling on the blanket, she looked around.

There were pines at her back, deep and green and thick all the way up the slope. A few feet away the water frothed at the rock, which had been worn smooth by wind and time. A single boat cruised in the distance, its sails full and white.

"It hasn't changed much." Smiling, she reached for the basket. "I guess the best things don't." She threw back the top and spotted a bottle of champagne. "Well." With a brow arched, she pulled it out. "Apparently we're going to have some picnic."

"Mae said you liked the French stuff."

"I do. I've never had champagne on a picnic."

"Then it's time you did." He took the bottle and walked back to dunk it in the water, screwing it down in the wet sand. "We'll let it chill a little more." He came back to her, taking her hand before she could explore deeper in the basket. He knelt. When they were thigh to thigh, he gathered her close and closed his mouth over hers.

Her quiet sound of pleasure came first, followed by a gasp as he took the kiss deeper. Her arms came around him, then slid up until her hands gripped his shoulders. Desire was like a flood, rising fast to drag her under.

He needed…needed to hold her close like this, to taste the heat of passion on his lips, to feel her heart thud against him. He dragged his hands through her hair, impatiently tugging it free of the braids. All the while his mouth ravaged hers, gentleness forgotten.

There was a restlessness in him, and an anger that she couldn't understand. Responding to both, she pressed against him, unhesitatingly offering whatever he needed. Perhaps it would be enough. Slowly his mouth gentled. Then he was only holding her.

"That's a very nice way to start a picnic," Charity managed when she found her voice again.

"I can't seem to get enough of you."

"That's okay. I don't mind."

He drew away to frame her face in his hands. The crystal drops at her ears swung and shot out light. But her eyes were calm and deep and full of understanding. It would be better, he thought, and certainly safer, if he simply let her pull out the sandwiches. They could talk about the weather, the water, the people at the inn. There was so much he couldn't tell her. But when he looked into her eyes he knew he had to tell her enough about Roman DeWinter that she would be able to make a choice.

"Sit down."

Something in his tone sent a frisson of alarm down her spine. He was going to tell her he was leaving, she thought. "All right." She clasped her hands together, promising herself she'd find a way to make him stay.

"I haven't been fair with you." He leaned back against a rock. "Fairness hasn't been one of my priorities. There are things about me you should know, that you should have known before things got this far."

"Roman—"

"It won't take long. I did come from St. Louis. I lived in a kind of neighborhood you wouldn't even understand. Drugs, whores, Saturday night specials." He looked out at the water. The spiffy little sailboat had caught the wind. "A long way from here, baby."

So the trust had come, she thought. She wouldn't let him regret it. "It doesn't matter where you came from, Roman. It's where you are now."

"That's not always true. Part of where you come from stays with you." He closed a hand over hers briefly, then released it. It would be better, he thought, to break the contact now. "When he was sober enough, my father drove a cab. When he wasn't sober enough, he sat around the apartment with his head in his hands. One of my first memories is waking up at night hearing my mother screaming at him. Every couple of months she'd threaten to leave. Then he'd straighten up. We'd live in the eye of the hurricane until he'd stop off at the bar to have a drink. So she finally stopped threatening and did it."

"Where did you go?"

"I said she left."

"But…didn't she take you with her?"

"I guess she figured she was going to have it rough enough without dealing with a ten-year-old."

Charity shook her head and struggled with a deep, churning anger. It was hard for her to understand how a mother could desert her child. "She must have been very confused and frightened. Once she—"

"I never saw her again," Roman said. "You have to understand that not everyone loves unconditionally. Not everyone loves at all."

"Oh, Roman." She wanted to gather him close then, but he held her away from him.

"I stayed with my father another three years. One night he hit the gin before he got in the cab. He killed himself and his passenger."

"Oh, God." She reached for him, but he shook his head.

"That made me a ward of the court. I didn't much care for that, so I took off, hit the streets."

She was reeling from what he'd already told her, and she could barely take it all in. "At thirteen?"

"I'd been living there most of my life anyway."

"But how?"

He shook a cigarette out of his pack, lighting it and drawing deep before he spoke again. "I took odd jobs when I could find them. I stole when I couldn't. After a couple of years I got good enough at the stealing that I didn't bother much with straight jobs. I broke into houses, hot-wired cars, snatched purses. Do you understand what I'm telling you?"

"Yes. You were alone and desperate."

"I was a thief. Damn it, Charity, I wasn't some poor misguided youth. I stopped being a kid when I came home and found my father passed out and my mother gone. I knew what I was doing. I chose to do it."

She kept her eyes level with his, battling the need to take him in her arms. "If you expect me to condemn a child for finding a way to survive, I'll have to disappoint you."

She was romanticizing, he told himself, pitching his cigarette into the water.

"Do you still steal?"

"What if I told you I did?"

"I'd have to say you were stupid. You don't seem stupid to me, Roman."

He paused for a moment before he decided to tell her the rest. "I was in Chicago. I'd just turned sixteen. It was January, so cold your eyes couldn't water. I decided I needed to score enough to take a bus south. Thought I'd winter in Florida and fleece the rich tourists. That's when I met John Brody. I broke into his apartment and ended up with a .45 in my face. He was a cop." The memory of that moment still made him laugh. "I don't know who was more surprised. He gave me three choices. One, he could turn me over to Juvie. Two, he could beat the hell out of me. Three, he could give me something to eat."

"What did you do?"

"It's hard to play it tough when a two-hundred-pound man's pointing a .45 at your belt. I ate a can of soup. He let me sleep on the couch." Looking back, he could still see himself, skinny and full of bitterness, lying wakeful on the lumpy sofa.

"I kept telling myself I was going to rip off whatever I could and take off. But I never did. I used to tell myself he was a stupid bleeding heart, and that once it warmed up I'd split with whatever I could carry. The next thing I knew I was going to school." Roman paused a moment to look up at the sky. "He used to build things down in the basement of the building. He taught me how to use a hammer."

"He must have been quite a man."

"He was only twenty-five when I met him. He'd grown up on the South Side, running with the gangs. At some point he turned it around. Then he decided to turn me around. In some ways he did. When he got married a couple of years later he bought this old run-down house in the suburbs. We fixed it up room by room. He used to tell me there was nothing he liked better than living in a construction zone. We were adding on another room—it was going to be his workshop—when he was killed. Line of duty. He was thirty-two. He left a three-year-old son and a pregnant widow."

"Roman, I'm sorry." She moved to him and took his hands.

"It killed something in me, Charity. I've never been able to get it back."

"I understand." He started to pull away, but she held him fast. "I do. When you lose someone who was that much a part of your life, something's always going to be missing. I still think about Pop all the time. It still makes me sad. Sometimes it just makes me angry, because there was so much more I wanted to say to him."

"You're leaving out pieces. Look at what I was, where I came from. I was a thief."

"You were a child."

He took her shoulders and shook her. "My father was a drunk."

"I don't even know who my father was. Should I be ashamed of that?"

"It doesn't matter to you, does it? Where I've been, what I've done?"

"Not very much. I'm more interested in what you are now."

He couldn't tell her what he was. Not yet. For her own safety, he had to continue the deception for a few more days. But there was something he could tell her. Like the story he had just recounted, it was something he had never told anyone else.

"I love you."

Her hands went slack on his. Her eyes grew huge. "Would you—" She paused long enough to take a deep breath. "Would you say that again?"

"I love you."

With a muffled sob, she launched herself into his arms. She wasn't going to cry, she told herself, squeezing her eyes tight against the threatening tears. She wouldn't be red-eyed and weepy at this, the most beautiful and exciting moment of her life.

"Just hold me a moment, okay?" Overwhelmed, she pressed her face into his shoulder. "I can't believe this is happening."

"That makes two of us." But he was smiling. He could feel the stunned delight coil through him as he stroked her hair. It hadn't been so hard to say, he realized. In fact, he could easily get used to saying it several times a day.

"A week ago I didn't even know you." She tilted her head back until her lips met his. "Now I can't imagine my life without you."

"Don't. You might change your mind."

"Not a chance."

"Promise." Overwhelmed by a sudden sense of urgency, he gripped her hands. "I want you to make that a promise."

"All right. I promise. I won't change my mind about being in love with you."

"I'm holding you to that, Charity." He swooped her

against him, then drained even happy thoughts from her mind. "Will you marry me?"

She jerked back, gaped, then sat down hard. "What? *What?*"

"I want you to marry me—now, today." It was crazy, and he knew it. It was wrong. Yet, as he pulled her up again, he knew he had to find a way to keep her. "You must know somebody, a minister, a justice of the peace, who could do it."

"Well, yes, but..." She held a hand to her spinning head. "There's paperwork, and licenses. God, I can't think."

"Don't think. Just say you will."

"Of course I will, but—"

"No buts." He crushed his mouth to hers. "I want you to belong to me. God, I need to belong to you. Do you believe that?"

"Yes." Breathless, she touched a hand to his cheek. "Roman, we're talking about marriage, a lifetime. I only intend to do this once." She dragged a hand through her hair and sat down again. "I guess everyone says that, but I need to believe it. It has to start off with more than a few words in front of an official. Wait, please," she said before he could speak again. "You've really thrown me off here, and I want to make you understand. I love you, and I can't think of anything I want more than to belong to you. When I marry you it has to be more than rushing to the J.P. and saying I do. I don't have to have a big, splashy wedding, either. It's not a matter of long white trains and engraved invitations."

"Then what is it?"

"I want flowers and music, Roman. And friends." She took his face in her hands, willing him to understand. "I want to stand beside you knowing I look beautiful, so that everyone can see how proud I am to be your wife. If that sounds overly romantic, well, it should be."

"How long do you need?"

"Can I have two weeks?"

He was afraid to give her two days. But it was for the best, he told himself. He would never be able to hold her if there were still lies between them. "I'll give you two weeks, if you'll go away with me afterward."

"Where?"

"Leave it to me."

"I love surprises." Her lips curved against his. "And you...you're the biggest surprise so far."

"Two weeks." He took her hands firmly in his. "No matter what happens."

"You make it sound as though we might have to overcome a natural disaster in the meantime. I'm only going to take a few days to make it right." She brushed a kiss over his cheek and smiled again. "It will be right, Roman, for both of us. That's another promise. I'd like that champagne now."

She took out the glasses while he retrieved the bottle from the water. As they sat together on the blanket, he released the cork with a pop and a hiss.

"To new beginnings," she said, touching her glass to his.

He wanted to believe it could happen. "I'll make you happy, Charity."

"You already have." She shifted so that she was cuddled against him, her head on his shoulder. "This is the best picnic I've ever had."

He kissed the top of her head. "You haven't eaten anything yet."

"Who needs food?" With a sigh, she reached up. He linked his hand with hers, and they both looked out toward the horizon.

Chapter 10

Check-in on Tuesday was as chaotic as it came. Charity barreled her way through it, assigning rooms and cabins, answering questions, finding a spare cookie for a cranky toddler, and waited for the first rush to pass.

She was the first to admit that she usually thrived on the noise, the problems and the healthy press of people that proved the inn's success. At the moment, though, she would have liked nothing better than having everyone, and everything settled.

It was hard to keep her mind on the business at hand when her head was full of plans for her wedding.

Should she have Chopin or Beethoven? She'd barely begun her list of possible selections. Would the weather hold so that they could have the ceremony in the gardens, or would it be best to plan an intimate and cozy wedding in the gathering room?

"Yes, sir, I'll be glad to give you information on renting bikes." She snatched up a pamphlet.

When was she going to find an afternoon free so that she could choose the right dress? It *had* to be the right dress, the perfect dress. Something ankle-length, with some romantic touches of lace. There was a boutique in Eastsound that specialized in antique clothing. If she could just—

"Aren't you going to sign that?"

"Sorry, Roger." Charity pulled herself back and offered him an apologetic smile. "I don't seem to be all here this morning."

"No problem." He patted her hand as she signed his roster. "Spring fever?"

"You could call it that." She tossed back her hair, annoyed that she hadn't remembered to braid it that morning. As long as she was smelling orange blossoms she'd be lucky to remember her own name. "We're a little behind. The computer's acting up again. Poor Bob's been fighting with it since yesterday."

"Looks like you've been in a fight yourself."

She lifted a hand to the healing cut on her temple. "I had a little accident last week."

"Nothing serious?"

"No, just inconvenient, really. Some idiot joyriding nearly ran me down."

"That's terrible." Watching her carefully, he pulled his face into stern lines. "Were you badly hurt?"

"No, only a few stitches and a medley of bruises. Scared me more than anything."

"I can imagine. You don't expect something like that around here. I hope they caught him."

"No, not yet." Because she'd already put the incident behind her, she gave a careless shrug. "To tell you the truth, I doubt they ever will. I imagine he got off the island as soon as he sobered up."

"Drunk drivers." Block made a sound of disgust. "Well, you've got a right to be distracted after something like that."

"Actually, I've got a much more pleasant reason. I'm getting married in a couple of weeks."

"You don't say!" His face split into a wide grin. "Who's the lucky man?"

"Roman DeWinter. I don't know if you met him. He's doing some remodeling upstairs."

"That's handy now, isn't it?" He continued to grin. The romance explained a lot. One look at Charity's face settled any lingering doubts. Block decided he'd have to have a nice long talk with Bob about jumping the gun. "Is he from around here?"

"No, he's from St. Louis, actually."

"Well, I hope he's not going to take you away from us."

"You know I'd never leave the inn, Roger." Her smile faded a bit. That was something she and Roman had never spoken of. "In any case, I promise to keep my mind on my work. You've got six people who want to rent boats." She took a quick look at her watch. "I can have them taken to the marina by noon."

"I'll round them up."

The door to the inn opened, and Charity glanced over. She saw a small, spare man with well-cut auburn hair, wearing a crisp sport shirt. He carried one small leather bag.

"Good morning."

"Good morning." He took a brief study of the lobby as he crossed to the desk. "Conby, Richard Conby. I believe I have a reservation."

"Yes, Mr. Conby. We're expecting you." Charity shuffled through the papers on the desk and sent up a quick prayer that Bob would have the computer humming along by the end of the day. "How was your trip?"

"Uneventful." He signed the register, listing his address as Seattle. Charity found herself both amused and impressed by his careful manicure. "I was told your inn is quiet, restful. I'm looking forward to relaxing for a day or two."

"I'm sure you'll find the inn very relaxing." She opened a drawer to choose a key. "Either Roman or I will drive your group to the marina, Roger. Have them in the parking lot at noon."

"Will do." With a cheerful wave, he sauntered off.

"I'll be happy to show you to your room, Mr. Conby. If you have any questions about the inn, or the island, feel free to ask me or any of the staff." She came around the desk and led the way to the stairs.

"Oh, I will," Conby said, following her. "I certainly will."

*   *   *

At precisely 12:05, Conby heard a knock and opened his door. "Prompt as always, DeWinter." He scanned down to Roman's tool belt. "Keeping busy, I see."

"Dupont's in cabin 3."

Conby decided to drop the sarcasm. This was a big one, much too big for him to let his personal feelings interfere. "You made a positive ID?"

"I helped him carry his bags."

"Very good." Satisfied, Conby finished arranging his ebony-handled clothes brush and shoe horn on the oak dresser. "We'll move in as planned on Thursday morning and take him before we close in on Block."

"What about the driver of the car who tried to kill Charity?"

Always fastidious, Conby walked into the adjoining bath to wash his hands. "You're inordinately interested in a small-time hood."

"Did you get a confession?"

"Yes." Conby unfolded a white hand towel bordered with flowers. "He admitted to meeting with Block last week and taking five thousand to—to put Miss Ford out of the picture. A very minor sum for a hit." His hands dry, Conby tossed the towel over the lip of the sink before walking back into the bedroom. "If Block had been more discerning, he might have had more success."

Taking him by the collar, Roman lifted Conby to his toes. "Watch your step," he said softly.

"It's more to the point for me to tell you to watch yours." Conby pulled himself free and straightened his shirt. In the five years since he had taken over as Roman's superior he had found Roman's methods crude and his attitude arrogant. The pity was, his results were invariably excellent. "You're losing your focus on this one, Agent DeWinter."

"No. It's taken me a while—maybe too long—but I'm focused just fine. You've got enough on Block to pin him with conspiracy to murder. Dupont's practically tied up with a bow. Why wait?"

"I won't bother to remind you who's in charge of this case."

"We both know who's in charge, Conby, but there's a difference between sitting behind a desk and calling the shots in the field. If we take them now, quietly, there's less risk of endangering innocent people."

"I have no intention of endangering any of the guests. Or the staff," he added, thinking he knew where Roman's mind was centered. "I have my orders on this, just as you do." He took a fresh handkerchief out of his drawer. "Since it's apparently so important to you, I'll tell you that we want to nail Block when he passes the money. We're working with the Canadian authorities on this, and that's the way we'll proceed. As for the conspiracy charges, we have the word of a bargain-basement hit man. It may take a bit more to make it stick."

"You'll make it stick. How many have we got?"

"We have two agents checking in tomorrow, and two more as backup. We'll take Dupont in his cabin, and Block in the lobby. Moving on Dupont any earlier would undoubtedly tip off Block. Agreed?"

"Yes."

"Since you've filled me in on the checkout procedures, it should go very smoothly."

"It better. If anything happens to her—anything—I'm holding you responsible."

Charity dashed into the kitchen with a loaded tray. "I don't know how things can get out of hand so fast. When have you ever known us to have a full house on a Wednesday night?" she asked the room at large, whipping out her pad. "Two specials with wild rice, one with baked potato, hold the sour cream, and one child's portion of ribs with fries." She rushed over to get the drinks herself.

"Take it easy, girl," Mae advised her. "They ain't going anywhere till they eat."

"That's the problem." She loaded up the tray. "What a time for Lori to get sick. The way this virus is bouncing around, we're lucky to have a waitress still standing.

Whoops!'' She backed up to keep from running into Roman. ''Sorry.''

''Need a hand?''

''I need two.'' She smiled and took the time to lean over the tray and kiss him. ''You seem to have them. Those salads Dolores is fixing go to table 5.''

''Girl makes me tired just looking at her,'' Mae commented as she filleted a trout. She lifted her head just long enough for her eyes to meet Roman's. ''Seems to me she rushes into everything.''

''Four house salads.'' Dolores was humming the ''Wedding March'' as she passed him a tray. ''Looks like you didn't need that dynamite after all.'' Cackling, she went back to fill the next order.

Five minutes later he passed Charity in the doorway again. ''Strange bunch tonight,'' she murmured.

''How so?''

''There's a man at table 2. He's so jumpy you'd think he'd robbed a bank or something. Then there's a couple at table 8, supposed to be on a second honeymoon. They're spending more time looking at everyone else than each other.''

Roman said nothing. She'd made both Dupont and two of Conby's agents in less than thirty minutes.

''And then there's this little man in a three-piece suit sitting at 4. Suit and tie,'' she added with a glance over her shoulder. ''Came here to relax, he says. Who can relax in a three-piece suit?'' Shifting, she balanced the tray on her hip. ''Claims to be from Seattle and has an Eastern accent that could cut Mae's apple pie. Looks like a weasel.''

''You think so?'' Roman allowed himself a small smile at her description of Conby.

''A very well-groomed weasel,'' she added. ''Check it out for yourself.'' With a small shudder, she headed toward the dining room again. ''Anyone that smooth gives me the creeps.''

Duty was duty though, and the weasel was sitting at her station. ''Are you ready to order?'' she asked Conby with a bright smile.

He took a last sip of his vodka martini. It was passable, he supposed. "The menu claims the trout is fresh."

"Yes, sir." She was particularly proud of that. The stocked pond had been her idea. "It certainly is."

"Fresh when it was shipped in this morning, no doubt."

"No." Charity lowered her pad but kept her smile in place. "We stock our own right here at the inn."

Lifting a brow, he tapped a finger against his empty glass. "Your fish may be superior to your vodka, but I have my doubts as to whether it is indeed fresh. Nonetheless, it appears to be the most interesting item on your menu, so I shall have to make do."

"The fish," Charity repeated, with what she considered admirable calm, "is fresh."

"I'm sure you consider it so. However, your conception of fresh and mine may differ."

"Yes, sir." She shoved the pad into her pocket. "If you'll excuse me a moment."

She might be innocent, Conby thought, frowning at his empty glass, but she was hardly efficient.

"Where's the fire?" Mae wanted to know when Charity burst into the kitchen.

"In my brain." She stopped a moment, hands on hips. "That—that insulting pipsqueak out there tells me our vodka's below standard, our menu's dull and our fish isn't fresh."

"A dull menu." Mae bristled down to her crepe-soled shoes. "What did he eat?"

"He hasn't eaten anything yet. One drink and a couple of crackers with salmon dip and he's a restaurant critic."

Charity took a turn around the kitchen, struggling with her temper. No urban wonder was going to stroll into her inn and pick it apart. Her bar was as good as any on the island, her restaurant had a triple-A rating, and her fish—

"Guy at table 4 wants another vodka martini," Roman announced as he carried in a loaded tray.

"Does he?" Charity whirled around. "Does he really?"

He couldn't recall ever seeing quite that glint in her eye. "That's right," he said cautiously.

"Well, I have something else to get him first." So saying, she strode into the utility room and then out again.

"Uh-oh," Dolores mumbled.

"Did I miss something?" Roman asked.

"Man's got a nerve saying the food's dull before he's even had a taste of it." Scowling, Mae scooped a helping of wild asparagus onto a plate. "I've a mind to add some curry to his entrée. A nice fat handful of it. We'll see about dull."

They all turned around when Charity strolled back in. She was still carrying the platter. On it flopped a very confused trout.

"My." Dolores covered her mouth with both hands, giggling. "Oh, my."

Grinning, Mae went back to her stove.

"Charity." Roman made a grab for her arm, but she evaded him and glided through the doorway. Shaking his head, he followed her.

A few of the diners looked up and stared as she carried the thrashing fish across the room. Weaving through the tables, she crossed to table 4 and held the tray under Conby's nose.

"Your trout, sir." She dropped the platter unceremoniously in front of him. "Fresh enough?" she asked with a small, polite smile.

In the archway Roman tucked his hands into his pockets and roared. He would have traded a year's salary for a photo of the expression on Conby's face as he and the fish gaped at each other.

When Charity glided back into the kitchen, she handed the tray and its passenger to Dolores. "You can put this back," she said. "Table 4 decided on the stuffed pork chops. I wish I had a pig handy." She let out a laughing squeal as Roman scooped her off the floor.

"You're the best." He pressed his lips to hers and held them there long after he'd set her down again. "The absolute best." He was still laughing as he gathered her close for a hug. "Isn't she, Mae?"

"She has her moments." She wasn't about to let them know how much good it did her to see them smiling at each other. "Now the two of you stop pawing each other in my kitchen and get back to work."

Charity lifted her face for one last kiss. "I guess I'd better fix that martini now. He looked like he could use one."

Because she wasn't one to hold a grudge, Charity treated Conby to attentive and cheerful service throughout the meal. Noting that he hadn't unbent by dessert, she brought him a serving of Mae's Black Forest cake on the house.

"I hope you enjoyed your meal, Mr. Conby."

It was impossible for him to admit that he'd never had better, not even in Washington's toniest restaurants. "It was quite good, thank you."

She offered an easy smile as she poured his coffee. "Perhaps you'll come back another time and try the trout."

Even for Conby, her smile was hard to resist. "Perhaps. You run an interesting establishment, Miss Ford."

"We try. Have you lived in Seattle long, Mr. Conby."

He continued to add cream to his coffee, but he was very much on guard. "Why do you ask?"

"Your accent. It's very Eastern."

Conby deliberated only seconds. He knew that Dupont had already left the dining room, but Block was at a nearby table, entertaining part of his tour group with what Conby considered rather boring stories. "You have a good ear. I was transferred to Seattle eighteen months ago. From Maryland. I'm in marketing."

"Maryland." Deciding to forgive and forget, she topped off his coffee. "You're supposed to have the best crabs in the country."

"I assure you, we do." The rich cake and the smooth coffee had mellowed him. He actually smiled at her. "It's a pity I didn't bring one along with me."

Laughing, Charity laid a friendly hand on his arm. "You're a good sport, Mr. Conby. Enjoy your evening."

Lips pursed, Conby watched her go. He couldn't recall anyone having accused him of being a good sport before. He rather liked it.

"We're down to three tables of diehards," Charity announced as she entered the kitchen again. "And I'm starving." She opened the refrigerator and rooted around for something to eat, but Mae snapped it closed again.

"You haven't got time."

"Haven't got time?" Charity pressed a hand to her stomach. "Mae, the way tonight went, I wasn't able to grab more than a stray French fry."

"I'll fix you a sandwich, but you had a call. Something about tomorrow's delivery."

"The salmon. Damn." She tilted her watch forward. "They're closed by now."

"Left an emergency number, I think. Message is upstairs."

"All right, all right. I'll be back in ten minutes." She cast a last longing glance at the refrigerator. "Make that two sandwiches."

To save time, she raced out through the utility room, rounded the side of the building and climbed the outside steps. When she opened the door, she could only stop and stare.

The music was pitched low. There was candlelight, and there were flowers and a white cloth on a table at the foot of the bed. It was set for two. As she watched, Roman took a bottle of wine from a glass bucket and drew the cork.

"I thought you'd never get here."

She leaned back on the closed door. "If I'd known this was waiting, I'd have been here a lot sooner."

"You said you liked surprises."

"Yes." There was both surprise and delight in her eyes as she brushed her tumbled hair back from her forehead. "I like them a lot." Untying her apron, she walked to the table while he poured the wine. It glinted warm and gold in the candlelight. "Thanks," she murmured when he offered her a glass.

"I wanted to give you something." He gripped her hand, holding tight and trying not to remember that this was their last night together before all the questions had to be answered. "I'm not very good with romantic gestures."

"Oh, no, you're very good at them. Champagne picnics, late-night suppers.'' She closed her eyes for a moment. "Mozart.''

"Picked at random,'' he admitted, feeling foolishly nervous. "I have something for you.''

She looked at the table. "Something else?''

"Yes.'' He reached down to the seat of his chair and picked up a square box. "It just came today.'' It was the best he could do. He pushed the box into her hand.

"A present?'' She'd always liked the anticipation as much as the gift itself, so she took a moment to study and shake the box. But the moment the lid was off she snatched the bracelet out. "Oh, Roman, it's gorgeous.'' Thoroughly stunned, she turned the etched gold, watching the light glint off the metal and the square-cut amethyst. "It's absolutely gorgeous,'' she said again. "I'd swear I'd seen this before. Last week,'' she remembered. "In one of the magazines Lori brought me.''

"You had it on your desk.''

Overwhelmed, she nodded. "Yes, I'd circled this. I do that with beautiful things I know I'll never buy.'' She took a deep breath. "Roman, this is a wonderful, sweet and very romantic thing to do, but—''

"Then don't spoil it.'' He took the bracelet from the box and clasped it on her wrist. "I need the practice.''

"No.'' She slipped her arms around him and rested her cheek against his shoulder. "I think you've got the hang of it.''

He held her, letting the music, her scent, the moment, wash over him. Things could be different with her. He could be different with her.

"Do you know when I fell in love with you, Roman?''

"No.'' He kissed the top of her head. "I've thought more about why than when.''

With a soft laugh, she snuggled against him. "I'd thought it was when you danced with me and you kissed me until every bone in my body turned to water.''

"Like this?''

He turned his head, meeting her lips with his. Gently he set her on fire.

"Yes." She swayed against him, eyes closed. "Just like that. But that wasn't when. That was when I realized it, but it wasn't when I fell in love with you. Do you remember when you asked me about the spare?"

"The what?"

"The spare." Sighing, she tilted her head to give him easier access to her throat. "You wanted to know where the spare was so you could fix my flat." She leaned back to smile at his stunned expression. "I guess I can't call it love at first sight, since I'd already known you two or three minutes."

He ran his hands over her cheeks, through her hair, down her neck. "Just like that?"

"I'd never thought as much about falling in love and getting married as I suppose most people might. Because of Pop's being sick, and the inn. I always figured if it happened it would happen without me doing a lot of worrying or preparing. And I was right." She linked hands with him. "All I had to do was have a flat tire. The rest was easy."

A flat, Roman remembered, that had been deliberately arranged, just as her sudden need for a handyman had been arranged. As everything had been arranged, he thought, his grip tightening on her fingers. Everything except his falling in love with her.

"Charity..." He would have given anything to be able to tell her the truth, the whole truth. Anything but his knowledge that in ignorance there was safety. "I never meant for any of this to happen," he said carefully. "I never wanted to feel this way about anyone."

"Are you sorry?"

"About a lot of things, but not about being in love with you." He released her. "Your dinner's getting cold."

She tucked her tongue in her cheek. "If we found something else to do for an hour or so we could call it a midnight supper." She ran her hands up his chest to toy with the top button of his shirt. "Want to play Parcheesi?"

"No."

She flicked the button open and worked her way slowly, steadily down. "Scrabble?"

"Uh-uh."

"I know." She trailed a finger down the center of his body to the snap of his jeans. "How about a rip-roaring game of canasta?"

"I don't know how to play."

Grinning, she tugged the snap open. "Oh, I have a feeling you'd catch on." Her laugh was muffled against his mouth.

Her heated thoughts of seducing him spun away as he dragged her head back and plundered her mouth. Her hands, so confident an instant before, faltered, then fisted hard at the back of his shirt. This wasn't the gentle, persuasive passion he had shown her since the night they had become lovers. This was a raw, desperate need, and it held a trace of fury, and a hint of despair. Whirling from the feel of it, she strained against him, letting herself go.

He'd needed her before. Roman had already come to understand that he had needed her long before he'd ever met her. But tonight was different. He'd set the stage carefully—the wine, the candles, the music—wanting to give her the romance she made him capable of. Then he'd felt her cool fingertips on his skin. He'd seen the promising flicker of desire in her eyes. There was only tonight. In a matter of hours she would know everything. No matter how often he told himself he would set things right, he was very much afraid she wouldn't forgive him.

He had tonight.

Breathless, she clung to him as they tumbled onto the bed. Here was the restless, ruthless lover she had known existed alongside the gentle, patient one. And he excited her every bit as much. As frantic as he, she pulled the loosened shirt from his shoulders and gloried in the feel of his flesh under her hands.

He was as taut as wire, as explosive as gunpowder. She felt his muscles tense and tighten as his mouth raced hungrily over her face. With a throaty laugh she tugged at his jeans while they rolled over the bed. If this was a game they were playing, she was determined they would both win.

A broken moan escaped him as her seeking hands drove him toward delirium. With an oath, he snagged her wrists, yanking them over her head. Breath heaving, he watched her face as he hooked a hand in the top of her shirt and ripped it down the center.

She had only time for a gasp before his hot, open mouth lowered to her skin to torment and tantalize. Powerless against the onslaught, she arched against him. When her hands were free, she only pressed him closer, crying out as he sucked greedily at her breast.

There were sensations here, wild and exquisite, that trembled on but never crossed the thin line that separated pleasure from pain. She felt herself dragged under, deep, still deeper, to windmill helplessly down some dark, endless tunnel toward unreasonable pleasures.

She couldn't know what she was doing to him. He was skilled enough to be certain that she was trapped by her own senses. Yet her body wrapped around his, her hands sought, her lips hungered.

In the flickering light her skin was like white satin. Under his hands it flowed like lava, hot and dangerous. Passion heated her light floral scent and turned it into something secret and forbidden.

Impatient, he yanked her slacks down her hips, frantically tasting each new inch of exposed flesh. This new intimacy had her sobbing out his name, shuddering as climax slammed impossibly into climax.

She held on to him, her nails digging in, her palms sliding damply over his slick skin. Her mind was empty, wiped clear of all but sensation. His name formed on her lips again and again. She thought he spoke to her, some mad, frenzied words that barely penetrated her clouded brain. Perhaps they were promises, pleas, or prayers. She would have answered all of them if she could.

Then his mouth was on hers, swallowing her cry of release,

smothering her groan of surrender, as he drove himself into her.

Fast, hot, reckless, they matched rhythms. Far beyond madness, they clung. Driven by love, locked in desire, they raced. Even when they tumbled back to earth, they held each other close.

Chapter 11

With her eyes half closed, her lips curved, she gave a long, lazy sigh. "That was wonderful."

Roman topped off the wine in Charity's glass. "Are you talking about the meal or the preliminaries?"

She smiled. "Both." Before he could set the bottle down, she touched his hand. It was just a skimming of her fingertip over his skin. His pulse doubled. "I think we should make midnight suppers a regular event."

It was long past midnight. Even cold fish was delicious with wine and love. He hoped that if he held on hard enough it could always be like this. "The first time you looked at me like that I almost swallowed my tongue."

She kept her eyes on his. Even in candlelight they were the color of morning. "Like what?"

"Like you knew exactly what I was thinking, and was trying not to think. Exactly what I wanted not to think. Exactly what I wanted, and was trying not to want. You scare the hell out of me."

Her lazy smile faltered. "I do?"

"You make too much difference. All the difference." He took both of her hands, wishing that just this once he had smooth words, a little poetry. "Every time you walk into a room..." But he didn't have smooth words, or poetry. "It makes a difference.'' He would have released her hands, but she turned them in his.

"I'm crazy about you. If I'd gone looking for someone to share my life, and my home, and my dreams, it would have been you.''

She saw the shadow of concern in his eyes and willed it away. There was no room for worries in their lives tonight. With a quick, wicked smile, she nibbled on his fingers. "You know what I'd like?''

"More Black Forest cake.''

"Besides that.'' Her eyes laughed at him over their joined hands. "I'd like to spend the night making love with you, talking with you, drinking wine and listening to music. I have a feeling I'd find it much more satisfying than the slumber parties I had as a girl.''

She could, with a look and a smile, seduce him more utterly than any vision of black lace or white silk. "What would you like to do first?''

She had to laugh. It delighted her to see him so relaxed and happy. "Actually, there is something I want to talk with you about.''

"I've already told you—I'll wear a suit, but no tuxedo.''

"It's not about that.'' She smiled and traced a fingertip over the back of his hand. "Even though I know you'd look wonderful in a tux, I think a suit's more than adequate for an informal garden wedding. I'd like to talk to you about after the wedding.''

"After-the-wedding plans aren't negotiable. I intend to make love with you for about twenty-four hours.''

"Oh.'' As if she were thinking it through, she sipped her wine. "I guess I can go along with that. What I'd like to discuss is more long-range. It's something that Block said to me the other day.''

"Block?'' Alarm sprinted upward, then centered at the base of his neck.

"Just an offhand comment, but it made me think.'' She moved her shoulders in a quick, restless movement, then settled again. "I mentioned that we were getting married, and he said something about hoping you didn't take me away. It suddenly occurred to me that you might not want to spend your life here, on Orcas.''

"That's it?'' He felt the tension seep away.

"It's not such a little thing. I mean, I'm sure we can work it out, but you might not be crazy about the idea of living in a…well, a public kind of place, with people coming and going, and interruptions, and…'' She let her words trail off, knowing she was rambling, as she did whenever she was nervous. "The point is, I need to know how you feel about staying on the island, living here, at the inn.''

"How do you feel about it?''

"It isn't just a matter of what I feel any longer. It's what we feel.''

It amazed him that she could so easily touch his heart. He supposed it always would. "It's been a long time since I've felt at home anywhere. I feel it here, with you.''

She smiled and linked her fingers with his. "Are you tired?''

"No.''

"Good.'' She rose and corked the wine. "Just let me get my keys.''

"Keys to what?''

"The van,'' she told him as she walked into the next room.

"Are we going somewhere?''

"I know the best place on the island to watch the sun rise.'' She came back carrying a blanket and jiggling the keys. "Want to watch the sun come up with me, Roman?''

"You're only wearing a robe.''

"Of course I am. It's nearly two in the morning. Don't forget the wine.'' With a laugh, she opened the door and crept down the steps. "Let's try not to wake anyone.'' She winced a little as she started across the gravel in her bare feet. With a muttered oath, Roman swung her up into his arms. "My hero,'' she murmured.

"Sure.'' He dumped her in the driver's seat of the van. "Where are we going, baby?''

"To the beach.'' She pushed her hair behind her shoulders

as she started the van. Symphonic music blared from the radio before she twisted the knob. "I always play it too loud when I'm driving alone." She turned to look guiltily back at the inn. It remained dark and quiet. Slowly she drove out of the lot and onto the road. "It's a beautiful night."

"Morning."

"Whatever." She took a long, greedy gulp of air. "I haven't really had time for big adventures, so I have to take small ones whenever I get the chance."

"Is that what this is? An adventure?"

"Sure. We're going to drink the rest of the wine, make love under the stars and watch the sun come up over the water." She turned her head. "Is that all right with you?"

"I think I can live with it."

It was hours later when she curled up close to him. The bottle of wine was empty, and the stars were blinking out one by one.

"I'm going to be totally useless today." After a sleepy laugh, she nuzzled his neck. "And I don't even care."

He tugged the blanket over her. The mornings were still chilly. Though he hadn't planned it, the long night of loving had given him new hope. If he could convince her to sleep through the morning, he could complete his assignment, close the door on it and then explain everything. That would let him keep her out of harm's way and begin at the beginning.

"It's nearly dawn," she murmured.

They didn't speak as they watched day break. The sky paled. The night birds hushed. For an instant, time hung suspended. Then, slowly, regally, colors seeped into the horizon, bleeding up from the water, reflecting in it. Shadows faded, and the trees were tipped with gold. The first bird of the morning trumpeted the new day.

Roman gathered her to him to love her slowly under the lightening sky.

She dozed as he drove back to the inn. The sky was a pale, milky blue, but it was as quiet now as it had been when they'd left. When he lifted her out of the van, she sighed and nestled her head on his shoulder.

"I love you, Roman."

"I know." For the first time in his life he wanted to think about next week, next month, even next year—anything except the day ahead. He carried her up the stairs and into the inn. "I love you, Charity."

He had little trouble convincing her to snuggle between the sheets of the rumpled bed once he promised to take Ludwig for his habitual run.

Before he did, Roman went downstairs, strapped on his shoulder holster and shoved in his gun.

Taking Dupont was a study in well-oiled police work. By 7:45 his secluded cabin was surrounded by the best Sheriff Royce and the F.B.I. had to offer. Roman had ignored Conby's mutterings about bringing the locals into it and advised his superior to stay out of the way.

When the men were in position, Roman moved to the door himself, his gun in one hand, his shoulder snug against the frame. He rapped twice. When there was no response, he signaled for his men to draw their weapons and close in. Using the key he'd taken from Charity's ring, he unlocked the door.

Once inside, he scanned the room, legs spread, the gun held tight in both hands. The adrenaline was there, familiar, even welcome. With only a jerk of the head he signaled his backup. Guarding each other's flanks, they took a last circle.

Roman cautiously approached the bedroom. For the first time, a smile—a grim smile—moved across his face. Dupont was in the shower. And he was singing.

The singing ended abruptly when Roman yanked the curtain aside.

"Don't bother to put your hands up," Roman told him as he blinked water out of his eyes. Keeping the gun level, he tossed his first prize a towel. "You're busted, pal. Why don't you dry off and I'll read you your rights?"

"Well done," Conby commented when the prisoner was cuffed. "If you handle the rest of this as smoothly, I'll see that you get a commendation."

"Keep it." Roman holstered his weapon. There was only

one more hurdle before he could finally separate past and future. "When this is done, I'm finished."

"You've been in law enforcement for over ten years, DeWinter. You won't walk away."

"Watch me." With that, he headed back to the inn to finish what he had started.

When Charity awoke, it was full morning and she was quite alone. She was grateful for that, because she couldn't stifle a moan. The moment she sat up, her head, unused to the generous doses of wine and stingy amounts of sleep, began to pound.

She had no one but herself to blame, she admitted as she crawled out of bed. Her feet tangled in what was left of the shirt she'd been wearing the night before.

It had been worth it, she thought, gathering up the torn cotton. Well worth it.

But, incredible night or not, it was morning and she had work to do. She downed some aspirin, allowed herself another groan, then dived into the shower.

Roman found Bob huddled in the office, anxiously gulping laced coffee. Without preamble, he yanked the mug away and emptied the contents into the trash can.

"I just needed a little something to get me through."

He'd had more than a little, Roman determined. His words were slurred, and his eyes were glazed. Even under the best of circumstances Roman found it difficult to drum up any sympathy for a drunk.

He dragged Bob out of his chair by the shirtfront. "You pull yourself together and do it fast. When Block comes in you're going to check him and his little group out. If you tip him off—if you so much as blink and tip him off—I'll hang you out to dry."

"Charity does the checkout," Bob managed through chattering teeth.

"Not today. You're going to go out to the desk and handle

it. You're going to do a good job because you're going to know I'm in here and I'm watching you.''

He stepped away from Bob just as the office door opened. ''Sorry I'm late.'' Despite her heavy eyes, Charity beamed at Roman. ''I overslept.''

He felt his heart stop, then sink to his knees. ''You didn't sleep enough.''

''You're telling me.'' Her smile faded when she looked at Bob. ''What's wrong?''

He grabbed at the thread of opportunity with both hands. ''I was just telling Roman that I'm not feeling very well.''

''You don't look well.'' Concerned, she walked over to feel his brow. It was clammy and deepened the worry in her eyes. ''You're probably coming down with that virus.''

''That's what I'm afraid of.''

''You shouldn't have come in at all today. Maybe Roman should drive you home.''

''No, I can manage.'' He walked on shaking legs to the door. ''Sorry about this, Charity.'' He turned to give her a last look. ''Really sorry.''

''Don't be silly. Just take care of yourself.''

''I'll give him a hand,'' Roman muttered, and followed him out. They walked out into the lobby at the same time Block strolled in.

''Good morning.'' His face creased with his habitual smile, but his eyes were wary. ''Is there a problem?''

''Virus.'' Bob's face was already turning a sickly green. Fear made a convincing cover. ''Hit me pretty hard this morning.''

''I called Dr. Mertens,'' Charity announced as she came in to stand behind the desk. ''You go straight home, Bob. He'll meet you there.''

''Thanks.'' But one of Conby's agents followed him out, and he knew he wouldn't be going home for quite a while.

''This virus has been a plague around here.'' She offered Block an apologetic smile. ''I'm short a housekeeper, a waitress and now Bob. I hope none of your group had any complaints about the service.''

"Not a one." Relaxed again, Block set his briefcase on the desk. "It's always a pleasure doing business with you, Charity."

Roman watched helplessly as they chatted and went through the routine of checking lists and figures. She was supposed to be safe upstairs, sleeping deeply and dreaming of the night they'd spent together. Frustrated, he balled his hands at his side. Now, no matter what he did, she'd be in the middle.

He heard her laugh when Block mentioned the fish she'd carried into the dining room. And he imagined how her face would look when the agents moved in and arrested the man she thought of as a tour guide and a friend.

Charity read off a total. Roman steadied himself.

"We seem to be off by...$22.50." Block began laboriously running the numbers through his calculator again. Brow furrowed, Charity went over her list, item by item.

"Good morning, dear."

"Hmm." Distracted, Charity glanced up. "Oh, good morning, Miss Millie."

"I'm just on my way up to pack. I wanted you to know what a delightful time we've had."

"We're always sorry to see you go. We were all pleased that you and Miss Lucy extended your stay for a few days."

Miss Millie fluttered her eyelashes myopically at Roman before making her way toward the stairs. At the top, he thought, there would now be an officer posted to see that she and the other guests were kept out of the way.

"I get the same total again, Roger." Puzzled, she tapped the end of her pencil on the list. "I wish I could say I'd run it through the computer, but..." She let her words trail off, ignoring her headache. "Ah, this might be it. Do you have the Wentworths in cabin 1 down for a bottle of wine? They charged it night before last."

"Wentworth, Wentworth..." With grating slowness, Block ran down his list. "No, nothing here."

"Let me find the tab." After opening a drawer, she flipped her way efficiently through the folders. Roman felt a bead of sweat slide slowly down his back. One of the agents strolled over to browse through some postcards.

"I've got both copies," she said with a shake of her head. "This virus is really hanging us up." She filed her copy of the receipt and handed Block his.

"No problem." Cheerful as ever, he noted the new charge, then added up his figures again. "That seems to match."

With the ease of long habit, Charity calculated the amount in Canadian currency. "That's $2,330.00." She turned the receipt around for Block's approval.

He clicked open his briefcase. "As always, it's a pleasure." He counted out the money in twenties. The moment Charity marked the bill Paid, Roman moved in.

"Put your hands up. Slow." He pressed the barrel of his gun into the small of Block's back.

"Roman!" Charity gaped at him, the key to the cash drawer in her hand. "What on earth are you doing?"

"Go around the desk," he told her. "Way around, and walk outside."

"Are you crazy? Roman, for God's sake—"

"Do it!"

Block moistened his lips, keeping his hands carefully aloft. "Is this a robbery?"

"Haven't you figured it out by now?" With his free hand, Roman pulled out his ID. After tossing it on the desk, he reached for his cuffs. "You're under arrest."

"What's the charge?"

"Conspiracy to murder, counterfeiting, transporting known felons across international borders. That'll do for a start." He yanked one of Block's arms down and slipped the cuff over his wrist.

"How could you?" Charity's voice was a mere whisper. She held his badge in her hand.

He took his eyes off Block for only a second to look at her. One second changed everything.

"How silly of me," Miss Millie muttered as she waltzed back into the lobby. "I was nearly upstairs when I realized I'd left my—"

For a man of his bulk, Block moved quickly. He dragged Miss Millie against him and had a knife to her throat before anyone could react. The cuffs dangled from one wrist. "It'll only take a heartbeat," he said quietly, staring into Roman's eyes. The gun was trained in the center of Block's forehead, and Roman's finger was twitching on the trigger.

"Think about it." Block's gaze swept the lobby, where other guns had been drawn. "I'll slice this nice little lady's throat. Don't move," he said to Charity. Shifting slightly, he blocked her way.

Wide-eyed, Miss Millie could only cling to Block's arm and whimper.

"Don't hurt her." Charity stepped forward, but she stopped quickly when she saw Block's grip tighten. "Please, don't hurt her." It had to be a dream, she told herself. A nightmare. "Someone tell me what's happening here."

"The place is surrounded." Roman kept his eyes and his weapon on Block. He waited in vain for one of his men to move in from the rear. "Hurting her isn't going to do you any good."

"It isn't going to do you any good, either. Think about it. Want a dead grandmother on your hands?"

"You don't want to add murder to your list, Block," Roman said evenly. And Charity was much too close, he thought. Much too close.

"It makes no difference to me. Now take it outside. All of you!" His voice rose as he scanned the room. "Toss down the guns. Toss them down and get out before I start slicing into her. Do it." He nicked Miss Millie's fragile throat with the blade.

"Please!" Again Charity took a step forward. "Let her go. I'll stay with you."

"Damn it, Charity, get back."

She didn't spare Roman a glance. "Please, Roger," she said again, taking another careful step forward. "She's old and frail. She might get sick. Her heart." Desperate, she stepped between him and Roman's gun. "I won't give you any trouble."

The decision took Block only a moment. He grabbed Charity and dug the point of the blade into her throat. Miss Millie slid bonelessly to the floor.

"Drop the gun." He saw the fear in Roman's eyes and smiled. Apparently he'd made a much better bargain. "Two seconds and it's over. I don't have anything to lose."

Roman held his hands up, letting his weapon drop. "We'll talk."

"We'll talk when I'm ready." Block shifted the knife so that the length of the blade lay across Charity's neck. She shut her eyes and waited to die. "Get out, now. The first time somebody tries to get back in she dies."

"Out." Roman pointed to the door. "Keep them back, Conby. All of them. There's my weapon," he said to Block. "I'm clean." He lifted his jacket cautiously to show his empty holster. "Why don't I hang around in here? You can have two hostages for the price of one. A federal agent ought to give you some leverage."

"Just the woman. Take off, DeWinter, or I'll kill her before you can think how to get to me. Now."

"For God's sake, Roman. Get her out of here. She needs a doctor." Charity sucked in her breath when the point of the knife pierced her skin.

"Don't." Roman held up his hands again, palms out, as he moved toward the crumpled form near the desk. Keeping his movements slow, he gathered the sobbing woman in his arms. "If you hurt her, you won't live long enough to regret it."

With that last frustrated threat he left Charity alone.

"Stay back." After bundling Miss Millie into waiting arms, he rushed off the porch, fighting to keep his mind clear. "Nobody goes near the doors or any of the windows. Get me a weapon." Before anyone could oblige him, he was yanking a gun away from one of Royce's deputies. With the smallest of gestures Royce signaled to his man to be silent.

"What do you want us to do?"

Roman merely stared down at the gun in his hand. It was loaded. He was trained. And he was helpless.

"DeWinter..." Conby began.

"Back off." When Conby started to speak again, Roman turned on him. "Back off."

He stared at the inn. He could hear Miss Millie crying softly as someone carried her to a car. The guests who had already been evacuated were being herded to safety. Roman imagined that Royce had arranged that. Charity would want to make sure they were well taken care of.

Charity.

Shoving the gun into his holster, he turned around. "Have the road blocked off a mile in each direction. Only official personnel in this area. We'll keep the inn surrounded from a distance of fifty feet. He'll be thinking again," Roman said slowly, "and when he starts thinking he's going to know he's blocked in."

He lifted both hands and rubbed them over his face. He'd been in hostage situations before. He was trained for them. With time and cool heads, the odds of getting a hostage out in a situation of this type were excellent. When the hostage was Charity, excellent wasn't nearly good enough.

"I want to talk to him."

"Agent DeWinter, under the circumstances I have serious reservations about you being in charge of this operation."

Roman rounded on him. "Get in my way, Conby, and I'll hang you up by your silk tie. Why the hell weren't there men positioned in the back, behind him?"

Because his palms were sweating, Conby's voice was only more frigid. "I thought it best to have them outside, prepared if he attempted to run."

Roman battled the red wave of fury that burst behind his eyes. "When I get her out," he said softly, "I'm going to deal with you, you bastard. I need communication," he said to Royce. "Can you handle it?"

"Give me twenty minutes."

With a nod, Roman turned back to study the inn. Systematically he considered and rejected points of entry.

Inside, Charity felt some measure of relief when the knife was removed from her throat. Somehow the gun Block was pointing at her now seemed less personal.

"Roger—"

"Shut up. Shut up and let me think." He swiped a beefy forearm over his brow to dry it. It had all happened so fast, too fast. Everything up to now he had done on instinct. As Roman had calculated, he was beginning to think.

"They've got me trapped in here. I should've used you to get to one of the cars, should've taken off." Then he laughed, looking wildly around the lobby. "We're on a damn island. Can't drive off an island."

"I think if we—"

"Shut up!" He shouted and had her holding her breath as he leveled the gun at her. "I'm the one who needs to think. Feds. That sniveling little wart was right all along," he muttered, thinking of Bob. "He made DeWinter days ago. Did you?" As he asked, he grabbed her by the hair and yanked her head back to hold the barrel against her throat.

"No. I didn't know. I didn't. I still don't understand." She could only give a muffled cry when he slammed her back against the wall. She'd never seen murder in a man's eyes before, but she recognized it. "Roger, think. If you kill me you won't have anything to bargain with." She tasted fear on her tongue as she forced the words out. "You need me."

"Yeah." He relaxed his grip. "You've been handy so far. You'll just have to go on being handy. How many ways in and out of this place?"

"I—I don't really know." She sucked in her breath when he gave her hair another cruel twist.

"You know how many two-by-fours are in this place."

"Five. There are five exits, not counting the windows. The lobby, the gathering room, the outside steps running to my quarters and a family suite in the east wing, and the back, through the utility room off the kitchen."

"That's good." Panting a bit, he considered the possibilities. "The kitchen. We'll take the kitchen. I'll have water and food there in case this takes a while. Come on." He kept a hand in her hair and the gun at the base of her neck.

His eyes on the inn, Roman paced back and forth behind the barricade of police cars. She was smart, he told himself.

Charity was a smart, sensible woman. She wouldn't panic. She wouldn't do anything stupid.

Oh, God, she must be terrified. He lit a cigarette from the butt of another, but he didn't find himself soothed as the harsh smoke seared into him.

"Where's the goddamn phone?"

"Nearly ready." Royce pushed back his hat and straightened from where he'd been watching a lineman patch in a temporary line. "My nephew," he explained to Roman with a thin smile. "The boy knows his job."

"You got a lot of relatives."

"I'm lousy with them. Listen, I heard you and Charity were getting married. That part of the cover?"

"No." Roman thought of the picnic on the beach, that one clear moment in time. "No."

"In that case, I'm going to give you some advice. You're wrong," he said, before Roman could speak. "You do need it. You're going to have to get yourself calm, real calm, before you pick up that phone. A trapped animal reacts two ways. He either cowers back and gives up or he strikes out at anything in his way." Royce nodded toward the inn. "Block doesn't look like the type to give up easy, and Charity sure as hell's in his way. That line through yet, son?"

"Yes, sir." The young lineman's hands were sweaty with nerves and excitement. "You can dial right through." He passed the damp receiver to Roman.

"I don't know the number," Roman murmured. "I don't know the damn number."

"I know it."

Roman swung around to face Mae. In that one instant he saw everything he felt about himself mirrored in her eyes. There would be time for guilt later, he told himself. There would be a lifetime for it. "Royce, you were supposed to clear the area."

"Moving Maeflower's like moving a tank."

"I don't budge until I see Charity." Mae firmed her quivering lips. "She's going to need me when she comes out.

Waste of time to argue,'' she added. ''You want the number?''

''Yes.''

She gave it to him. Tossing his cigarette aside, Roman dialed.

Charity jolted in the chair when the phone rang. Across the table, Block simply stared at it. He had had her pile everything she could drag or carry to block the two doors. Extra chairs, twenty-pound canisters of flour and sugar, the rolling butcher block, iron skillets, all sat in a jumble, braced against both entrances.

In the silent kitchen the phone sounded again and again, like a scream.

''Stay right where you are.'' Block moved across the room to answer it. ''Yeah?''

''It's DeWinter. Thought you might be ready to talk about a deal.''

''What kind of deal?''

''That's what we have to talk about. First I have to know you've still got Charity.''

''Have you seen her come out?'' Block spit into the phone. ''You know damn well I've got her or you wouldn't be talking to me.''

''I have to make sure she's still alive. Let me talk to her.''

''You can go to hell.''

Threats, abuse, curses, rose like bile in his throat. Still, when he spoke, his voice was dispassionate. ''I verify that you still have a hostage, Block, or we don't deal.''

''You want to talk to her?'' Block gestured with the gun. ''Over here,'' he ordered. ''Make it fast. It's your boyfriend,'' he told Charity when she stood beside him. ''He wants to know how you're doing. You tell him you're just fine.'' He brushed the gun up her cheek to rest it at her temple. ''Understand?''

With a nod, she leaned into the phone. ''Roman?''

''Charity.'' Too many emotions slammed into him for him to measure. He wanted to reassure her, to make promises, to beg her to be careful. But he knew he would have only seconds and that Block would be listening to every word spoken. "Has he hurt you?"

"No." She closed her eyes and fought back a sob. "No, I'm fine. He's going to let me fix some food."

"Hear that, DeWinter? She's fine." Deliberately Block dragged her arm behind her back until she cried out. "That can change anytime."

Roman gripped the phone helplessly as he listened to the sound of Charity's sobs. It took every ounce of control he had left to keep the terror out of his voice. "You don't have to hurt her. I said we'd talk about terms."

"We'll talk about terms, all right. My terms." He released Charity's arm and ignored her as she slid to the floor. "You get me a car. I want safe passage to the airport, DeWinter. Charity drives. I want a plane fueled up and waiting. She'll be getting on it with me, so any tricks and we're back to square one. When I get where I'm going, I turn her loose."

"How big a plane?"

"Don't try to stall me."

"Wait. I have to know. It's a small airport, Block. You know that. If you're going any distance—"

"Just get me a plane."

"Okay." Roman wiped the back of his hand over his mouth and forced his voice to level. He couldn't hear her any longer, and the silence was as anguishing as her sobbing. "I'm going to have to go through channels on this. That's how it works."

"The hell with your channels."

"Look, I don't have the authority to get you what you want. I need to get approval. Then I'll have to clear the airport, get a pilot. You'll have to give me some time."

"Don't yank my chain, DeWinter. You got an hour."

"I've got to get through to Washington. You know how bureaucrats are. It'll take me three, maybe four."

"The hell with that. You got two. After two I'm going to start sending her out in pieces."

Charity closed her eyes, lowered her head to her folded arms and wept out her terror.

Chapter 12

"We've got a couple of hours," Roman murmured, continuing to study the inn and the floor plan Royce had given him. "He's not as smart as I thought, or maybe he's too panicked to think it through."

"That could be to our advantage," Royce said when Roman shook his head at his offer of coffee. "Or it could work against us."

Two hours. Roman stared at the quiet clapboard building. He couldn't stand the idea of Charity being held at gunpoint for that long. "He wants a car, safe passage to the airport and a plane." He turned to Conby. "I want you to make sure he thinks he's going to get it."

"I'm aware of how to handle a hostage situation, De-Winter."

"Which one of your men is the best shot?" Roman asked Royce.

"I am." He kept his eyes steady on Roman's. "Where do you want me?"

"They're in the kitchen."

"He tell you that?"

"No, Charity. She told me he was going to let her fix some food. Since I doubt eating's on her mind, she was letting me know their position."

Royce glanced over to where Mae was pacing up and down the pier. "She's a tough girl. She's keeping her head."

"So far." But Roman remembered too well the sound of her muffled sobbing. "We need to shift two of the men around the back. I want them to keep their distance, stay out of sight. Let's see how close we can get." He turned to Conby again. "Give us five minutes, then call him again. Tell him who you are. You know how to make yourself sound important. Stall him, keep him on the phone as long as you can."

"You have two hours, DeWinter. We can call for a SWAT team from Seattle."

"We have two hours," Roman said grimly. "Charity may not."

"I can't take responsibility—"

Roman cut him off. "You'll damn well take it."

"Agent DeWinter, if this wasn't a crisis situation I would cite you for insubordination."

"Great. Just put it on my tab." He looked at the rifle Royce had picked up. It had a long-range telescopic sight. "Let's move."

She'd cried long enough, Charity decided, taking a long, deep breath. It wasn't doing her any good. Like her captor, she needed to think. Her world had whittled down to one room, with fear as her constant companion. This wouldn't do, she told herself, straightening her spine. Her life was being threatened, and she wasn't even sure why.

She rose from where she had been huddled on the floor. Block was still sitting at the table, holding the gun in one hand while the other tapped monotonously on the scrubbed wood. The dangling cuffs jangled. He was terrified, she realized. Perhaps every bit as much as she. There must be some way to use that to her advantage.

"Roger...would you like some coffee?"

"Yeah. That's good, that's a good idea." He took a firmer grip on the gun. "But don't get cute. I'm watching every move."

"Are they going to give you a plane?" She turned the burner on low. The kitchen was full of weapons, she thought.

Knives, cleavers, mallets. Closing her eyes, she wondered if she had the courage to use one.

"They're going to give me anything I want as long as I have you."

"Why do they want you?" Stay calm, she told herself. She wanted to stay calm and alert and alive. "I don't understand." She poured the hot coffee into two cups. She didn't think she could swallow, but she hoped that sharing it would put him slightly more at ease. "They said something about counterfeiting."

It didn't matter what she knew. In any case, he had worked hard and was proud of it. "For over two years now I've been running a nice little game back and forth over the border. Twenties and tens in Canadian. I can stamp them out like bottle caps. But I'm careful, you know." He gulped at the coffee. "A couple thousand here, couple thousand there, with Vision as the front. We run a good tour, keep the clients happy."

"You've been paying me with counterfeit money?"

"You, and a couple other places. But you're the longest and most consistent." He smiled at her, as friendly as ever—if you didn't count the gun in his hand. "You have a special place here, Charity, quiet, remote, privately owned. You deal with a small local bank. It ran like a charm."

"Yes." She looked down at her cup, her stomach rolling. "I can see that." And Roman had come not to see the whales but to work on a case. That was all she had been to him.

"We were going to milk this route for a few more months," he continued. "Just lately Bob started getting antsy."

"Bob?" Her hand fisted on her lap. "Bob knew?"

"He was nothing but a nickel-and-dime con man before I took him on. Working scams and petty embezzlements. I set him up here and made him rich. Didn't do badly by you, either," he added with a grin. "You were on some shaky financial ground when I came along."

"All this time," she whispered.

"I'd decided to give it another six months, then move on,

but Bob started getting real jumpy about your new handyman. The bastard set me up.'' He slammed the cup down. ''Worked a deal with the feds. I should have caught it, the way he started falling apart after the hit-and-run.''

''The accident—you tried to kill me.''

''No.'' He patted her hand, and she cringed. ''Truth is, I've always had a liking for you. But I wanted to get you out of the way for a while. Just testing the waters to see how DeWinter played it. He's good,'' Block mused. ''Real good. Had me convinced he was only interested in you. The romance was a good touch. Threw me off.''

''Yes.'' Devastated, she stared at the grain in the wood of the tabletop. ''That was clever.''

''Sucked me in,'' Block muttered. ''I knew you weren't stringing me along. You haven't got it in you. But De-Winter... They've probably already taken Dupont.''

''Who?''

''We don't just run the money. There are people, people who need to leave the country quietly, who pay a lot for our services. Looks like I'm going to have to take myself on as a client.'' He laughed and drained his cup. ''How about some food? One of the things I'll miss most about this place is the food.''

She rose silently and went to the refrigerator. It had all been a lie, she thought. Everything Roman had said, everything he'd done...

The pain cut deep and had her fighting back another bout of weeping. He'd made a fool of her, as surely and as completely as Roger Block had. They had used her, both of them, used her and her inn. She would never forgive. She rubbed her hands over her eyes to clear them. And she would never forget.

''How about that lemon meringue pie?'' Relaxed, pleased with his own cleverness, Roger tapped the barrel of the gun on the table. ''Mae outdid herself on that pie last night.''

''Yes.'' Slowly Charity pulled it out. ''There's a little left.''

Block had ripped the frilly tiebacks from the sunny yellow curtains, but there was a space two inches wide at the center.

Silently Roman eased toward it. He could see Charity reach into a cupboard, take out a plate.

There were tears drying on her cheeks. It tore at him to see them. Her hands were steady. That was something, some small thing to hold on to. He couldn't see Block, though he shifted as much as he dared.

Then, suddenly, as if she had sensed him, their eyes met through the glass. She braced, and in that instant he saw a myriad of emotions run across her face. Then it was set again. She looked at him as she would have looked at a stranger and waited for instructions.

He held up a hand, palm out, doing his best to signal her to hold on, to keep calm. Then the phone rang and he watched her jolt.

"About time," Block said. He was almost swaggering as he walked to the phone. "Yeah? Who the hell's this?" After listening a moment, he gave a pleased laugh. "I like dealing with a title. Where's my plane, Inspector Conby?"

As quickly as she dared, Charity tugged the curtain open another inch.

"Over here," Block ordered.

She dropped her hand, and the plate rattled to the counter. "What?"

He gestured with the gun. "I said over here."

Roman swore as she moved between him and a clear shot.

"I want them to know I'm keeping up my end." Block took Charity by the arm, less roughly this time. "Tell the man I'm treating you fine."

"He hasn't hurt me," she said dully. She forced herself to keep her eyes away from the window. Roman was out there. He would do his best to get her out safely. That was his job.

"The plane'll be ready in a hour," Block told her after he hung up. "Just enough time for that pie and another cup of coffee."

"All right." She crossed to the counter again. Panic sprinted through her when she looked out the window and saw no one. He'd left. Because her fingers were unsteady, she fumbled with the pie. "Roger, are you going to let me go?"

He hesitated only an instant, but that was enough to tell her that his words were just another lie. "Sure. As soon as I'm clear."

So it came down to that. Her heart, her inn, and now her life. She set the pie in front of him and studied his face. He was pleased with himself, she thought, and she hated him for it. But he was still sweating.

"I'll get your coffee." She walked to the stove. One foot, then the other. There was a buzzing in her ears. It was more than fear now, she realized as she turned the burner up under the pot. It was rage and despair and a strong, irresistible need to survive. Mechanically she switched the stove off. Then, taking a cloth, she took the pot by the handle.

He was still holding the gun, and he was shoveling pie into his mouth with his left hand. He thought she was a fool, Charity mused. Someone who could be used and duped and manipulated. She took a deep breath.

"Roger?"

He glanced up. Charity looked directly into his eyes.

"You forgot your coffee," she said calmly, then tossed the steaming contents into his face.

He screamed. She didn't think she'd ever heard a man scream like that before. He was half out of his chair, groping blindly for the gun. It happened quickly. No matter how often she played back the scene in her mind, she would never be completely sure what happened first.

She grabbed for the gun herself. Block's flailing hand caught her across the cheekbone. Even as she staggered backward there was the sound of glass breaking.

Roman was through the window. Charity landed on the floor, stunned by the blow, as he burst through. There were men breaking through the barricaded doors and rushing into the room. Someone dragged her from the floor and pulled her out.

Roman held the gun to Block's temple. They were kneeling on the shattered glass—or rather Roman was kneeling and supporting the moaning Block. There were already welts rising up on his wide face. "Please," Roman murmured. "Give me a reason."

"Roman." Royce laid a hand on his shoulder. "It's over."

But the rage clogged his throat. It made his finger slippery on the trigger of the gun. He remembered the way Charity had looked at him when she had seen him outside the window. Slowly he drew back and holstered his gun.

"Yeah. It's over. Get him the hell out of here." He rose and went to find Charity.

He found her in the lobby, wrapped in Mae's arms.

"I'm all right," Charity murmured. "Really." When she saw Roman, her eyes frosted over. "Everything's going to be fine now. I need to speak with Roman for a minute."

"You say your piece." Mae kissed both of her cheeks. "Then you're going to get in a nice hot tub."

"Okay." She squeezed Mae's hand. Strange, but it felt more like a dream now, as if she were pushing her way through layers and layers of gauzy gray curtains. "I think we'll have more privacy upstairs," she said to Roman. Then she turned without looking at him and started up the stairs.

He wanted to hold her. His fingers curled tight into his palms. He needed to lift her against him, touch her hair, her skin, and convince himself that the nightmare was over.

Her knees were shaking. Reaction was struggling to set in, but she fought it off. When she was alone, Charity promised herself. When she was finally alone, she would let it all out.

In her sitting room she turned to face him. She would not, could not, speak to him in the intimacy of her bedroom. "I imagine you have reports to file," she began. Was that her voice? she wondered. It sounded so thin and cold, so foreign. Deliberately she cleared her throat. "I've been told I'll have to make a statement, but I thought we should get this out of the way first."

"Charity." He started toward her, only to be brought up short when her hands whipped out.

"Don't." Her eyes were as cold as her voice. It wasn't a dream, she told herself. It was as harsh and as brutal a reality as she had ever known. "Don't touch me. Not now, not ever again."

His hands fell uselessly to his sides. "I'm sorry."

"Why? You accomplished exactly what you came to do. From what I've been able to gather, Roger and Bob had quite a system going. I'm sure your superiors will be delighted with you."

"It doesn't matter."

She dug his badge out of her pocket, where she had shoved it. "Yes." She threw it at him. "Yes, it does."

Struggling for calm, he pushed it into his pocket. He noted dispassionately that his hands were bleeding. "I couldn't tell you."

"Didn't tell me."

There was a faint bruise on her cheekbone. For a moment all his guilt and impotent fury centered there. "He hit you."

She ran a fingertip lightly across the mark. "I don't break easily."

"I want to explain."

"Do you?" She turned away for a moment. She wanted to keep her anger cold. "I think I get the picture."

"Listen, baby—"

"No, *you* listen, baby." Her composure cracking, she whirled around again. "You lied to me, you used me from the first minute to the last. It was all one huge, incredible lie."

"Not all."

"No? Let's see, how can we separate one from the other? A convenient flat." She saw the anger in his eyes and shoved a chair out of her path. "And George, good old lucky George. I suppose it was worth a few thousand dollars to get him out of the way and leave you an opening. And Bob—you knew all about Bob, didn't you?"

"We couldn't be sure, not at first."

"Not at first," she repeated. As long as she kept her brain cold, she told herself, she could think. She could think and not feel. "I wonder, Roman, were you so sure of me? Or did you think I was part of it?" When he didn't answer, she spun around again. "You did. Oh, I see. I was under investigation all the time. And there you were, so conveniently on the scene. All you had to do was get close to me, and I made it so easy for you." With a laugh, she pressed her hands to her face. "My God, I threw myself at you."

"I wasn't supposed to get involved with you." Fighting desperation, he paced his words carefully. "It just happened. I fell in love with you."

"Don't say that to me." She lowered her hands. Her face was pale and cool behind them. "You don't even know what it means."

"I didn't, until you."

"You can't have love without trust, Roman. I trusted you. I didn't just give you my body. I gave you everything."

"I told you everything I could," he shot back. "Damn it, I couldn't tell you the rest. The things I told you about myself, about the way I grew up, the way I felt, they were all true."

"Do I have your word on that? Agent DeWinter?"

With an oath, he strode across the room and grabbed her arms. "I didn't know you when I took the assignment. I was doing a job. When things changed, the most important part of that job became proving your innocence and keeping you safe."

"If you had told me I would have proven my own innocence." She jerked out of his hold. "This is my inn, and these are my people. The only family I have left. Do you think I would risk it all for money?"

"No. I knew that, I trusted that, after the first twenty-four hours. I had orders, Charity, and my own instincts. If I had told you who I was and what was going on, you would never have been able to keep up a front."

"So I'm that stupid?"

"No. That honest." Digging deep, he found his control again. "You've been through a lot. Let me take you to the hospital."

"I've been through a lot," she repeated, and nearly laughed. "Do you know how it feels to know that for two years, *two years*, people I thought I knew were using me? I always thought I was such a good judge of character." Now she did laugh. She walked to the window. "They made a fool out of me week after week. I'm not sure I'll ever get over it. But that's nothing." She turned, wrapping her fingers around the windowsill. "That's nothing compared to what I feel when I think of how I let myself believe you were in love with me."

"If it was a lie, why am I here now, telling you that I do?"

"I don't know." Suddenly weary, she dragged her hair away from her face. "And it doesn't seem to matter. I'm wrung dry, Roman. For a while today I was sure he was going to kill me."

"Oh, Charity." He gathered her close, and when she didn't resist he buried his face in her hair.

"I thought he would kill me," she repeated, her arms held rigidly at her sides. "And I didn't want to die. In fact, nothing was quite so important to me as staying alive. When my mother fell in love and that love was betrayed, she gave up. I've never been much like her." She stepped stiffly out of his hold. "Maybe I'm gullible, but I've never been weak. I intend to pick up where I left off, before all of this. I'm going to keep the inn running. No matter what it takes, I'm going to erase you and these last weeks from my life."

"No." Furious, he took her face in his hands. "You won't, because you know I love you. And you made me a promise, Charity. No matter what happened, you wouldn't stop loving me."

"I made that promise to a man who doesn't exist." It hurt. She could feel the pain rip through her from one end to the other. "And I don't love the man who does." She took a small but significant step backward. "Leave me alone."

When he didn't move, she walked into the bedroom and flipped the lock.

Mae was busily sweeping up glass in the kitchen. For the first time in over twenty years the inn was closed. She figured it would open again soon enough, but for now she was content that her girl was safe upstairs in bed and the coffee-guzzling police were on their way out.

When Roman came in, she rested her arms on her broom. Mae had rocked Charity for nearly an hour while she'd cried over him. She'd been prepared to be cold and dismissive. It only took one look to change her mind.

"You look worn out."

"I..." Feeling lost, he glanced around the room. "I wanted to ask how she was before I left."

"She's miserable." She nodded, content with the anguish she saw in his eyes. "And stubborn. You got a few cuts."

Automatically he lifted a hand to rub at the nick on his temple. "Will you give her this number?" He dropped a card on the table. "She can reach me there if— She can reach me there."

"Sit down. Let me clean you up."

"No, it's all right."

"I said sit down." She went to a cupboard for a bottle of antiseptic. "She's had a bad shock."

He had a sudden mental image of Block holding the knife to her throat. "I know."

"She bounces back pretty quick from most things. She loves you."

Roman winced a little as she dabbed on the antiseptic, but not from the sting. "Did."

"Does," Mae said flatly. "She just doesn't want to right now. You been an agent for long?"

"Too long."

"Are you going to make sure that slimy worm Roger Block's put away?"

Roman's hands curled into fists. "Yes."

"Are you in love with Charity?"

He relaxed his hands. "Yes."

"I believe you, so I'm going to give you some advice." Puffing a bit, she sat down next to him. "She's hurt, real bad. Charity's the kind who likes to fix things herself. Give her a little time." She picked up the card and slipped it into her apron pocket. "I'll just hold on to this for now."

She was feeling stronger. And not just physically, Charity decided as she jogged along behind Ludwig. In every way.

The sweaty dreams that had woken her night after night were fading. It wasn't nearly as difficult to talk, or to smile, or to pretend that she was in control again. She had promised herself she would put her life back together, and she was doing it.

She rarely thought of Roman. On a sigh, she relented. She would never get strong again if she began to lie to herself.

She *always* thought of Roman. It was difficult not to, and it was especially difficult today.

They were to have been married today. Charity veered into the grass as Ludwig explored. The ache came, spread and was accepted. Just after noon, with the music swelling and the sun streaming down on the garden, she would have put her hand in his. And promised.

A fantasy, she told herself, and nudged her dog back onto the shoulder of the road. It had been fantasy then, and it was a fantasy now.

And yet... With every day that passed she remembered more clearly the times they had spent together. His reluctance, and his anger. Then his tenderness and concern. She glanced down to where the bracelet shimmered on her wrist.

She'd tried to put it back in the box, to push it into some dark, rarely opened drawer. Every day she told herself she would. Tomorrow. And every day she remembered how sweet, how awkward and how wonderful he'd been when he'd given it to her.

If it had only been a job, why had he given her so much more than he had needed to? Not just the piece of jewelry, but everything the circle of gold had symbolized? He could have offered her friendship and respect, as Bob had, and she would have trusted him as much. He could have kept their relationship strictly physical. Her feelings would have remained the same.

But he had said he loved her. And at the end he had all but begged her to believe it.

She shook her head and increased her pace. She was being

weak and sentimental. It was just the day...the beautiful spring morning that was to have been her wedding day.

What she needed was to get back to the inn and keep busy. This day would pass, like all the others.

At first she thought she was imagining it when she saw him standing beside the road, looking out at the sunrise over the water. Her feet faltered. Before she could think to prevent it, her knees weakened. Fighting her heart, she walked to him.

He'd heard her coming. As he'd stood in the growing light he'd remembered wondering if he came back, if he would stand just there and wait for Charity to run to him.

She wasn't running now. She was walking very slowly, despite the eager dog. Could she know, he wondered, that she held his life in her hands?

Nerves swarmed through her, making her fingers clench and unclench on the leash. She prayed as she stopped in front of him that her voice would be steadier.

"What do you want?"

He bent down to pat the squirming dog's head. "We'll get to that. How are you feeling?"

"I'm fine."

"You've been having nightmares." There were shadows under her eyes. He wouldn't make it easy on her by ignoring them.

She stiffened. "They're passing. Mae talks too much."

"At least she talks to me."

"We've already said all there is to say."

He closed a hand over her arm as she started by him. "Not this time. You had your say last time, and I had a lot of it coming. Now it's my turn." Reaching down, he unhooked the leash. Free, Ludwig bounded toward home. "Mae's waiting for him," Roman explained before Charity could call the dog back.

"I see." She wrapped the leash around her fisted hand. "You two work all this out?"

"She cares about you. So do I."

"I have things to do."

"Yeah. This is first." He pulled her close and, ignoring her struggling, crushed his mouth to hers. It was like a drink after days in the desert, like a fire after a dozen long cold nights. He plundered, greedy, as though it were the first time. Or the last.

She couldn't fight him, or herself. Almost sobbing, she clung to him, hungry and hurting. No matter how strong she tried to be, she would never be strong enough to stand against her own heart.

Aching, she started to draw back, but he tightened his hold. "Give me a minute," he murmured, pressing his lips to her hair. "Every night I wake up and see him holding a knife at your throat. And there's nothing I can do. I reach for you, and you're not there. For a minute, one horrible minute, I'm terrified. Then I remember that you're safe. You're not with me, but you're safe. It's almost enough."

"Roman." With a helpless sigh, she stroked soothing hands over his shoulders. "It doesn't do any good to think about it."

"Do you think I could forget?" He pulled back, keeping his hands firm on her arms. "For the rest of my life I'll remember every second of it. I was responsible for you."

"No." The anger came quickly enough to surprise both of them. She shoved at his chest. "*I'm* responsible for me. I was and I am and I always will be. And I took care of myself."

"Yeah." He ran his palm over her cheek. The bruise had faded, even if the memory hadn't. "It was a hell of a way to serve coffee."

"Let's forget it." She shrugged out of his grip and walked toward the water. "I'm not particularly proud of letting myself be duped, so I'd rather not dwell on it."

"They were pros, Charity. You're not the first person they've used."

She pressed her lips together. "And you?"

"When you're undercover you lie, and you use, and you take advantage of anything that's offered." Her eyes were closed when he turned her around to face him. "I came here to do a job. It had been a long time since I'd let myself think beyond anything but the next day. Look at me. Please."

Taking a steadying breath, she opened her eyes. "We've been through this already, Roman."

"No. I'd hurt you. I'd disappointed you. You weren't ready to listen." Gently he brushed a tear from her lashes. "I hope you are now, because I can't make it much longer without you."

"I was too hard on you before." It took almost everything she had, but she managed a smile. "I was hurt, and I was a lot shakier than I knew from being locked up with Roger. After I gave my statement, Inspector Conby explained everything to me, more clearly. About how the operation had been working, what my responsibilities were, what you had to do."

"What responsibilities?"

"About the money. It's put us in somewhat of a hole, but at least we only have to pay back a percentage."

"I see." Roman laughed and shook his head. "He always was a prince."

"The merchant's responsible for the loss." She tilted her head. "You didn't know about the arrangements I've made with him?"

"No."

"But you work for him."

"Not anymore. I turned in my resignation when I got back to D.C."

"Oh, Roman, that's ridiculous. It's like throwing out the baby with the bathwater."

He smiled appreciatively at her innate practicality. "I decided I like carpentry better. Got any openings?"

Running the leash through her hands, she looked over the water. "I haven't given much thought to remodeling lately."

"I work cheap." He tilted her face to his. "All you have to do is marry me."

"Don't."

"Charity." Calling on patience he hadn't been aware he possessed, he held her still. "One of the things I most admire about you is your mind. You're real sharp. Look at me, really look. I figure you've got to know that I'm not beating my head against this same wall for entertainment. I love you. You've got to believe that.''

"I'm afraid to,'' she whispered.

He felt the first true spark of hope. "Believe this. You changed my life. Literally changed it. I can't go back to the way it was before. I can't go forward unless you're with me. How long do you want me to stand here, waiting to start living again?''

With her arms wrapped around her chest, she walked a short distance away. The high grass at the water's edge was still misted with dew. She could smell it, and the fragile fragrances of wildflowers. It occurred to her then that she had blocked such small things out of her life ever since she'd sent him away.

If it was honesty she was demanding from him, how could she give him anything less?

"I've missed you terribly.'' She shook her head quickly before he could touch her again. "I tried not to wonder if you'd come back. I told myself I didn't want you to. When I saw you standing in the road, all I wanted to do was run to you. No questions, no explanations. But it's not that simple.''

"No.''

"I do love you, Roman. I can't stop. I have tried,'' she said, looking back at him. "Not very hard, but I have tried. I think I knew under all the anger and the hurt that you weren't lying about loving me back. I haven't wanted to forgive you for lying about the rest, but— That's just pride really.'' Perhaps it was simple after all, she thought. "If I have to make a choice, I'd rather take love.'' She smiled and opened her arms to him. "I guess you're hired.''

She laughed when he caught her up in his arms and swung her around. "We'll make it work,'' he promised her, raining kisses all over her face. "Starting today.''

"We were going to be married today.''

"Are going to be.'' He hooked his arm under her legs to carry her.

"But we—''

"I have a license." Closing his mouth over hers, he swung her around again.

"A marriage license?"

"It's in my pocket, with two tickets to Venice."

"To—" Her hand slid limply from his shoulder. "To *Venice?* But how—?"

"And Mae bought you a dress yesterday. She wouldn't let me see it."

"Well." The thrill was too overwhelming to allow her to pretend annoyance. "You were awfully sure of yourself."

"No." He kissed her again, felt the curve of her lips, and the welcoming. "I was sure of you."

* * * * *

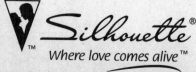

Have you ever wanted to be part of a romance reading group?

Be part of the Readers' Ring,
Silhouette Special Edition's
exciting book club!

The third title in the promotion is

THE ACCIDENTAL PRINCESS

by Peggy Webb

Silhouette Special Edition
#1516 (January 2003)

Encourage your friends to get together to engage in
lively discussions with the suggested reading-group
questions provided at the end of the novel. Also, visit
www.readersring.com for some exciting interactive
materials related to this novel.

Available at your favorite retail outlet.

Where love comes alive™

SPECIAL EDITION™

From *USA TODAY* bestselling author

SHERRYL WOODS

comes the continuation of the heartwarming series

Coming in January 2003

MICHAEL'S DISCOVERY

Silhouette Special Edition #1513

An injury received in the line of duty left ex-navy SEAL
Michael Devaney bitter and withdrawn. But Michael hadn't
counted on beautiful physical therapist Kelly Andrews's healing
powers. Kelly's gentle touch mended his wounds, warmed
his heart and rekindled his belief in the power of love.

Look for more Devaneys coming in July and August 2003,
only from Silhouette Special Edition.

Available at your favorite retail outlet.

New York Times bestselling author

DEBBIE MACOMBER

weaves emotional tales of love and longing.

Here is the first
of her celebrated
NAVY series!

NAVY *Wife*

Dare Lindy risk her heart

Visit Silhouette at www.eHarlequin.com